After studying English at Oxford, Phillipa Ashley worked as a copywriter and journalist. Her first novel, *Decent Exposure*, won the RNA New Writers Award and was made into a TV movie called *12 Men of Christmas* starring Kristin Chenoweth and Josh Hopkins. Phillipa lives in a Staffordshire village and has an engineer husband and a scientist daughter who indulge her arty whims. She runs a holiday-let business in the Lake District, but a big part of her heart belongs to Cornwall. She visits the county several times a year for 'research purposes', an arduous task that involves sampling cream teas, swimming in wild Cornish coves, and following actors around film shoots in a camper van. Her hobbies include watching *Poldark*, Earl Grey tea, prosecco-tasting, and falling off surfboards in front of RNLI lifeguards.

You can discover more about the author at http://phillipa-ashley.com

CHRISTMAS AT THE CORNISH CAFE

Christmas will be slightly less turbulent than summer, won't it? Demi certainly hopes so. She and Cal are keeping their fledgling relationship under wraps for now. But then Kit Bannen, a hunky, blond and somewhat mysterious writer, arrives at Kilhallon Resort — and Cal is sure he's hiding something. Demi is busy baking festive treats for the newly opened Demelza's Cafe, but when Cal's ex Isla arrives to shoot scenes for her new drama, Demi can't help but worry that things aren't quite over between them. Kit flirts with both women, fuelling Cal's suspicions that Kit has hidden motives for staying on at Kilhallon. Then Cal has to go to London, leaving Demi and Kit to decorate the cafe for Christmas — all by themselves. A storm is brewing in more ways than one . . .

Books by Phillipa Ashley
Published by Ulverscroft:

WISH YOU WERE HERE
IT SHOULD HAVE BEEN ME
SUMMER AT THE CORNISH CAFE

PHILLIPA ASHLEY

CHRISTMAS AT THE CORNISH CAFE

Complete and Unabridged

CHARNWOOD
Leicester

First published in Great Britain in 2017 by
Avon
A division of HarperCollins*Publishers* Ltd
London

First Charnwood Edition
published 2018
by arrangement with
HarperCollins*Publishers*
London

A catalogue record for this book is available from the British Library.

ISBN 978–1–4448–3638–7

For Charlotte and James,
Nadelik Lowen Ha Bledhen Nowyth Da
(Merry Christmas and a Happy New Year)

And in memory of Rowena Kincaid
1975–2016

Prologue

Tuesday October 1st
Demi

'Good morning, friends! This is Greg Stennack, your favourite local DJ on your favourite local station, Radio St Trenyan. I'll be bringing you all the latest tunes and news from our great little corner of Cornwall and cheering you up on this wet and windy October the first. Hey, did I just say it was October? Seems like only yesterday that we were slapping on the suncream and stretching out the beach towels to catch some rays. Oh, wait — that was only yesterday! Hey, never mind, people. Christmas is only eighty-five sleeps away. Now, let's kick off this wild autumn day with 'Here Comes the Rain Again' by the Eurythmics . . . '

Hey, thanks, Greg, I've nothing against Annie Lennox, but I think I'll pass.

With a groan, I bash the radio alarm 'off' button with my palm and pull the duvet over my head. That was a mistake. Now that Greg's not blaring down my ear, I can hear the rain lashing against the windows and battering the roof of my tiny terraced cottage. A moment later, I throw the duvet off me, shivering in the cool October morning. I say 'morning', but it might as well be evening it's so dark and gloomy in my bedroom. The late September heatwave we'd been

1

enjoying at Kilhallon Park broke late last night when a massive storm blew in from the Atlantic and settled over our corner of far-west Cornwall.

The bedroom door bangs against the wall and four paws land squarely on my legs and a rough tongue licks my face.

'Oof!'

My dog, Mitch, stands on my stomach, tongue lolling. 'Thanks, boy, but I'd rather have a wash myself. In the bathroom, preferably.'

Mitch woofs and jumps onto the floor, wagging his feathery tail.

'I know, I know. You want a walk, but have you heard that wet stuff falling from the sky outside?'

Mitch leaps off the bed, and stands by, tilting his head this way and that, as if to say: 'Wuss'.

I give up all thought of staying in bed. 'OK. You win.'

As I swing my legs off the bed, Mitch scampers to the doorway, hardly able to contain himself, excited at the prospect of a walk. After I've pulled on old jeans and a fleece, I trot downstairs, grab a quick glass of juice and pull open the curtains. It's still bucketing down, and the rain is driven by strong winds off the sea, so it's almost horizontal.

I grab an old waxed jacket from a peg by the back door and pull the hood over my head. Not only does Mitch need a walk, I need to check that nothing's blown away from our brand-new guest cottages. I also need to make sure that our new cafe, Demelza's, is still in one piece ready for its opening day on Thursday.

Since I arrived at Easter, my boss, Cal

Penwith, and I have been working hard to transform Kilhallon Park from a run-down caravan site into a boutique holiday resort. With the help of our friends — and despite the efforts of our foes — our cottages and glamping site officially open for business today.

Then there's Demelza's.

I persuaded Cal to convert the old storage barn by the coastal path into a cafe. He decided to name it after me, so I'm determined to make it a success — come hell or high water.

And on that note . . . Outside the front door, the drumming of the rain and the howls of the wind almost drown out Mitch's woofs. He dashes outside and scampers through the puddles while I linger in the doorway watching raindrops bounce off the cobbles of the yard. But it's not the downpour that's stopping me from taking that step outside; it's the realisation that today's the day that Kilhallon — and Cal and I — take our leap into the unknown.

I step into an old pair of Hunters that used to belong to Cal's cousin Robyn. I'm wearing her old coat too: everyone mucks in and shares what they have here. I've become part of the Kilhallon tribe since Cal invited me to work for him, even though my own family have become lost to me. I've also made some good friends who've stuck with me through thick and thin. One of them — Cal — is more than a friend, but we'll see where that leads.

Mitch dances round my wellies and barks joyfully, as if to say: 'Come on, what are we waiting for?'

After the tough times we've overcome, and the challenges that await us, there's no going back now. I let out a deep breath and step into the deluge. If you want to see a rainbow, as my Nana Demelza would have said, you have to put up with the rain . . .

1

'Hello there! Welcome to Kilhallon Park. How was your journey?'

The man scowls from beneath the hood of his jacket and tosses his car keys on the shiny new reception desk at the front of Kilhallon House. He can't be more than thirty and his face would be handsome if his expression wasn't even more thundery than the weather. 'Does it ever stop raining down here?' he grumbles. 'It's been pouring all the way from London and I've had a nightmare of a journey.'

'I'm sorry about that, sir, it must have been awful, but I'm so glad you're here now and the forecast did show the weather brightening up later this afternoon. We should have a much drier day tomorrow. Would you mind filling in this card with your car registration while I collect your keys and welcome pack so I can show you to your cottage?' With a smile, I hand him a pen.

He pushes his hood off his face. His dark blond fringe is stuck to his forehead and a raindrop trickles down his nose as he takes the pen and frowns at the card. Meanwhile, I collect his cottage keys and welcome pack from the drawer below the reception desk, hoping that the rain will stop. Instead, a rumble of thunder shakes Kilhallon House and our guest glances around him as if we're about to be zapped by aliens.

He pushes the card towards me. His writing looks like a drunken spider has been doing the salsa with the felt tip, but I'm not going to ask him to redo it. 'Your website said there's a cafe on site. I'd like some lunch. Can you show me the way?' His voice is tight and the news I'm about to deliver isn't going to help his mood one bit.

'I'm afraid the cafe doesn't open until the day after tomorrow . . . Mr Bracken.'

'It's not Bracken. It's *Bannen*. Kit Bannen,' he adds, stressing each word as if I'm a toddler. Mind you, I don't blame him, our first guest and I've got his name wrong. I should have spent more time preparing, instead of baking.

'What's that about the cafe being closed?' he goes on. 'The on-site cafe is one of the reasons I chose this place and I've held off from having lunch. It looked great on your website and I didn't dare stop once I finally got moving after all the hold-ups. I'd hoped to grab a late lunch as soon as I arrived.'

'I'm sorry, Mr Bannen, but we'll be open for coffee on Thursday morning. The website and information we sent you does say our opening days are Thursday to Sunday in the autumn and winter.'

'That's no good to me, is it?'

'I appreciate that, sir, but it's only two days away . . . less than that, technically speaking,' I say, aware that the hours are ticking by fast.

Mr Bannen cuts across me. 'Is there a pub or a restaurant close by?'

'The pub's just over a mile away at the

6

crossroads. You'll probably have to drive.' Oh dear, this is *not* going well. I can understand that he's tired and grouchy, but there's no need to be rude.

'Great. I've just spent seven hours crawling down here in the car from London and now I have to get straight back in it.'

'I'm so sorry, Mr Bannen, but the good news is that there's a welcome hamper in your cottage, with fresh bread, butter, eggs and cheese and some milk and a bottle of wine. They're basic but high-quality supplies and enough to rustle up a sandwich or an omelette.'

He glares at me, then frowns. 'Did you say there was wine?'

'Yes, a bottle of red from a local vineyard, though I can swap it for a white if you'd prefer. I do have a chilled bottle in the fridge here. There are tea- and coffee-making facilities ready in your cottage, of course, and some Cornish apple juice in your own fridge, if it's too early for wine . . . '

'It isn't too early for wine!'

I half expect the reception desk to shake.

He sighs and flashes me an apologetic smile. 'Look, I'm not always this grouchy but I've had a fraught time at work and the journey from London was even more crap than I'd expected and it's pouring down and I'm starving.'

'I understand, Mr Bannen, and I'm sorry the cafe's not open yet, but if you like I could sell you some of the spinach and ricotta quiche I made this morning to add to the supplies in your luxury, free welcome pack?'

'Quiche, you say?'

I smile. 'Uh huh. Homemade here at Kilhallon.'

'Hmm. Well, thanks, I may just do as you say and stay in. I do need a break.'

'Good idea. Now, if you want to follow me in your car, your cottage is only a few hundred yards up the lane to the left of the main farmhouse. I'll get your keys and show you around Enys Cottage. Would you like some mince pies with your quiche, by the way?'

He frowns. 'Mince pies? But we're barely into October.'

'Yes, um, I've been practising some recipes for when the cafe opens.'

'Practising?'

'Trialling,' I correct myself, because he seems worried again. 'I've created a new boozy mincemeat recipe actually, and I've been trying out different toppings for the pies. I've made glazed stars and cinnamon and orange crunchy crumble tops . . . the crumble ones are particularly delicious, and I was just about to make some Viennese topped ones when you rang the reception bell . . . ' I clam up, realising that I've been babbling because I'm nervous and rattled by our first guest not being in the holiday mood that I'd expected.

Mr Bannen peers at me like I'm mad and then wrinkles his nose, sniffs the air and unexpectedly, breaks into a smile that transforms his face from grumpy pants to golden surf boy.

'I thought I could smell something good. You know, I think a mince pie and wine is just what I need after the time I've had at work.'

'What do you do?' I ask, relieved he's simmering down.

'Oh, this and that. Boring admin-type stuff, mostly.'

So, he doesn't want to tell me. Well, that's fine. 'If you'd like to wait here for a moment, I'll get the food and my coat and you can follow me in your car up to Enys Cottage.'

He humphs in reply, but it's the quiet humph of a man who's calming down and feeling a bit guilty for ranting at me. At least, I think it's that — as he's our first guest, I have a lot to learn.

I grab my wax jacket from the peg in the hallway that separates the reception area from Kilhallon House, the old farmhouse that forms the heart of the Cornish holiday complex where I work. Then I find the quiche in the fridge and pop it into a square, cardboard cake box — luckily I have some in, ready for the cafe opening. I transfer four mince pies of different types from their tin to another box and carry them into reception.

Mr Bannen is nowhere to be seen.

Oh dear. I hope he hasn't decided to do a runner after all.

After zipping up my jacket and collecting the keys to the Land Rover, I carry the boxes outside. Mr Bannen is standing at the far side of the gravelled car park by the fence, looking out over the fields that, next spring, will become our camp site. For now, we only have four yurts situated in the little copse just out of view of the car park.

9

Mr Bannen has his hands spread wide, gripping the wooden rail, and I could be wrong, but think he's taking some deep breaths of Cornish sea air. It's still raining, but not as hard, as I stow the quiche and mince pies on the passenger seat. Mr Bannen shows no signs of returning to his car, a large silver BMW that seems too big for one man, but is probably just right for a stressed-out angry person. I haven't asked, though I have wondered, where his family or friends are.

I pull up my own hood and wait by the Land Rover.

The rain is definitely easing as Mr Bannen finally turns away from the view and trudges back towards me. He seems sad now rather than furious.

'Sorry,' he says, reaching me. 'I needed a bit of fresh air.'

'I don't blame you. Are you ready to follow me to your cottage now?'

He nods. He pushes his hood off again. The edges of his dark blond hair are soaked but I can tell his hair brushes his neck. He also has a thin gold loop earring through one lobe, like the fishermen in St Trenyan. He doesn't look like he does boring admin-type stuff; I'd have said he was the creative type, more advertising or graphic design or something. He's probably here for the surfing, though there's no board on the roof rack of the car.

He turns back towards the sea and I follow his gaze. Our soon-to-be camping field slopes very gently down to the boundary of the park. It's separated by a low hedge from the coastal footpath that skirts our land. A few yards beyond the path, the jagged cliffs plunge down to the Atlantic. He turns to me again, his voice gentler. 'I'm sorry. You must have lots to do and I shouldn't have kept you waiting, but the view drew me. I stare at four walls for most of my working life and this is pretty special, even in the rain.'

'We like to think so,' I say, delighted that we finally have a visitor and fascinated by the change in him since he saw the Cornish scenery in its full glory.

Mr Bannen shades his eyes and points upwards. 'Bloody hell, am I imagining things or is that a patch of blue sky over there?'

I follow his outstretched arm and smile to myself. There's still a hint of rain in the air, and the breeze is bending the branches of the oak trees in the field, but a sliver of blue has opened up between the billowing grey clouds over the sea.

'It looks like the weather front is blowing in sooner than was forecast. Things can change very quickly at Kilhallon,' I say, seeing the place through fresh eyes. The same way I saw it the day I first arrived here at Easter, only this time, it's with pride and not the shock I felt when I saw the rundown mess it was in then.

'Wow,' he says, still shading his eyes as a shaft of sunlight breaks out and the chasm of blue widens. I push my own hood off my head and jingle my keys discreetly. I'd love to stand and appreciate the beauty of Kilhallon but I was in the middle of baking when Mr Bannen arrived. It's just dawned on me how much I still have to do to get the other cottages, not to mention Demelza's Cafe, ready for our other visitors.

'Mr Bannen? Would you like to follow me through the gate to the left and to your cottage?' I ask, noting the puddles that have formed in the car park and thinking of the guests who'll be staying under canvas, albeit luxurious canvas, in our new yurts. I saw Cal earlier this morning, heading out in the deluge to check they hadn't leaked.

Mr Bannen takes the hint and pulls his own keys from the pocket of his Berghaus. 'Thanks . . . and please, it's Kit . . . Well, Christopher, actually but everyone calls me Kit.' He takes another lingering look at the view before he climbs into his silver BMW. 'You know, even in the lashing rain with a howling gale and no licensed premises within spitting distance, I can see why you'd want to escape here.'

2

'All I want for Christmas . . . is youuuuuu!'

Humming along to Mariah Carey, I do a little jig in front of the Aga in Kilhallon House, waiting for the kitchen timer to ping. A few more minutes should just about do it.

I came straight back to my baking after I'd shown Mr Bannen — sorry, Kit — the basics of Enys Cottage. Enys is our cosiest cottage, perfect for two or, in his case, one — so my first guest tour didn't take too long. I left him not exactly smiling, but opening a bottle of wine and about to tuck in to the quiche. I'm glad that my boss, Cal, and Polly his PA will be taking over management of the park after Thursday, leaving me to concentrate on my main passion, the cafe and its food, of course.

Cal texted me while I showed Kit to his cottage. He was about to greet a group from Surrey who have rented some of our glamping yurts. If Kit's journey was anything to go by, they'll be tired and frazzled too. The field is thick with mud after the storm so I don't envy him having to meet them, although hopefully this sunshine will lift their mood, not to mention the welcome hamper of treats that awaits them in their yurts.

Once all my mince pies are cooked and cooled, I need to set up some shots that I can upload to my Demelza's blog and use on social media to promote the seasonal menus. The more bookings we can get for lunches and events, the better. I need to repay Cal's faith in me, not to mention his investment in my cafe. It was my idea, after all.

A peek outside the kitchen door confirms to me that the weather is definitely warming up again, and there is now more blue in the sky than clouds. A late burst of sunshine is just what we need to attract customers to Demelza's Cafe; I hope it lasts for our opening day on Thursday, and over the weekend. We might get some last-minute bookings for Cal's cottages and yurts too.

And after the tough time we've both had lately, we're surely due a run of good luck now, right?

'All I want for Christmas is youooooooo!'

As Mariah hits an impossibly high note, the kitchen timer finally pings. The moment I open the Aga door, a wave of heat blasts my face, instantly followed by the overwhelming aroma of spices and dried fruit. The pies are a perfect shade of light golden brown, the honeyed blond of a surf dude's tint. The Viennese biscuit topping was a little time-consuming, if I'm honest, so I'm not sure if I'll add that to the cafe menu, but they look very pretty and smell gorgeous, so we'll see. Carefully, because the oven mitts in the kitchen of Kilhallon House have seen some action lately and need replacing, I extricate the pies from the oven, knowing I'm about seven seconds from scorched fingers.

I straighten up, clutching the tray in one hand,

while closing the door with the other.

'Phew, it's roasting in here.'

A familiar voice behind me makes my pies wobble alarmingly. Just in time, I save them from sliding onto the quarry-tiled floor where my dog, Mitch, looks on hopefully from his bed by the back door.

If I thought Kit was wet, Cal looks like Mitch after he's had a dip in the sea. Water drips from his coat.

'How was he, then, this Mr Bannen?' he asks, peeling off his waxed jacket.

'Oh, you mean Kit?'

Cal raises an eyebrow. 'First name terms, already, eh? And Kit? Sounds like a dog's name . . . or a hamster's.'

'I promise you there's nothing cute and furry about Mr Bannen, and the Kit is short for Christopher. He was stressed out, tired and pissed off about the cafe not being open, but he seemed happy enough when I showed him into Enys Cottage and gave him some free mince pies'

'Funny that he's on his own for two whole weeks.' Cal holds up his jacket with a grimace. The rain has seeped down his collar to his T-shirt, leaving a large damp patch over the chest. The grey cotton is plastered across his broad shoulders and pecs, and his nipples are like tight little currants. A taut-yet-melty feeling stirs low in my stomach.

Did I say Cal was my boss and more than a friend? That might have only been part of the truth . . .

'What's up?' he asks.

The second batch of pies will definitely be burned if I let on to him how turned on I am. 'Nothing. Just thinking how wet you are, that's all.'

He glares at me, but even his glares are sexy. 'It's not funny.'

'I think you looking like a drowned rat — or hamster — is very funny.'

With another stern look that turns me into a puddle, he bends down to take off his Hunters. 'Any more cheek, Ms Jones, and I may have to sack you.'

The mention of cheek makes me think of his gorgeous bottom, not to mention the warmth of his hand on mine. His arse is thrust into the air as he pulls off his wellies, grunting with the effort. I scoop up his jacket from the tiles and add it to the others hanging in the vestibule that separates the reception area from the main Kilhallon House. Cal pops his mud-spattered Hunters in the drip tray by the kitchen door.

'I wonder if there's a Mrs Bannen somewhere,' he says.

'He didn't mention one.'

'No girlfriend or boyfriend? Both?' His espresso-coloured eyes hold a hint of mischief.

'He did say 'everyone calls me Kit' so he must have some friends and family. He definitely didn't want to talk about his work though, so I think he's had a stressful time in London.'

'Tell me about it,' Cal says, standing on the tiles in his woolly hiking socks with a grimace on his tanned face. Even the sight of those rugged

16

socks are turning me on which must mean I've got it *very* bad. At least he doesn't know quite *how* bad. Cal and I have been rubbing along in this relationship for the past few weeks. It's as rocky and twisty-turny as the coastal path, and as uncertain as the weather in our part of the county. One day there are storms between us, the next clear blue skies — and sometimes four seasons in one day. There's no formal arrangement between us and I have no intention of moving into Kilhallon House itself, but while Polly is away, we sneak nights together in his bed.

You see, Cal may be more than a boss but he's also not *entirely* mine. Not that he's actually sleeping with anyone else, but only part of him belongs to me. His socks, perhaps . . . if I'm lucky. You see, I still suspect his heart lies with his ex, even though he said that I'd made a mark on him and he begged me to stay just a few weeks ago.

My stomach clenches at the reminder of how new and fragile our relationship is. I remind myself not to start getting any stupid ideas about Cal that involve hearts and flowers, let alone love and marriage.

'How were the group who've rented the yurts?' I ask him, refocusing on the business at hand, not his sexy socks or his top-notch arse. 'I was wondering how you'd got on with them. How horrible for them that they travelled here in this crap weather.'

'They weren't quite as easily pacified as your mate 'Kit'. In fact, judging by their faces and the fact the kids were crying and begging Mummy to take them 'to a proper house with real walls', I'm not sure they're entirely happy. I've had to leave them to settle in, and at least the weather's improving, they should cheer up soon.'

He lifts up his foot. 'Damn it, my socks are soaked. I think my boxers might be wet too.'

The heat from the Aga curls around us and steam rises from Cal's damp T-shirt.

I can't hide my giggle. 'You look like Mitch after he's jumped in a rock pool. You'd better get changed while I make a hot coffee, then you can tell me all about the yurt people.'

'And you can tell me more about your mate Kit.'

'He's not my mate.'

I can't see Cal's face as he heads out of the kitchen but I can picture that self-satisfied grin of pleasure at winding me up. At least he *cares* that Kit might have chatted me up, even if all Kit was really interested in was getting some alcohol and calories down his neck as fast as possible.

Ten minutes later, the tinny intro to 'Last Christmas' tinkles through the kitchen. Cal leans against the door frame, drying his hair on a towel. Thank goodness he decided to put a T-shirt on. He frowns. 'What are you doing? And why the crappy music?'

'The crappy music you're referring to, though that's open to debate, is my Christmas cafe mix and I'm getting into the festive spirit.'

His gaze travels slowly and deliberately from my toes, past my skinny jeans and Kilhallon Park T-shirt to my face.

'In an elf apron and a Santa hat?'

I plant my hands on my hips. 'Are you complaining?'

'Not at all,' he says, with the lop-sided smile that never ceases to make my insides tingle. His voice is as rich and delicious as the spices in my mincemeat, though I'd rather die than tell him either of those things, of course.

'You can give me a hand with these,' I say, nodding to the cooling rack on top of the Aga and handing him a tray from the oven. While Cal transfers the mince pies from the tin to the rack, I rescue the second and final batch from the oven.

'Is that the last batch?' Cal asks, dumping the empty pie tins in the Belfast sink.

'Yes, thanks.' While I untie the strings of my apron and hang it on the back of the door that leads into the hallway, I know Cal's eyes will be fixed on my rear, which is a delicious thought although it makes me self-conscious. By the time I turn back to him, however, he's holding up a cake net and sniffing the plate of crumble-topped pies that was under it.

'You've been busy. It smells great in here.'

'I've been trying out some recipes for the cafe in between checking in the guests. You know we're going to do most of our own baking, but we'll have to buy in some of it from outside. Sheila's going to provide the pasties and the St Trenyan bakery will help with the bread. There's a young food blogger near St Just who's going to help out too, when we're really busy.'

'What about this lot? Do I get to try some?'

His hand snakes towards the cooling rack. I bat it away. 'I'm not complaining, but isn't it a bit early for mince pies?'

'That's what Kit said, but these are for work, not pleasure. I'm going to take some shots for our social media pages. Twitter, Instagram and the blog, you know? Maybe make some promotional memes on Canva and I must upload the pics to Pinterest. Have you forgotten that Demelza's opens the day after tomorrow? I've been trialling some seasonal bakes and we need to get people in the mood for booking festive breaks.'

'I hear you about the cafe, but Pinterest? Canva memes? I've absolutely no idea what you're talking about.'

'Yes, you do. You just pretend you don't so you don't have to spend hours on the Internet.'

He sneaks a pie and bites into it. 'Fu . . . ow! Thasstillverhot.' He pants and dances the other half of the stolen pie from one palm to the other. Crumbs scatter onto the tiles.

'Serves you right. You couldn't wait, could you?'

He winks. 'You know me so well.'

Correction, I think, I know him *better*. Since I started working at Kilhallon at Easter, I've come to realise that no one knows Cal well, not even the people who've grown up with him in the little Cornish village of St Trenyan. I don't think his own family know him completely. Which makes me a total novice in the ways of Cal Penwith, apart from the ways in which I now know him intimately, of course.

Cal blows on the other half of the pie and finishes it in a couple of bites while I cover the rest of them with a clean tea towel and switch on the kettle. After baking all morning, and checking in Kit, I'm more than happy to take a break with Cal while I have the chance. Once the cafe is open and our other guests start arriving over the next few days, I doubt if we'll have a moment to breathe, let alone share a mince pie and coffee.

'Want a coffee and another sample?'

'Thanks, but I'll make the coffee.'

He scrapes his chair back and fills the kettle while I clean up the table. The oak surface is dusted with flour and scraps of pastry plus the debris of my baking: a beige pastry bowl, old-fashioned scales, a floury wooden rolling pin and old-fashioned pastry cutters in the shape of stars and hearts. I rescued them all from various corners of the farmhouse kitchen and outbuildings when we cleared out decades of junk while we were refurbishing Kilhallon Park over the summer. Cal's family hadn't thrown anything away for fifty years, judging by the junk that was piled high in the old barn and workshop and offices.

I hand Cal a flowery china plate with a crumble-topped tart on it. It just happens to have a heart-shaped crust.

He pushes away the Kilner jar of mincemeat to make room for the plate. 'My, this is posh.'

'It was one of your mum's, I think. I found the service in the back of the dresser in the sitting room.'

'Yes, I remember it . . . it was a wedding present from Uncle Rory and Auntie Fiona, but Mum never wanted to use it. I think it's called Old Country Roses. Dad put it away after she died. He said it might get broken, but I think the real reason was because he couldn't bear to be reminded of her.' Cal brushes his finger over the gold rim. 'Probably felt guilty,' he adds.

Cal's father died a couple of years ago, and his mum passed away when he was still a teenager. His parents' marriage was a troubled one. His father worshipped his mum but still had a string of affairs. Sometimes I wonder if that's why Cal's own love life has been stormy too. As for losing our mothers when we were young — we have that in common. Mine lost her battle with cancer when I was a teenager and I haven't seen my dad and brother for ages, but that's by choice. I ran away from home when I was eighteen. Some people might say that's why we're drawn to each other, Cal and I: we share a bond; troubled childhoods, less than ideal family lives.

He pulls me into his arms for a long, warm snog that makes me tingle from head to toe. Phew, it's not only the Aga that's making it so hot in here.

'The pies pass the test then?' I say when I can finally breathe again. 'The mincemeat is homemade from my Nana Demelza's recipe, but I added a local fruit cider for a Cornish twist.'

He licks his lips. 'Mmm. Cider mincemeat. Nice. They're delicious, but I may have a burnt tongue.'

I roll my eyes. 'As if I care.'

'You know you do.' With another wicked smile, Cal kisses me again. Tiny flakes of pastry cling to his lips. His mouth is still warm from the pie and tastes sweet and buttery. If I don't push him away now, we might end up in bed in the middle of the day and I have way too much to do.

With the greatest reluctance, I end the kiss, but Cal keeps his hands around my waist and they feel as if they belong there — have always belonged there — which is a dangerous thought. Cal belongs to no woman or man.

'Cal, I have so much to do. As well as the cafe stuff, the other guests will be here on Friday afternoon and the other two cottages still aren't ready. With Polly away, we need to dress the beds and finish hanging the curtains in the bedroom of Warleggan and I still need to do extra shopping for the welcome hamper.'

'I'll help you with the curtains and Polly will be back from her daughter's tomorrow to lend us a hand. So now you have no excuse not to get naked with me.'

'Naked? What if one of the guests turns up in reception and finds us in bed in the middle of the afternoon?' I say, picturing Kit Bannen dinging the bell and being answered by creaking floorboards and a *When Harry Met Sally* re-enactment.

Cal waggles his eyebrows. 'Who mentioned bed? I was thinking of taking you in the kitchen.'

'You can't!' But even the mention of bed and taking me in the kitchen is driving me insane. My body zings with a peppery lust that's both sharp and delicious. He blows softly in the v-neck of my T-shirt, cooling the hot skin of my cleavage, but heating up every other part of me.

'I have to face the yurt family as soon as we're finished. Come on, this may be our last chance for a while . . . ' Cal says.

Now, this, I cannot deny.

'Not for long, then . . . '

He runs his palm over my bare thigh. 'Oh, don't worry, the way you're making me feel, it won't take long . . . but would you mind very much if we do it without the Santa hat?'

3

On Wednesday morning I skip down the farmhouse stairs after taking a shower in the bathroom of Kilhallon House. Polly arrives later today so I stayed over at the farmhouse last night while I had the chance. Cal lives in the main house, but, of course, I have my own little cottage across the yard. It's tiny and the décor's straight from the seventies: a crazy mix of clashing florals, but I love having my independence.

My place is one of a row of old farm buildings that was converted for the staff that used to work at the original caravan site in the seventies. We're converting two of the others into low-cost guest accommodation because Cal wanted to offer something at Kilhallon to suit all budgets, not only catering for people with more cash to spend on their holidays. For those who can afford luxury, there are also four larger 'premium' cottages on the estate that have been renovated over the summer ready for our first guests — one of which is occupied by Kit.

When I walk into the kitchen, Cal is scrolling through his phone. His hair is still damp from the shower and he's pulled on a crumpled but clean blue long-sleeved T-shirt and cargo pants. Bare footed, he pads over the tiles and pours a glass of water from the tap. Mitch wanders into the kitchen from the yard too and also heads straight for his water bowl, slurping noisily and splashing droplets over the tiles.

The morning sun streams in through the open door. It's warmer in here than yesterday, or perhaps I'm glowing after my night-time 'exercise'. Cal puts down his glass of water and kisses me. The scent of his woody body spray fills my senses, but Cal pulls a regretful face. 'Sorry I have to leave you, but I need to go down to the yurt field to make sure our guests haven't decided to leave after the overnight showers. How about dinner here at the house tonight? There's a nice bottle of Cornish fizz in the fridge.'

'That's a free sample from the vineyard that I was going to put in one of the welcome hampers for the guests. Sorry, but I'll be way too busy to stop for dinner. The cafe's opening tomorrow and there's still stuff to do.'

'What stuff?'

'I need to clean the floor because the tiler only finished yesterday and it's still dusty. Then there's the blackboard to chalk up with the specials because I won't have time tomorrow, and there's still a drinks delivery to put away and I need to email everyone to make sure they're still going to turn up and that no one's had cold feet about working for us.'

Cal opens his mouth. 'Why would — '

'And the courier dropped off the new cafe uniforms here yesterday and they all need ironing. And I still haven't written a blog post about opening day or scheduled my tweets and I'll have to upload some photos to Instagram and I need to email the ad department at *Cornish Lifestyle* to say we do want to be in their pre-Christmas dining feature because the copy deadline was last night and I'm already late.'

Cal holds up both hands. 'Whoa.'

'So I can't have dinner with you this evening no matter how much I'd love to.'

He puts his hands on my shoulders. 'I've worked that much out for myself. Tell you what, why don't we take a picnic down to the cafe and I'll help you get ready.'

'*You'll* write the ad copy and upload my photos?'

'No, but I'll clean the floor, put away the drinks order and iron the aprons.'

'You do ironing?'

He tuts. 'That's sexist, Ms Jones. I can iron. I did work in a warzone for several years, you know.'

'Yes, but I don't expect there was much call for ironing in the desert, was there?'

He smiles. 'Not often, no. Either way, we're in this together. I'll deal with the yurt people and clean the washroom block.'

I pull a face, glad this isn't my job.

'And then I'll meet you at the cafe.'

By late afternoon, the sun is sinking and the horizon is tinged with orange and pink. The lights are on in Demelza's, highlighting the sparkling clean floor as Cal hangs the last of the freshly pressed Demelza's aprons on a peg in the staff room.

All our perishables and groceries are stored in the correct places and the new steel kitchen

27

gleams so brightly you can see your face in the surfaces, I've double checked the fresh and chilled stores and chalked up the specials on the blackboard. In the end, Cal helped me write some copy for an ad and he's now sending a 'friendly' mass text to make sure the staff are OK and ready for tomorrow.

Throughout the day, I've been working on my blog and scheduling some posts for social media. I suspect that it's going to take all my 'days off' when the cafe is closed to get through the admin and marketing.

Cal scrolls through his phone where he keeps an app to keep track of the park bookings. 'Great. We've just had an Internet booking for Poldark Cottage and had an enquiry about two of the yurts from a family who want to celebrate a fortieth birthday party here next weekend. I'll have to tell the large party that they can have the yurts at the far end of the copse, away from the other two. We don't want complaints when we've promised people peace and tranquillity, but we don't want to lose a big booking like this.'

'Oh. If it's a party, they might want catering provided too.'

'I'm sure they will, but don't take too much on yet. You've got enough to do with the cafe opening tomorrow. I don't want the cafe manager having a meltdown in the middle of us launching the empire, do I?'

'You're all heart,' I say, but I know he means it and I must admit, I've been feeling knackered lately, even though I'm 'living the dream' right now. I've come so far from the day I lost my job and my home and ended up sleeping in the doorway of a fish and chip shop in St Trenyan.

Mitch woofs a hello from the corner. He seems totally at home in the cafe, which is great. Canine comfort is one of our USPs. Demelza's is even going to have a special doggy treats menu for all the four-legged guests who will stay at the park and take their owners on a walk along the coastal path that runs past the cafe.

Cal crouches down to stroke Mitch's ears. Mitch turns his head this way and that, closing his eyes in pleasure at Cal's touch. Did I say Mitch was *my* dog? Even though he's faithful to me and has stuck with me through a tough couple of years, he's rapidly becoming *our* dog: mine and Cal's dog, even Polly's dog at times, though she pretends she doesn't like animals at all, apart from her hens. I caught her sneaking him a treat from the jar when she thought I wasn't looking, and she let him sit next to her on the sofa while she was watching *Countryfile* on iPlayer the night before she went to visit her daughter.

Mitch and I, we've become as much a part of Kilhallon as the stone house, or the holiday cottages or the cafe.

'How are the opening-day plans going? Is there anything else I can do to help?' Cal says.

'I'm sure there'll be tons tomorrow. We'll be chasing our own tails,' I reply, and Mitch wags his as if he can understand me. 'I've tried to think of everything but there are bound to be hitches and teething problems until we've actually served some real customers.'

'Let's hope the weather keeps improving so we have lots of people out on the coastal path. The walking festival run by the tourist board should help,' Cal says.

'I hope that dog-friendly cafe-trail website and leaflet I signed up to pays off. It's hard knowing what marketing is worth spending my precious budget on. I'm bombarded with sales people and emails wanting me to part with cash all the time. I guess we're going to make mistakes along the way. Although I've worked in a few cafes now and done so much research and talked to other owners, I still have so much to learn.'

'Will Eva Spero be coming?' Cal pops the leftover crust of a cheese and bacon pasty in his mouth. We ate them cold with pickles and salad, washed down with cider.

'I don't know. She's still a bit miffed with me for turning down her job offer, although she said we can work together on the homemade dog treats book and possibly launch them into the market. I've had to put it on hold for now, until I've got Demelza's up and running.' I shrug off a pang of regret about turning down Eva Spero's offer of a job at her restaurant in Brighton. It was my decision, even though Cal also wanted me to stay here at Kilhallon and run Demelza's. Then, of course, there's the small matter of my being in love with him . . .

Cal pulls me into his arms and for a few moments I enjoy the warmth and comfort of his gorgeous body against mine. I can't believe how far I've come. The project I've started over-whelms me sometimes and I have the urge to run away instead of facing down the great big wave that's rushing towards me, faster and faster.

'I'd better get some work done,' I say, escaping his embrace before I'm lost again. 'Then I really *do* need an early night.'

He folds his arms, a gesture that only shows off his magnificent guns, honed by all the outdoor work and labour he's put in on the renovation of the park since he returned from working in a refugee camp in the Middle East. 'Of course,' he says with the kind of serious face that's even sexier than his smile. Despite all my resolve, I know an early night will mean going to bed with him.

Cal scratches Mitch's belly. 'If the cottages let, they let, and if they don't, then we mustn't panic. Same with the customers for the cafe. It's going to take time to build up our custom and reputation . . . and it might be better not to have full occupancy to start with while we learn the ropes.'

I turn away to find the keys, ready to lock up.

'By the way, I meant to tell you, Isla called me earlier,' he says.

At the mention of this name, my stomach tightens. 'Did she?'

'She's coming down here from London in a couple of weeks' time.'

Mitch snickers and yips like Scooby Doo on Red Bull as Cal fusses him. My stomach ties itself in even tighter knots. I knew it had to come sometime. I knew that she'd be back, but I haven't heard Cal talk about his ex-girlfriend and childhood sweetheart since she left Cornwall a few weeks ago. Even though Isla has been kind to me in the past, part of me hoped she might not come back at all.

I keep my voice casual. 'Does she still want to use Kilhallon for the film shoot?'

Cal glances up at me. Is that relief on his face that I haven't reacted to his news, or have I imagined it?

'Yes. She wants to use the ruined tin mine as a backdrop, and possibly the exterior of the cafe for the filming. Isla says that the far, gabled end could still double up as a farm barn for some of the scenes. She said that Bonnie and Clyde will also want to come and visit to discuss their hand-fasting arrangements at some point.'

These are codenames we're all using for the very famous and very actor friends of Isla's. Did I mention she's a film producer? A stunning, blonde, award-winning film producer with some seriously A-list mates. Two of her friends plan on holding their wedding celebrations at Kilhallon next year, although the engagement is secret for now.

'Why did Polly call them Bonnie and Clyde — who *are* Bonnie and Clyde?' I ask Cal.

'They were gangster lovers so I think the nicknames are Polly's little joke. I don't think she approves of hand fasting. What the hell is a hand fasting, anyway? Sounds like a cross between a DIY skill and an obscene practice. If it is rude, even I've never heard of it.'

Cal succeeds in making me laugh out loud even though the thought of catering for a

32

celebrity wedding makes me nervous.

'So you're cool with Isla and her crew descending?' Cal adds, laughing as Mitch moans in delight under his expert belly rubs. How, I ask myself, did my faithful hound turn into such a tart?

'Sounds great,' I say, trying to make myself feel as enthusiastic as I sound. The publicity that would come from a film being made here is exactly what we need for the resort and my cafe. In fact it's priceless and I should be welcoming Isla and her crew with open arms. 'We should have any teething problems ironed out by the time they get here.'

Cal gives Mitch's turn a final tickle then straightens up. 'Isla said she didn't want to disrupt business any more than was strictly necessary. She asked me if you'd email her or call to arrange the best time for her visit. It's better if you two liaise together rather than me passing on messages. I'd probably get it wrong anyway and then I'd be in trouble with both of you.'

'True. Who knows what havoc you'd create if we left the arrangements to you.' My smile makes my jaw ache, along with my heart and conscience, but I can see that Cal's pleasure at my apparent approval is genuine. Even though Isla has made it clear she's no longer interested in Cal beyond 'friendship', I'm not convinced. Cal has been honest enough to admit he couldn't simply 'unlove' Isla.

And if *I'm* honest, I never expected him to.

He knows I really like him and the sex is

amazing, but does he have any inkling that I'm crazy in love with him? I don't think it would be a great idea for him to find out.

'Demi?' Cal touches my arm. 'Are you OK?'

'Fine. It's been a long day and there's an even bigger one coming tomorrow.'

I'm already thinking of throwing caution to the wind and dragging him off to bed when Cal says, 'Are you *really* too tired for some therapy?'

'Perhaps you're right. It might do me good.'

His face lights up and we lock up the cafe, and Mitch scampers ahead on our way back to the house. He doesn't have a care in the world and I envy him his simple doggy life sometimes.

I don't want to be part of a love triangle, because someone always gets the sharp end. Isla and her fiancé, Luke — who was Cal's best mate years ago — have moved to London from Cornwall, to 'make a fresh start'. Apparently, Isla suspected that Luke was having an affair with a local 'property developer' called Mawgan Cade. I wouldn't put *anything* past Mawgan, but I can't see why Luke would jeopardise his relationship with Isla for a woman like Mawgan. But what do I know? Mawgan is manipulative and would sell her granny if it achieved her aims. Plus, Luke's a weak and selfish character if you ask me; and Isla deserves better. As long as 'better' doesn't turn out to be Cal again.

He hugs me and his chest is warm and firm against my body. If I let my guard down too far, I could easily start thinking how wonderful it would be to spend the rest of my life at Kilhallon with Cal. It's an idyllic place that sucks you in, just like Cal draws people to him. Just like the wreckers who used to shine their lights to lure people onto the rocks in storms. Except that was a myth. I need to get real and, reluctantly, I slide out of his embrace. 'Do you think we can cope?' I say.

'Of course I think we can cope. We've come a long way — both of us — and everything will be OK. Wasn't that what you were always telling me when we started work on the place? When we were refused planning permission and the appeal failed because of the Cades' opposition? When I ripped my hands open demolishing the walls? When the tree fell through the farmhouse window? When you almost walked out on me to work for Eva Spero in Brighton?'

'Maybe I should have,' I joke, thinking of how close I came to quitting and heading off to Brighton before the place had even opened. 'This is a massive thing for me, Cal. It's very exciting, but I'm also terrified.'

He slides his hand under my hair, lifting it from my neck, caressing my skin. His palm is rough from the work he's been doing, yet the effect is like being stroked with warm velvet.

'Shh,' he says in that gentle, half-amused voice that turns me on and irritates me at the same time. 'It's OK to be nervous, but the important thing is that you stick with me. That's what we're going to carry on doing: sticking together.

Even as I close my eyes and abandon myself to his touch and soothing words, there's a part of me holding back. A part that can't forget the Cal who left a trail of broken hearts when he went away to the Middle East. The teenage Cal breezing his way through the girls of St Trenyan: Isla, even Mawgan Cade. Even his father was sleeping with half the women from here to Truro, if you believe the rumours. My friend Tamsin warned me about him and even Mawgan said he'd break my heart. She may be right about that one.

'I promise you Kilhallon will succeed and Demelza's will be open for business as scheduled, and nothing's going to stop us.' Cal pours soothing words into my ear. 'Now come to bed before I explode.'

Me too, I think. Mitch settles down in his bed in the farmhouse kitchen. Cal takes my hand and leads me, trembling, up to his room again. He's right, of course, I mustn't expect too much of the business; but even more importantly, I mustn't expect anything at all from him.

4

Coffee machine: on.

Air conditioning: on.

Ovens: on.

Sunshine: off, for now, but judging by the pale-blue patches peeking through the clouds, it's clearing up, which is just what we want to tempt customers out onto the coastal path and into the cafe for our opening day.

I repeat the words again, because I don't believe them: It's opening day at Demelza's. Opening day at *my* cafe. Six months ago I had no job, no home and no prospects and now look at me: manager of my own tiny empire.

Nina shouts from the side door. 'Demi! Demi! Come quick. Mitch has done something terrible!'

I run after her to the rear of the cafe, picturing Mitch with his teeth sunk into a toddler. The white fishmonger's van is parked outside. Harry, the driver, is cursing and shaking his fist at Mitch, who's chomping his way through a pack of fish from a safe distance.

'There goes your smoked mackerel order,' Harry says. 'Only turned away for a minute to get the shellfish out of the van for Nina and the crafty hound had the polystyrene off the packs and was wolfing them down.'

Plastic wrappers and polystyrene snow litter the grass. Mitch licks his chops and looks up at us as if to say, 'You have a problem?'

'I tried to grab them off him but he was too quick for me,' Nina wails. 'I'm sorry, Demi. Shall I tell everyone that the Fisherman's Lunch is off? We've got bit of smoked salmon, but that won't last long.'

'Leave it on until we run out of the salmon, then tell everyone we've sold out. I don't want to take something off the menu on our first day.'

I glare at Mitch, though, from the way Nina shouted, I'm relieved that his antics are nothing worse. 'Mitch, you're in trouble when I get hold of you. You can forget coming anywhere near my bed tonight. Your breath will stink for a week!'

Harry carries the rest of the order into the back of the cafe. We can't afford to waste expensive food, but I guess if Mitch guzzling the mackerel is the worst thing that happens on opening day, we'll be doing OK. With my nostrils closed, I tether Mitch in the shade by the back door with a bowl of water and his rope chew. I'll ask Robyn to take him when she turns up. I go back inside the cafe with a smile that says I'm cool about 'little mishaps' like losing a small fortune's worth of smoked mackerel.

The team is buzzing about in the cafe, servery and kitchen, preparing for our first day. My breath catches at the sight that greets me. They all look super smart in their teal-blue Demelza's Cafe aprons — and Jez the chef, who's in whites. His charcoal-coloured ponytail dangles from the back of his teal chef's cap. He's pushing forty, but still a lean, mean type who lives to surf. He also happens to be a very good chef. We were lucky to get him, but the part-time hours enable him to make the most of the gnarly surfing conditions and quiet beaches during the autumn and winter.

Nina's back behind the server, checking the operation of the till for the umpteenth time. I met her when we both worked as waitresses at a ball earlier this year. She's the same age as me and helps her mum run a kennels and dog rescue centre over the moor from Kilhallon. With all the dog walking and her triathlon training, she's super fit. Her spiky orange hair reminds me of a pixie.

Shamia, currently filling the condiment area, is my order taker. She's wearing a teal-blue headscarf to match her apron. She looks the most confident of anyone, to be honest. She's a former dinner lady and now a food blogger. She will be lending us a hand on weekdays while her little boy goes to nursery school, and at the weekends when her husband can babysit.

My official title is Cafe Manager, but I'm also the general dogsbody, greeting people, clearing tables and helping out on the counter. I love the baking and cooking, but I've had to leave most of the hot food prep to Jez.

There's only one person missing.

Just as I think Robyn Penwith, Cal's cousin, has cold feet about helping us, there's a rap on the glass door of the cafe. My shoulders slump in relief and I unlock the door. She's in jodhpurs and riding boots.

'Um. Sorry, I'm late. I had to call at Bosinney on my way here and tack up Ruby, then settle her in Kilhallon House stables.'

'It's fine. You're here now,' I say as we exchange a hug. Robyn's clothes smell faintly of horse, but that's fine. She keeps her mare at her dad's house even though she lives with her girlfriend, Andi, now. Andi's cool apart from the small matter of her sister being Mawgan Cade.

Cal has placed two advertising boards outside where the path skirts our land to catch walkers coming in both directions — from the far west and from St Trenyan in the east. You can see the cafe building and Kilhallon Farm from miles away too, thanks to the undulating path. Robyn's been drafted in to hand out flyers and free samples of ginger fairing biscuits on the path today and at the weekend.

The doughy, fruity scents of croissants, pains-au-chocolat and cinnamon swirls start to fill the air as the ovens heat up the first batch of baked goods. I clap my hands. 'OK, now we're all here, can we have a quick coffee and a chat, please? I won't keep you long. Why don't we all have one of these lime shortbreads, because it's going to be difficult to grab a break later.'

'Yes, boss!' voices chorus from the four corners.

We all gather for a very quick coffee — instant — and homemade lime shortbread around the large refectory table on one side of the cafe floor. Huddled in her padded riding gilet, even though it's warm in here, Robyn is nibbling her purple nails. Nina is trembling like a newborn pup. Shamia cradles her mug casually. Jez seems cool enough with it all — but he's experienced and, to be honest, I think he'd be chilled even if the place was on fire.

Our voices echo off the beams that support the high ceiling. The stone building is at least two hundred years old, and it was a storage barn until I persuaded Cal to let me convert it. It's a cool morning so we've made the cafe a little too warm for our comfort, but there's nothing worse for the customers than a cold welcome and the door's going to be open a lot, fingers crossed. Most people will arrive in layers and we want them to feel they can take them off, not be desperate to keep them on.

Nestling my own mug in both hands to stop them from shaking, I throw out an encouraging smile to my team.

'So, here we are. D-Day, which stands for Demelza's Day. Thanks to everyone for not running off and for turning up on time.'

They laugh dutifully, even Jez manages a smile. Robyn glances down guiltily.

'It's our first day and I'm not expecting that everything will run perfectly or to plan but as long as we get things 99.9 per cent right, I won't have to sack anyone.'

More laughter and an eye roll from Jez.

'You think I'm joking?'

Nina's mouth opens in horror and, for a moment, I wonder if she actually will run off and never come back.

I pat her arm, feeling way too young to be leading a team of staff, but if I don't put on a show of confidence, what hope do we have? 'It's fine, hun. I really am joking. We're all on a learning curve, apart from Jez, I guess.'

His mouth twitches, amused. Without him on side, we'd be done for.

'We're all here to help you. You'll be an old hand by the end of the day,' I reassure her.

She brightens.

'Now, as you all know, it's the first day of the West Cornwall Walking Festival, which is partly why we chose to open today. We're expecting even more ramblers than usual and a lot of dogs. I've put up a sign explaining everything but if anyone asks, the first three tables by the door are dog-friendly and, of course, the terrace.

'Most people will probably want to sit outside if the weather stays dry, and the dog owners are sure to prefer to be out there while it's fine. By the way, you'll find extra water bowls and doggy menus in the storeroom, if anyone needs them. If there's any canine aggro, or human aggro for that matter, call me immediately. Robyn, Mitch, and Nina's mum, plus a few of her rescue dogs, will be stationed on the coast path throughout the day to lure people in to the cafe.'

'I've put the collecting tin for the dog rescue centre next to the till,' Shamia says.

'Great, thanks. Can someone please pin a notice about the Christmas bookings on the notice board and arrange some of Cal's leaflets about weddings at Kilhallon on the window ledges?'

Nina raises her hand. 'I'll do that, Demi.'

'I'll collect Mitch,' Robyn pipes up, obviously eager to be out in the fresh air.

'Thanks, Robyn. OK, I've almost finished. You

all know your roles and we've had plenty of practice and a rehearsal so it should be fine. I trust you all and I know you'll work your guts out and won't let me down. So, one more time, let's hear it.'

Everyone groans, but I hold up my hand, excitement and adrenaline taking over.

'We are all awesome and Demelza's rocks!' they chorus, even Jez, before they dissolve into laughter and Jez rolls his eyes again. It was Nina who originally made up the cheesy mantra for a joke, but now we've all latched on to it. I don't care how crappy it sounds, if it releases the tension, that's fine by me.

Cal arrives, stooping under the weight of two large crates of veg. 'Hi there. The delivery guy from the market garden dropped these off at the farmhouse. Where do you want them?' he says, resting the crates on the table.

'In the storeroom.'

Cal looks around him. 'It looks great, Demi. You've done a fantastic job.'

'No, *we* have. All of us.'

'It's your baby and you should be proud.' His eyes shine. I don't think I've seen him quite so happy since the day he showed me the sign for the cafe and persuaded me to stay here at Kilhallon. For a moment, I'm too choked with emotion to reply, then I remember that the staff are relying on me today.

'Well, I can't think of a cafe with a better view for miles. It's a huge selling point if we can just let people know we're open,' I tell Cal, feeling the rising sense of panic that I've been subduing for the past few days about to overwhelm me like a great big wave. 'I hope they come.'

'I think you might have trouble keeping them away. Look.'

He nods to a man and a woman peering through the glass door, as if we're animals in the zoo.

My pulse leaps. 'OK. Our first customers are here. Do you want to let them in?' I call to Nina.

'No way. It's your cafe,' she says with a broad smile that tells me she's a lot more calm and collected than I feel.

'I think you should have the honour,' says Cal. 'Demelza.'

With a deep breath, and on slightly wobbly legs, I hurry to the door and open it. The couple, a sprightly pair of pensioners in matching hiking boots and navy fleeces, have big grins on their weather-beaten faces.

'So you *are* open. We thought you might be training or something.'

'No. We're open. Welcome to Demelza's Cafe. In fact you're our first ever customers.'

'Really? We're the first?'

'The very first. Look, you can have your pick of the seats. There are menus on the tables and a specials board above the counter over there.'

'We'd love a nice big pot of tea, Graham?' the woman says to her partner as they walk into the centre of the room, eyeing the scrubbed oak tables, the oak settles and vintage china.

'I'd like a latte, I think,' says Graham, sitting down at the table by the window. 'What a view. Have you really only just opened?'

'This very minute. If you'd like to place your order at the counter, you can collect your drinks and we'll bring any food orders across to you. Have you come far?'

'We were up at sparrow-fart and traipsed from the cove on the other side of St Trenyan. Linda said it would only take an hour but we've already been going nearly two. She always gets the timing way out. Thinks I won't notice she's trying to con me into believing it's only a stroll.'

'Don't start, Graham. You're the one who said we shouldn't take any notice of the walking app and swore blind you knew a short cut. I'll never forgive you for making me walk through that field of bullocks.'

'They won't do you any harm.'

'Then why were they following us and giving us funny looks?'

'You're safe in the cafe, I can promise that,' I cut in before we have our first full-blown domestic. 'We've got some amazing homemade cakes today and there's a brunch special. It's local bacon, sausages from the farm up the hill and eggs from our own hens here at Kilhallon.'

'Do you do those bacon and avocado toast combos? Our grandkids love those when we're visiting them in London and we're hooked,' Linda chirps up, much to my amazement.

'We do have some avocado. In fact it's on the menu,' I say, glad I've done my research, even though I'm not the greatest fan of this latest fad. Cal pulled an icky face when he tried it out and even Mitch refused to touch his bite-size sample.

'Not for me. I'm going to have a massive slice

45

of this here figgy obbin. Not had any of that since we used to motor down here in the Cortina with the kids.' Graham holds up the menu.

'Well, please join the queue,' I say, gesturing to Nina, standing alone behind the counter, fidgeting with her hat.

Before Graham's placed his order, the door opens again and a party of ramblers troops in, sighing with relief at reaching us, debating over which table to choose and asking where the toilets are.

'Thank goodness you're open!' declares a middle-aged woman in a yellow cagoule. 'I'm gagging for a coffee and a wee. Oh, are those homemade apricot scones? I've walked bloody miles this morning so I deserve one of those.'

'We've only done a thousand steps from the car park by the main road,' her friend whispers, showing me her FitBit.

I usher them to the table by the window and listen to them admiring the view. As part of the renovation of the old barn, the doors on one side have been replaced with a large glass window that gives an amazing view over the Atlantic Ocean. From our window seats and terrace, it almost feels as if you could touch the sea. On a stormy day, if the swell is big enough and the wind in the right direction, we might even have some spray on the windows.

It's only as I put more menus on the outside tables that I realise Cal has gone and left me in charge, but there's no time to think or worry. More customers drift in and out, some with dogs, some with babies in carriers, some with walking poles and even one in an all-terrain mobility scooter though goodness knows how he made it along the coast path. Jez is calling orders from the kitchen, Shamia's dealing with a queue of people at the counter and Nina is racing about clearing tables and serving people as if she's in a triathlon. In no time, we're dishing up Cornish goat's cheese paninis, and pasties, quiche salads and sandwiches to an array of people relaxing, chatting, checking their iPads, and all drinking our teas, coffees, and ciders while they scoff our cakes and savouries.

There's one moment when I have to stand outside the kitchen door to the rear and take a huge gulp of fresh Kilhallon air and pinch myself.

'Demi — it's four o'clock.' Nina pulls me aside as I fly into the kitchen with more dirty plates.

'You're joking?'

'No. Look.' She points to the clock on the wall, just above the health and safety notice.

'What? I thought it was about half-past two.'

'No. It really is. We've stopped taking orders.' Jez pops his head round the door of the staff cubby hole. His whites have been replaced by board shorts, a hoodie and flip-flops. 'I'm off shift. Hope you're pleased with how it went?'

'Yes. Wow. Thanks so much, Jez. But *four* o'clock? I can't believe it. I've been so busy clearing tables outside that I hadn't noticed.'

'Shall I put the closed sign on the door?' Nina enquires.

'Yes, I guess so, but we still have people eating,

47

inside and out. I'll go and tell everyone we're shutting soon.'

I feel strangely light-headed as I float into the cafe and inform the few stragglers that we're now closing. One man grumbles but the other customers seem OK and start to finish their food. Has the day really flown by so fast? Can it be real?

I turn over the closed sign on the door and step outside to clear the final tables when a man sprints onto the terrace.

'Damn it. I knew I'd be too late!'

5

Kit Bannen's face is red and he's breathing hard. 'Am I too late? I *am* too late, aren't I?'

'Yes.'

'Damn!'

I laugh. 'It's fine. We're open again tomorrow.' *It's only a cafe*, I want to add.

'I wanted to be here on your opening day. I was all set to be a difficult customer.'

I lower my voice. 'Don't worry, we've already had the customer from hell.'

I throw a wave and a smile at a couple from London who are staying in our cottages. Their toddler, George, had a screaming tantrum lasting half an hour and threw every piece of food they offered him onto the floor. George's wails of protest pierce the air as his parents attempt to strap him into his luxury all-terrain buggy.

Kit winces and we both laugh.

'Come in and have some coffee,' I say, reminding myself that he's a guest and that he was seriously pissed off that the cafe was shut when he checked into Kilhallon. One extra customer won't matter.

'I don't want to get in the way.'

'It's OK, as long as you don't mind the staff clearing up around you.'

He smiles. 'I'll make myself useful.'

'You don't have to do that. You're a guest

here.' My smile is fixed on by now. It's been a long and exciting day and to be honest, all I want to do is clear up and have a debrief with the team then collapse in my cottage.

'No way. It's my fault I'm late so I insist on giving you a hand.'

Too tired and frazzled to object further, I cave in. 'OK, but I warn you, I'm a horrible boss and if you're so keen, you can help me clear the last of the stuff from the outside tables.'

It's twenty-past four and a few people had lingered outside, draining their teapots and chatting in the last precious rays of the afternoon sun. However, the clouds are rolling in, so even they start to pack up and leave. Kit helps me gather up the dirty crockery, empty sugar packets and pots of strawberry jam and clotted cream.

'Looks like you've had a busy opening day,' he says, following me to the bin store at the rear of the kitchens.

'Yes, the walking festival brought us some good custom and once the sun came out, we had passing trade. Plus George, of course. I need to warn you that he and his mum and dad are staying in Penvenen Cottage. It's the other end of the row from you, though, so you shouldn't hear him.'

'I wouldn't be too sure.' Kit holds up the bin lid while I throw in the rubbish. 'If I do, I'll have to get some ear plugs or turn up my music to full volume.'

I wince. 'Sorry about George. I'm guessing you came here for some quiet away from the office.'

He glances away from me then throws me a pained smile. 'Actually, I may have been economical with the truth about working in an office. I tend to take my office with me wherever I go. I'm a writer.'

I resist shouting 'Yessss', because I knew he did something creative and arty. Instead I ask politely. 'Oh, do you write books?'

'Yes. Thrillers. Correction: *a* thriller. I haven't even finished my first yet, though my deadline's racing up fast.'

'Sounds exciting. Do you have a pen name?' I ask him. To be honest, I'm doing most of the clearing up while he talks but I'd much rather it was that way.

'I will do, I expect. I don't know for sure because I've only just got my first book deal and it's all new to me. I was a journalist before I became an author and before you ask, it was as an editor for a very dull trade publication about renewable energy. My new thriller is about a woman scientist who finds a way to generate power from water that's going to change the whole world and do away with the need for fossil fuels. Naturally a lot of countries with less than ideal human rights records aren't very pleased about that, while others would do anything to get their hands on her research.'

'That sounds . . . intriguing,' I say. 'I don't have tons of time to read anything except recipe and business books at the moment, but your book sounds right up Polly's street. She loves crime and thrillers, the gorier the better. Sometimes I worry she might secretly be plotting to murder us all in our beds.'

Kit's sea-green eyes glint with humour. 'I've already met Polly earlier today. I popped up to your reception to pick up some leaflets about the local area. She's certainly an interesting woman. I reckon I could get enough material for a whole series of novels from her tales about the local area, if I wanted to set a book here.'

'She's definitely unique,' I say, surprised that Kit has charmed Polly so fast, and even more surprised that she's made such an impression on him. Polly is a hard woman to please and can be plain speaking to the point of rudeness, but Kit is a guest so she was obviously being polite.

Kit is silent, thoughtful, for a second or so, toeing a clump of grass with his running shoe. 'Look, I'm sorry I was such a grumpy sod when I turned up yesterday. You must have thought 'miserable git, hope all the guests aren't going to be like this'.'

'No . . . I was thinking poor you, arriving in stinking weather after a terrible journey.'

'You're a good fibber, Demi.' He opens the bin again for me to throw in the final bits of rubbish.

'No fib. It's true.' Or half-true, I think. I was sorry for him, but I also did think he was a miserable git.

'OK, you're good at the customer relations, then. I'd never be any good at serving the public. I'd cause any place that I ran to be closed down or I'd be bankrupt within a week. I'm not very good at hiding my feelings, you see. It's a good job my work requires me to be where people are not.'

'Isn't it very exciting, being an author?'

He smiles again, as if I've missed a huge point. 'Most of the time it's squalid. Spending far too much time in your own company, with the terror of the blank page. You know how it is . . . '

'Not really. I tend to have terror of the soggy bottom.'

He does a double take.

'Of my pies and pasties. If you don't get the temperature right.'

'Ah.' He laughs politely at my lame joke. 'You do have a proper job, however, whereas I make up stories for a living. Or not, at the moment. I've been struggling with my plot lately. And my characters. And the actual words.' He grimaces but in a charming way, a *tiny* bit like Cal. He really is handsome when he smiles, though nothing like as handsome as Cal, and of course Kit is blond, whereas Cal has dark, brooding good looks. I guess blonds can be brooding too. I snap out of my thoughts as Kit goes on.

'You must have thought I'd come here to get away from work, but the reason I was so tetchy was because I've come here *to* work. Normally, I tend to avoid telling people I'm a writer because they ask all sorts of awkward questions. Some people think having a book published is like winning the lottery: just an unexpected lucky windfall you landed on top of your regular job, but you know yourself that any degree of success takes a lot of hard work,' he says with a nod at the cafe.

'That's true. I imagine some people think that running a cosy little tea room would be a great way of escaping a real job too. I've worked in catering before so I had an idea of what was involved, but it's a completely different ballgame being responsible for the cafe rather than simply serving customers'

He nods and pauses, looking awkward. 'Sorry I was grumpy when I arrived. I promise to behave from now on.'

'It's fine. I know how to handle tricky customers.'

'Yes, I've experienced your people skills first hand. You were very good at calming me down. In fact, you're very good at all of this.'

He waves a hand at the cafe and the park. I feel myself blushing. I'm not used to the flattery, and not sure I like it that much.

'I think that will do for out here. Let's go back inside,' I say.

Kit follows me in. Shamia is wiping down the last few tables inside the cafe while Nina washes up the items that can't or didn't fit into the dishwasher. Without the spurts and gurgles of the coffee machine and the buzz of customers, it seems quiet. The dishwasher hums softly and there's the odd thunk and clink of pots being washed as a backdrop. Jez has gone so the girls chat to each other about some of the stranger requests and comments we've had today. Robyn offers to check the online review sites. I think she cajoled her student friends into writing a few. I'm not sure I can face reading them, but I know I *have* to, to get some feedback and politely respond to any negative comments.

That thought makes me feel faintly sick. I

remember Sheila ranting when she steeled herself for her weekly reviewers' ordeal. That pleasure's now all mine. Suddenly, I feel like a wrung-out dishcloth, but there's still work to do. Closing the door on the customers is only the start of the end of our day.

'I need to mop the floor,' I say, feeling as if I don't even have the energy to lick an envelope.

'Don't take this the wrong way, but you do look like you need a break,' Kit says.

'I don't have time.'

'Yes, you do. Do as he says.' Nina pulls back a chair from the table.

'She hasn't stopped all day and hasn't eaten anything,' Shamia tuts.

'I had that broken fairing at lunchtime.'

Kit smiles. 'Not enough to keep a flea alive. I think you should do what your staff say, boss.'

'But the floor needs a mop. I can't sit around while the team are working.'

'Chill. We'll manage to clean the floor round you both. Now, sit down! We're going to bring you a nice apple and elderflower presse and there's one slice of bacon and tomato quiche left.' Nina turns to Kit, every inch the seasoned professional. She's blossomed in just one day. 'And what can we get you, sir?'

'I'll have a cider, please, and thanks for the offer of food but I already ate in St Trenyan. My research trip took longer than I'd expected.'

'Not even an apricot scone?'

Kit pauses then says. 'Oh, go on then. I can't resist.'

Delighted to have persuaded him, Nina

55

scuttles off to the kitchen. The moment my bum makes contact with the seat, I realise how knackered and weak I feel. I haven't eaten or drunk much and I've been running on adrenaline and excitement since six o'clock this morning.

It's weird to sit in the cafe with the staff working around me, chatting to a guest about how I started the cafe business and Kilhallon, but this is my life now: it's begun to sink in that I'm in charge and living my dream, even if that dream is harder work than I ever imagined. Slowly, the tension ebbs from my body and in between devouring the quiche and the slice of figgy obbin that Nina brings me for dessert, I finally begin to relax and realise that for today, at least, it's job done.

'This is a stunning location,' Kit says, accepting his scone from Nina with a dazzling smile that brings pink to her cheeks. 'I can see why you and Cal fought so hard to keep it going.'

His remark catches me off guard. It seems a bit funny that he's talking about Cal as if he knows us already but I suppose Polly's been gossiping to him and we *should* make the guests feel like old friends.

'You wouldn't believe the difference between the park today and when Cal first showed me round at Easter. The location itself is fantastic. The views are incredible, even when you've lived round here all your life, you realise that. The moment I saw the barn that was here, I knew it would make a great cafe.'

'I chose this place because it had last-minute availability and it was good value, thanks to your opening offers. It also seemed to be out of the way of distractions, apart from the Internet, that is. Sadly, I need that to keep in touch with my agent and editor and I still do a bit of freelance work for my old trade publication.'

'I knew you must do something creative, even though you said it was boring admin. I thought you'd had enough of work and didn't want to talk about it.'

'Yes, and no.' He grins. 'Talking of which, I was going to ask you a favour.'

'Ask away,' I say, suddenly wondering — I don't know why — if he's going to ask me out for a drink or something. No, that would be silly. He would never do that here with everyone around and he's not here for long and he *must* have guessed I'm 'with' Cal — except I'm not, in any formal sense. We're not living together or even acting like a couple in public. Which I'm fine with, I remind myself.

'Miraculously, I've managed to get on with my novel pretty well so far this week and I put that down to the peace and tranquillity here. People can hardly drop in and ask me for a pint or to help them fix their bikes. The setting's inspirational too. Even the storm and the rain. Especially the rain.'

Tell that to the yurt people, I think, although judging by the noise last night, they were having a good time.

'Glad you're enjoying it,' I say, wondering where the conversation is leading and thinking it doesn't sound like he's about to ask me on a date.

'And I know I only intended to stay for two weeks but I was wondering if you might be willing to negotiate on a longer-term let. It's a long shot because you may be booked up.'

Relief floods through me. 'I'm not sure. I know Enys is booked at half term but it might be free until then and afterwards, it's our quiet season so I can probably let you have a discount then.' I harden my heart, knowing I can't do him a deal until after half term. 'How long were you thinking of staying?' I ask.

'Until the week before Christmas, if you have the availability.'

'Christmas!'

He breaks into a grin. 'Don't sound so surprised. There are worse places to stay, you know.'

'I know. Kilhallon's great but it won't be cheap . . . and what about your place in London?' I say, knowing I'm doing a terrible job of selling the site. Out of the corner of my eye, I catch Nina and Shamia watching us from the servery.

'I've a friend who'd be happy looking after my flat. He's just finished a contract abroad and wants a short-term place to stay in London while he hunts for a new job and his rent will cover my stay here. Plus there are trains, you know, if I can't face the drive back when I need to go to a meeting.'

'I didn't mean to be nosy. Of course, Kilhallon's perfect for peace and quiet and I'm sure we can come to some arrangement. I'd have to ask Cal, of course.'

'Of course, if you need to square things with him, as he's your boss . . . '

Something in Kit's tone irritates me and I remind myself that I don't need Cal's permission to take a booking from a guest. 'I'll check the bookings when I go back to the house. I've got the live booking chart on my phone, but the signal's not great down here.'

Kit puts his hand on my arm to stop me leaping to my feet, not that I could leap, my legs feel wobbly. 'No rush,' he says. 'Later will do and as for the phone signal: that's another reason for staying here. My agent can't keep ringing me to ask how the book is going, and no one else can reach me either.'

'OK. I'll come round or call you later when I've checked, but it should be fine for a long-term let, even if you have to move cottages halfway through.'

'That won't bother me. Great. Now that I know I'm staying, I can settle into my novel. It's a relief, to be honest, I was dreading having to go back to the smoke. There's something about Kilhallon that really inspires me.' He flashes me a smile then tips the cider bottle to his lips. He really is very good-looking when he turns on the charm, but I can't quite fathom him out. When he first arrived, you'd have thought he was furious with the whole world.

He reminds me of Cal a little: one moment sunshine and the next showers, but Cal doesn't seem to be able to switch the seasons on and off in the same way that Kit does. I'm not sure Cal's so in control of his climate, and to be honest, I prefer it that way. Cal's unpredictable in a predictable way, but Kit's just unpredictable ... Oh sod it, he's only a guest. As long as he doesn't start wailing the place down and chucking food on the floor like George, he can be as quirky as he likes. More importantly, his money's as good as anyone else's and it looks like we're going to get rather a nice chunk of it.

6

Our opening long weekend of trading has been exhausting, but that's way better than having to stand around with nothing to do. My marketing efforts are paying off and word has got round that we're now up and running. I know a lot of locals will have turned up out of curiosity over the weekend and that we need to work hard to keep them coming back, as well as attracting tourists, but I was so happy to see the cafe buzzing on Friday, Saturday and Sunday. There's no time to let up, however, and I've spent today — Monday — trying to catch up with admin, ordering and planning.

I must admit I could have quite happily collapsed in my cottage this evening, but tonight is another important occasion for Kilhallon. We've opened Demelza's especially to host a meeting of the St Trenyan Harbour Lights committee. The Harbour Lights Festival, held on the last Friday in November, attracts thousands of people to the village, both from Cornwall and further afield at a time of year when St Trenyan really needs a boost.

'I still can't believe Kit Bannen wants to stay here for so long,' Cal says to me midway through laying out mince pie cookies on a table in the cafe.

'Until the week before Christmas, according to Kit. I meant to tell you sooner, but we've both

61

been so busy with work that I forgot. The resort's your job, of course, but I checked out the booking calendar while you were at the wholesalers and I've already said he can have Enys Cottage. We had another couple booked into Enys for half term but it's easier to upgrade them to Penvenen than move Kit out just for a week. Was that OK?'

'I guess so but this longer-term stay will cost him a lot of money. Why does he want to hunker down in the middle of nowhere at this time of year?'

'Boy am I glad you're not doing the marketing for this place,' I say with an eye roll.

'You know what I mean. I can understand him staying a couple of weeks but why would a metrosexual like him want to be away from London?'

'A metrosexual? Kit? Nah. He's much too rugged for that. He wears a Berghaus coat, for a start.'

Cal eyes me sharply and raises an eyebrow at my comment.

'Stop laughing at me. He just doesn't strike me as a hipster. He's too blokey for the self-obsessed trendy type.'

' 'Rugged' and 'blokey' eh? Not that *you're* interested in the blond hunk, Kit Bannen, of course. He's *only* a guest.' Cal swipes a mince pie cookie from the plate.

'I didn't say he was a 'hunk', *you* did and *actually* he has a deadline on his book and he said he can get on with it better away from the distractions in London. It's a techno-thriller.'

Cal huffs. 'A techno-thriller? He obviously talks to you more than me. He hardly even bothers to nod a hello at me if we come across each other, not that I'm bothered, as long as he pays the bill. You must have charmed him.'

'No. Kilhallon has charmed him.' Do I detect a hint of jealousy from Cal? That would be nice . . . then I snap out of my fantasies. Kit isn't interested in me and vice versa, and I doubt Cal's really jealous.

'What else do we need?' he asks.

'Nothing. I'll set the coffee machine going just before we have a break and bring it out here. People can help themselves to hot water from the machine for their teas.'

'I'm sure they'll be impressed. This place looks great and the smell of these cookies is delicious.'

'I thought the spices would get everyone in the mood. Thanks for helping me. I can't ask the staff to stay on. They've done enough this week.'

'It's no problem.'

Cal chats to me about the accommodation bookings while we push some tables together to make one long 'boardroom-style' table for the meeting. We still need to fill two of the cottages for Christmas, and Warleggan is vacant at New Year. The yurt season will be over after half term until next Easter.

Cal goes into the kitchen to collect some mugs and plates while I add a jug of milk and sparkling white bowls of demerara sugar cubes to the refreshment table. It may be only a meeting, but I want everything to look perfect tonight. One of the tourist officers is coming, along with influential locals, to discuss plans for the highlight of the St Trenyan calendar.

The festival starts with a lantern procession to the harbour before the big switch-on. The old harbour is decorated with lights in the shape of boats, Christmas trees, stars, shells and starfish, all made up of thousands of jewel-bright bulbs. It's quirky, random and very pretty. Until Twelfth Night, the quay and nearby pubs, shops and houses are illuminated, the colours reflected in the coal-black waters of the sea.

There are stalls selling hot food and drink, gifts and a mini funfair on the quayside. The evening ends with sing-along carols with the St Trenyan Fisherman's Choir. It's a massively popular tradition with everyone, and it marks the 'real' start of Christmas, even though all the shops will already be selling gifts and cards well before then.

I spot myself reflected in the large window, almost perfectly mirrored by the blackness outside, and think of a time, less than a year ago, when I wasn't part of the celebrations but an outsider left in the cold. A lump forms in my throat.

'How many are you expecting?' Cal calls to me from the servery where he's filling two jugs with water.

Shaking off the memory of darker times, I join him. 'A dozen, maybe a few more. I looked at the list and recognised a few of the names. Local businesspeople, councillors, fishermen and the vicar. Are you definitely staying for the meeting?' I ask Cal.

'Normally I'd rather stick pins in my eyeballs than join a committee, but I'll make an exception for this one. A lot of the people coming will want to ask questions about Kilhallon. Some of them came to our promo event in August and they'll be keen to see how we're doing. Or not.' He smiles wryly, knowing a couple of the committee members run holiday-let businesses themselves.

He tears open a blue bag of ice and empties the cubes into the water jugs. 'Besides, Mum was on the committee for a few years before she became ill. She helped with the fundraising and used to really enjoy it. I think it was a welcome distraction from Dad's shenanigans.'

Cal doesn't mention his late mother very often but I know he misses her. 'I didn't know she was part of it. She'd be pleased you're keeping up the tradition.'

'Yeah, well, Dad couldn't be arsed to help out so maybe I should do it, if only to show them how much Kilhallon has changed. We should mention our bookings are healthy, of course, even if it's not *strictly* accurate, but that we also want to do our bit for community spirit.' He winks at me. I envy his lashes, damn him.

'There are some lemon slices in a tub at the bottom of the fridge,' I say, feeling myself growing warm again as I think of Cal's eyes on me, and his hands too.

Cal finds the tub and drops the lemon slices into the water while I select a large bottle of apple juice from the chiller. 'November's looking a bit thin, but that's always a dead time of year

65

and hopefully the Christmas lights will lure people into the cottages for the final week of the month, especially now the cafe's open,' he says.

I try to refocus on the business in hand. 'I must blog about the meeting and post some pics of last year's lights and some menus for the pop-up cafe we're having at the festival.'

I fill another jug with the apple juice and we carry them to the table. The first of the committee will start to arrive in a few minutes. There's a small parking area behind the cafe that should accommodate most of their cars. Cal opens his tablet and nods at me to look at the Harbour Lights website. It's a 'homemade' site but I think the quirkiness is part of its charm. The photos of the twinkling snowmen and a giant shark fixed on the harbour walls make us both smile. 'I loved the harbour lights when I was little, even when I was a teenager we looked forward to going down into St Trenyan with our mates.'

'You and Luke? I'd have thought you were too cool for fairy lights.'

'No way. It was a chance for Luke, Isla, Tamsin and me — plus a few others from school — to go down into St Trenyan for a night out without our parents keeping an eye on us. When we were in the sixth form whoever had a car would drive us down and the rest of us would try to sneak into the pubs or persuade someone over eighteen to buy us drinks that we could take outside. There were so many people around drinking and eating in the streets and the stalls that no one would notice. One year we got lashed on dodgy mulled wine from a stall and were as sick as dogs.'

'Serves you right,' I say, realising that Cal has definitely cut down on his drinking lately. Polly used to nag him about it when he first got home from the Middle East and was even worried, but since Isla left for London — and even before then — the empties have greatly reduced. I didn't like to see him so pissed every night: it reminded me of my dad, who was even more of an ogre when he'd had a few drinks. After Mum died, he hit the bottle hard, met a new girlfriend and eventually I couldn't stand the situation any longer and left home.

'I haven't been to the lights switch-on since I was young, though. I was either away at uni, or too cool or working abroad. Last year, the Christmas lights were the last thing on my mind.'

His tone takes on a bitter edge; the same edge that I used to hear all the time when I first came to Kilhallon. It surfaces less frequently now but I know that his disappointment gnaws at him. His father passed away not long before he went to the Middle East on an aid project. Although that was two and half years ago, he's bound to miss his dad and regret that they didn't have a closer relationship. Then there's the loss of Isla, of course, but there's something else that causes him pain. Memories, worries, something to do with what he saw or went through in the Middle East. Something unimaginable that I'm sure still affects him way more than he ever lets on.

He pushes the tablet away. 'What about you?'

'I never really took much notice of the lights. My main aim last year was finding a warm place for Mitch and me to stay. I'd just lost my job in Truro and was sofa surfing around friends and friends of friends. On the night of the lights, I was between sofas and hanging about until the people had left and the lights had been turned off until sundown the next day.

He winces. 'I had no idea.'

'I remember how I felt *after* the lights went off and everyone had gone home. The place seemed twice as dead as it had before the switch-on. Mitch and I bunked down in an alley not far from Tamsin's Spa.' I also remember the smells of hot food, buttered rum punch, stollen, saffron cake, spicy mulled apple cider, rich hot chocolate, and the way they curled around me and drove me insane. Plus the feeling that I'd never been so lonely or such an outsider. Cal gathers me into his arms. Perhaps I didn't hide the shiver as well as I thought I had.

'I'm sorry. It must have been tough.'

Tears sting my eyes and make me wish I'd never mentioned last November. I genuinely don't want Cal's sympathy — so why did I have to say so much? 'Some of the poor people I saw had so many problems, I could have cried for them. Some will never get off the streets. I'm the lucky one. Look at me now: hosting an event for the village bigwigs. Who'd have thought it?'

He smiles briefly. 'Even so . . . Feel free to hit me, but have you given any more thought to contacting your family? Your father? Your brother? Sorry, I don't even know his name.'

'It's Kyle. My dad's called Gary.'

'OK . . .'

'And you're right, I have given it some more thought and I still don't want to speak to them. I don't know exactly what Kyle's doing now or even where he is and I refuse to ask my dad.'

'But you know where your dad and his partner live?'

'Near Redruth, as far as I know, that's where they were living when I last spoke to him. Last I heard, Kyle joined the army. He left home before I did and went to share a flat with a mate in Truro, but I'm not sure that worked out, so he signed up. We weren't close and he used to spend as much time as he could out of the house at his mates.'

'Your dad must have been on his own a lot after your mum died.'

'I suppose so. I was in the house though; he could have spoken to me if he'd wanted to. He just used to sit in his chair and drink cans and channel surf. I may as well have not existed, but he's got her now. Rachel.' I slap on a smile, feeling I've already raked over far too many old memories. 'I thought *you* were in the army, remember, when I first saw you with the combats and bag?'

Cal rolls his eyes. 'Yeah, I do, but I wasn't.'

'Do you remember where you were this time last year? During the Christmas lights?'

He glances out of the window into the darkness. 'I wasn't exactly having a fun time, either.'

His phone buzzes from the table, the sound

69

magnified by the table top and the high ceiling of the empty cafe. He grimaces, then glances at the screen.

'Aren't you going to answer it?'

He turns back to me, a grin on his face. Goosebumps prick my skin: I know what that look means.

'No. I was thinking we might have time for a quick bite before the committee arrive. A hot vampire bite.' He bares his teeth and while I pull a face at him, warm feelings stir at the jokey reminder of the nickname I had for him when we first met. He grazes the skin at the side of my neck with his teeth and it tingles. His breath is warm and I close my eyes in pleasure, trying to blot out the insistent throb of the mobile phone.

'There's no time,' I murmur. 'The committee will be here in twenty minutes.'

'So? I like living dangerously. You told me to do it.' His phone stops buzzing. 'I told you, they can wait.'

He kisses me, it's deep and hot and it sparks a swirling sensation low in my stomach. I'm shaky with lust. He tangles his hands in my hair, tugging at the roots without realising, but so gently that the tension just drives me even more crazy.

'Come on. Into the staff room.' His voice is husky with desire as he leads me through the kitchen and into the store-cupboard-sized room that serves as our staff room. It's warm in there, and the air smells of the pine disinfectant we keep in the cupboard. He backs me against the lockers and they rattle loudly.

'What if they're early?'

'They can wait.'

He shuts the door behind us while I pull off my Demelza's sweatshirt and T-shirt. Cal unzips his jeans and slips them down, along with his boxers. Still standing, with me braced against the lockers, Cal lifts me onto him. We're face to face and then he's inside me. I melt like butter on a hot scone under his touch and close my eyes to everything around me. The cafe, the lights, the dark night, the world, all are gone in those few intense, nerve-jangling seconds. There's only me and Cal, one person, for a brief, dark, hot moment. I wish it could go on and on.

'Whew.'

My face rests on his shoulder, my cheek skimming the soft wool cotton of his sweater. His fingers rest lightly on my back, beneath my shoulder blades and he whispers to me as I come back to awareness, like a swimmer surfacing in the cove to the sky.

'Demi, I've been thinking.' His voice is tender, serious and I'm not used to that.

'Always dangerous,' I breathe, still half-drowsy after the intensity.

'That maybe, we should think about, if you don't mind, well . . .'

My eyes are open. His phone buzzes again. It's closer now. I hadn't realised he'd even picked it up or brought it with him.

'Damn it.' Almost falling over, tangled by the jeans still around his ankles, he pulls up his jeans and delves in the pocket. 'Bloody thing.'

Leave it, I say silently. *Leave it and say what's on your mind.*

He glares at his phone, and he mouths at me, 'Sorry' then: 'Hello, Isla, no, I'm not busy. How are you?'

I don't think he's realised that he's turned his back on me as if he doesn't want me to hear his conversation. While he's talking to her, his jeans slip down his hips again, leaving his pants halfway up his muscular bottom. I struggle back into my top and sweatshirt and slip past him into the tiny washroom. I close the door but can hear him, 'hmm-ing' and 'OK-ing' and the odd 'fine' and the final 'OK, take care, see you soon'.

He comes out into the cafe while I scoop coffee into the filter machine. There's no time to make cappuccinos and lattes tonight.

'Sorry for that,' he says. 'It was Isla, making arrangements to come down for the shoot in a few weeks' time. It means opening the cafe especially, because she asked if you'd cater for the cast and crew for the day. It's extra work, but they have a decent budget and she thought we might as well have the business rather than handing it over to the outside caterers. Will that be OK?'

'That's awesome.' I try to sound cheerful, because we do need the business and the publicity during and after the shoot and when the series — a historical drama about a highwayman and his aristocratic mistress — is aired will be priceless. Isla's going to be here anyway so we may as well profit from it. It is good of her to help us — Cal — out.

'It's only for a day, possibly a day and a half, depending on the weather.'

'Great. Did you know your flies are still undone?'

'Hell. No.' He glances down and then up at me, a wicked grin on his face. 'That would have shocked the vicar. She's on the committee.'

'I'm sure she's seen it all before. Is that headlights?'

Through the window, I spot twin white beams wavering as a vehicle makes its way over the bumpy track from the farm. The road will serve as access to the camping field in the summer but it's not exactly public-highway standard yet. Behind the lights, I spot two more sets of lamps. The first car stops a few feet from the cafe.

Cal goes to unlock the door and groans. 'Please, no . . . '

'What?'

'That's Mawgan's car.'

'No. God, I had no idea she was on the committee.'

'She isn't, according to the minutes they sent me. What the hell is she doing here?'

'I don't know, but we're about to find out.'

7

'Hello, Demi, how nice to see you again.'

'Mawgan,' I reply through gritted teeth while she pulls off crimson leather gloves. 'What a surprise. We didn't know you were on the Harbour Lights committee.'

She throws us an angelic smile. 'Well, strictly speaking, I'm not, because I'm far too busy for a regular commitment, but Cade Developments is making a significant contribution to the fund this year so the chairwoman invited me to join you tonight.'

'Great,' says Cal, his voice dripping with sarcasm.

'Cade Developments takes its responsibility to the local community very seriously,' Mawgan adds, dropping her gloves on a table and peering over Cal's shoulder at the cafe.

Yeah, by hiking up rents, blocking our plans and intimidating local people, I think, not that we can prove any of it. I'm amazed the Harbour Lights committee has allowed Mawgan to contribute, though I guess they can't afford not to, in all kinds of ways.

'Cade Developments only has a responsibility to make money no matter what the cost to the community,' Cal replies. 'So what are you really doing here, Mawgan. Spying?'

'Cal. We have more customers. Help yourself to refreshments,' I say to Mawgan, steering Cal towards the door before we all come to blows, verbal or otherwise.

A glamorous forty-something lady in a leather biker jacket, pointy snakeskin boots and a dog collar sashays in. It's the Reverend Beverley Fritton, the vicar of St Trenyan. If the Rev Bev recognises me, she doesn't let on. She once bought me a coffee and gave Mitch a meal, all without trying to convert me to anything other than *Game of Thrones*. She and her much younger curate, who I suspect is also much more than her assistant, made me hot rum chocolate and let me and Mitch bunk down in her snug for the night. She may have forgotten me, but I haven't forgotten her.

'Wow, this is awesome,' she declares in her broad Birmingham accent, her auburn ponytail swinging round as she does a 360-degree twirl in the middle of the cafe. She sniffs the air and sighs in ecstasy. 'And what is that amazing smell? Did I forget to set my alarm and wake up on Christmas Eve?'

'They're mincemeat cookies: very easy to make. I can let you have the recipe.'

'I'd love it, though I can barely boil an egg. This place was a wreck of an old barn when I was last up here. What an amazing transformation, isn't it, Mawgan?'

Though I can tell it's killing her, even Mawgan wouldn't be openly catty in front of the Rev Bev and she grinds out a reply. 'It is. Who'd have ever thought a wreck like Kilhallon would scrub up so well?'

My reply, also involving scrubbers, is a

nanosecond from escaping my lips, but it's Cal's turn to shoot me a warning glance and the Rev Bev continues to torture Mawgan by lavishing praise on the 'a-maz-ing' job we've done on the cafe. The door opens again and more of the committee troop in. I recognise the harbourmaster — or should I say, harbourmistress — and Josh, the boat skipper, who used to deliver seafood to Sheila's. Thank goodness Mitch is safely snoozing at the farmhouse, I'd hate him to spend the evening sniffing Josh's trousers.

'Have a look round and help yourselves to drinks and cookies while I get the coffee,' I tell everyone, glad to have something to do that will keep me out of Mawgan's way. More people arrive and Cal greets them. Soon, the noise level in the cafe is deafening as people help themselves to cookies and drinks, 'oh-ing' and 'ah-ing'.

St Trenyan's harbourmistress is chairing the meeting and calls everyone to order. Cal joins in, agreeing to make a modest donation to the cost of the lights, though we can't match Mawgan's contribution. I pluck up the courage to mention our 'pop-up' Demelza's stall at the festival, which will sell hot food and drinks and showcase Kilhallon as a resort, and manage to wangle a great position for it right on the quayside by the Fisherman's Choir.

The harbourmistress thanks Mawgan for her 'generous' support, which is met by grudging mutterings of thanks. I glance sideways at Cal and see him with his lips pressed tightly together. Mawgan might have backed off from destroying our plans for Kilhallon, but there's no way she's given up hating us. I distract myself by working out the menu I can offer at the switch-on. Jewelled cookies to match the lights, perhaps ... mulled cider ... caramel sea salt brownies ...

When the meeting breaks up, most people hang around, helping themselves to more cookies and 'networking', aka gossiping. I gather up the used crockery onto a tray and take it into the dishwashing area in the kitchen.

Mawgan appears in the doorway to the kitchen, holding out her empty mug.'

'This is cosy.'

'Can I help you, madam?' I say, sarcastically. I know she's trying to provoke me and she can't behave too nastily in this company, especially when she's trying to act the generous local businesswoman, but I'm on my guard. Most of the people here loathe the Cades, but some rent their business premises from Mawgan's lettings company and can't afford to upset her. Even though she's backed off from some of her worst practices, I don't believe for a moment that she's given up on hurting Cal by destroying Kilhallon or wrecking his life some other way. Mawgan's view of relationships and family is warped to say the least.

She dumps her mug on the drainer. 'No, thanks. I see you've carved out a nice comfortable little niche for yourself up here. You and Cal. So, how's business? Made your first million, yet?'

'Forgive me for speaking frankly, Mawgan, but our business is actually none of your business.'

'Fair enough, but I just thought I'd remind you that you're here — you and Cal — only because I decided that Kilhallon wasn't part of my development plans.'

I just resist snorting out loud. Only Mawgan and I know the real reason she changed her mind about ruining us: because I gave her hell about her behaviour towards us and to Andi and Robyn. Even so, I was gobsmacked that she listened to me. Even though she claimed it was a business decision, I know I touched a very raw nerve with her. Her mum had an affair with Cal's father and that has led to bad feeling between the families, that and the fact Cal refused to go out with her when they were younger.

'It's too late now. We're here to stay.'

Mawgan runs her finger over the stainless steel prep table. 'Possibly. We'll see.'

'I'm sorry, but customers aren't really allowed in the kitchen area. Regulations.'

'I bet you allow that dirty dog of yours in here.'

'Actually we don't allow any hygiene hazards in here, human or animal.'

Mawgan has a hide like a rhino so ignores me. 'I heard Isla was coming back from London.'

'How do you know that? She only told Cal the other day.' I kick myself at revealing this snippet of information, but it's too late; Mawgan's eyes gleam with delight.

'I have my sources,' she says.

Does that mean she's still in touch with Luke, Isla's fiancé? They left Cornwall to keep out of

Mawgan's way, because Isla suspected that Luke and Mawgan were getting too close. I doubt it very much, but I wouldn't put anything past her. Only Mawgan and I know what went on between us in the summer and that our 'chat' about her personal life led to her removing her objections to us redeveloping Kilhallon Park.

Laughter drifts in from the cafe and a car engine fires up outside. I hold out my hand, to show her the door. 'I don't want to be rude but the meeting's over and we need to lock up.'

Blocking my way to the door, she lowers her voice, 'I could still hurt Cal. I could ruin him. If I want to.'

'How?'

'I have my ways. You just bear it in mind. Just because you came to me begging me to save him doesn't change a thing between any of us, and it isn't only me who thinks he's a selfish bastard.'

'You may be bitter and twisted and blame him for your mum leaving you, but any reasonable person would see it's not his fault.'

'It's not only me, and the amateur psychology you spouted when you turned up at my house uninvited had nothing to do with my decision to back off.'

'Drop the act, Mawgan. If you want me to think you gave up your opposition to our plans for financial reasons, that's fine, but we both know there was more to it than that. You just can't admit you found you had a conscience after all.'

'I've no idea what you're referring to, but I told you that our conversation was private.'

No one can hear us in the kitchen, but I lower my voice anyway. 'It was and it is. I kept my word. Cal has no idea that I came to see you or what we spoke about. As far as I'm aware, he also has no idea about your mum and his dad.'

She snorts. 'Really?'

'I think he would have mentioned it if he did.'

'He tells you everything, does he?' she says.

'Not everything. I don't share everything with him either, but I would have thought that considering the trouble you tried to cause over the summer, he might have told me about the situation if he knew.'

She sniffs, and seems at a loss for words for a few moments, then her lip curls. 'I couldn't care less anyway. You can relax. I've decided not to waste my time with little people like you and Cal.'

'That suits us fine,' I say, glad she can't see my stomach drop to my shoes. If I never see Mawgan Cade again it will be too soon. Judging by the sneer on her face, I'm guessing she hates having betrayed any weakness to me. I could tell her that it wasn't weak to allow her sister some happiness, or to let go of her bitter feud with Cal — but she wouldn't listen.

'Mawgan! We're going. I'd like a word with you before we leave.'

Mawgan presses her lips together as Rev Bev pops her head round the door. 'Goodnight,' she says tightly. 'I'm sure we'll meet again soon.'

Shouldering her neon-pink ostrich-effect bag, she wobbles out of the kitchen on her pointy heels. I focus on loading the dishwasher, reminding myself that Mawgan is full of crap. I won't let her empty threats hurt me because that's exactly what she wants. I'm a successful cafe owner, I've a film crew to deal with in a few weeks, and Cal was going to say something nice too, although he didn't *actually* say it.

8

Cal

My head throbs as I reach for the clock by the bed. The green digits glow in the gloom. Wednesday 9 October. 09.23. Shit. Is it that late? I need to get up. Those old staff cottages won't renovate themselves.

I lift my head off the pillow and instantly regret it. Pain pulses in my temples. I'm shivering yet sheened in sweat. No wonder, I've woken up to find I'm lying on top of the duvet in my boxers. Last night, after I staggered home from the Tinner's Arms in the small hours, I must have collapsed on top of the bed. At least I had the presence of mind to get undressed, which is amazing considering I was off my face. I haven't been to one of the pub's lock-ins for months. I'd already started to cut back on my drinking since Demi and I got Kilhallon off the ground, and I'm almost back within the so-called 'healthy' limit now. Correction, I *was* in the healthy limit until last night's lapse.

Last night Demi went out with her mates to see a film in Penzance. I could and should have spent the evening doing the accounts for the resort, but I needed a break too. I only intended to have a quick pint at the pub, but one turned into two, then more, plus a few whiskies as well. Before I knew it, the landlord had locked the doors, joined his regulars for a game of poker and the evening had become early morning.

Snatches of conversation from the night before slowly come back to me, along with scenes from my nightmare and memories of my time in Syria. I remember someone talking about the Harbour Lights Festival in the bar. They reminded me of my conversation with Demi on Monday night before the committee meeting.

I told her I wasn't having a fun time during last year's festival. A slight understatement. I remember *exactly* where I was on that day. I was working in a refugee camp a couple of miles from the front line of a conflict zone, trying to do what I could for hundreds of wounded and displaced people. The sights, the sounds and smells will never leave me. Although I pretend to the people around me that I've put that time behind me and it doesn't affect me, I'm lying.

I'm fully awake now. After I crashed out, some of the events from Syria came back to haunt me in a nightmare; albeit in a bizarre, jumbled way, like a story where the chapters have been swapped around or are missing altogether. I'm not sure why I had a nightmare or why the memories are so vivid and troubling now. Since I returned to Kilhallon, I've tried to lock my time in Syria away so I can try to get on with daily life, but it's impossible to forget. The guilt I feel about what happened that day will never leave me, and perhaps it never should.

Lying in my bed now, I tell myself that my bad dream was probably just the result of too much Doom Bar, too many whisky chasers and a very stupid urge to scoff bacon, egg and black pudding at two o'clock in the morning when I eventually staggered into Kilhallon. I lift my head and see a tangle of sheets at the foot of the bed. I must have kicked them off while I was fighting imaginary attackers in my dream. The new sash window is open a few inches and the curtains flutter against the frame. A cold wind keens around the farmhouse, changing pitch every now and then and making my head hurt even more. It was only a dream, I remind myself, as my throbbing temples send a bolt of nausea straight to my stomach.

Yet the images from that day are still vivid now I'm awake. I remember my friend Soraya lying on top of a pile of bricks and broken furniture. A red checked tablecloth covered her legs; it must have fallen on top of her when the mortar round hit her home. She didn't have a mark on her beautiful face and her eyes were closed as if she'd lain down to rest and pulled the cloth over her. Her upper body was covered with a fine powder, just as though someone had shaken icing sugar over her.

I'd been blown off my feet by an explosion and when I came round, I spotted her in the clouds of smoke and dust. From a few metres away, I'd almost believed she was asleep. I'd started to cough, my eyes stinging, and then I looked around for her little girl, Esme.

No matter how hard I looked, I couldn't see her anywhere.

The sounds and smells come back to me, along with the scene of devastation all round.

84

Clouds of dirt and debris rose up like a fog, yet one that was hot and acrid and burned my throat. My eyes were raw and streaming. Rumbles like thunder shook the ground to one side and the chatter of gunfire echoed on the other. A soldier loomed out of the dust and yelled at me: 'We're going. Come with us now or die here.'

I could not move. All I could do was stare at Soraya sleeping on her rubble bed, knowing she'd never wake up. And then I knew what to do and my feet moved: not to run after the soldier but to clamber over the rubble piles to search for Esme. I knew I had to find her and take her back with me to safety.

I clawed at the rubble, looking for her. My knuckles were bleeding. I couldn't find her. Then I heard the soldiers again, their voices, and realised that they weren't 'our' side, but the insurgents who had shelled the town. I had to leave, or be killed. Instinct told me to run and hope I could find Esme at our camp. So I ran, tears streaming down my face. It was too late. Too late for Soraya, for Esme and for me.

Suddenly, another scene from my nightmare floods my mind and merges with my memories. I was in a dusty room, the sun beating down on the tiled roof, shafts of light piercing the cracks and shining on the dust and blood on the earth floor. A man held my ankles down, the pressure was unbearable. Another face appeared above me with a hose. I remember feeling so thirsty. I couldn't speak, but I didn't want this water. I opened my mouth to scream but he pushed a rag

85

over my nose and mouth and the water poured down. I tried to scream but I was drowning — like I was in the cove this summer, only this time there was no Demi to reach in and pull me out.

Bloody hell, just *how* much did I have to drink last night?

Thank God Demi wasn't staying over with me . . . Or maybe if she had been, I wouldn't have stayed so long at the Tinner's. Demi helps me keep off the booze and from dwelling on the dark times as often as I might do. Trouble is, now that Polly's here and the businesses demand our time and energy, we've had precious few chances to get together, apart from a couple of snatched moments of passion at the cafe.

I also remember that after Demi and I had made out in the cafe, I was going to ask her to go public and move into Kilhallon House with me. After last night's talk in the pub, I'm not so sure it's a good idea, for Demi or for me.

The bedroom door rattles in a gust of wind. I must get the latch fixed. Anyone could walk in.

Oh God, it's 09.45. I *have* to get up and get on with my jobs, even though hammering and drilling is the last thing my head needs. I suppose it's some kind of justice for getting pissed last night.

Still in my boxers, I scuttle downstairs in search of black coffee. There's singing coming from the kitchen. Something about it being 'time to say goodbye'. When I walk in, Polly stops her impromptu Il Divo karaoke and stares at me from the sink. She holds a very sharp pair of

86

scissors and is surrounded by leaves, roses and cellophane.

'My God. You look bloody awful, Cal Penwith.'

'Thanks, Polly.'

Talking hurts. My throat feels like the bottom of a birdcage. Maybe that's why I dreamed I was choking from the dust and sand.

She purses her lips at me as if a cockroach has just crawled into the kitchen. Any minute now I expect her to grab the broom and sweep me out of the door.

'I speak as I find. Rough night, was it?'

'I've had better.' Aware that I'm wearing only boxers, I reach for a pair of old trackie bottoms from the nearby laundry basket.

'You've no need to get dressed on my account. I've seen you naked in your paddling pool and changed your nappy, remember?' she declares. Nonetheless, she eyes my boxers with obvious distaste, like I'm hiding a scorpion down there or something. Despite my hangover, it *is* still first thing.

Her scissor blades glint in the sunlight.

'No, I don't remember,' I growl.

I pull on the trackie bottoms, cringing as Polly continues to observe me.

'Well, I've no sympathy if you've been drinking again *and* you should keep off the fry-ups late at night. I've washed up your greasy pan and the plate, but don't expect it to become a regular thing.'

She points at the upturned frying pan on the drainer.

'I never expected you washing up to be a 'thing' at all,' I growl. 'And you should have left it to me. It's my mess. Aren't you meant to be on reception duty?'

'In a minute, yes. I came over early to arrange these.' She holds up a long stemmed rose.

'Who bought you those?' I grunt, but only because she wants me to ask her.

'One of the guests.'

'That's good of them.'

With a smile, she snips the bottom of the stem and strips off the lower leaves. I drag myself to the sink and she moves aside so I can fill the kettle.

'It was Kit Bannen. He brought them round this morning.'

'How nice,' I say, feeling too shitty and too bloody minded to enquire why Kit the-sun-shines-out-of-his-arsehole Bannen has brought expensive flowers for my PA. 'Want a coffee?' I ask her, though the effort of moving my jaw to speak makes my temples throb.

'No time. I have to get these in a vase and get to work.'

Polly finishes snipping and ripping the roses as I drag back a chair. The scrape of wood on tile is like someone playing a violin out of tune inside my ear.

'Right,' she says as the kettle clicks off. 'Those will have to do.' She holds up the vase to the light. 'I could have kept them at home, but I thought 'no', I'll have them on display in reception where everyone can enjoy them.' She glares at me. 'There's some Alka Seltzer in the

88

medicine cupboard. And I hope you don't mind me saying, but you need a shower. You stink of beer.'

Polly bustles off, proudly carrying her vase. I pour water on some instant coffee and add an extra spoon for good measure. My first sip almost makes me gag. The discarded ends of the stems, with their thorns, still lie on the draining board.

Bloody Bannen. I don't like him one bit. The way he's inveigled his way into Demi's heart, and Polly's too, in such a short time. And now I remember the worst thing about my nightmare, which only goes to show how crazy it all was: I swear the guy holding me down had Kit Bannen's face.

9

Demi

'Wow. What amazing flowers!'

'They're from Kit.' Polly beams at me as Mitch snuffles around the reception area, picking up the trail of strange smells left by strange boots.

I drink in the sweet perfume. The flowers add a touch of summer. There must be a dozen of them, of the palest, almost translucent pink, arranged in a vase with greenery from Polly's garden. The scent of roses filled my nose when I walked into the reception area. The lights are on even though it's after ten because it's misty outside.

'He asked me to call him Kit. He says that 'Mr Bannen' makes him feel old and he bought me the roses as a thank-you for sorting out his Wi-Fi the other day. They're from the proper florist in St Just, not from a petrol station,' Polly says proudly. She may be referring to the flowers Cal gave her after their latest 'difference of opinion' over the cleaner we've taken on to help with the changeovers. They still had the yellow reduced sticker on them, even though he'd obviously made a half-hearted attempt to pick it off.

'*You* sorted out Kit's Wi-Fi?'

Polly tuts. 'Don't sound so amazed, madam. I know how to reboot a router. Not that Kit needed to give me any flowers for doing that, but I suppose he's been brought up properly, unlike some.' She peers at me over the rim of her specs. 'He's such a *nice* man. So polite. Handsome too. If you like blonds, which I don't as a rule. He's a bit of a sex bomb.'

'Really? I hadn't noticed.' I'm gobsmacked at Polly's reference to Kit as a 'sex bomb', not that he isn't cute in a wannabe surfer-boy way, but she's never said that about anyone else apart from the guys in her favourite 'band', Il Divo. Is she trying to match-make me and Kit? She doesn't like the idea of Cal and I getting together, that's for sure, but I'm not clear on who she's trying to protect, me or Cal.

'I really hadn't taken any notice.'

'You're always saying that you don't take any notice of Cal.' She peers at me again, this time with pursed lips. She must know there's something going on between us, even if we're careful not to drop any hints when Polly or the customers — or anyone — are around.

'Have to go. Must take Mitch for his walk then plan the menus for this film shoot. Bye . . . '

Leaving Polly wittering on about Kit and Cal, I jog after Mitch down the fields and over the stile towards the coast path that leads away from the cafe and St Trenyan and towards the ruined engine house and old mine workings. The mist is thicker towards the cliffs and clings to my skin. In patches it's so dense I can only see a few yards ahead, but in other places, I can see up to the sky, where a few watery splashes of blue are trying to break through the gloom. The mist should clear later but at this time of year, you never know for sure. The days are getting shorter, fast — the cue for St Trenyan Radio to start its 'festive' advertising. Half-term week is coming up and we're opening longer hours to make the most of the business.

Mitch stays close, sniffing the gorse and stopping to paw at a hole that might be a rabbit burrow.

'Ouch!'

A man runs round a bend in the path, slamming into me, knocking me into the gorse. Sharp prickles graze my exposed skin.

'Ow! You should be more . . . Kit?'

I stop, recognising the face above me, which switches from furious to agonised the moment that he recognises me. Kit holds out his hand to help me up from the spiky bush. Mitch starts barking, and not in a friendly way.

'Oh God, I'm so sorry. I'm such a bloody idiot. Did I scare you?'

'You startled me. I didn't see or hear you coming.' The mist swirls around us and Mitch barks even louder. 'Settle down, Mitch. It's OK, I'm fine.'

With a final warning yip, Mitch closes his jaws and stands by me protectively. Kit rubs his hand over his face, the way I've seen Cal do when he feels guilty. He's wearing grey Lycra running tights and a charcoal top, not the easiest thing to spot in a sea fog.

'Are you sure you're OK? I should have slowed down on the bend, but I was trying to make it to the top of this steep section. It's so early, and I thought no one would be out in this weather. I was in two minds whether to go for a run at all this morning, but I was hoping it would clear while I ran.'

Gradually my heart rate returns to normal. 'It might burn off later, though the forecast wasn't promising. I probably wouldn't have walked this way in this mist unless I knew the path well.'

'You're right, of course, but I needed some fresh air and if I don't get out early before I'm into my writing, I probably won't be able to tear myself away from the keyboard until it's dark. This mist gets into your bones. Are you sure I didn't hurt you?'

'I'm fine, but you'll get cold now you've stopped moving.'

'I'm almost back at Kilhallon now,' he says, pointing back along the path. Somewhere, a few hundred yards behind us, shrouded in the mist, is the cafe. 'Are you going down to the cove?' he adds. 'I have to say that it's possibly even worse down there than here. The path's very slippery, not that I'm trying to stop you — this is your territory.'

I consider for a moment. 'I was going to stay high, to be honest.' The truth is my arm's a bit sore after falling into the bushes and even I don't fancy tackling the steep cove path in these conditions, but I'm not going to tell Kit that. 'Mitch won't mind going up onto the moor for a change.'

We turn back towards Kilhallon along the coast path. To our right, the bushes rise gently up to the open moorland above our park. The sea is on our left. Kit walks ahead of me, and Mitch stays behind, snuffling around my heels. At least I thought he was behind me. The mist swirls around us and when I turn, Mitch has disappeared, but I can hear him bark at an imaginary — or real — rabbit.

'Mitch. Come back here now!'

There's a skittering nearby and Mitch emerges from the gorse between the path and the cliff edge. The constant crash of the waves on the rocks many metres below us seems muffled and even the telltale scent of seaweed and ozone is gone today.

'You'll have to go on your lead if you run off again,' I say rattling the lead at him. Mitch hangs his head and squeezes his shaggy coat against my legs. 'Mitch hates the lead, he hardly ever needs it, but it's too dodgy to let him loose in a fog like this, even so close to home.'

'I'm sure he's safer than either of us and knows the path better too, but you're right to be careful,' says Kit, slipping behind me as we reach a narrow section that's rocky underfoot. The path twists and climbs steeply for a few yards, then we reach the top of the cliff and it broadens out.

There's more space between the path and the edge here, so Mitch runs a few feet in front of us and Kit walks alongside me.

'There's been a lot more cliff falls of late. Cal said he was surprised at how different the route looked when he came home. He thinks the path's going to crumble into the sea one day soon.'

Kit moves alongside. 'Home? Had Cal been away long, then?'

'A couple of years.'

'That's a long time. Was he living abroad?'

'He worked for a charity in Syria.'

He blows out a breath. 'I'm impressed. Sounds dangerous.'

'I don't know about that. He doesn't talk about it much.'

'Perhaps that's because it *was* dangerous. I should imagine he's seen things he'd rather forget.'

'Maybe. Like I say, I've no idea. He's focused on running Kilhallon now. Look, we're back at the park.'

I kick myself, feeling I've said more than I should have already. People are going to find out that Cal was an aid worker anyway, because he agreed to the photo shoot for the magazine in the summer and it's scheduled to appear sometime soon. Yet saying that Cal doesn't talk about his time there *is* a personal comment; and more than I wanted to reveal.

Aware that Cal might think I've *already* said too much, I'm happy to see the cafe building looming on the other side of the hedge. Mitch trots ahead, sniffing at the ancient granite gateposts at the entrance of Kilhallon land. On the cafe terrace, dew coats the wooden tables and benches. The terrace gives an amazing view over the coastline, not that you can even see beyond the gorse that marks the cliff edge at the moment. It seems strange that the tables will soon be full of customers again, all eating their

95

cream teas. Mitch runs off to investigate rabbit holes.

'I've just realised why the cafe is called Demelza's.' Kit's voice breaks into my thoughts and he points to the sign on the stone wall of the cafe. 'After you, I presume? That's what Demi is short for, is it? Or are you named after the American actress?'

Looking at the name, I can still hardly believe it myself, and I can't resist a smile. 'The cafe's named after my Nana Demelza who inspired my love of cooking. I was always known as Demi at home and, strictly speaking, it's Cal's cafe because he owns Kilhallon Park. I'm only an employee.'

He tuts. '*Only* an employee? Come on now, I'm sure Cal sees you as much more than that. I've seen you in reception, chatting to guests, running all over the place. You seem indispensable to me. I bet Cal thinks so.'

I feel uncomfortable, because I'm not quite sure what Kit is getting at and as a guest, there's no way I'm going to say anything unprofessional. 'You'd have to ask him,' I say with what I hope is a charming smile. Mitch darts out from the hedge and sniffs around Kit's Lycra-clad rude bits.

'Mitch! Come here, now!' I dash forward to grab his collar but Kit laughs.

'He's only being friendly and doing what dogs do.'

'He's a bit too friendly at times. Not all the guests like dogs.'

'Luckily, I do. I had a cocker spaniel when I

96

was little. Couldn't look after one now in my flat in London. Couldn't swing a cat in there, let alone a spaniel.'

Clicking his tongue, he rubs Mitch's ears the way Cal does. But Mitch doesn't know Kit as well as Cal, and while he enjoys the ear rub, he's not about to roll over and ask for a belly tickle. I'm relieved, I don't want Mitch getting too intimately acquainted with our visitors.

'Is everything OK at the cottage? We haven't wanted to disturb you, but we like to know that our guests are happy. Do you need any tips for good places to eat in St Trenyan?' Mitch takes off in the direction of a scuffling noise in the gorse.

'Everything's fine, thanks. Polly, your reception manager, sorted out a problem with my Wi-Fi.'

'So I heard.' I try not to sound too amazed but I still am. Polly's never been too keen on the idea of taking her turn on reception and is always grumbling about the computer system and our Internet service provider and the keyboard and the blah-di-blah. 'She was very impressed with the roses you gave her.'

He smiles. 'Well, I'm going to be here for a while so I want to get on Polly's side; I should imagine it's not a good idea to end up in her bad books.'

'You imagine right.'

'And I was very grateful for her help. She did a reboot of the main router or something. I don't know much about tech and as long as I can get my work done, that's all I care about, but she seems to know what she's doing. Interesting woman; 'old school' as my mum would say. She told me she's worked for the Penwith family for years. Are you connected with the family?'

I laugh out loud at the idea of me being a Penwith. 'No. I only work for them, or rather what's left of the Penwiths. There's only Cal now on his side of the family. He owns the site, and his parents before him, but that was years ago.'

'I remember it. Never stayed here but walked by a few times when I was a little boy. Lots of static caravans, if I remember, but the site did seem a bit run-down.'

'It was probably on its last legs when you were little, but we're back now,' I say.

'Looks great now. Polly said the Penwiths have owned this land for centuries. They used to farm here, she said, and then there were the mines, of course. The guidebook in my cottage says that it was a tin miner's home at one time?'

'Yes, it was, but there was probably a family of ten living in it then.'

'Hard times, but fascinating,' he says. 'Shame that Cal's father lost interest in the holiday park, though. Still, these things happen.'

'Did Polly tell you that?' Even though Polly loves to gossip, I'm surprised she revealed a detail like that to a new guest.

'She said the late Mr Penwith was busy with his other interests.'

'Oh. Did she?'

I daren't say any more. Surely Polly hasn't revealed to a complete stranger what Mr Penwith's 'other interests' were? She wouldn't tell a guest about his affairs with women, would

98

she? I'll have to speak to her and find out exactly what she has told Kit and our other visitors.

Much to my relief, wavering headlights appear through the fog at the end of the field, and a red transit van lumbers down the track towards the cafe.

'Good. The electricians are here early. I need to have a word with them about fixing a glitch with the kitchen extractor system.'

'And I'm getting cold,' says Kit, hugging himself. 'See you later.' He gives a little bow, as charming now as he was grouchy when he first turned up a few weeks ago, and jogs across the field towards his cottage. Book or no book, Kilhallon has obviously worked some kind of magic on him.

10

Isla and her production company turned up at six o'clock this morning. It's now been almost three weeks since we opened and it's amazing how quickly we've all settled into the routine of daily cafe life, but looking after a film crew is a fresh challenge. Being a Monday, we've opened specially to cater for them and the guys and I have been up since five, making the cafe into a warm, welcoming haven for the cast and crew. We had coffee and pastries ready for them when they rolled into Kilhallon Park. Their vans and costume and make-up trailers have taken over our small parking area and the main car park.

Isla's doing us a big favour by using Demelza's to feed the crew, instead of a professional location caterer, so we have a lot to live up to. By seven a.m., a queue of hungry actors and crew members snakes back from the counter. I had no idea it took so many people to shoot a few short scenes — or how hungry they got.

'Hi, Demi, thanks for opening so early for us. It smells amazing in here.' Isla reaches the counter.

'Thanks.' I smile back, but it's not easy when you've been awake half the night worrying, and dragged yourself out of bed in the pitch black, a howling gale and lashing rain. 'Can I get you any breakfast?'

'A bacon roll, please. They look delicious.'

Despite also being up at the crack of dawn, Isla is rosy-cheeked and gorgeous, her blond hair piled up in a messy but chic up-do. She wears navy Hunters and a waxed jacket similar to Cal's. I didn't even have the energy to take my make-up off last night and my mascara-clogged eyelids must make me look as if an inky spider had crawled over my face.

'There you go.' Handing her two crisp rashers of organic Cornish bacon cushioned between two halves of an artisan soft white roll, I think how surreal it is to be dishing up bacon butties and croissants to people dressed in frock coats and corsets.

'There's ketchup and brown sauce on the tables, next to the serviettes and cutlery. Help yourself to tea and coffee too. You were right about serving everyone a simple breakfast menu and letting them help themselves to hot drinks,' I tell Isla.

'Glad it's working out. It's lovely and cosy in here, and we all need warming up. The wind's bitter, but at least the rain has stopped. Last night I thought we might have to cancel and do some interior shots. The forecast never said anything about a storm.'

'My Nana Demelza always used to say, 'Rain before seven; fine before eleven.' I never believed it, but I guess she was right this morning.'

Although the storm that raged half the night has blown away, the sky is still marred by clouds as lumpy and grey as an old pillow. As if to remind us of what it could unleash, the wind wails around the cafe.

101

Isla smiles. 'Actually, this is exactly what we want today. Wild, untamed, authentic Cornwall. The weather matches the mood of the scene perfectly. Not too sunny and bright but not too much of a safety risk to the cast and crew.' She lowers her voice. 'Can you spare a minute for a chat?'

I can't really spare a second, but this must be important so I follow her over to a corner table and sit down.

'Have you seen Cal this morning?'

'Not yet. I headed straight down here from my cottage.'

I'm not sure if she's fishing to find out if I spent the night with Cal. She must have guessed by now that there's something going on between us, even if Cal hasn't told her straight out that we're officially together yet. Nothing is 'official' anyway. The truth is that Cal and I haven't spent the night together since our encounter in the cafe before the Harbour Lights. All we've managed is a few quick snogs and even then Cal seemed half-hearted about it. In fact, he's seemed more distant generally since that night I went to the cinema and he had a skinful at the Tinner's. I wonder if someone said something to him about us in the pub that's upset him, not that he usually takes any notice of village gossip.

'Really? Oh, of course. You had an early start. It doesn't matter. I expect he'll pop down to see how we're getting on at some point.'

'He's bound to.'

'Luke's in London. I'm staying at Bosinney House to keep Uncle Rory company. He misses

102

Robyn since she moved in with Andi Cade, but I know he's relieved to see her happy. I'm so glad they're together now. I hope my visit to you in the summer helped iron out your problems?'

She sips her coffee. I'm pretty amazed to hear her refer to what happened earlier this summer. Mawgan used Isla's fiancé, Luke, to persuade Robyn to end her relationship with Mawgan Cade's younger sister, Andi. Luke was in financial trouble with the Cades and didn't dare to defy them but Isla decided to intervene and tell me that Luke was putting unfair pressure on the girls. It was a tough call, but I decided to let them know that Mawgan was the real person trying to split them up. Andi and Robyn were shocked and hurt, but they're together now — partly because I told Mawgan just what I thought of her toxic interference in other people's lives and, amazingly, made her think again.

'It's incredible that Mawgan had an attack of conscience and gave her blessing for the girls moving in together after all, isn't it? Perhaps she's not as bad as I thought,' Isla says.

'Maybe.' I shrug, squirming a little. Isla has no idea that I confronted Mawgan and Cal suspects that it was Isla's intervention that made the difference, which suits me. 'Who knows what goes on in Mawgan's mind, eh?'

'No. It's a mystery. Anyway, I must let you get back to work. Thanks again for putting up with us. I know everyone appreciates a cosy haven to retreat to. See you later.'

A tall man who I think is the director, joins

103

Isla and I go back to serving. I recognise a couple of the actors in the queue. Whether they're well known or not, the stars seem to line up with the extras and the lowliest crew member. The lead actor and actress didn't bother with the cooked breakfast, opting for fresh fruit bowls and black coffee. They're sitting in the far corner, studying scripts.

I caught them huddled inside their Puffa coats by our bins earlier this morning, grabbing a sneaky fag in the dark. Now I know how they stay that thin. Their life — at least on set — isn't that glamorous after all. I also think they're more than colleagues, judging by the way they were giggling and whispering in each other's ears. The lead actor, Dylan, is an up-and-coming star and has attracted a following of fans already. He's quite cute, I guess, but he's not really my type. He also seems very nervy and strung out.

After breakfast, most of the cast and crew clear out, although a few of the 'extras' linger. The dishwasher hums and Radio St Trenyan blares out from the kitchen where Jez and I are doing prep for lunch: a choice of pasties and a veggie quiche, with jackets and salad, plus different sandwiches. Trays of homemade figgy obbin, flapjacks, fly pastry, cereal bars, posh popcorn and fresh fruit are already laid out for the breaks in filming, alongside bottled water, presses, a selection of teas, coffee and hot-chocolate sachets.

During the morning, people pop in and out constantly, grabbing drinks and snacks to eat on the go. A few of the extras huddle in a corner, waiting to be called, gossiping about the productions they've worked on and the stars they've met, according to Nina who's still star-struck and eavesdropping.

After the shoot is finished, Isla has suggested we can use some exclusive pictures on our social media pages. With the photo shoot we did in the autumn set to be published very soon, the publicity should be a big boost to bookings and business.

Cal turns up around eleven o'clock. 'Hi, I came to see how you were doing and brought some more milk and take-out cups.'

Wiping my hands, I meet him in the middle of the customer area. 'Great, thanks.'

'How's it going?'

I lower my voice. 'Busy. Very hard work, but exciting.'

'Good. If you need an extra pair of hands, shout up. I'm clearing out the old staff cottages next to yours and I'm going to start repainting them ready for next season.'

'OK. I think we can manage.'

'Well done,' he says, with a wink. 'I've got the stuff in the Land Rover. Do you want to come and collect it?'

He knows how busy I am, so I guess he wants to have a word with me away from the film people.

He opens the tailgate and pulls out a box. 'That should keep you going for the rest of today and tomorrow, but let me know if you need anything and I'll nip to the cash and carry.'

'Thanks.'

He hands me the box. 'Oh . . . I asked Isla to dinner with us at Kilhallon House tonight after the shoot wraps for the day. She's looking forward to having more time to talk to you.'

'Dinner with us? Both of us?'

He smiles. 'Don't worry. I'm cooking. I thought you'd need a break after slaving away here all today. You will come over, won't you?'

'Yes. Sure. As long as we're finished here. I need to clear up and get ready for tomorrow before I can leave.'

'I'll help you clear up.'

'Won't you be busy doing dinner?'

'Hmm. I suppose so. It could take me some time. I'll see you around eight-ish, or later, if it's easier?'

'It'll be nearer half-past.'

'OK.'

Cal opens the rear doors to the Land Rover, just as Isla walks onto the terrace. 'Oh hello, Cal.'

Her eyes light up and she kisses him on the cheek.

'Isla. Hi.'

He tries not to sound too excited or happy to see her. I try to be sensible and not look for something that isn't there. Cal explained to me how he feels for her — and for me — and I mustn't become fixated on worrying about them.

Kit Bannen jogs past the cafe on the coast path and waves, then stops, turns and walks onto the terrace. 'Hello,' he says with a smile.

Cal grunts a 'hi'.

OK. It looks like I'll have to make the

106

introductions. 'Isla. This is Kit Bannen. He's staying in one of our cottages. He's a writer.'

'Really? What do you write?' Isla asks Kit.

'Techno-thrillers,' Kit replies with a sheepish grin, but Isla seems impressed.

'Wow.'

Cal's lips are pressed tightly together, but Kit either hasn't noticed his disapproval or doesn't care. I feel embarrassed by Cal's attitude, to be honest.

'This is a bit cheeky as we've never met, but as a writer I wanted to say how brilliant I thought your adaptation of *Dark Blue* was,' Kit tells Isla. 'I've read the book, of course, and I thought it was a superb adaptation, the best I've ever seen. No wonder it won a BAFTA.'

'Thank you. That's high praise from a writer. What's your book about?'

Is Isla just being polite to Kit? I wonder.

'It's about a scientist who has to run for her life after discovering a way of producing energy from water. Just about everyone on the planet is looking for her for one reason or another. Don't worry, I'm not here to ask you to adapt my book, even though that would be fantastic. I couldn't resist saying congratulations. I've a copy of the behind-the-scenes guide in the cottage. I know this might come across as cheesy, but I wondered if you'd sign it?'

Somehow I don't need to look at Cal to visualise his expression.

'Of course I'll sign it.' Isla's charming, and I can see she's used to doing this.

'I'll pop down later with it. I'd go up and fetch

it now, but I'd better have a shower first.' His crooked apologetic smile is a little like Cal's. There the resemblance ends, because Cal isn't smiling at all. I'm not sure why he's acting so jealous.

Isla sips her coffee. 'I'm impressed by you running along the cliffs. This is a rough section of coast path. Known for being tough. Where did you run to?'

'Oh, only as far as the lighthouse,' Kit says with a breezy wave at the far headland, which is at least three miles away. 'And you're right, the terrain is hard going for someone like me, used to the flat streets of London.'

'Which part of London?'

'Hammersmith.'

She nods. 'I happen to know it well, In fact, my fiancé and I have a flat there.'

Cal glances down at his boots, his arms folded.

'You don't say?' says Kit in a tone of amazement, though I'd have thought lots of people live in Hammersmith.

'Yes, we live not far from the Highwayman Tavern.'

Kit gasps. 'Wow. You're only five minutes from me. I have a ground-floor flat round the corner from the station, by that funny little tapas bar with the rusty tables outside.'

'Gosh, yes, I know that place. It's never been open when I've walked past, but Luke said he'd seen people sitting outside with Sangrias in the summer.' Isla smiles again, then seems to catch sight of her watch and winces. 'Ouch. It's later than I thought. I'm sorry, I'll have to go back to work, I'm afraid. It would have been great to chat some more.'

'I mustn't keep you from your work — any of you,' Kit says, with a charming smile at me and at Cal — who suddenly decides to take an intense interest in the conversation. 'And I need to have my shower and grind out some words. I'll bring *The Making of Dark Blue* down later.'

'OK. We'll probably take a break for lunch around two, but it depends how the shoot's going. If we don't, why not bring the book up to the farmhouse later and leave it for me to sign? I'm sure Cal won't mind, will you?'

Cal looks like a bomb about to go off.

'So you two know each other?' Kit asks, as if he's amazed.

'Yes, Cal and I are old friends — Demi too,' says Isla.

'I knew you were from this part of the world. I didn't know you were good friends with Cal. It's a small world, huh?' He directs this at Cal who has a fixed smile on his face though I suspect he's enjoying the conversation as much as Mitch enjoyed his trip to the vet's to get the snip.

'Isn't it?' Cal says, with a long drawn-out sigh. 'And, sadly, I have to go and get on with my work too. Such a shame we can't chat some more about the eateries of West London, but maybe another time. See you later,' he directs this at me and Isla. 'You too, *Kit*.'

Kit smiles and nods. 'Cal.'

In that exchange there's something so charged a spark would blow everything sky high. I'm not

109

sure why Cal has it in for Kit.

Kit jogs away and once he's out of hearing, Isla raises an eyebrow to me. 'Well, if that's the class of guest you're getting, you're doing OK.'

'Depends on your point of view,' Cal growls.

I cut in. 'Kit's more than a holidaymaker. He's staying here until Christmas to finish his book.'

'If he's bothering you, just let me know and I'll get him to back off,' Cal directs his comment at Isla.

'He's not bothering me. He only said hello and asked me to sign his book. He's a writer, you know what they're like.'

'No. Actually I don't. I'm not the creative type, as you both well know, and I really can't stand around gossiping. I'll see you later then, at the farmhouse, when you're finished. Don't expect haute cuisine, either of you. It's a casserole so it won't matter if it's in the Aga for a longer amount of time.'

'Sounds great,' says Isla. 'You'd better go, we don't want to waste your time with gossip, do we, Demi?'

'Wouldn't dream of it,' I say, surprised but amused by Isla's sarcasm. Cal deserves it.

Jez pops his head around the corner of the cafe. 'Hey, Demi. Sorry to bother you, but I could do with a hand with preparing the salads for the lunch service.'

'See. I have my work too. Bye.'

Feeling guilty for abandoning Jez to chat with Cal and Isla, yet secretly longing to stay and hear the rest of their conversation, I follow Jez inside and leave them alone together on the terrace.

11

Cal

Damn Bannen. Still, at least Isla didn't invite him for dinner as well as to sign that bloody book in person. He brought it round earlier, according to Polly, and she's left it on the dresser for Isla. He's slipped his business card inside it — I had a look and I don't feel the slightest bit guilty about it. It says: Kit Bannen, Author and Journalist — and includes his office phone and mobile number, of course. I wouldn't put it past him to hope Isla slips him her card in return.

She wouldn't, would she?

No way.

Isla arrives before Demi, while I'm checking the garlic and rosemary potatoes aren't burned. They're golden brown and the herby scent fills the kitchen. It was my mother's recipe, but I've tried it before and everyone seems to like it so I hope I'm on to a winner. I'm making a classic beef bourguignon from an old Mary Berry cookbook — from when she was famous the first time. The book is dog-eared and was handed down to my mother from my grandmother.

Isla walks straight through the back door, of course, because she's virtually family. She's changed into jeans and a chunky, oversized Arran sweater that hangs off her slender frame.

'Hello. Wow, that smells good,' she says.

'I hope so. Can you leave the door open a bit. It's warm in here.'

'Sure.' There's pink in her cheeks from a day spent out in the wind. She looks happier than I've seen her for a while. Work suits her, obviously, but then it has always suited us both.

'How are you?' Isla asks while I collect two glasses from the dresser. The book lies next to my mum's photo.

I turn to her. 'Good. Like I said, we're busy but could be even busier — though it's all going well.'

'No, not how's business. How are *you*?'

'OK. How are you?'

'OK. Do I look OK?'

What the hell am I supposed to say to that? 'You look better. Less tired and healthier.'

She laughs. 'Ever the charmer. You look good, Cal. The extra weight suits you.'

I laugh. 'You always thought I was well fit.'

'Ha ha. Yes, and didn't you know it, but you *do* look well.'

'Ditto.' I say and she smiles and I do. I can say it now, without her telling me off or thinking I'm going to dive on her. These days, I'm more in control; anchored to the bottom like sea kelp, yet able to sway with the tide. I think that means I'm immune to her now. God, I don't know . . .

She sits down at the table. 'Where's Demi?'

'She was late finishing up at the cafe. She texted me to say she'll be here in ten minutes, after she's changed.'

'She's done incredibly well with Demelza's.

You both have. I can hardly believe it was the old storage barn, and apparently the first few weeks have gone very well.'

'Yes. She's worked her guts out for it so she deserves it. Thanks for doing us a favour by using it for the catering.'

'I wasn't doing anyone a favour. The crew and cast are very happy to have great food and somewhere comfortable to escape. Even my stars were happy.'

'Thanks anyway. I want Demi to succeed. She deserves it after tackling Kilhallon head on, sticking with us through thick and thin and putting up with my moods.' I can't hide my smile as I empty the remains of the Côtes du Rhône I used for the casserole into two glasses. 'She deserves a medal.'

'You really like her, don't you?' Isla focuses on me.

'*Like* her?' I roll my eyes. 'Yeah, I like her when she's not driving me mad.'

'You're a terrible liar, Cal. I know you too well, remember? I know when you have feelings for someone.'

'For you?' I keep my tone light.

'For anyone. I can tell how you feel about Demi,' Isla says. 'I've seen the way you look at each other, and the way you don't look at each other when you think other people are watching you. You and Demi are an item, aren't you? Perhaps more than that?'

I laugh, squirming a little under her scrutiny, but knowing there's no hiding place any more. Isla moving to London has put space between us, or, perhaps, it's simply time passing. I don't know.

'An item? That makes me feel like I'm a parcel . . . but I guess we are together, sort of, but we're not making a big thing of it. Demi has her own life, with the cafe, the publicity and new opportunities coming her way.'

'Opportunities which Demi turned down?'

'How do you know about that?'

'Robyn told me that Demi was offered a job at Spero's in Brighton, but decided to stay here.'

'I tried not to persuade her to stay.'

'Not hard enough, by the look of things.'

'You'd be surprised. I almost drove Demi away. I wanted her to stay but it was selfish of me to keep her here. I still think it was selfish of me and that I won't keep her long.'

Isla shakes her head at me. 'It's OK to admit you're in love with her. It's not a betrayal,' she says.

'In love?' I laugh. 'It's nothing like that. It's not that simple . . . '

'It seems very simple to me. You've fallen for Demi but you're scared to either let go or keep her. Both freak you out in their own ways. You're scared to show her how you feel, and of losing someone else that you love.'

'You give me credit for being more sensitive than I really am.'

'On the contrary, I think you're way more sensitive than you'd ever admit.'

'I'm a lost cause, then.'

She puts down her glass and covers my hand with hers, letting it rest there. She's right: it

114

would feel like a betrayal to admit how much I feel for Demi. It would also feel like a fresh loss to truly move on. My own glass abandoned, I catch her fingers in mine before she can pull them away. I brush my lips over them; it's such an innocent gesture, chaste compared to the intimacy we once enjoyed together, but it's all I dare risk. Anything else would be a betrayal of Isla, Luke and Demi. Of my own conscience.

'You're not lost. Not yet,' Isla whispers, gently withdrawing her hand. 'Make a fresh start . . . I think, perhaps, that it was a mistake to do the shoot here, even to help you and Demi out. I should have stayed in London and found another location.'

'No. You can't hide away from me. You should come here. I need you to, if only to prove to myself that I can behave normally around you.'

'But it's not a game, Cal. There's Demi to consider too. You can't use me to test your resolve . . . or mine,' she adds softly.

She stands up before I can fully realise the impact of her words and crosses to the open doorway as if she's about to make a run for it. 'Oh, look. There's Demi — and she's with that writer guy, Kit.' Isla sounds relieved, but all I feel is annoyed and confused.

She steps outside and I join her in the yard. Across the car park, the security light on the barn reveals two figures standing close together, talking. 'Kit's only a guest,' I tell her.

'Yes, and he's staying until Christmas, which seems like a very long time to be only a guest. He looks like a permanent fixture to me, and he seems to like Demi.'

Kit laughs. Demi laughs the way she does when Mitch does something to amuse her, or a customer pays her a compliment about the food in the cafe — though I don't think Kit Bannen is talking about her scones, judging from their expressions. I'm not sure I make her laugh like he just has. I don't praise her enough, and I definitely don't let her know how good she makes me feel. Is that because I'm not sure how I feel or because, as Isla says, I'm too afraid to go out on a limb again with any woman?

'Are you sure he's only a guest?' Her breath mists the night air as she repeats her theory to me.

'Those potatoes won't wait any longer. Come on, it's getting cold, let's go inside.'

Demi arrives a few minutes later, smiling and looking hot in denim shorts, woolly tights and a pair of suede ankle boots with cute fringes that I find inexplicably sexy. Her chestnut hair is loose around her shoulders and she joins Isla and me around the table in the sitting room.

So: I'm having dinner with two beautiful women, both of whom I've slept with, both of whom I feel passionately about, yet I don't have a clue how either of them really feels about me. I don't know how they feel about each other — are they jealous? Indifferent? Hurt?

Some men might not care — my father obviously didn't or he would never have kept on betraying and hurting my mother.

I haven't betrayed anyone, yet, so I should be a happy man, but something is niggling me, gnawing at the fringe of my consciousness while we eat and laugh and pretend to be friends, while knowing that 'friends' could never describe the relationship between any of us.

There's something that they don't know about me, and can never know, that gnaws at me too, hardly ever stops gnawing at me. In the end, it may eat me up, and make the fact that I'm in love with Demi meaningless.

I'm in love with Demi.

Right in the middle of dinner, with a fork halfway to my mouth, I've admitted it. Not out loud of course, but to myself — and with Isla here. Isla shares some risqué gossip with Demi about some actor. I love the way Demi's eyes light up in wonder. I love the way she gasps in amazement at being let into the secrets of a world of glamour and privilege she could never have dreamed of a few months ago. I love her freshness and lust for life; even though she's had a tough go of it, she isn't jaded and cynical like me. She showed me that I could make a fresh start and I want it to be with her.

A lump forms in my throat and I make a sharp exit to the kitchen, on the pretext of fetching another bottle. I need a few moments on my own before I come back, a smile on my face and a tale of my own from our schooldays that makes Isla and Demi laugh. I may be ready to admit my feelings for Demi to myself, but I'm not ready to share them with her. I need time . . . more time . . . there are issues I need to resolve before then, things I need to face and come to terms with.

Can I do that? Do I deserve to?

While we laugh together and drink too much wine in the sitting room, Kit Bannen's name comes up more than once, from Demi and from Isla. Before she leaves for Bosinney House, Isla signs Bannen's book about her last drama with a personal message and puts his card in her handbag without comment. Robyn calls for her in the Mini and Demi walks back to her cottage at the same time, without a kiss or any comment to me. She's seemed quiet but not subdued this evening, more relaxed in Isla's presence than I've seen her before, and it went way better than I could have hoped.

I shut the kitchen door behind them, leaving it unlocked as I always have — as all the Penwiths always have — but tonight I wonder for a second or two if I should lock it. I've no idea why: maybe that stupid nightmare rattled me more than I realised. I put the book on the reception desk so that Polly can hand it to Bannen when he calls tomorrow morning, without having to come in here to find it. Not that she'd invite him into my house, but you never know.

Possibly — probably — I'm being completely paranoid, but I have the feeling that Kit Bannen is definitely not 'only a guest'. I do believe that he's an author of techno-thrillers or a journalist on a solar energy trade publication. But I'm also one hundred per cent certain that he's a chancer who would love to get in Demi's knickers — and possibly Isla's too. I'm convinced he'd say anything to charm anyone who might be of use to him, including Polly and Mitch.

118

Beyond those facts, I'm not sure about anything where Bannen's concerned, but I'm bloody well going to find out.

* * *

In my study the following afternoon, I'm trying to grapple with the accounts for the holiday park when Isla arrives. She finds me peering at the laptop and getting nowhere.

'Sorry to disturb you, but I didn't want to leave without saying a proper goodbye. We're finished up here now.' She hovers in the doorway to the study as if she's not quite sure how deep she dare venture into my space.

'You're not disturbing me. I'm grateful for the distraction.'

She steps inside and shuts the door behind her.

'Thanks again for letting us use Kilhallon. I've already thanked Demi and her team for their catering, which was awesome, and I'll send her some flowers and a card too from the whole cast. She can start blogging and tweeting about us being here now we're gone. We have to be more secretive these days because my leads, Dylan and Jojo, are becoming hot property and it's hard to work when the hordes descend, even though most are harmless and we're glad of the publicity.'

I shake my head. 'I've spent the past hour unblocking a toilet because a toddler called George insisted on stuffing his soft toys down it. Yours is a very different world.'

She perches on a chair. 'Sometimes I would definitely swap.'

'No, you wouldn't.'

'Oh, I would. I yearn for a simpler life and have those 'how the hell did I get here?' thoughts. It's weird. But aren't you going to be splashed all over the press soon, anyway? Demi said the magazine fashion piece is coming out any day.'

'Is it? I hadn't even thought about it. Demi handles all the PR stuff and I don't think 'all over the press' is right. It's only one Sunday features magazine that a handful of bored people flick through while their quail are roasting. Or whatever.'

Isla laughs. 'She's one in a million.'

'Yes.' I decide to plunge in now we're alone again and can't be overheard. If I don't ask this now I may never do it.

'Isla, there's something I have to thank you for.'

'Thank me for?'

'Yes. Last summer, I don't know how you did it, but somehow you persuaded Mawgan Cade to drop her opposition to our plans for Kilhallon, I thought it was impossible, but whatever you did, it made a massive difference to us. To me and to Demi. She wouldn't be running the cafe and have her dream now, if you hadn't intervened.'

Isla frowns. 'Cal, no . . . '

'Don't try to deny that you stepped in to help us. I knew it was you, Mawgan likes you and whatever you think about her and Luke having an affair, she listened.'

'Stop. You have it all wrong. I didn't speak to Mawgan about changing her plans. I swear it.'

'What? But I thought . . . '

'No. I promise it wasn't me.' She crosses her heart. 'And Luke and Mawgan weren't having an affair, you were right. I shouldn't have come whining about my problems to you and saying I'd made a mistake with Luke. It was very wrong of me. I do love him, Cal. I really do.'

I wait for the kick in the guts at hearing those words but I feel only mild regret and amazement at Luke's good fortune.

'I need to tell you that I went to see Demi while you were out and told her about the pressure he'd been putting on Robyn to leave Andi,' she goes on, toying with a glass bird paperweight that my father gave my mother.

I catch my breath at her words. 'You went to see Demi? When was this?'

'One morning in the summer while Mawgan Cade was trying to block your plans for developing Kilhallon. Luke told me that Mawgan wanted to stop Andi and Robyn from moving in together. She persuaded Luke to put pressure on Robyn to end the relationship. Mawgan has always been unstable, but she's turned into a truly bitter and twisted woman.'

I shake my head. 'I already knew the depths Mawgan could plumb, but I didn't realise the Cades had such a tight grip on Luke.'

'They owned your Uncle Rory and Luke's business premises and they'd loaned money to the actual business too. What Luke did was wrong but he was under enormous pressure and

121

not thinking straight . . . ' Isla says, her cheeks tinged with pink. She's obviously ashamed of Luke's actions, although they're not her fault. 'Luke told me that he'd go bankrupt and we'd lose everything if Robyn took Andi away from Mawgan and her father. I thought the information might help Demi put things right for Robyn and Andi, somehow,' she adds.

'Now I know why you and Luke were so keen to move to London.'

'Luke and Rory sold all of their assets and with my help they were able to pay off the Cades. Luke's working for a financial advice company in London and he seems much happier. Now we're in London and Rory has sold up, we're out of the Cades' reach. Making a fresh start was the best thing we ever did.'

Although I can, just about, understand Luke's motives for treating Robyn and Andi so cruelly, I can't understand how Demi fits in. Or why she let me assume Isla had helped me. 'What did you think Demi could do with the information? Does Luke know you came to talk to her?'

Isla shrugs. 'I don't know. I wasn't thinking straight at the time myself. I suppose I hoped she might tell Robyn and Andi. Perhaps Andi was so upset she finally made Mawgan see sense about what really mattered to her family. I remember that I was desperate to help in any way I could. I care about Kilhallon, the history and heritage and everyone here. I've betrayed Luke in one way, but I'd do the same again, because in the end, things turned out OK, didn't they?'

She looks around her at the study which looks

no different to how it always has, even though so much has changed in the past few months.

'Thank you for telling me this,' I say, stunned by her revelation.

'I'm not sure my interference had anything to do with the outcome. Someone else saved you, Cal, not me.'

She stands up. 'Now, I have to go. I'm staying over at Rory's again this evening and I promised to have dinner with him and Robyn. Despite his new lady friend coming over these days, your uncle still misses having family and friends around the house.'

'Is that a hint? You're right and I'll make time to visit him. I've been too wrapped up in working here lately.'

I get up and we embrace. Isla kisses my cheek. She smells of the cold, clear Cornish air and leaves me with memories neither of us can afford to dwell on any longer.

She walks away and I walk in the opposite direction. Is it wrong of me to still fancy her like crazy? To think of what might have been? Is it wrong to be sad to see her walk out of my life again, even though she'd never walked back into it? I can't rejoice in the idea of her with another man, my best mate, a man who's not worthy of her — not that I ever was either.

Is it wrong not to be as eaten up as I would have been six months, or even six weeks, ago?

Is it wrong that, as Isla leaves the car park in her Jeep, I'm thinking — longing — for another woman who drives me just as crazy? Even though I suspect she may love me, and I could hurt her the way I hurt Isla.

I've done a lot of bad things in my life. It's time I did the right thing. But I'm damned if I know what the right thing is where Demi is concerned.

12

Monday November 4th
Demi

After the crew left last Tuesday morning, I had Wednesday off and we were back into the 'normal' cafe opening session from Thursday to Sunday. On Monday, so many families descended for the half-term holidays that we decided to open for the rest of the week to make the most of the business while we could. I've had no choice but to work most of the days straight through, even though Cal, Robyn and Polly tried to help as much as they could.

By yesterday evening — Sunday — I was so worn out I virtually crawled home to the cottage and didn't wake up until eleven o'clock this morning, a grey and gloomy Monday. In all the mayhem of the past weeks, I was too busy and tired to blog about the filming, so Robyn and Andi wrote the post for me and finally uploaded it last night, a week late, along with some 'exclusive' photos from the shoot for social media channels. With a bit of luck it should attract a few more bookings and customers.

Now I'm finally awake, I crunch on a piece of toast in my cottage and switch on my tablet.

Wow and wow. The hits on the Demelza's Cafe and Kilhallon blog have rocketed and I can't even begin to reply to or even like all the retweets of the photos on our Twitter account. We've almost doubled our followers on Instagram and our Facebook page likes have soared. The photos of the shoot have been shared hundreds of times, possibly thousands. In a way, I'm relieved we didn't blog about it until now because I don't think we could have coped with all the extra custom and attention during the busy half-term week.

Checking the Kilhallon Park booking app, I see that lots of new reservations for the cottages have already come in and Christmas and New Year are now full. My phone hardly stops ringing with enquiries from people wanting to arrange festive lunches and afternoon teas in the cafe.

Just when I think there will be time to grab a sandwich while I start on the cafe accounts, a copy of next week's Sunday magazine supplement pings into my inbox from Eva Spero's journalist friend. It's in the lifestyle section and combines a fashion shoot with a short feature on Cal and me, and Kilhallon.

The photos have been retouched, of course, and made meaner and moodier. I expected the Photoshop effects, but I barely recognise the figures as us. There's me in a floaty dress sitting on the platform of the engine house, and lying in the meadow wearing a pair of dungarees (and nothing else). Oh God, you would almost see my nipples in one picture, if it wasn't for a well-placed shadow.

Then there's Cal. As far as I'm concerned, he needs no grooming or enhancement to look red hot, but the photos have taken his natural rugged sexiness and raised it to superheated level. To me, he's far more gorgeous than the star of Isla's drama. It's weird to think these photos will be on thousands of doorsteps and probably thousands of tablets and mobile phones all over the world. In fact, I'm not sure I like sharing him with so many people.

I'm a bit nervous of how he's going to react when he sees the photos, even if it does mean good news for the business. I've been worried about him. Ever since Isla left, he hasn't been himself. He seems subdued and quiet. No matter how much I tell myself not to be silly, their relationship is over — and I can't do a damn thing about it if it isn't — and that I shouldn't expect anything more from Cal than I already have. I can't help but get goosebumps.

It has to be done, though, and instead of forwarding the pictures, I take my tablet up to the house and show him myself.

He goes deadly quiet as he scrolls through the PDF of the feature. There are three pages of it, with the headline 'The Cream of Cornish'.

'It's amazing, isn't it?' I say cheerily, as he toggles back and forth through the photos. 'Bookings have gone through the roof since the film shoot and this magazine hasn't even landed on people's doorsteps yet.'

He grunts, flicking over the pages and back again. It's all I can do to not explode with the agony.

'Well?' I say, cracking.

'You look great. Very sexy . . . ' he mutters.

'I don't think I look like that in real life,' I say.

'Well, you can wander around in skimpy dungarees for me any day.'

'Cal!'

A smile tugs at his mouth, then disappears. He shoves the tablet away as if he's ashamed. 'I look a right pillock.'

'Pillock isn't exactly the word I'd use,' I say, unable to bring myself to tell him that I'm surprised the screen hasn't set alight.

He pulls the tablet to him again and starts poring over the words. He frowns, mutters a rude word every so often and then puts down the tablet with a gasp of disgust.

'That's not true. They've made up some total crap about me 'risking my life to save others in a war-torn hell hole'. I *never* said that. I told the reporter I was part of a charity team, but this piece make it seem as if I'm boasting about having saved the world single-handedly.'

'Hmm. I must admit I was a bit surprised when I saw some of the quotes.'

'Oh Jeez . . . what's this?'

He pokes a finger at a section of text on the tablet. 'This so-called quote from me makes me sound like a sanctimonious twat to boot.' He glares at me. 'Did you tell them anything?'

'As if! Don't overreact. I don't think you come across like a boastful hero or sanctimonious twat, but I was surprised you'd given them any quotes at all about your work, even though Eva said that it would make a good story.'

'A good story? It was real life for those people who had to live and die there.'

'Cal, calm down. I'd never say anything to

128

strangers or anyone else about your time in Syria, mainly because I haven't got a clue what did or didn't happen to you. I just think they've taken the bones of the story and stretched the truth.'

He snorts. 'Stretched it? There's nothing true in here.'

'But it won't matter, will it? This is a lifestyle feature. It's the publicity for Kilhallon that counts. You can't deny that Kilhallon looks incredible. Added to the buzz over the film shoot, this feature will be fantastic for business. We need all the help we can get to take us through winter into next season.'

'I guess so, but I'm still pissed off about them making up this rubbish. I don't like people thinking I'm some kind of hero. Do you think it's too late to change it?'

'Probably, and I don't think journalists like interviewees having approval of their articles. It gets in the way of their story.'

He puts down the tablet, still shaking his head. 'The thing is, I'm going to be meeting up with some of my old buddies from the charity sooner than I thought.'

'Meeting up? When?'

'I've got to go to London next week. The group is having a reunion and I want to go along and catch up with a few old friends afterwards, though God knows what they'll make of this rubbish when they see it.'

'I'm sure your mates will know what journalists are like and you can explain to them in person that the reporter's used poetic licence.

That's if they ever see this article. I doubt they're the type of people who'd bother to read this lifestyle supplement, are they?'

'God, I don't know.' He glances at the tablet again and sighs. 'Shit.'

I put my arms around him. 'You worry too much. When are you going to London?'

'Next Monday. Will you be OK here on your own while I'm away?

'I won't be on my own. I have Polly, Mitch and the guests, and I think I can manage without you.'

He rolls his eyes at my sarcasm but I'm glad he can't read my mind. There's no way I would voice my fears about him being persuaded to go back to work in the Middle East again.

I don't even know why I think that myself. Perhaps it's his passionate reaction to the magazine shoot. Working in a warzone in life or death situations must have been an incredibly intense experience. I often wonder if he misses it.

But surely Cal wouldn't abandon Kilhallon now, after expending so much blood, sweat and tears reviving it? Yet I know his time there has left him with scars we don't know about, inside and out. When I first met him he was thin and tired and nursing some injuries. It looked like he'd had an accident or been wounded, but he didn't say anything about it and I didn't ask. Polly and Robyn both think he suffered a breakdown or post-traumatic stress disorder and had to be sent home, and he did mention to me something about having to be rescued once so I suspect he was airlifted out of a bad situation.

The prospect of reliving his time out in the warzone, even if it's only by seeing people he worked with and hearing about all the latest troubles, is bound to bring back bad memories.

'Does it bother you, being reminded of what you did and saw out there?' I'm dying to ask him exactly what happened.

'Mind? Why would I? It's not as if I'm going on assignment. It's only a meeting . . . even if it is in that highly dangerous zone they call London.' He smiles. 'You'll be lucky to get me back in one piece now I'm a celebrity. I must admit, I'm revising my opinion of those photos by the second. I think I look pretty damn hot. In fact, even I'd shag me.'

'Cal!' I have to hit him, but he grabs my wrist, gently, and wrestles me back onto the sofa. He pulls me onto his lap and gently teases my hair out of the collar of my jumper. My scalp tingles and desire swirls low in my belly. Warmth spreads all over my body. I know he's trying to distract me, but I don't mind. It's such a relief to be so close again.

'Don't worry about me,' he says seriously. 'I'll be back before you even miss me.'

'Why would I miss you?' I tease, gazing into those deep dark eyes. 'I'm far too busy to miss you. In fact I can probably get loads done without you here thumping about and distracting me.'

He strokes my thigh. 'There hasn't been enough distraction for either of us lately.'

'You think?' My skin heats deliciously.

'I *know*.' Gently pushing me off his lap, he

locks the door of the study and draws the heavy curtains. Soon, the magazine and his impromptu trip to London are forgotten in a kiss that turns my limbs liquid. My concerns about him can wait for now. They won't go away, but I'm going to make sure I forget them for a little while.

13

A week later, Robyn takes Cal to the station so that we can use the Land Rover while he's away in London. He's staying with an old uni friend, a doctor who volunteers with the charity in London, to save money on hotels. It's the first time he's left Kilhallon since I came to work here. I've spent hundreds of nights on my own and slept on the streets, but it still seems strange for Cal not to be around.

Even though Demelza's is closed today, Polly, Shamia, Nina and I meet in the building at lunchtime to firm up our plans for the pop-up Demelza's at the Harbour Lights Festival launch in just over two and half weeks, on the last Friday in November. We tried to work out how much stock we'll need so we don't run out halfway through the evening, or worse, have waste left over. Polly suggested we borrow Jez's mate's van for the evening. I think she's getting into the idea of the festival and has started reminiscing about the days when Cal's mum was on the committee. I'm not sure she would have done that if Cal had been here.

★ ★ ★

Tuesday is my chance to call into St Trenyan to do some shopping and have lunch with Tamsin at Sheila's Beach Hut where I used to work. It's

133

great to chat to Sheila and see how she is, and to be waited on for a change. Knowing Cal will be home tomorrow, I spend this evening with Robyn and Andi at the Tinner's, playing pool in the bar and just chilling out. Despite my work and friends, I *do* miss Cal and I can't deny it. I had a text from him on Monday afternoon telling me he arrived safely at Paddington and a quick phone call before I went to bed. He sounds like he's been busy catching up with old friends and colleagues, although I wouldn't say he sounds happy. Cal's not one for sending lots of OTT messages and I'm sure he can look after himself.

Finally, it's Wednesday afternoon and I have to admit that today has crawled by. Cal texted me to say his train arrives at Penzance at 9.30 and that he is looking forward to seeing me. I had a lazy morning, did some little jobs in the cafe then came home to my cottage and wrote a piece for the cafe blog. Maybe it's the weather — it's been dreary and damp all the time Cal's been away — but despite trying to concentrate, I can't settle to anything properly. Even Mitch is getting the twitches. Outside, darkness has fallen and it's still four hours until I need to set out for Penzance. I feed Mitch and reheat some leftover pasta bake for myself to eat in front of my tiny TV.

'This is no good, Mitch, I can't sit around in here any longer. Tell you what? Shall we go and hang some of the Christmas decorations at the cafe?'

I shipped the decorations down to the cafe this

morning and was going to wait until tomorrow and ask Nina or Shamia and Polly to give me a hand with them before we opened, but now's as good a time as any. Making the cafe look Christmassy will be a nice way to pass the time before I have to leave for the station. Mitch trots after me as I plunge into the mist and trudge down to the cafe. It's thickened a little as night has drawn in and is cold and damp on my face. I haven't bothered with a torch — it's not far and I know my way almost as well as Mitch, but I'm still glad to reach the doors and switch on the lights.

Soon, I realise that I should have brought the step ladder for hanging the festive-themed bunting I bought at the St Trenyan Christmas market. I'm going to need help. However, I can manage most of the jobs myself and I start up my 'Christmas Mix' on the iPad.

What else would I choose but 'Christmas Wrapping' by the Waitresses, an oldie but goodie that's my all-time-top festive tune. The empty cafe makes a natural theatre and singing along to these old favourites lifts my mood despite the gloomy evening outside. Mitch lies in a corner, chewing a toy, as I unpack the decorations from the box.

I decide less is more, opting for a few strategically placed festive decorations in natural colours. The fresh holly and mistletoe sprigs will be boosted by some lush faux-fir and berry garlands, which I think complement the beamed interior of the barn better than over-the-top tinsel and dancing Santas. Not that I'm against

135

all the festive glitz and shiny stuff, but I can go to town on twinkly decorations in the cottage and farmhouse if Cal doesn't scream too loudly. Even if he does, I don't care. Polly told me she likes to go the whole hog from December the 1st in her own place and that Cal's mum always had a real tree, with a collection of family ornaments on it that go way back.

From feeling low earlier, I now can't stop grinning.

Christmas is coming up fast and this year I'll be spending it in a proper home, not on a friend's sofa or, like last year, in a shop doorway. Polly's going to spend a couple of days with her family, so Cal and I will able to chill out at Kilhallon House, tucking into turkey and all the trimmings. We can open our presents — well, he can open the present I'll get him, when I've decided what it is. I don't actually expect anything from him. Then we can drink and eat and shag ourselves into oblivion for the rest of the day. I hope the guests don't need us for anything, because we're bound to be too knackered from all the stuffing and sex to do anything.

The fiddle intro to 'Fairytale of New York' bursts into life. Mitch jumps up as I belt out the rude bits and he stares at me while I jog about to 'Christmas Rapping' by Kurtis Blow. The cafe is looking quite festive now. I stop back to admire my handiwork, a little out of breath, and then it comes on: 'I Saw Mommy Kissing Santa Claus'. I don't know who it's by, it must be half a century old and the scratchy recording sounds like something from a museum. Yet I know every word and sing them softly while Mitch looks at me as if I'm loopy. It's a very silly tune, but it was Nana Demelza's favourite. When I was very little, I'd stand on her giant furry-slippered feet and she'd dance around the front room while we sang it.

It was always obvious to me that Santa Claus was the girl's dad. How stupid was she not to know her father was snogging her mum?

'Oh, puhleaase,' I say to Mitch, shaking a bunch of mistletoe in his face and making him yip in surprise.

He licks my hand and looks up at me with soulful eyes. I drop the mistletoe and hug him. The old song has brought back memories of my mum as well as my nan. They were happy times. Why did they have to go?

I have Mitch now, and Cal, Polly, Robyn and my friends. I'm way luckier than most, but I can't help the thick, full feeling in my throat. I wish Mum and Nana Demelza could see me now. I wish . . .

Before I burst into tears, I let go of Mitch and get up to rip a paper towel from the roll in the servery.

'*Demi?*'

'Oh my God!'

Sharp barks echo round the cafe. Kit stands in the doorway, in a black trench coat like Sherlock's with a trapper hat pulled over his ears.

'Are you OK? I saw the lights on from my place. I was a bit bored so I wandered down here

137

and heard the music — thought I'd come and see if there was any craic to be had.'

I feign a laugh although my heart is beating fast from the shock of him walking in without me hearing him. 'I'm not sure my solo karaoke counts as craic.'

Taking off his hat, he joins me on the other side of the servery counter. 'I'm sorry I startled you.' He frowns. 'You look as if you've been crying.'

'No. No, I think I'm going down with a cold.' I sniff dramatically.

He raises his eyebrows. 'Then you should be tucked up in your cottage, not working late here.'

'Decorating the cafe isn't work and I wanted to pass the time before I collect Cal from the station. I'll only lie about, watching rubbish telly and necking Lemsips if I'm not here.' At least part of that statement is true.

Recognising Kit and now happy with his presence, Mitch wanders back to his corner and his dog chew.

The music mix kicks in, I have it on a loop. It's Wham — again.

Kit puts his hat on a table next to the decorations. 'Ouch.'

I groan. 'Not you too? You're as bad as Cal.'

'You mean Cal doesn't like Wham either?'

'He hates this one.'

He starts to take off his coat. 'Then we have more than one thing in common. Are you sure I can't give you a hand here? I can see a spare box of garlands on the table.'

'I need the steps to loop them over the beams

138

and I can't be bothered to fetch them in the dark.' Whoops, I hope that doesn't sound like a girly plea. 'I mean, I could get the steps if I wanted. I didn't mean I want you to get them for me.'

He smiles. 'I know. The fog's thick and it's cold too, I don't fancy it either, but if I stand on a chair I think I can throw the garlands over the beams without the steps.'

'Oh, I couldn't let you do that.'

'Why not? Because I'm a guest? I thought we'd gone past that stage.' His green eyes twinkle.

'No. Because of health and safety. I don't want you suing us if you fall off and break your neck.'

He laughs. 'Thanks. But I promise I won't sue, even if I do break something. Which won't happen. I'll be very careful.'

I hesitate. There's not long until I have to leave for the station, but it would be great to see the place finished and it will save time tomorrow. It won't do any harm. 'OK, thanks, but please be careful. It's a long wait for the paramedics down here and the air ambulance won't be flying tonight.'

'You're all heart,' says Kit and starts taking off his boots. I wonder if there's a girlfriend — or boyfriend — on the scene, but there can't be or surely she or he or both would have visited him by now. Maybe he's come to Kilhallon to escape from a breakup, not only to write his book.

With the help of a chair and the countertop and bar stools, we manage to loop the garland over the beams with only a few wobbly close

139

shaves. When we stand back and admire our handiwork, we're both surprisingly out of puff.

'Not bad, eh?'

'No. Who'd have thought hanging Christmas decorations could be such hard work,' Kit replies. 'Worth it though. The place looks very festive.'

He's right. The greenery might be artificial but it does look fabulous against the reclaimed oak beams. The high-quality decorations were worth every penny from my budget. By the time the tree arrives next week and I've added some more holly, and the cafe's filled with the aromas of my seasonal menu, I think we'll be rocking Christmas at the cafe.

Together, we carry the holly in from the buckets outside the rear door. Robyn brought some of it from Bosinney House yesterday, but I hadn't had the chance to display it yet.

'I saw all the publicity about the film shoot online. That must be good for business,' Kit says, following me in with the second bucket.

'It already has been. The cottages are fully booked over Christmas and New Year and we've had lots of advance bookings for the new season for the yurts too.'

'I'm glad about that. I expect the magazine feature helped too.' He picks up a stray piece of holly. 'I bought a copy in the coffee shop down in St Trenyan. Sorry, I don't always use Demelza's.'

'I'll forgive you.' He hands me the holly and I stick it in one of the old stone cider jars I rescued from the barn this summer.

'What does Cal think of being a celebrity?' Kit asks as I arrange the sprigs in the jar.

'He doesn't think of himself as a celebrity. He's in London at the moment and I expect that feature is the last thing on his mind.'

'Oh really? I have to pop back myself next week to see my publicist. Business trips are a pain, aren't they? Especially with the traffic.'

'Cal took the train. I don't think he could face driving into central London.' I decide not to tell him where Cal's actually gone. It is none of his business, after all, no matter how friendly he's become.

'Probably the best idea, especially in this weather. You must miss him, then, being all on your own.' I'm pretty sure Kit is angling to find out more about my situation with Cal but I won't be drawn in.

'I haven't had the chance to miss him. I'm going to decorate the cafe and launch our Christmas menus, then there have been a lot of extra bookings to process since we had the film people here. I need to get online and make the most of the extra publicity. And I'm not alone. I have Polly and Mitch and the staff for company, not to mention the guests.'

'Sounds like you're too busy to miss your boss.'

I glance at the big iron clock that says *Dreckly* on it, a Cornish word meaning sometime later or maybe never. 'Wow. It's late. I'd better lock up here and fetch Cal.'

'Do you want a hand closing up?'

'Thanks, but you've been a huge help already.

141

The staff will have a big surprise when they get in tomorrow. Be careful on your way back to the cottage,' I warn.

'I will,' Kit says. 'Goodnight then. You take care driving to the station too. It's a real pea souper out here now.'

With a wave, he steps outside and the fog swallows him. I scoop up my keys from the serving counter, still wondering about Kit. Apart from being a bit nosy at times — which could be because he's a writer — he isn't so bad. He could have flirted with me and made me feel uncomfortable, which was the real reason for my reluctance to let him help, but he was nothing beyond friendly. Cal's jealousy is just silly.

'Come on then, Mitch.'

I think I hear a snuffling in the kitchen. I hope he hasn't nicked any food and the fact he's wormed his way in there at all is a massive hygiene no-no.

'Mitch! Get out of there!'

I must have imagined the snuffling noise, or perhaps it was a bird or rabbit in the fog outside, because there's no Mitch in the kitchen. 'You'd better not be in the storeroom, you devil,' I call as I walk deeper into the kitchen area towards the storeroom and staff cubby hole. Both are still locked and the rear exit is also locked. I shut it myself after Kit and I brought in the holly — Mitch was still in the main cafe area then. I'm sure he was. If he'd slipped out while we collected the holly I'm sure we'd have noticed him.

'Mitch? Where the hell are you hiding?'

I hunt around the whole cafe area, checking under tables although I know there's nowhere for him to hide in there. I even check under the serving counter again, even though he wasn't there the last time I looked, thirty seconds ago. Yet he was there half an hour ago, when Kit and I started to hang the garlands. I heard him yipping softly as he dozed, dreaming of rabbits and running along the coast path, nose to the ground, on the trail of doggy scents. I saw him, twitching happily as he dreamed.

The cafe door squeaks. Is that him?

It swings open the tiniest crack though there's barely a breath of wind or the fog wouldn't be so thick. Yet the door is open, from when Kit left me. Or from when he arrived . . .

A tiny shiver runs through me. Mitch *must* have slipped outside when Kit and I were chatting. I hurry out onto the terrace, expecting to hear a bark, or spot two eyes glowing in the fog, or feel the rasp of a wet tongue on my hand.

'Mitch!'

I listen hard, hoping for a clatter of claws or a snuffle, but get nothing. I go back into the cafe and call for him one last time before I head out into the fog to search for him. But all I get is silence: a bigger, emptier silence than I've ever heard in the cafe before, as if it's wrapped in a foggy duvet that muffles all sounds of life.

14

Polly answers her door in tartan pyjamas and a fleecy dressing gown. Her cottage stands apart, behind Kilhallon House. Made of Cornish granite, it's sturdy and forbidding — just like Polly can be, unless you know her well. Tonight I need her, because it's been fifteen minutes since I left the cafe to look for Mitch and I still haven't found him. I'll be late meeting Cal's train at this rate.

'Sorry to disturb you this late, Polly, but have you seen Mitch?'

She frowns. 'No. Why would I have?'

'I don't know . . . I just . . . I'm trying not to panic, but I can't find him. I was at the cafe with Kit a while ago and he must have slipped outside while we were hanging the decorations. I've shouted and called to him but there was no answer and then I went back to my place because I was sure he'd be waiting for me, but he wasn't there and now I wonder if he's sneaked into the farmhouse for some reason, because you know the back door is always open and he might have smelled something or gone in there and maybe the door shut behind him and — ' I gulp in air ' — I don't know where he could have got to!'

'Whoa. Whoa. Steady, Draw breath!'

I gulp in a huge breath, and another, but I still feel as if I've been racing the hundred metres. I have been running, or as close to running as I could get in fog that swirls around me and clings to my clothes.

'Come in out of this mist. It's freezing.'

'I can't. I have to go and look for Mitch. He could be anywhere, and in this weather you can't see more than a few yards. Oh, damn, I have to collect Cal from the station too but I can't leave Mitch.'

'I'll call him and ask if he wants me to arrange a taxi to meet him. You come in while I get dressed and I'll help you look. Have you checked the farmhouse? The offices? The barn?'

'Not the barn, nor the workshop. I never thought of that.'

'I'll help you. Wait a minute while I get changed and find the torches.' Polly practically drags me inside.

Hardly able to contain myself, I pace Polly's sitting room while the floorboards creak and groan above me. After what seems an agonising wait, she comes downstairs in jeans and a fleece, grabs her coat and pulls on her wellies.

She pats my back and hands me a torch. 'You check the barn and I'll have a look in the workshop. He's bound to be hanging round here somewhere. Did you say you were with Kit Bannen when you last saw the silly hound?'

'Yes. He was helping me decorate the cafe and I think Mitch must have slipped out. I hope he hasn't gone onto the cliffs.'

She shakes her head. 'I bet you anything he's wandered back up to Kilhallon House looking for food. Have you asked Kit if he saw him when

145

he walked back to his cottage?'

'I didn't want to disturb him, but I think I might have to.'

'OK,' she replies. 'Let's have a quick look in the farmhouse first. You know Mitch loves to hide under Cal's bed.'

'Oh, yes. He could be there.'

I search Cal's room first, lifting the valance to look under the new bed, even opening the wardrobe. Calling his name, I try the bathroom — though God knows why Mitch would run in there, he's not one of these toilet-water-drinking dogs. The doors to two of the spare bedrooms are shut but I look inside anyway. One is kept relatively tidy as a guest room but the other is crammed with 'stuff', like old lamps, furniture, packing cases, and books. Mitch isn't hiding in any of them.

I check everywhere else in the farmhouse, trying the ground floor first. There was no Mitch in Cal's study, nor in the snug or the kitchen. 'Mitch? Mitch! Where are you?'

'No luck, then?' Polly meets me outside the back door.

'No.'

'He isn't out in the car park. I even walked up to the entrance gates to the park and I can't see him.'

'Thanks.' I feel faintly sick, then I remember Cal. 'Did you get through to Cal?' I ask Polly.

'No. His mobile went straight to answer phone, but I left him a message and sent him a text. Don't worry about him, he managed to find his way back from a warzone so he can make it home from Penzance on his own. Now, let's give these outbuildings a good going over.'

Calling Mitch's name, we separate. The barn and workshop have lights we can switch on and, though full of equipment, it doesn't take long for us to realise that Mitch isn't hiding in either or he'd have answered to his name. That is, of course, if he *can* answer. A shiver runs down my spine but I tell myself that thinking the worst won't help Mitch if he is lying injured somewhere.

'Where next?' I ask.

Polly sighs. 'I don't know. He might be wandering around different places while we move about so we could all be chasing our tails. Your cottage is surely the most likely place he'll head for as that's where he expects to be fed. I just hope the silly dog hasn't gone and got himself lost in the fog.'

Fear clutches at my stomach. I might be sick. 'Mitch wouldn't get lost even on a night like this. He can smell his way home.' Looking out at the whirling mass of black and grey around us, I don't even believe my words myself.

'Hello!' A beam penetrates the mist and Kit Bannen emerges. 'Everything OK? I went out to my car and thought I could hear people shouting. Why are you out on a night like this?'

'Mitch has run off,' says Polly grimly.

The knot tightens in my stomach. 'When I was locking up, I couldn't find him. I thought he was inside the cafe with us but he must have sneaked out.'

'No. He wouldn't do that, surely? I presume

you've checked your cottage and Kilhallon House?'

'We've checked the farmhouse, my cottage, the outbuildings, offices and reception and I hunted around the cafe building for ages,' I say, trying to stay calm. 'It's been well over an hour now.'

'That's not long, but I can understand why you're worried about him, even if he won't be worried about you,' Kit says gently.

'He's never taken off like this before. He's missed his dinner and that's not like him.'

Polly and Kit exchange glances.

'What? Why are you looking at each other like that? You think he's fallen over the cliff, don't you?' My voice rises and I'm struggling to hold it together now. The tears are so close.

'Calm down, my bird,' says Polly, slipping her arm around my shoulders. 'We don't think anything of the sort, but it's so dark and foul out here, you've no chance of stumbling across him, even if he has wandered off Kilhallon land. You're far better waiting for him to run home to the farmhouse or to your cottage.'

'Polly's right, and you said yourself that Mitch is far more able to find his way around than we ever could be. He'll be sniffing his way back right now, especially if he's hungry. He's probably having a fine old time.' Kit tries to sound reassuring and fails because I've already imagined every horrible scenario.

'Have you thought he might be back at your cottage while we've been hunting around?' Polly suggests.

'Oh, he might. Oh, I hope so. I'll run down there now.'

'Be careful! I'll wait in the farmhouse,' Polly calls after me. 'If you're hell bent on going out, keep in touch with me. I'll wait here in case the stupid hound decides to run home.'

'I'll come with you,' Kit shouts, but I'm already running to the cottage again. My heart pounds, expecting to hear Mitch scrabbling at the door of my cottage to be let in. Of course, I tell myself, he's been wandering around the farmyard, and finally got hungry and come home. Even so, I wish Cal were here, not that he could do any more than we are, but still I wish he were here.

The fog is so thick, I'm almost on the cottage before I see the lights shining through the front windows, but the door is shut firmly and it's obvious Mitch can't have come home, or if he has, he's run off again in search of us. He's a big dog, and brave, but he must be so confused now, running around in the fog, wondering where we all are, hungry and cold. The disappointment is so much, I only just stifle a howl. Kit catches me up and stands helplessly by my side. Squashing down a sob, I pull myself together. Me going to pieces won't help Mitch. Only action will.

'I'm going to look for him by the cafe again.'

Kit shakes his head. 'It's much too dangerous for you to go out to the cliffs on your own. I'm sure Mitch is fine; he knows this place inside out and he has four paws not two, but for humans, it's not safe. Those cliffs will be treacherous.' He puts his hand briefly on my shoulder. 'I mean it, Demi.'

I've been thinking the same thing: maybe Mitch wouldn't have run over the cliff in the fog, but some dogs do. It's happened to visitor's dogs occasionally in other parts of the coast. Mitch wouldn't do that, would he?

'Honestly, the best thing you can do is stay at the cottage and wait. He'll be back soon,' Kit adds.

'But what if he *isn't*?'

'He will be and you should be here for him. He'll be confused and wanting his mistress.'

'True . . . ' The fog is dense, almost suffocating. Kit's right. I sit on the sofa, trying not to look at the empty dog bed by the front door.

'Do you want me to stay with you?' he asks.

'No! I mean, thanks, but no.'

'OK. OK. I'll go and check around the reception and car park again. How's that?'

'Thanks. Kit, I really appreciate this. You're a guest, no matter what you say, and this is meant to be your holiday.'

Kit touches my arm. 'I may be only a guest, but I'll do anything I can to help. Call me if he comes back.'

'If I can get a signal, I will, but I might have to come up to your cottage to tell you.'

'OK. I'll go and look around the yard. I bet you a tenner he's back here before I come across him.'

Everything that Kit and Polly have told me makes perfect sense, but by now my worries have taken control of me — and when it comes to Mitch's safety, I'd do anything.

A minute after Kit leaves, I jump off the sofa, grab the torch and head out into the fog. While I still have a signal, I text and try Cal's phone again. I get his answer phone.

The torch beam only serves to show how thick the mist is, but I don't care. I know Kilhallon land so well, I can find my way down to the cafe without too much trouble. I left the cottage door open a crack. I don't call for Mitch until I'm sure I'm out of earshot of the guest cottages and farmhouse. I don't want Kit or Polly following me and dragging me back home again.

My main theory is that Mitch must have scented a rabbit outside the cafe and chased after it. He's part terrier and he may have simply found the chase too tempting and either became disorientated or got stuck in a rabbit hole. The alternatives — that he's fallen over the cliff and is injured on a ledge, or worse — don't bear thinking about. There's also a slim chance that he's become trapped in a snare. I've seen one or two on the cliffs around St Trenyan, set by cruel people, but none on Kilhallon land. What if Mitch is lying bleeding and in pain, with a snare cutting into his leg? Fighting back the urge to throw up, I press on past the cafe, calling his name.

The fog coats my throat and clings to my face. It muffles me, like a damp, chilly blanket. It swirls as I trace the coast path towards Kilhallon Cove. I'm on top of the cliff here and the path is almost flat but it will soon start to slope down to the beach, at first gently, then steeply, twisting and turning. I don't know how I'm going to climb down there in the fog and the dark so I hope I find Mitch first.

'Mitch!'

I stumble, curse and stub my foot on a granite pillar of the stile. I scramble over it and my torch falls to the ground with a soft thud, the beam illuminating the brambles at the edge of the path. I pick it up again and press on, calling. When I'm not calling, the silence is as thick as the fog.

'Mitch!!'

A rustling in the brambles on the cliffside startles me and I edge towards it. Thorns scratch my hands but there's no Mitch. My heartbeat jumps around like mad.

'Mitch!'

I reach a fork in the path and decide to stay high on the heathland rather than clambering down to the cove. If Mitch was hunting rabbits, he's more likely to be up here where they like to hide and burrow among the old tin-mine workings.

'Whoa!' The stone monster of the engine house looms out of the mist with no warning, and I almost fall over a sofa-sized lump of granite. This was where we posed for the photo shoot in the summer. The fog is so thick and low, I can barely see the broken chimney stack high above me.

'Mitch! Where are you?'

There's more rustling and scratching to my left, then the call of a night bird. My pulse speeds up and I stop. I balance the torch on a lump of granite and try to calm my breathing and listen . . . now I can hear the sea breaking gently on the rocks below Kilhallon Cove. Even the sound of the waves is muffled.

'Mitch? Please come home.'

Ahead of me, out of sight, I think I heard a snuffle.

There it is again.

A whine. Faint but definite.

'Mitch! Over here!'

An answering woof, louder but still weak.

I forge on, stumbling over stray stones and spoil, which was left by the miners and has lain here for over a hundred years, and trampling over brambles and bracken. The barks are louder, but where is he? Why hasn't he come to me? He must be hurt. A snare, maybe, a fall. My heart pounds. I *have* to reach him.

'I'm coming, Mitch. Hold on.'

My torch beam wavers over a Mitch-sized hump in the dark a few yards below me, in one of the hollows in between the overgrown mining spoil heaps. Could that be him or am I now so desperate that I'm imagining him as any old lump of rock or bush. No! The lump moved. I swear it whimpered.

'Mitch!'

Ignoring the scratches from the brambles, I run towards the sound. The lump barks. It is Mitch. He barks, but oh God, he sounds so hoarse. He must have barked and barked for me until his throat is raw. Tears run down my face. 'I'm coming, boy! Hang on!'

Ignoring the gorse tearing at my clothes and hands, I clamber through the undergrowth. Mitch barks again. Oh God, he must be seriously hurt not to be able to come to me. My heart is in my mouth, I want to scream but he needs me. Prickles scratch my flesh and face as I fight my way through the undergrowth towards him. Oh, thank God, I'm almost on him now. I can see his eyes glowing through the fog about six feet below me. He tries to get up, collapses and barks. I have to reach him. I slither down a bank, clutching at the undergrowth, not caring about my bleeding hands.

'Oh, Mitch, I'm so glad I — arrghh!'

The ground gives way under my feet and I plunge into darkness.

15

Cal

Oh shit, Demi is going to *kill* me for making her wait so long. Stepping down off the train onto the platform, my heart sinks. The announcer said we'd reached Penzance but we could be anywhere, the fog is so thick. It's half-past eleven and the station waiting room is closed.

I hope she hasn't been waiting for me on the platform all this time, but she must have been. My train has been delayed by two hours, first due to an 'operational failure' near Reading and then at Bodmin due to the fog. I suppose you can't blame the train company for the fog delay, but eight hours to get from Paddington to Penzance is enough to drive anyone insane.

I know I'm entirely to blame for leaving my phone charger in my room. My mobile battery died just after Tiverton Parkway.

Getting home late and upsetting Demi is the last thing I need. There were a couple of reasons why I went to London, and they didn't all have to do with a reunion of the charity personnel I used to work with. I went to try and see if there was any more news of Esme, the little girl I tried to find after her mother was killed. My ex boss, Carolyn, said that the rest of the team had continued to try to find her after I'd been released from the people who captured me.

Carolyn said she would put out more enquiries now.

'She could be anywhere, Cal,' Carolyn told me when we had a private drink together. 'That's anywhere between Africa and the UK. There are millions of people displaced and while we'll do our very best to find out through all the official channels and NGOs, the likelihood is that we'll probably never know what happened to her. I'm sorry, but you're going to have to accept that she's lost.'

I told Carolyn that I'd never accept that fact and asked her to keep searching for Esme. She asked me why I was so eaten up with guilt about this one little girl; she told me it wasn't my fault. But she doesn't know the full story. She told me to let Esme go and to focus on my new life.

She asked me about Kilhallon and I told her about our plans. I spoke about it a lot more than I expected. She joked that I had 'mentionitis' about 'this Demi'. I laughed at her and said she was winding me up.

I jog out to the station car park, hearing the engines of cars start and the moans of disgruntled passengers. I scope out the car park, expecting to spot the Land Rover at any moment. Damn this fog. It's like a chilly veil has descended on the whole of Cornwall. By the time I've done two more circuits of the car park, the place is deserted and it's clear Demi isn't here. Perhaps she checked the train company website and realised I'd be delayed. That must be it, and I'm glad because it means she won't have been hanging around here. Any moment

156

now, the Land Rover will rumble into the car park . . .

Twenty minutes later, a church clock is striking midnight and there's still no sign of Demi. Christ, I hope she hasn't had an accident in the fog. Thank God the station still has a call box. Finally, I punch in Demi's number and it connects.

The call goes straight to answer phone so I leave a message and try Polly's number. Polly must be sitting on top of her phone because she picks up almost immediately.

'Cal, thank God I've got you!'

'Hello, Polly. Is everything OK?'

'No, and we've been trying to reach you all night. Where the heck have you been?'

'My train was delayed by the fog and my mobile battery's dead. Where's Demi? She hasn't turned up at the station.'

'The *station*? Of course she isn't at the station! She never even left here. She's gone missing.'

I wonder if my hearing's defective. '*Missing?* What? Where is she?'

'If we knew that, she wouldn't be missing, would she! We don't know where she is, or Mitch, the stupid hound. He ran off earlier while Demi was down at the cafe and she must have gone to look for him, the silly girl. The pair of them don't have an ounce of common sense between them.'

My heart thumps. 'Why did you let Demi go after the dog in these conditions?'

'Don't you blame us. We tried to stop her, but she sneaked off and you know how rubbish the

157

signal is on the cliffs. Kit's gone to look for her but I had to stay here in case you called.'

My stomach twists painfully. 'I have to get home.'

'Yes, and I would have called Tremayne's Cabs if I'd known for sure that your train was delayed.'

'It's OK. I can walk to the rank. There's still a couple of drivers hanging about having a fag.'

'Good. Get back here as soon as you can.'

The journey back to Kilhallon counts as one of the longest and most agonising of my life. The fog was patchier inland but still bad enough for the driver to have to stick to a painfully slow speed. He did lend me his phone and I was able to talk to Polly again. Apparently, Mitch vanished after Demi had been hanging Christmas decorations in the cafe.

Polly was beside herself and made no attempt to hide her fears about what might have happened to the pair of them. She said that Demi had promised she'd wait in her cottage for Mitch, but when Polly called her, there was no answer, so she went down to the cottage and found the door open and the lights on. That's when she fetched Kit and he must still be searching for Demi now.

With no phone signal, the three of them could be anywhere. I feel light-headed. This fog, it reminds me of the dust after the explosion. After I lost Soraya and Esme disappeared. Jesus, I can't lose Demi too. Then I tell myself this is Cornwall, not a warzone, and if Demi saw me panicking, she'd probably wet herself laughing and tell me to get a grip.

Even so, the second the taxi pulls up on the Kilhallon car park, I'm out of it. Polly's standing by the front door of the farmhouse with a blanket and torch. She rushes to me and gives me a huge and totally out of character hug.

'Still no sign?' I ask as the taxi driver rumbles away into the fog.

She lets me go, but clasps her hands together. 'No. Thank God you're home. I'm so worried. Mitch has been gone for hours now, and Demi almost as long.'

'Oh God, why did you let her go?'

'I didn't let her go! We tried to make her wait in the cottage, Kit and I. We told her it was pointless and dangerous going out in this fog, but you know her, she does what she wants, the daft bird. She must have sneaked out after Kit had left her and now he's been gone over an hour and he could have met the same fate.'

'Polly,' I say gently, struggling to keep a grip on my own darker thoughts. 'No one has met their fate. Knowing Demi she's just determined not to come home until she finds her dog and, in fact, they could walk back into the yard at any moment.'

'I told Demi that earlier to reassure her but I'm worried sick for them both now. You know what those cliffs are like in a pea souper like this, and there's all the old mine workings . . . '

'They were filled in a long time ago. More likely they've found Mitch and need to carry him home.' My stomach turns over even as I say it. 'He might have been chasing a rabbit and become disorientated. The works have all been

159

made safe, as far as we can tell, but the ground is very uneven with some steep slopes and deep hollows in places.

If I've lost Demi . . .

'Kit's a star, but he doesn't know the area that well and I'd have called the cliff rescue by now if it wasn't for this fog. How can I get anyone out to help in this? And I keep hoping they'll come back. Oh Lord, I don't know what to do for the best.'

I lay a calming hand on Polly's arm. 'I'll go and look for them. I know this place better than anyone. If I don't come across them quickly, then we'll have to call the police and cliff rescue, no matter what the conditions.'

Polly lets out a squeak of panic.

'But I'm sure there won't be any need for that. I know some of the places Mitch likes to hunt rabbits by the engine house. I'll check there first. Try not to panic yet, Polly. I'll find them.'

I transfer the blanket and spare torches to my backpack while Polly makes a flask of hot coffee and collects the first aid kit from the farmhouse kitchen. It occurs to me to call Robyn or Uncle Rory to come and help, but I don't want to put anyone else in danger. No matter what I think of Kit Bannen, I really hope he *has* done his hero act and will emerge at any second from the fog, with Mitch and an adoring Demi by his side. God, I do hope so . . . any other scenario is beyond imagination.

I may know Kilhallon as well as the back of my hand, but even I'm struggling in the fog and darkness. The taxi driver charged my phone on

160

the drive home, though the signal's about as predictable as the fog, which shifts and wreathes round me. It's also cold, and getting colder by the minute. If Demi and Mitch are lying injured, hypothermia could set in very quickly. I have to find them.

I call for Demi and Mitch — and even Kit — as I make my way along the coast path towards the engine house. I try to call Demi a few times but only get her answer phone. Polly's given me Bannen's number so I even try that.

It's then I hear a ringing in the mist a few yards ahead. That's a mobile phone.

'Hello? Kit?'

'Over here! I'm coming.'

Kit pushes through a narrow gap in the gorse and is on me almost before I can speak again. His blond mane is soaked by the freezing fog. 'Any luck?' he asks.

'No.'

'Been here two hours now. I'm worried.'

'Not as worried as me. Let's go to the far side of the engine house. Be careful. Stick to the path and keep within shouting distance. The coverage is rubbish up here and we can't rely on it.'

'OK.' He rubs his hands together. 'I hope we find them soon. It's bloody freezing out here.'

'I know. We have to find them and we will.'

16

Demi

'Help! Kit! Polly! Can anyone hear me?'

Mitch has stopped joining in with my cries. He lies next to me, whimpering from time to time. I think he's broken his leg, judging by the strange angle it's lying at. I hope I haven't broken my ankle, I don't think so, though the pain is sharp when I move even the slightest bit and it throbs sickeningly when I'm not moving. When the undergrowth gave way, I almost fell on top of Mitch. I think we've fallen into a hole that used to hold some old winding gear for the engine house. One edge is overgrown with brambles, but in the daylight you'd probably have spotted it.

The moon shines down and I realise that the fog has lessened. Thank God for that. I would try my phone again but there's still no reception. This hole is a black spot in a black spot. Hugging Mitch gently for warmth, I press my cheek to his fur. His coat is thick but it's also damp and I started shivering an hour ago. With his injured leg, I don't know how long he can hold on. My throat is already hoarse, but I have two choices: lie here and keep Mitch warm and comfortable, hoping someone will find me soon, or try to climb out of the hole again and fetch help. Despite my coat, lying in the sodden leaves and bracken makes me shudder with the damp and cold.

Someone must be looking for us by now, but I'm worried — Mitch might not make it until morning in these conditions. I have to do something.

Gritting my teeth against the pain, I crawl away from Mitch. I clutch at the brambles for support and I clamber to my feet, ignoring the prickles scratching my hands. I know some people would say he's 'only' a dog, but he means everything to me. Him and Cal, they're the things that matter to me now. I wish Cal hadn't gone to London. I wish he'd stayed here. What if he's decided to go back to work for the charity? Or go back to the Middle East? Why would he, though, when he had such an awful time before? When he's said that Kilhallon is important to him? It's only the cold and my worries about Mitch that are making me think such crazy thoughts.

I have to get a grip. I've got us both out of sticky situations many times before, and this is just another one, although possibly stickier than most. Below me, Mitch lets out a whimper that stabs at my heart.

'It's OK, Mitch. Someone will find us soon.' I lift my face to the sky that's somewhere above this fog. 'Hey! Kit! Anyone! Helpppp!'

Holding on to the root of a bramble bush with one hand, I wave the torch around above my head, screaming until my throat burns.

'Hey there! We're here! Somebody help us!'

There's nothing. My ankle throbs and I almost

throw up as I try to clamber up the brambles. Why did I leave my gloves behind? Why did I fall down this hole? Why did I not watch Mitch more carefully when I was chatting to Kit?

'Arghh!'

My hands slip from the brambles and I tumble backwards onto the undergrowth again. My cry of pain draws a bark from Mitch. Winded, I lie on my back, staring up at swirling darkness. My ankle pulsates and I feel faint and see stars . . .

Real stars. Above me, the stars twinkle as if someone has torn a small and ragged hole in the fog. Seconds later, the hole is closed again and all is grey. I let out a yell of frustration and rage.

'For God's sake, will someone get us out of here?'

17

Cal

Bushes rustle and twigs snap a few yards to my side. The fog has swallowed up Kit and although I know it's him making his way over the heath a few yards from me, hearing but not seeing him is still an eerie experience.

How then must Demi feel, frantic and alone, looking for Mitch? Thinking her beloved dog might be hurt or worse. My guts twist sharply and I know that sickening sensation. It's the same one I felt every time they opened the door to the stinking room they held me in in the Middle East. I remember the bullet holes in the walls, the heat pressing down on me, the sun beating down on the tiled roof. The sound of their boots ringing on the hard earth as they came for me. Every time I thought it was the end.

'Cal!'

'Jesus!'

'Sorry I scared you.' Kit looms in front of me. He appeared as if from nowhere in the middle of the path.

'You didn't scare me. I was trying to listen.' He angers me although he's done nothing wrong.

'OK. Let's try again. You call and we'll both stand here and listen.'

'Demi!' I shout at the top of my voice. 'Mitch!' My pulse pounds in my head as I strain to listen but there's nothing. Kit looks at me enquiringly and I shake my head. He grimaces. 'You carry on searching that side of the path and I'll go this way,' I say. 'And don't go getting lost. We've enough on our plate. Keep within hearing distance,' I tell him again.

The gut punch subsides to a gnawing anxiety as we approach the engine house. I try to calm myself, wondering if Demi and Mitch have already made their own way home and are huddled by the fire in Kilhallon House, waiting for us to give up and return. But when should we give up? At some point, Kit or I are going to have to go somewhere with a decent mobile signal and ask Polly if they've returned on their own. Otherwise we'll go round in circles looking for each other. And if Demi isn't found soon, we really will have to call out the cliff rescue team.

If only I'd let her go to Brighton, she wouldn't be lost in this godforsaken place in this nightmarish weather. She'd be serving up *amuse bouches* at Eva Spero's and making her name as a chef or a cookery writer. Despite her passion for Demelza's, I haven't forgotten that things could still all go wrong here at Kilhallon, in a business sense and in a far worse one.

I've made a huge mistake in not seeing what was in front of me for far too long.

'Wait! What was that?'

Kit's torch sweeps over the wall of the inside of the engine house and back to me. I blink, dazzled by the beam. 'What was what?'

166

'Shhh.'

'*Help us!*'

Kit mouths, '*Demi?*'

I nod, straining my ears until my temples throb.

'Kit? Polly? Anyone? We're here!' The shout is followed by a faint but definite bark.

'It's them!' Kit says.

My heart rate takes off. 'I think they're over there on the other side of the engine house. Be careful, follow me!'

'Demi, we hear you!'

'Cal? Is that you?'

'Yes, me and Kit. Keep calling!'

'We're here in a big hole beyond the engine house. Mitch is hurt!'

'Hold on.'

All I can think is that she's alive and OK, and so is Mitch. Until this moment, I hadn't realised how terrified I was of any other outcome. I surge through the undergrowth, Kit behind me. Demi's voice grows louder and Mitch yips.

'Watch out. The edge of the hole gave way!'

Demi's voice seems to almost come from next to me but I still can't see her. Whoa. I stop suddenly almost overbalancing. I prod the bracken ahead of me with my toe and realise there's no solid earth under it. It must overhang a hollow. 'Be careful!' I warn Kit. 'They must have fallen through here into a pit. Looks like the depression left from the winding gear. I don't think it's the entrance to an old shaft, but you can't be too careful.

'Don't move!' I call to Demi.

167

'I can't bloody move! If I could, I'd have climbed out. My ankle's done for.'

Although I'm almost out of my mind with worry, I'm relieved to hear her back chat. She's going to be OK. Edging forward gingerly, I direct the torch into the darkness below. The beam shows the broken tendrils and roots of the brambles and, to my enormous relief, Demi's pale face peers upwards, six feet below. She has her arms around a very still and subdued Mitch who yips softly as he spots us. I let out a sigh and call to her. 'We're coming down.'

Thanking every star they're safe for now, though I'm worried about the state of Mitch, Kit and I scramble into the hole.

Demi grabs me and clings on for a second or two then pushes me away. 'You have to help Mitch. I think he's broken his leg. I don't know what I'd do if I lost him.'

Realisation slams into me, a punch to the chest that sucks away my breath: I was thinking exactly the same thing about Demi.

18

Demi

Annie, the emergency vet, settles a groggy Mitch in an overnight bed at Cooper's Surgery in St Trenyan. After Kit and Cal had helped us out of the hole, Kit carried Mitch and Cal lent me his arm so I could limp back along the cliffs to Kilhallon. The fog had cleared a bit, which made things slightly easier, but it was all I could do not to cry like a wuss. I was so worried about Mitch. As it is, I lost it when the vet finally told me the results of the X-ray she took while Mitch was sedated, but I'm calming down now.

Mitch lays his head on his paws and drifts off to sleep in the recovery cage.

'Are you sure he'll be OK?' I ask.

She smiles. 'Well, it's not broken, but it's a nasty strain. I'll strap it up and he should make a full recovery. He's still a young dog and he's fit. You need to get your ankle treated.'

'That's only a sprain too.'

Annie ignores me. 'It might be a hairline fracture. It looks very swollen to me.'

'You wouldn't X-ray it for me, would you?' I ask Annie.

'She's joking.' Cal takes my elbow. 'Come on, I'm taking you to A&E.'

'No way. There'll be a long wait and what if they keep me in for ages and I can't come and see Mitch when he comes round?'

'He'll be fine and you need some rest,' the vet says. 'Even if you won't go to hospital, strap it up and rest it and take some paracetamol.'

Cal's arm tightens on my elbow. 'I'll do it.'

'You?' I ask.

'I may only have done half a medical degree but I can deal with a twisted ankle, if it's only twisted, that is.'

'Whatever you decide, you should go home and rest it,' says Annie firmly. 'My nurse will take care of Mitch and we'll call you to come and collect him in the morning if he's fit to be released.'

Cal helps me to the car, and every step makes me wince in pain. Now the ordeal is over and I know Mitch will be safe, I'm also shaking like a leaf.

Gently, Cal helps me back into the car and drapes his wax jacket over me. 'Here, put this on,' he says gruffly.

On the drive home to Kilhallon, Cal is very quiet. I don't mind, I'm exhausted, hurting and still thinking about Mitch, even though I know he's going to be fine now.

'I don't know what I'd have done if you and Kit hadn't found me. Thanks.'

'It was luck. We heard you calling. You might have lain there all night otherwise. Why did you go after Mitch on your own?'

'Why do you think? He'd have died if I hadn't. He means everything to me.'

Cal glances at me briefly. 'You could have hit your head and been knocked out. We might not

170

have found you till it was too late.'

'I was fine,' I say, wondering why he's so quiet and distant. Now Mitch is safe, I've started to wonder what might have gone on in London.

We reach Kilhallon and find Polly and Kit still up, despite it being the small hours now, and drinking tea in the kitchen.

Kit jumps to his feet. 'How is he?'

'Fine.'

'Demi isn't. Look at that ankle,' Kit says.

Polly gasps. 'It's black and blue! You should have it X-rayed!'

Cal sighs. 'I've told her that until I'm hoarse.'

'It looks bad,' Kit says. 'Cal's right.'

'Will you all just leave me alone!'

Polly's face crumples with hurt.

I give her a brief hug. 'Sorry . . . Sorry, Polly. It's been a long night.'

Polly huffs and pats my back.

'You're exhausted and I need to do something with that foot. Sit down,' Cal orders.

'You should do as you're told, Kit says quietly. 'I'm glad you're safe and Mitch is on the mend. I'd better go and leave you to Cal's tender care.'

Cal's mouth is set in a line, but I manage a smile as Kit shrugs on his coat. 'Thanks.'

He smiles back. He is nice. Not as lovely as Cal, but kind under the awkward exterior. 'It was a pleasure.'

Cal turns round, holding the first aid kit. 'I think she should get some rest. I'll look after her now.'

'I know you will,' says Kit pleasantly enough,

but the air prickles between them.

'I'm getting back to my bed,' says Polly, clearly oblivious to the virtual cock fight going on in front of her. 'As you should be, Demi. I'll be round to see how you are first thing. You're welcome to come up here for breakfast.'

Cal says nothing but catches my eye. His are dark and intense, and threatening something, though I don't know what.

'Thanks,' I say, determined to have it out with him the moment we're alone.

Polly plants her hands on her hips. 'Are you sure you'll be OK?'

'Demi will be fine. She's staying here with me tonight.' Cal slips his arm around me while I sit in my chair and kisses the top of my head.

Polly's eyes widen and her mouth opens then closes. My heart sinks. Oh no, not here, not now. She must have known about me and Cal — she *must* have — but it's one thing *thinking* you know something and another finding out that Cal and I are a 'couple' in public, in front of a stranger. As for Kit . . . it was only a moment, but unmistakeable: the look on his face of anger, disappointment and bitterness. Surely he can't be jealous of Cal? Not *that* jealous?

'You do what you like,' Polly says tightly, hiding her hurt with brusqueness, as she often does. 'I'm off to bed. I suppose you'll be here anyway for breakfast then, Demi, if you're staying over,' she adds, her eyes drilling into me.

'I don't know . . . I have to collect Mitch.'

'Not that early,' Cal cuts across me. 'Demi needs a good night's sleep.'

'I expect she does, and she'd be better off in her own bed,' says Polly. 'Goodnight. Glad everything turned out all right. You know where I am if either of you wants me. Not that you will.'

'Thanks, Polly!' I say.

'I'm glad you're both safe,' she replies quietly, snatches up her coat and hurries out into the yard.

Keeping a hand on my shoulder, Cal turns to Kit. 'Thanks for coming out in this weather, mate. You're supposed to be a guest here. It wouldn't have looked good if you'd broken your neck.'

Mate?

Kit manages a smile but his eyes hold fury. 'Anyone would have done it,' he mutters.

'I don't think so,' I cut in, fuming inwardly at Cal's presumption, not to mention his arrogance, in 'claiming' me in front of Polly and Kit out of the blue. 'You were brave to go out in the fog when you don't really know the land that well. Anything could have happened.'

'Something did happen . . . ' he begins, directing all his words at me.

'But all's well that ends well,' Cal snaps. 'You'll have to come over for a meal with us, mate, as a thank-you. Won't he, Demi?'

'Yes. Yes, that would be lovely.' I try to say everything in a look, that I'm embarrassed, apologetic and shocked — all without being openly disloyal to Cal, although he deserves it.

Kit stops by my chair and looks down at me. Cal's fingers tighten subtly around my shoulder.

'Great. I expect I'll see you tomorrow then.

173

Let me know how Mitch is, will you? And take care of the ankle.'

Minutes later, it's just Cal and me in the sitting room. I'm gripping the handles of the armchair and trying not to wince while Cal kneels by the stool and straps up my ankle. He's not exactly rough, but he's definitely being businesslike, and I'd rather chop my foot off than let out as much as a squeak. He was right, he does know what he's doing, but I don't care.

He stands up. 'There. Keep your weight off it for as long as possible.'

'No chance. I have to open up the cafe in six hours time.'

'No, you don't.'

'Aside from any walkers who might drop in, I've got a twenty-strong WI group in for an early Christmas lunch and a full cream tea to serve to a dozen Americans on a *Poldark* tour. And I have to collect Mitch. How can I put my feet up when there's only Jez and Nina in?'

'Quite easily. You bloody well will *not* work in that cafe today. I already texted Jez, and Nina and Polly have offered to help me with your group bookings.'

'Polly! She'll frighten away all my customers. And you'd be the final nail in the coffin.'

'No, she won't, and I *can* behave. I look after the cottage guests and the yurt campers and they haven't complained so far, apart from that scary woman who wanted me to mow the camping field with my top off — but that was hardly relevant. Hell, you can't do everything, Demi, and I won't let you.'

'You won't *let* me? Since when did you start saying what I can and can't do?' I try to stand up but wobble after Cal's brand of first aid. 'And by the way, I can see why you never made a doctor. Your bedside manner is crap!'

'Crap? You're the worst patient in the world. Where do you think you're going?'

'To bed. *My* bed.'

'No way. You're staying in the farmhouse with me.'

'No, I'm not. What will Polly have to say about that? Did you see her face when you so kindly announced to the world that we're shagging each other?'

'I don't care. It's time we stopped hiding our relationship from everyone. I want you in my bed tonight.'

I shake my head. 'Is this about Kit?'

'What do you mean? About Kit?'

'You wanted him to know I was yours, didn't you? You don't like him, even though he risked himself to come after me while you were swanning off in London.'

He snorts. 'First, I was not 'swanning off' and second, this is nothing to do with Bannen. I'm not trying to score points off him. I *want you* to stay with me, and I'm sick of sneaking between the cottage and farmhouse and pretending we're just friends. I thought you were ready to take the next step and let people know we're together? Not that they haven't guessed. Isla saw straight through us and was amazed we aren't living together.'

'Isla? You mean you discussed me moving in

here with her before you asked me? That's great!'

'Don't make a big deal of this, Demi. You're tired and in shock. We both are.'

'What? I may be tired and in shock but I'm also furious that you talked to Isla about asking me to live with you before mentioning it to me. It would also have been nice, don't you think, if you'd asked me to stay the night, rather than informing me in front of Polly and Kit? And for the record, you are *so* wrong about Kit. He's a nice guy, kind, helpful, thoughtful — which is more than I can say for some people!'

'Thoughtful and helpful? Especially with hanging decorations, eh?'

'What's that supposed to mean?' I snap.

'Polly's told me that he was helping you put them up in the cafe. She said you two were in there when Kit left the door open and Mitch escaped.'

'Now you're being ridiculous. It's not Kit's fault that Mitch ran off. He probably took off after a rabbit and got lost. It could have been me who left it open or you — if you'd been here!'

'But I wasn't here, was I?'

'No, you weren't. You were in London.'

'You have a problem with me going to London? What is it with that? I had to go. I had no choice.'

I snort. 'I thought it was only a reunion. A social occasion. You could have stayed here.' Even though I'm angry, I also know I'm being unreasonable in this respect. I honestly don't mind Cal going to London, but I can't turn off the tap now. All my doubts and fears about Cal flood out. He is so unpredictable. I thought this uncertainty suited me, but now realise that it is the opposite of what I need in my life.

'This is getting us nowhere. I'll give you a hand to the cottage.'

'Don't change the subject. *How* could you do that? Ask me to stay over in front of Polly and Kit without warning me — without asking me first if it was OK?'

He shrugs. 'I assumed it would be.'

'Then you assumed wrong.'

'Why? You wanted me to tell Isla about us. You almost ran away because I didn't tell her we were sleeping together, so why is it different with Polly and Bannen? Because if you're bothered about what Polly might think, you're not the woman I thought you were. Don't you think that she's guessed already. She knew.'

'I don't care what Polly thinks of us sleeping together, but I think she was hurt that we hadn't told her officially that we're an item — I hate that word but you know what I mean. Instead, you just announced it in front of a stranger. No wonder Polly was taken aback.'

'Kit? A stranger? Hardly. Are you actually more worried about what Kit thinks than Polly? Do you care that he might be hurt?' Cal says sarcastically.

'You've got Kit all wrong.' I fire up again, even though my head has started to throb as hard as my ankle.

He snorts. 'I may still not know what he's doing here but I've got one thing about him absolutely right.'

'What does that mean?'

'Nothing.' He shoves his hands through his hair. 'Can we please stop talking about him? I asked you to stay with me because I was going to ask you to move into Kilhallon House with me, but now . . . '

I'd drop a sarcastic curtsey if I could, but instead I kick off again and I don't care who hears me. 'Don't do me a favour. I'm not some waif and stray you rescued. I work for you and I don't want to move in here.'

'Don't want to?'

He frowns, as if he's genuinely gobsmacked that I'm turning him down. My hands are shaky.

'Is it so hard to believe I might not want to?'

'I . . . thought you would. I thought . . . Why not?'

'Because . . . because I don't trust you, Cal. Because I want my independence. Because if I give that up, and give you everything, I'll only get hurt even harder when it all goes wrong. And then I'll have nothing, not even a space to call my own, and I've needed that for so long. When it all goes wrong between us, I want that space.'

Cal's jaw drops. He's stunned at my words. 'If . . . if that's how you feel . . . ' he squeezes the words out eventually.

'I can't do this. I have to go to bed.' I push myself out of the armchair, but feel as if I'm standing in a sinking rowing boat on a stormy sea.

'Let me help you,' he tries to take my arm.

I shrug it off. 'I can manage.'

'Don't be stupid.'

A look from me silences him. He steps back. 'Have it your way, if you must.'

'I think it's for the best.' Hurting even more inside than out, I limp past him. His face is agonised and angry, but I don't care. I refuse to let him help me.

I hobble out of the doorway. The fog has cleared but my feelings are as confused as they ever were. Cal wanted me to move in with him? Argh. The tears come now, and they sting my eyes, but I will not let him see me crying. I know he's watching me. I can see the light from the open doorway spilling out ahead of me. I'm half expecting, half hoping that Cal will follow me and that he'll come and hold me. But in the mood I'm in, I'll probably shove him away.

Behind me, the door closes and the light goes off. Every step is painful and when I finally reach my cottage, I virtually fall through the door and collapse onto the sofa. Hugging a cushion that's covered in hairs and smells of dog, I can't hold back the strain and worry of the past few hours. What if I hadn't found Mitch? What if Cal and Kit hadn't found me? Why did Cal have to behave so arrogantly in front of Polly and Kit?

Why am I so upset that he asked me to move in with him? Why don't I want to? *Do* I want to? *Do I love him?*

Moving in with him would mean taking a huge leap of faith and giving up my independence, but that's not why I'm holding back or so disappointed that he chose tonight to ask me, no, tell me that he wanted us to be 'an item'. I don't want to move in with him just so he can prove a point to Kit or to Isla — or to himself. I long to trust him with my heart, but I don't know if I ever can or will.

19

The night was a restless one for me — what was left of it — and I ease myself out of bed mid-morning to take a very careful shower before Nina arrives to give me a lift to the vet's. Before we leave, Cal drops by the cottage on his way to the cafe to see how I am, but the conversation is conducted in grunts on both sides and he only stays a few minutes. He's obviously still stinging from my refusal to move in with him and I'm upset that he can't understand my reasons.

Our problems will have to wait. Mitch is my priority for now. I almost weep in relief when we arrive at the vet's to find him enjoying a meal and being fussed by the veterinary nurse. He's definitely on the mend. However, I have strict instructions to keep him as quiet and still as possible, which is very difficult. He keeps trying to race around the place on his bandage support, almost giving me a heart attack. He looks so pathetic and makes me feel guilty every time I see his big brown eyes gazing up at me. It's so tempting to drop everything and spend the day cuddling him, but I daren't.

Finally, with Mitch settled in the farmhouse kitchen under Polly's watchful eye, I tear myself away and head for the cafe to see what havoc Cal has wreaked. Polly hasn't mentioned what passed between me and Cal last night but she

181

isn't exactly warm towards me. I don't know if that's because she can't bear the thought of another woman living in the house — and bedroom — that used to be Mrs Penwith's, or if she's worried that Cal and I will end up badly hurt.

My ankle is sore by the time I hobble through the rear door of the cafe around 2.30. Jez is finishing up after the lunch service while I hover between the kitchen and door to the service area, spying on Cal. I put my finger over my lips as Jez joins me. 'Shh. Don't tell him I'm here.'

The combined scent of cranberry sauce, Christmas pudding and custard wafts into my nose when I poke my head around the serving area for a sneaky look. The garlands look very festive and someone has placed extra vases of red-berried holly twigs and glossy greenery in the window alcoves. Carols from the local Fisherman's Choir are playing in the background, not that you can hear them over the din of women chatting and laughing.

Nina is serving coffee and mince pies to the WI group, while at the other end of the cafe Cal unloads a tray of cream teas. On any other occasion, the sight of him in an apron, dishing up scones while charming the knickers off the WI and a dozen American ladies, would make me drag him off to bed and shag him senseless.

Not today.

'How's the leg? I heard about last night. Nasty,' Jez whispers as I watch Cal.

'It's OK. A bit sore, but much better than I thought it would be.'

'How's Mitch?'

'Feeling slightly sorry for himself and lapping up the attention. The vet says he'll make a full recovery if we can stop him from racing about too soon. What about you and Cal? How's he doing?'

Jez pulls a face. 'Apart from us coming to blows several times, OK. Only joking! He's good front of house but he does try to be boss. Shall I call him into the kitchen?'

'No way. I want to watch this a while longer.'

'So tell us, just why do the Cornish have the jam on first?' a woman in a *Poldark* sweatshirt calls to Cal. She waggles a scone at him with a cheeky grin.

Cal has his back to me but I can picture him smiling back sweetly. The American lady is certainly agog at his gorgeous voice and brooding charm.

'Ah, now, that's a very good question. Some say . . . ' he begins.

Listening to Cal launch into a complicated and completely made-up explanation of why the Cornish have the jam on scones first, I ought to laugh, but his behaviour from earlier this morning has frozen any warm, fuzzy feelings I had for him. He does look gorgeous, though, his dark curls tangled, his blue shirt open just enough to reveal a glimpse of springy hair on his chest. Without letting Cal know I've even been in the cafe, I walk gingerly back to the farmhouse to check on Mitch. It's still only three o'clock, but the coral-pink sun is sinking low in the sky and the air is cooling rapidly under the clear skies. I doubt we'll have a frost this close to the sea, but inland it might freeze. Winter is coming and, after last night, everyone at Kilhallon has caught the mood.

20

Stars glimmer in the velvety sky above St Trenyan when Cal drops me off in the harbour car park the Monday after Mitch's accident. Since the night of the Great Fog, as Polly calls it, Cal and I haven't spoken about him asking me to move in with him and we definitely haven't slept together. I've only seen Kit in passing, and apart from a terse enquiry about my ankle and Mitch, he's kept well away from me and the cafe. He said his deadline was looming, but I think that was only an excuse to avoid contact.

Stray leaves blow in the gutters and I button up the top of my coat on my way down into town via the harbour. The ice-cream kiosk is shuttered and won't open until next Easter and the harbour deckchair man shut up shop weeks ago. Even the chip shop where I used to sleep in the doorway is shut. Like Demelza's, some of the larger cafes will only open weekends now, and a few of the guest-house and restaurant owners are grabbing a break somewhere warmer if they can afford it. The streets are the quietest I've ever seen them, only a few locals, fishermen and students venturing out for a pint or a pizza.

There are some signs of life. A small group of guys are clustered around a hi-lift cab that's hoisting up the final string of lights onto the wall of the harbour office. Lighting frames have already been fixed in place around the harbour walls and garlands of lights strung across Fore Street shiver in the wind. St Trenyan needs to spark back into life again. It's a good job the Harbour Lights switch-on is only ten days away.

I wobble down the steep cobbled streets in my heeled boots, still a little wary of my ankle. The warren of alleys between Fore Street and the main beach is the oldest part of St Trenyan. It's the heart of the town and is made up of terraced fisherman's cottages huddling together for shelter from the Atlantic storms. Their doors and tiny courtyards face inwards to escape the worst of the gales and high waves. Nowadays, almost all of the pastel-coloured buildings are second homes or holiday lets, and they cost a fortune to rent or buy. However, in one of the courtyards just off Fore Street is Tamsin's Spa, my destination this evening.

Tamsin convinced me that a manicure and make-up session would soothe my jitters, and I do need to carve out some time to look my best. I'm sure I won't have time for pampering when the festive-lunch season kicks in.

After I've had the facial and Tamsin has done my nails and make-up, we head off to a bar that is shoehorned between a gallery and a shell shop in the narrow back streets of St Trenyan, owned by a mate of Tamsin's.

It's called Sharky's and has a wooden sign in the shape of a shark suspended over the entrance so it looks like you're walking down the steps into the shark's mouth through razor-sharp teeth. St Trenyan spreads up and down a steep valley and many of the buildings are built on a slope. Even though the front entrance is on ground level, you descend a flight of steps into the bar area which has a huge window overlooking the town beach. The street lamps around the harbour are reflected in the black water.

We grab a couple of stools and I plant two cocktails on the high table. A Sea Breeze for me and for Tamsin something called a Cutthroat, presumably because it's lethal.

'Oh, thanks, hun. I need this,' says Tamsin.

'My treat. It's the least I could do after the free treatments. You know, I could get used to being pampered,' I say with a sigh. It's been ages since I had a night out with Tamsin. Running a business is brilliant, but there's so much to do, I could spend every moment at work.

Tamsin giggles. 'I do my own treatments. I only twitch and keep wanting to criticise if I visit other therapists. I guess we all have our own ways that we think are the best ones.'

'I'm the same about food now. If I eat out at another cafe, I can't help thinking how I'd have seasoned or presented the dish differently — or about adapting the ideas for Demelza's.'

We've already chatted a little about the cafe while Tamsin was doing my treatments. Even though I was supposed to be relaxing, we couldn't help talking 'shop'. I take a long sip of my Sea Breeze through the straw, trying not to think of how well it would accompany the themed food nights I plan to set up next summer. The combination of the vodka and tangy grapefruit and cranberry juices is totally

187

addictive. We have a licence to serve alcohol with meals, but we're just stocking a small range of locally brewed beers and some Cornish wines at the moment, so I daren't run before we can walk.

'You look like you needed that cocktail, my facial obviously didn't work its magic,' Tamsin says. 'How's things at Demelza's?'

'OK. Fine. Exciting. A bit scary when it goes quiet and when it gets too busy, but it's my dream.'

'Sounds normal to me. I was petrified when I left the country club spa to set up my own business.

'Were you?'

'Yup, kept wondering if I was mad, could I cover the rent on this place, would I make enough to pay my suppliers, would I get sued if something went wrong, would I have to move back to my parents if it all went pear-shaped.'

'The Cades don't own your building, do they?'

'Oh, no, thank goodness. They don't own everything in town, it only feels like it. Have they been giving you any more trouble since the summer? I heard Mawgan was on the Harbour Lights committee.'

'She is, but she hasn't done anything to us since she changed her mind about buying Kilhallon.'

'Miraculous. Thank God she decided it wasn't any good for her to develop.'

'Mawgan bears grudges longer than the mafia. I'm still wondering what she might have in store for us — me, Cal and Kilhallon — next. Part of me expects her to release a plague of rats in the cafe or sneak mouse droppings into someone's soup the day the hygiene inspector turns up. She has fingers in so many local pies . . . Hey, maybe she puts her enemies in pies like Sweeney Todd.'

Tamsin almost snorts her cocktail. She doesn't realise I'm serious about Mawgan holding a grudge and, while I don't think Mawgan would murder anyone, I do know a few of her weak spots and that makes her a very dangerous foe to have. Mawgan won't have forgiven me for finding out how hurt she was by her mother's affair with Cal's father. I touched a very raw nerve when I brought up that subject. Even though she relented and allowed Andi and Robyn to move into one of her properties, she'll be seething that my 'chat' with her had an effect.

'What about Cal? How's it going with him?' Tamsin lobs this question in like a pebble in a previously tranquil rock pool. I need to let the ripples settle before I consider my reply.

'OK. He's my boss. You know what it's like.'

'He's not just your boss, though, is he?' Tamsin has a mischievous gleam in her blue eyes. 'That's the rumour around St Trenyan, anyway.'

'Rumour? How can anyone possibly know what's going on between me and Cal?'

'Gotcha!' Tamsin smirks.

'Oh, God.' I slurp my Sea Breeze while I think of how to reply and how much to reveal. I haven't known Tamsin more than a few months, but she's lived in St Trenyan all her life and has known Cal since their schooldays. I *really* like

189

her and we're getting to know each other much better, I'm just not sure I'm ready to share my — or Cal's — intimate secrets with her yet. Although now Polly knows Cal and I are sleeping together, it might *well* be all over St Trenyan.

'Cal and me — it's complicated,' I say, at a loss for any other way of describing it.

'With Isla being on the scene, you mean? Or off it. She's gone back to London, hasn't she?'

'For now, yes, but she's bound to be back. I shouldn't complain, really, because the shoot she did has paid very well and the publicity will be worth masses to us after the series airs next year.'

'And?'

'And . . . Cal, I just don't understand him.'

'I did warn you, hun. What's he done now?'

'He asked me to move into the farmhouse with him.'

'Wow. That sounds serious.'

'Hmm.'

'And have you?'

'No. No, like I said, it's complicated. I do like him.'

'*Like?*'

'I like him a *lot*, but moving in is a big step. I've only just found my own place to stay. Me and Mitch, we value our independence and I feel I'm being dragged in deeper with a man who I don't know well enough yet.'

'And you're scared that it's going too fast?'

'Not only that. More that if it ends — when it ends — it will hurt worse if I'm living with him. I need to keep that distance.'

'I think you're right, but Cal . . . when he falls, he falls hard, and I guess that asking you to move in is a biggie for him. You're not still worried about Isla being a threat?'

'Not a threat, exactly. I do believe he's getting over her, but they're still very close.'

'Yes, but she's off the scene now since she moved to London. She's making a go of it with Luke from what I can work out, unless you know different?'

'I saw her when she brought her film crew to Kilhallon. She didn't say that much about Luke to me, but I got the impression they're doing OK.' For now, I remind myself.

'So you don't think the rumours that Luke was having an affair with Mawgan Cade were ever true?' Tamsin says.

'No . . . I don't think he'd be that stupid, do you?'

Tamsin snorts. 'Maybe not, but Mawgan definitely *would* if it suited her plans . . . Oh my God, talk of the devil. I thought we were safe in Sharky's.' Tamsin does a lemon-sucking face and nods at the entrance where Mawgan has just walked into the bar.

I groan. 'Quick, let's grab that booth in the corner so she can't see us.'

'OK, but I thought you weren't scared of her?' Tamsin says with a grin.

'I'm not, I just don't want any trouble.'

Even from here, I can hear Mawgan ordering drinks and laughing — it's hard *not* to hear her as she likes to be the centre of attention in any establishment — but we can't actually see her now and vice versa, with a bit of luck.

'Wow. Is that her new boyfriend?' Tamsin whispers, risking a none-too-discreet glance around the edge of the booth.

'I dunno. I didn't see who was with her. Please *don't* look at her.'

Ignoring my plea, Tamsin cranes her neck around the corner of the booth. 'I'm not looking at her, but *he's* worth a second glance. He's far too good for Mawgan!'

'He must be mad or brave or both,' I say, agreeing with Tamsin that most guys are too good for Mawgan, not because of any shallow thing about the way she looks, but because she's a vindictive, malicious cow.

'If I could only get my hands on those eyebrows,' Tamsin says between giggles. 'She'd look great if she went a bit more natural, but I suppose she loves the fake look.'

'I saw her without any make-up on once,' I say then wish I hadn't because I've vowed — sworn in blood — not to tell anyone what passed between Mawgan and me at her house earlier this summer.

'Really? When was that? Had she come out of her coffin during the day, then?'

'I was erm . . . passing her place and she was putting out the bins,' I say, hoping Tamsin won't realise my white lie. 'She was wearing a leopard-print onesie and I hardly recognised her,' I add, because this part of the story is at least the truth.

'Putting out the bins in a leopard-print onesie? Actually, I can imagine that, although I'd have thought the Cades kept a team of servants to do their chores,' says Tamsin, swirling the dregs of her Cutthroat with a swizzle stick then knocking it back. 'I think we both need another cocktail to get over the shock.'

'I agree but not in Sharky's. The atmosphere's gone way downhill for me. How the hell are we going to get out of here without Mawgan seeing us?'

'Hmm. Could be a problem although . . . wait . . . Mawgan and the hottie are taking their drinks over to the VIP area in the corner. Now's our chance.'

As I can't see anything, I have to take Tamsin's word for it. Grabbing my bag, I squeeze out of the booth while Tamsin checks the coast is clear. As we scuttle out, Mawgan's voice carries right across the bar. She's laughing — actually laughing — not cackling or sneering, which is her default setting when I'm around. Tamsin makes a dash for the exit and I follow but I can't resist a glance round.

'Oh my God!' I nearly trip over in the doorway.

Tamsin stops at the bottom of the stairs leading up to street level. 'What's up?'

'That man with Mawgan. I know him. Wait . . . '

Tamsin hisses at me as I hover in the entrance to the bar. 'I thought you said you don't want Mawgan to spot you.'

I crane my neck as a group of lads squeeze past me on their way inside. I *have* to know that my eyes weren't deceiving me, even if Mawgan

193

does see me, which isn't likely because she only has eyes for the man opposite her. She leans forward, gazing into his eyes like a puppy waiting for a chew from its owner. I can't see his face but I'd know that dark blond mane anywhere.

'It's Kit.'

'Who?'

'Kit Bannen,' I tell Tamsin as we hurry up the steps and out into the street. 'He's renting a cottage at Kilhallon but I have *no* idea what he's got to do with Mawgan.'

21

'Let me get this right. You saw Bannen in town with Mawgan Cade?'

Cal stops dead when I deliver the news on Tuesday morning while unloading the delivery of craft beers and cider we've ordered for the Harbour Lights Festival a week on Friday. After I got a cab back from St Trenyan last night, I lay awake into the small hours, wondering whether to tell him about Kit, because it will only feed his prejudices, but decided it was one secret I couldn't keep to myself.

'Yes, in Sharky's, that new bar off Fore Street.'

'What the hell were they doing in there?'

'Drinking together, I suppose. That's the point. I don't really *know*. I didn't see him for more than a few seconds, but it definitely *was* him.'

'And he was definitely *with* Mawgan, he didn't just happen to have rocked up next to her at the bar by a piece of terrible luck?'

'No. He walked into the place with her and they seemed chatty enough — according to Tamsin.'

Cal hisses. 'My God. So they're seeing each other?'

'I don't know about that. He didn't exactly have his hand on her bum or anything, or at least he didn't from the brief glimpses Tamsin got of him.'

'Mmm. Did he see you?'

'I don't think so.'

He humphs and drags his fingers through his messy hair. He looks tired, but I'm hardly the brightest bunny myself after burning the candle at both ends for the past few weeks and partying last night. Tamsin and I went on to another bar, then for pizza and then to St Trenyan's only club. I spent half the time wondering if Mawgan and Kit might walk in, but there was no sign of them. Cal was still up when I got home. I saw the lights on in the study window of Kilhallon House and it was after midnight. I crawled into bed, and was so tired that I didn't even have the energy to push Mitch off my bed. Then I lay awake, wondering the same things as Cal.

'He might have just bumped into her in town, you know. He is entitled to go out for a drink,' I say.

Call rolls his eyes. 'No one just bumps into Mawgan uninvited.'

'She could have picked him up in the pub or a cafe. Stranger things have happened,' I say, not believing it myself.

'Yeah . . . but he's not her type, surely?'

'And she's not his type.'

'I don't know what type he is . . . ' says Cal sharply then, as if he's regretted his tone, adds, 'In fact, we don't really know what he actually *does* all day, do we?'

'Writes his book, I suppose, and he goes out running and walking. He used to pop into the cafe and work on his laptop over a coffee, but he hasn't been over lately. Funnily enough, he never

196

has that much to say to me now.' Yes, there is sarcasm in that comment, but I don't care. Cal asked for it.

'He never says anything to me at all and it didn't look like he had nothing to say on Sunday morning. I saw you chatting to him for ages outside the cafe.'

'Not for *ages*, it was just for a few minutes while I cleared the tables and he was only asking whether he could have a packed lunch while he went on a walk. In fact, he's hardly spoken to me more than a couple of times since Mitch was lost in the fog. Anyway, how do you know? Have you been spying on me?'

He rolls his eyes. 'You're being paranoid. I never spy on people.'

I snort.

'Don't start a fight.'

'Me? You started it when you warned Kit to back off from me after Mitch went missing and broadcasted to the world that we were sleeping together.'

He looks at me with those intense dark eyes and I have to admit, longing stirs low in my stomach. 'Were sleeping together is the problem,' he says softly. 'I really miss you, Demi. Come back to the house. Polly knows now, so there's no need to sneak about. We can't go on avoiding each other and not talking about it.' He continues the Cal brooding stare and my knees almost go weak. Almost.

'What's '*it*' meant to be?'

'You know what 'it' is. It's the elephant in the room. Me asking you to move in with me. I'm

197

sorry I misjudged things between us.' He groans in frustration. 'Hell, I wish I'd never mentioned it. Now all I want is for us to go back to the way things were. You in my bed, the banter, the cheek, the hot sex.'

My skin tingles at the prospect of being back in Cal's bed. Of lying next to that warm, hard body. Waking up next to him, hot and naked and . . .

'Stop. Don't do it. Things can't be the same.'

'Why not? Because I tried to move things too fast for you?'

'No. OK, yes, but my reasons aren't only that things have moved too quickly between us. It's also the way you announced it in front of Kit, like you wanted to prove a point to him.'

He groans. 'Kit. Bloody Kit! What is it with him? Why does he matter so much to you? And I was right to be wary. There is something going on with him. It can't be a coincidence he was with Mawgan, you have to admit that much.'

'No. It might not be a coincidence but — Cal, can we drop this for now?'

'Fine by me. I can think of way better things to do than talk about Bannen, anyway.'

My lips clamp shut. I don't know what to say. I'm still angry with him even as feelings stir that I can't suppress, making my blood heat and my senses zing. I don't think I've felt fully alive since our row. I'd love to take him upstairs right now and strip him naked and feel that gorgeous body against mine. I'd love to melt into him and spend half the night making love and wake up, exhausted and happy all afternoon.

'It's a bad idea. We can't.'

'You mean you can't handle it. Can't handle me?'

'Of course I can handle you!'

'Then do it.' He grabs my hand and places it over his groin. 'You want me now.'

I snatch my hand away but not fast enough not to know exactly what he means. I feel the same way, shaky with lust for him but also furious. 'Stop it. Someone will see us out here.'

'Like Kit? Do you really care what he thinks of us now you've seen him snogging Mawgan?'

'He wasn't *snogging* her. He was listening to her. That's all I saw.'

Cal raises his eyebrows. 'Listening? You mean encouraging her?'

'He definitely wasn't kissing her, but she wanted to kiss him. An idiot could see that, but . . . '

'But what?'

I picture the scene in Sharky's again. Mawgan leaning over the table, drooling over Kit like Mitch does over a piece of steak. Kit leaning in on one hand, very close to Mawgan. I couldn't see his expression from behind but you can't mistake body language like that.

'I suppose he could have been flirting with her, in a way.'

'What way?'

'Paying her attention, leaning in towards her, as if she was the only girl in the room . . . ' My voice trails off because Cal is giving me a look that says he knows exactly what I'm thinking. I hate him for his smugness, but he *is* right. Kit

Bannen was behaving the same way with Mawgan that he has done with me sometimes. Even the way I've seen him with Polly.

'You know he could be as manipulative as Mawgan, but way more clever and subtle.'

'That's going too far. I agree there's something odd about him knowing Mawgan, but I don't think he's manipulative and I still think he could easily have met her by chance and she pounced on him.'

'Yes, but why?'

'Because he's good-looking and charming and hot in a blond way and he's an author.'

'Thanks.'

'You asked.'

'It was a rhetorical question, I didn't expect an answer.'

'Well, you got one so it serves you right.'

We're face to face, sparring like fighters in a boxing match. My heart's pounding, Cal's glaring down at me, bristling with frustration. Has he forgotten that it was him who said he didn't want to talk about Kit any more, yet he can't help himself.

'Demi.'

'Sorry, Cal. I have a hundred and one things to do. I run a business. So do you, and we ought to remember that.'

The crunch is: our row has reminded me that if it all goes wrong with Cal, even more than it has already, Demelza's will be all I have. No matter what happens, after all the work I've put in, I'm determined not to lose that too.

22

'Demi? Is it OK to take a booking for this new group?'

Nina's voice drifts into my ears as I'm taking a five minute break in the 'staff room' in the cafe the following Saturday afternoon. Although I meant to try and forget about Kit and Mawgan, I find I'm once again wondering why they were in Sharky's Bar together last Monday evening. 'Hmm.'

'So, I can go ahead and tell them 'yes'? It means opening on a Tuesday, specially.'

'Hmm.'

'Right. So we're all cool with serving the Naturists Club in the nude and we're happy to turn up the heat full and hang sheets up at the windows?'

'*Sheets? Nude?* Nina, what are you on about?'

A smirking Nina stands in the doorway with her hands on her hips. 'I was referring to the booking for afternoon tea next Tuesday from the Naturists Club. I knew you weren't listening.'

'*Naturists?* Are you serious?'

'No. It's a bunch of *naturalists*, actually, although Polly took the original call and was slightly confused until I worked it out. A local wildlife group want to book the cafe for tea after a winter walk. As we've already agreed to open for a large party from the St Trenyan Businesswomen's Lunch Club earlier in the day, I said I thought it would

201

be OK, but would confirm it with you.'

'Oh, yes. It's fine. Argh. You'll have to forgive me, I've been miles away.' I've snatched a break while we had a quiet period to update the Demelza's blog with some photos of the festive food menu, but my mind wandered on to Cal. And Kit. And weirdly, my parents. What would Mum have thought of Cal? What advice would she have had about me moving in with him? Sadly, I was still too young to really have discovered boys before she died. I wish she was here now.

'Are you sure you're OK? You haven't properly been with us for most of the morning. It's fine, hun. We're really busy and if you don't mind me saying, you look knackered. I wish I hadn't bothered you, but the secretary of the group needs an answer.'

I scrape up a smile, remembering that I'm in charge and it's me who should be motivating the staff, not vice versa. 'No, I'm good. It's great we're getting extra bookings and I should have known we'd have to extend our opening hours as Christmas gets closer. Are you sure you're OK to work a few extra days to help out with the festive functions?'

'Yes. I've also asked Shamia if she can help out too and she said she's happy to do that. Jez can't do one of the Christmas lunches but I thought you could step in if we can find someone else to work on tables and the counter.'

'Thanks, Nina. Really grateful that you're on the ball, even if I'm not.'

Snapping out of my daydreaming, I follow her into the counter area where a bunch of red-faced ramblers have just walked in, dripping water all over the stone floor. I hadn't even noticed it had started raining . . .

With a huge smile, I crack a joke about the weather and help Nina serve up their hot drinks and mince pies as they queue. With a bit of luck, they'll stay for lunch too. Every cloud has a silver lining, as Nana Demelza used to say.

After an early lunch, the walkers forged out into the rain and we had a couple of guests from the cottages and a small group of surfers on their way back from one of the far west beaches. But for the past twenty minutes the cafe has been empty and, as it's grown so dark, I half wonder about closing early. I'll give it until three, maybe. Jez has already finished the lunch service and we can manage the drinks and teas now. I'd better mop the floors, though, they're muddy again already.

While I clean the tiles as best I can, the door opens and a man in head-to-toe Gore-Tex walks in, shaking water from his hands. He pushes back his hood.

'Hello,' he says, flashing me a reluctant smile that reminds me of the first time I met him. Only now, I'm even more wary of him than I was then.

'Oh, hi, Kit.'

'Are you still open? I wondered if you'd bother in this weather, but then I saw the lights on and thought I'd chance it.'

'We're staying open until three at least.'

'Great. I can get a flat white and a sandwich, then? I've had no lunch yet, but I know it's too late for hot food.'

'We've got some broccoli and stilton soup left and I can get you that and a Cornish Brie and rocket baguette?'

'That's fine.'

'I'll bring it over.'

'No, I can fetch it from the servery.'

'Sit down before you tramp mud over my nice clean floor.'

He laughs. The ice is broken for now, but it's still awkward to see him.

While I dish up his soup and retrieve the last baguette, Nina makes the flat white. I take them both over to Kit myself. A handful of other customers have arrived so it looks like I won't have time to chat to him and honestly, I'm relieved about that.

In the end, he eats his late lunch and leaves without saying any more to me and now I'm in the farmhouse office with Cal, discussing what — if anything — to do next.

'What did he say to you?'

'Nothing. He had a quick lunch and then he left.'

'He's got a bloody nerve.'

'He has to eat, Cal! And he's no idea that we know about Mawgan and actually, there might be an innocent explanation.'

Cal drops his pen on the desk. 'Innocent, my arse.'

'So, do you actually have any reason to suspect Kit of doing anything wrong, apart from you being jealous and him having a drink with Mawgan?'

After a moment's hesitation, he shrugs. 'No.'

'Don't you think you're being overly suspicious of him? There are perfectly reasonable explanations for why he might have been with Mawgan in the bar. He could have been having a quiet drink, she bumped into him and put on an angelic act. He's probably already decided he never wants to see her again.'

'Possibly.' Cal looks doubtful.

'Or he might have met someone Mawgan knows and they introduced him to her. St Trenyan is a small place, he's here for weeks. Come to think of it, he did mention he'd gone along to a creative writing group to see how it was.'

He snorts. 'Are you saying that Bannen might have met Mawgan Cade at a creative writing group? The only creative writing she does is when she's falsifying her tax returns!'

'Well, I did think it was a remote possibility. We can speculate all we like. How are you going to find out the truth? You can't just come straight out and ask him.'

'No, but you could.'

I hold up my hands in protest. 'No way. He's a guest. We can't interrogate him about his private life.'

Cal's eyebrows shoot up. 'Want to bet?'

'I won't do it. I can't think of any way to ask him how he knows her that doesn't sound rude, intrusive and just plain weird.'

'Then we're going to have to be more subtle.' He sighs thoughtfully. 'We need to lull him into a false sense of security and get him off his guard.'

'Cal, you don't know if he's even *on* his guard.

Aren't you going over the top about this? I half wish I'd never told you I spotted them.'

'No, you don't, and we do need to get to the bottom of his association with Mawgan. It's too much of a coincidence that he rocks up here and stays for months and then you see him cosying up with her in town. I think we should ask him to dinner here as a thank-you for saving Mitch and for being a long-term guest.'

I snort. 'That's outrageous. You're being a hypocrite.'

'I don't care. He's told you he's almost a resident now, so let's treat him like one. We'll have him over here for dinner next week, ply him with a few whiskies and find out his secrets.'

'That's sneaky and unethical.'

'I don't care. I left my ethics behind in the Middle East.'

'No, you didn't, or you wouldn't have wanted Kilhallon to be an eco resort or given me a job or tried to help Robyn and Andi.'

'That still doesn't mean I'm not prepared to play dirty if I have to.'

'Fine, but *you* can ask him,' I say, wondering if I can cope with all this intrigue on top of the stress of organising our stall at the Harbour Lights Festival this coming Friday evening.

He shakes his head. 'No way. He'd be suspicious immediately if I asked him. You ask him.'

'No way! He'll think I've lured him over here for . . . well, he might get the wrong idea.'

'If I'm here too, he won't get the wrong idea, will he?' Cal says with a smirk. 'There's definitely something going on with him and Mawgan. I know it and it makes my skin crawl.'

With common or garden jealously, I think, but dare not say. 'OK. I will ask him but he won't want to join us, if he has any sense or doesn't want to play wallflower.'

'Oh, I don't think Kit Bannen is a wallflower.'

'Whatever. He won't come. I bet you fifty quid.'

23

'Hello, Kit. Glad you could make it,' Cal says as he shows Kit into the farmhouse sitting room on Monday evening. In the end, Cal invited him to dinner out of range of my hearing, thank goodness, and to my amazement, Kit agreed. Instead of telling Kit to use the back door, however, he's made him ring the bell and brought him into the house via reception and the vestibule. We keep the kitchen entrance for family and close friends and it's obvious Cal considers him neither of those things. Cal probably wants Kit to know that.

I'm squirming, frankly, because I still think there's a totally boring explanation for why Kit was with Mawgan in town, and I hate the idea of spying on a guest in this way.

Cal told me that as he'd won the bet that Kit would accept the invitation to dinner, I had to spend the whole of Sunday afternoon naked in bed with him. Apparently I can't even leave the bedroom from noon until midnight and Cal has sworn he's going to confiscate my bra and knickers and lock them in the filing cabinet in his office. Even thinking about my 'penalty' makes me squirm with lust. Of course, I'm still annoyed with him for declaring to Polly and Kit that we are sleeping together so I shouldn't feel obliged to repay my debt. But I am thinking about it. Very, very seriously.

Kit, looking cool and smooth in black jeans, a soft brushed shirt and sleek Puffa jacket, hands over a bottle of white wine. A very nice one too, and freshly chilled.

'Oh, thanks. That'll go wonderfully with our dinner,' I say, trying to sound like the perfect hostess while cringing inside. We've tidied up a bit, though Kit probably can't tell. The fire crackles in the hearth and the rich smell of my fish pie is very inviting, even if I do say so myself. It all feels very welcoming, which makes me feel doubly guilty about conning him.

'Pleasure, and thanks for asking me. Must admit I feel a bit guilty for interrupting your evening. I'd no idea you two were together when I first arrived at Kilhallon. Now I feel like I'm butting in.'

'You're not butting in, mate. Is he, sweetheart?'

Cal puts his arm around my waist and it's my turn to grit my teeth. *Sweetheart?* Cal never calls me sweetheart, or darling, or anything that cheesy — or complimentary. Longing to hit him with the fish slice, I slip smartly out of his embrace.

'I just have to see how the fish pie is doing and open the wine.'

Kit sniffs the air. 'Thought I smelled something good, although I reckoned Cal might have given you the night off from cooking.' The firelight reflects in Kit's green eyes, making them gleam. He must have guessed there's something going on.

'It's my day off and, actually, Cal's made the

pud so we've shared the duties. I'll be back in a sec. Cal, aren't you going to offer Kit a beer or something?'

'Yeah. Sorry, forgot. What'll it be, mate? Doom Bar? Lager? Cider?'

'A lager, thanks.'

Kit has a twist of amusement on his lips. He doesn't seem too jealous to me, but he is obviously delighted to have caught us 'at home' and in full-on couple mode. Actually I think I'd be more relaxed if he *had* seemed jealous of Cal's possessive gesture. Maybe Cal is right about him after all: there is something peculiar about his moods.

I leave 'the boys' discussing craft beers while I check the pie and put some broccoli on to boil, but a few minutes later, I hear Cal rummaging in the old pantry off the kitchen where he keeps a crate of beer and I store the welcome-pack wines on permanent chill.

I pour myself a large glass of Kit's white, sensing I'm going to need it.

When I walk back into the sitting room, the boys are once more drinking from bottles and looking, on the surface at least, like mates. Mates, my arse, I think. They're still standing up, Cal lingering 'casually' in front of his hearth every inch the lord of the manor, while Kit looks around admiringly.

'Wow. Great room. I thought it had character from the outside, but I'd no idea it was this old. Eighteenth century, is it?'

'Sixteen seventy-five or thereabouts,' Cal replies casually. I did know something of the

210

history of the Kilhallon estate, because I had to research it when I was trying to get some words together for the website.

'And it's always been in Penwith hands throughout all that time?'

'Yeah, as far as the records tell us. There was another place here before it, which dated back another three hundred years, but that burned down, apparently.'

'Wow, and I thought Enys Cottage was old.'

'That row of cottages was built after the farmhouse, for the senior mine captain and officials and their families. My Granddad Penwith added the reception area to the main farmhouse in the late sixties, but apart from a lick of paint, it's been the same ever since. We could have rebuilt it when we refurbished the park, but we settled for another repair and repaint. We had other priorities, didn't we, sweetheart?'

'Yes, we did, *darling.*'

I cross to Cal and put my arm around him, groping his bum behind Kit's back to see how *he* likes being treated like a possession. Judging by the grin on his face, I think he's actually enjoying himself.

Kit wanders up to a painting on the wall of a proud middle-aged man, standing on a wind-swept cliff with a chocolate Labrador at his feet. 'That's him, is it? Your granddad?'

'No, that's his father. My great granddad. This is my granddad and dad.'

Cal picks up a photo, a seventies print that was already rosy hued and is faded almost to sepia now. He hands it to Kit. I know the one: Cal's grandfather, older now and stooped, but still with his stick, and Cal's father, in his late thirties, handsome, with Cal's thick dark hair hidden by a tweed cap. They're standing in front of reception and in the background you can spot the rows of static caravans marshalled in ranks like soldiers.

Kit holds it, his face expressionless, then hands it back to Cal. 'I heard your father passed away a few years ago. I'm sorry for that, he wasn't very old, was he? After losing your mother when you were so young, that must have been a terrible blow.'

'It was, but what can you do? We all have to manage with what life hands us, no matter how crap.'

Kit nods. 'True.'

'Your mum and dad live in London, don't they?' Cal says. 'Polly told me,' he adds.

Kit smiles. 'Yes. Not far from my flat, actually.'

'What do they think of you being down here for so long?'

'They're not surprised at anything I do these days, and I am a grown-up even though it may not always seem like it.'

'Yeah, but parents don't always believe it, do they?'

'No, but I'm lucky to have them. Unlike you and Demi. I read about your losses in the magazine feature and I'm sorry. For both of you. You've done well to rebuild this place and your lives, if you don't mind me saying.'

'Thanks.' Cal sniffs the air extravagantly and

212

gets up from the chair. 'By the smell of it, I think that fish pie must be more than ready. I'll help Demi dish up if you want to sit at the table. Make yourself at home, mate. We don't stand on ceremony here.'

Kit takes a seat and I corner Cal in the kitchen.

'It's no good, I'm not asking him!' I declare. 'It's devious and rude.'

'In that case,' Cal says, snatching a fresh bottle of wine. '*I* will.'

Shortly after, Kit 'ohs' and 'ahs' enthusiastically as I bring in the pie and place it on the table.

'Wow, that smells amazing. That mash looks interesting. Are those herbs?'

'No, it's salad seaweed from a local company. Sounds weird but I promise it's delicious.'

'I can't wait. You're a woman of many talents, Demi.'

Cal throws me what I can only describe as an 'adoring' grin. 'She certainly is,' he croons.

Ignoring Cal, I hold a dish under our guest's nose. 'Have some broccoli. How's your book going, by the way?'

After several glasses of wine, a fish pie and a lot of talk about writing, I almost start to relax. Kit has some funny stories about being an author and the weird things people think and say to him. Even Cal laughs at the one about the woman who asked him why he still did his own shopping in Tesco and the man asked him to write his life story about being a loss adjuster in return for half the profits. Cal opens another bottle and I bring in a dish of spiced pears baked in cider. Anyone would think we were three old mates, enjoying a cosy reunion together after not seeing each other for ages. The whole time, however, I keep remembering that we're only softening up Kit so we can ask him about Mawgan.

'That smells incredible. What's in there?' he asks as I lift the lid of the casserole dish and the heady scent of alcohol and spices fills the room.

'Local cider, cinnamon sticks, nutmeg. It's very festive, isn't it?'

'Amazing.'

'Hold on.' I return from the kitchen with a plastic carton and a scoop. 'This is delicious with it.'

'What's that?'

'Christmas Pudding ice cream.'

'I think I've died and gone to heaven,' says Kit.

Cal serves up the pears and ice cream and we tuck in. For a few minutes the only sounds are 'mms and 'wows' and spoons scraping on bowls. Cal and Kit have seconds of the ice cream and I take the carton back to the freezer. As Kit's finishing his seconds, Cal refills his glass with the last of the wine.

'I've been wondering. Don't you get bored, down here? It's very isolated and quiet in the winter,' he asks Kit.

The hairs on the back of my neck prickle.

'No. I want to be bored. That means I can finish my book. I've written more words down here than I ever do in London.'

'But you must miss your friends in the smoke.'

'Yes and no. It's because of my friends in the smoke that I keep being distracted from my work. There's always someone wanting me to go to the pub or a gig or a play or to the football. All I have here is a walk and the odd pint in the Tinner's.'

'The Tinner's? I'd have thought it was a bit local for a London sophisticate.' Cal smiles, but my stomach clenches as I fear a fresh sparring contest about to take place.

'You're not a regular?'

'Not as regular as I used to be.' I can see Cal recalling the lock-ins he used to go to after hours. 'It's a decent pub.'

'Cal's cousin works behind the bar. She's a goth.'

'Ah, Robyn. She's a laugh. I like her. I hadn't really made the connection. She's only doing a couple of nights now, isn't she? She said she's too busy with her course and hoping to start up her own jewellery-making business when her course finishes. Her dad's recently retired, hasn't he? I guess he must be your uncle?'

'Yes. Rory Penwith's my uncle.'

'Hmm. Now you come to mention it, there is a likeness between you and Robyn. Even withstanding the eyeliner.'

Cal rolls his eyes. I can feel that he's inwardly fuming.

Kit licks the last trace of ice cream from his spoon. 'This really is fantastic. I have to have the recipe.'

'I'll send you a link. Cal — let's chill out by

the fire again.' I get up and start to clear some plates from the table.

'I'll get the whisky. Don't load the dishwasher,' Cal says. 'Come and have a nightcap.'

'Don't worry. I had no intention of it. I'll leave that to you guys. I don't want any whisky though.'

After dumping the plates by the dishwasher, I go back to the sitting room to find Cal unscrewing the paper from a new bottle of single malt.

'So, have you met any other interesting local characters while you've been here?' he says, pouring a generous measure into a tumbler for Kit. 'In St Trenyan, for instance?'

Oh my God, Cal's going for the killer blow. Kit picks up his glass, mouths cheers and says, 'The locals are friendly enough I suppose, but I don't spend much time in St Trenyan.'

Cal smiles. 'What about with Mawgan Cade?'

Kit pauses with the glass halfway to his mouth, or am I imagining it? 'Mawgan?' he asks.

'Mawgan Cade. I saw you with her at Sharky's the other night,' I say quickly.

'Oh, yes, I *was* there with Mawgan, but I didn't spot you.' He smiles. 'If you saw us, why didn't you come over and say hello?'

'I didn't want to butt in, and anyway I was out with a mate and we couldn't stop because she was in a rush to get back. Her sister wasn't very well,' I babble, squirming at my white lie. I could *kill* Cal.

'Is Mawgan a friend of yours, then?' Kit says, sitting back in his chair and smiling at me.

'We were going to ask you the same thing,' says Cal, cradling his own glass.

216

'Mawgan's more of a business acquaintance,' I add. 'She's on the St Trenyan Harbour Lights committee. They meet at the cafe once a week, and Cal went to school with her.'

'Really?'

'Didn't she mention it?'

'No, but then we hadn't long met. She came along to the talk I gave to St Trenyan Writers and asked me to meet her for a drink.'

'Mawgan went to a writers' group?'

Cal has a coughing fit.

'Malt a bit potent for you?' Kit grins at him and swills the amber liquid around the bottom of his glass. 'Too good to water down, though, eh? Your father had very good taste.'

Cal frowns. 'In some things.'

I sense a dangerous atmosphere.

'So, you were saying you met Mawgan at a writers' group . . . ' I ask.

'Is that so strange? They knew I was here from a crime writers' forum and they invited me to give a talk. I didn't like to say no so I agreed and Mawgan went along.'

'What's she writing?' Cal asks.

'I'm not really sure. She mentioned something about a bonk-buster. You know, Jackie Collins style. It's not really my thing, and I'm not sure how serious she is, but she came up to me after and asked if I'd meet her for a drink, so I said, 'Why not?' He sips his drink then looks at Cal. 'I haven't committed some terrible faux pas, have I? She's not got a big hairy fisherman boyfriend who's going to beat me up and feed me to the gulls?'

'I don't think she needs anyone for that,' Cal says.

'Sorry, we must seem really nosy,' I cut in. 'But I was just curious. I didn't know Mawgan was interested in writing a book. She doesn't seem the type.'

'No one ever does,' says Kit. 'I gave her a few tips and we had a good time, but doubt if I'll have time to see her again. I have to go back to London in mid-December, you see. I have meetings with my publisher and my agent's arranged for me to speak at a book festival and attend a crime writers' conference. It makes sense for me to leave sooner than I'd expected. I won't ask for a refund.'

'We will refund you as you've stayed so long at a quiet time of year,' I say. 'So, will we still see you at the Harbour Lights this Friday?'

Kit smiles. 'Oh, yes, I wouldn't miss that for the world.'

The talk turns to the lights and how the festival and traditions started, and the pop-up cafe we're opening on the night. Cal joins in readily enough, but I can tell by his body language that he's puzzled and confused and pissed off. I just want the night to be over.

The old long case clock strikes ten and Kit gets up. 'Sorry to be a party pooper but I need an early start in the morning. I want to get a run in before I set to work. And I don't want to keep you both from your bed.'

'We mustn't keep you from yours either,' Cal adds.

Is it me or does he emphasise the word 'bed',

as in one bed: ours? Seeming amused, Kit goes on. 'I think we all need our beauty sleep, apart from Demi, of course. If I don't see you before, I'll see you at the Harbour Lights, if you can bear the excitement.'

Cal grins and, almost, rubs his hands together. 'Oh I think so. Actually, I can't wait. I think it's going to be an absolutely fascinating evening.'

24

'*Ten, nine, eight . . .* '

Thousands of voices join Greg Stennack, Radio St Trenyan's breakfast show DJ, in the countdown to the switch on. '*Seven, six, five . . .* '

The customers queuing at our pop-up cafe turn to face the harbour like everyone, holding their breath as Greg's voice rises.

'*Four, three, two . . . one!*'

A huge 'ohh' ripples through the crowds as the mayor throws the switch and St Trenyan explodes into multi-coloured, glittering life. Cheering and applause erupts for the thousands of bulbs and displays twinkling in the streets. The harbour walls are decorated with illuminated Christmas trees, presents, stockings, candles and even a shark (sponsored by Sharky's, of course). There are little boats made up of frames wired with neon bulbs in red, green, yellow, orange, violet and blue. They shimmer like rainbows against the dark waters of the harbour, transforming St Trenyan from the out-of-season gloom into a fairytale seaside village.

We managed to book a prime spot on the harbour for our stall. The location is almost opposite Santa's grotto and not far from Sheila's cafe where I worked, briefly, before I lost my job because of a spat with Mawgan Cade. Sheila's

Beach Hut is open, of course, but I don't expect to see Sheila herself tonight. We're all way too busy, but I can see the glow of the patio heaters on her terrace from our stall and I'm so happy she's making a success of the business after her problems with the Cades, her landlords-from-hell.

Most of our stall is given over to a pop-up Demelza's while Cal and Polly have taken one end to promote Kilhallon Resort to the visitors who have come to Cornwall to enjoy the lights. We're full for Christmas and New Year now, but hopefully we can lure them down for longer holidays in spring.

Since the event officially kicked off at four o'clock, we've been doing a roaring trade before the switch-on, with queues down the street for our mulled cider, hot turkey pasties and mince pies, but the few minutes around the switch-on gave us a quick breather. Nina is helping me to look after the lines that are forming again. Robyn's right next to us, helping Polly and Cal on the Kilhallon stall. Andi's coming to help later too, and if Mawgan sees her on our stall, it will be fun.

Robyn gazes around her, wide-eyed. 'Wow. The lights are amazing. I know it's so uncool, but I never get fed up of seeing them. I love Christmas.'

She's like a little kid, and to be honest, even I have a lump in my throat. Last year, I watched this happen from above the town. I was between jobs and Mitch and I slept in a doorway later that night. I could never share this with Robyn,

221

and if I do, I may cry.

'It's great. Good for business too.'

Cal catches my eye and mouths 'OK?'

I nod back, and smile at the young family at the head of the queue. The little girl clutches a *Frozen* helium balloon. 'Hello, oh, what a lovely balloon,' I say to the girl. 'What can I get you?' I ask the mum.

All around us, children shriek and chatter, their parents laugh and smile and even the teenagers sound excited. You'd think they'd never seen Christmas lights before. There is something magical about St Trenyan's lights. Maybe it's the setting and the reflections in the harbour, or the fact that so many local people have worked to make tonight happen, or the sounds of the Fisherman's Choir or the tang of the sea in the air. Whatever the reason, the lights have woven a spell over thousands of people from all over Cornwall and across the Tamar, and beyond. There are German, French and Dutch accents, even Americans and Australians mingling with the crowds.

The brief lull in our queue is over and people are lined up again at the stall for hot pasties, mince pies, mulled cider and apple juice. With Nina helping we can just about cope, although the queue for the stall seems to be getting longer. People seem prepared to wait, although I'm a bit worried that we're going to run out of stock before the end of the event at nine. It's non-stop, though I manage to send Nina off for a ten-minute break. When she comes back, Robyn catches my arm.

'Polly asked if you want a hand? Cal can manage the Kilhallon stall and she can see how busy we are. Shall I take over and give you a chance to grab a bite to eat? Do a bit of Christmas shopping?' Robyn says.

'Me? Do Christmas shopping?'

'Yes. You'll want to get Cal something, won't you?'

'I . . . I hadn't thought about it.'

Robyn rolls her eyes. 'Of course you will, but good luck with choosing something. I decided to make him a necklace — a shark's tooth set in silver on a leather cord with a matching woven wristband. I hope he likes them.'

'I'm sure he will,' I say, but realise I've no idea what Cal will think, or what to get him myself. I haven't bought Christmas gifts for anyone for years, and I haven't had any myself for even longer. I'd like to get Polly something too, and Robyn, and Tamsin and what about Nina and the girls at the cafe? I've been so busy serving up Christmas to everyone else, that I haven't even thought about it myself.

Polly bustles over and starts helping Nina to serve customers while Robyn lays out mince pies on a tray. 'It's good to see Cal here. He was away from home last Harbour Lights and for Christmas itself of course,' she says.

'He told me he was on one of his aid missions.'

'Yes. It wasn't a very happy time because we were all worried sick about him. We'd only had the odd email up to — and after — Christmas but we'd guessed he was horrendously busy. I can't imagine what it must have been like working out there. Then after the New Year, the messages stopped altogether. Dad contacted the charity a few times and they said he was in a remote place and was probably too busy to speak to us or out of contact. But that's all over now, he's back and he looks soooo much better. More like his old self, only maybe happier.'

'Do you think so?'

She nods. 'Oh, God, yes, I was so worried about him when he turned up at Bosinney at Easter. He'd lost too much weight and he was so troubled and unhappy but you've worked a miracle on him. You are together now, aren't you?'

'Yes, I guess so . . . '

Robyn lowers her voice while Polly is engrossed in conversation with a woman from her zumba class. 'Polly was right then. She said Cal wants you to move in with him but you haven't yet.'

'That's mine and Cal's business.'

'Oh, don't be too hard on her. She thinks she's Cal's mum, maybe yours too now. She only means well.'

'Yeah, I know, but maybe I'll get her a CCTV system for Christmas so she can watch us all the time.'

Robyn laughs. 'So will you? Move in with Cal, I mean. He's never asked a girl to do that before. Not even Isla.'

'I don't know, and I've told Cal no, for the moment.'

'Oh, I see . . . I'm being very nosy, aren't I?

It's your decision but Cal must really care about you.'

Polly moves on to speak to some holidaymakers. Robyn changes the subject. 'Anyway, I have some exciting news of my own. Andi and me, we're going to visit her mum in Australia for Christmas. Dad says he's cool about it and he's spending the day with his new woman, Moira.'

'That's fantastic, Robyn. But what do Mawgan and Clive Cade think? They won't be very happy about you visiting Mrs Cade — and you are living in one of Mawgan's flats now.'

'Andi's mum paid for her flight and my dad paid for mine, so it's none of Mawgan's business. She said she didn't care what we do, but Andi thinks she'd secretly like to come with us and see her mum again. It's sad how Mawgan's turned into such an evil cow. Fancy cutting off your mum like that when you could go and see her and at least try to patch things up. Andi said Mawgan loved her mum to bits until she ran off to Australia. Mr Cade won't have any pictures of her in the house, but Andi says Mawgan keeps one at the back of her knicker drawer.'

Luckily, Nina saves me from hearing any more about Mawgan's knicker drawer, but I was right, Mawgan must still love her mum, even if, as Mawgan views it, she ran off and abandoned her and Andi.

'Go and take a break, boss,' Nina orders.

'That's exactly what I was telling her,' Robyn says smugly.

'OK. I will then, but I'll be back soon.'

I untie my apron, find my coat and join the

crowds in the streets. The lights are dazzling, the smells of food and mulled wine fill my nose, music of all kinds mixes with the 'festive sounds' being played by the Radio St Trenyan road show. Outside one of the pubs in the back streets, there's a hog roast and a Celtic band, while the Fisherman's Choir are setting up outside the lifeboat station. Last year, I watched and listened to all of this like I was watching a TV documentary. Even though I was born and bred in Cornwall, I didn't feel part of it.

Yet I'm not an outsider any more, I'm at the heart of tonight's events. A few people nod and smile at me as I make my way through the streets. There will be plenty of time to do more shopping after tonight, although I do spot a gorgeous purple sarong on an ethnic stall. I can't resist buying it for Robyn. If she's going to Oz for Christmas she'll need it before she goes. I think of my meagre but growing savings. I'm so busy I hardly have time to spend my salary so it's built up. I can afford to spend some on presents. Now Robyn has put the idea in my head, it surprises me how excited I feel about doing my Christmas shopping. It's what normal people do.

Normal people usually spend Christmas with their families too. Even the Cades will be together, sort of. Mawgan with her dad — what a festive scene that conjures up in my mind; both of them checking their bank balances at the dinner table while some flunkey serves up the biggest turkey Waitrose could supply. Yet Mawgan does love her dad, in her own weird way, whereas the thought of spending Christmas with mine sends shudders down my spine. Not that he ever actually physically hurt me or my brother; but I don't see any way back for us after how things went downhill between us when Mum died. My father was never the most affectionate man and he liked a drink. After my mum passed away, he hit the bottle and I may as well not have existed most of the time. For all I know, he might have drunk himself to death by now.

Oh God, I hope not. I don't want that, because I do care about Dad, no matter how much I pretend I've washed my hands of him.

Before such thoughts derail my whole night, I plunge back into the Christmas market on a mission to get Cal a gift. Soon I'm lost among the festive tat and trinkets: bobble hats, scarves, faux-fur gilets, flashing reindeer ears, packets of chocolate seagull droppings, mulled cider truffles, Rudolphs made of shells, snow globes with trawlers inside, and singing Santas who drop their trousers to show their bums. Everything you need, in fact, for a perfect family festive season.

It's no good, I can't see anything for Cal and I daren't be away any longer, so I wind back towards the stall. The break has been exactly what I needed but I've already been away far too long. What if Robyn and the girls have had a disaster while I've been shopping and daydreaming? They need me.

Mitch and I have a home, a job I love, I'm almost my own boss, and I do have friends who are even better than family, I have Cal . . . If I want to. If I *dare*.

I spot him ahead, walking towards me up the narrow alley that's a shortcut from Fore Street to the harbour area where our stall is. The sounds of the festival are muted here, and we're alone for the first time this evening.

'Hi there. Is everything OK?' he asks.

'It's fine. Robyn and Andi are looking after the stall. I didn't really need a break, but Nina forced me.'

Cal nods at the bag in my hand. 'What have you bought?'

'A sarong for Robyn. I've been doing a bit of Christmas shopping.'

He smiles. 'So it's not for me?'

'I don't think purple batik is your thing.'

'You look and smell great.'

'Of cider and pasties?'

'Of course.'

He steps forward and before I know where I am, he's kissing me deeply. It's the first time I've been in his arms since our row and it feels amazing. If his kiss wasn't delicious enough, he tastes of chocolate and mulled cider. I mean, what's a girl to do with a combination like that? He cradles my face in his hands and his fingers are warm against my chilly skin. I pull him against me, greedy for the pressure of his body against mine. The tensions between us are forgotten in this moment.

In the background, the voices of the Fisherman's Choir drift into my consciousness as we end our kiss and simply stand together in

228

the alley. Cal wraps his arms around me and I rest my cheek against his jacket. The choir starts an old Cornish folk song, 'Trelawney'. I recognise it from a CD my mum bought my Nana Demelza. I wish they were both here now. My heart feels as if it might crack in half.

'What's up?' Cal whispers into my hair. I know I'm making his coat damp with my tears.

'Nothing. I was only thinking of what a difference a year makes.'

He squeezes me tighter. I think he senses what I'm going through and why. Perhaps he's feeling it too. 'I know.'

'Sometimes I don't think that my life now can be real. Perhaps I'm going to wake up in a shop doorway or discover I've jumped into another girl's shoes by mistake and that I've got to hand them back and have my old worn-out ones.'

'You won't have to give anything back or let it go. You've made it all happen. And I promise you, you're real.' He squeezes my bottom, making me snap up and look him in the eyes.

'You have a cheek, Cal Penwith!'

'Not as cute as yours.' He squeezes my bum again and stifles any protest with a glorious snog. His mouth is warm and he tastes spicy and delicious. His tongue darts into my mouth and he pulls me against him. It's so good to be back in his arms, I don't want it to end.

'Shall we abandon the stalls and go back to Kilhallon to bed?'

'I'd like that.'

His eyes shine. 'So will you think again about my offer? I'm making it now, in private, as I should have done the first time. I'm so sorry about that, I was wrong. So move in with me, Demi. The nights are cold and long without you and Mitch. There's a bed for him in the kitchen.'

'Mitch won't approve. He might not want to live in the farmhouse.'

'He will. You know he'd do anything for me after I saved his life and yours.'

I gasp. 'It wasn't that dramatic!'

'Don't spoil it.' He tucks a lock of hair under my hat. 'Say you will.'

'I will *think* about it. But not tonight.'

His face falls. 'At least promise that you'll spend Christmas Day with me. It'll be just the two of us because Polly's going to her daughter's, Robyn's in Australia with Andi and Uncle Rory's going to his girlfriend's. The holiday guests will be too drunk and stuffed to need anything. It can just be us, together, having a cosy Cornish Christmas. I'll even cook Christmas dinner if you promise to look after me for the rest of the day.'

His wink tells me how he'd expect me to look after him. My throat tightens.

'And,' he says, 'you still have to repay my bet.'

'What bet's that?'

'I think it involved a filing cabinet and your knickers.' He raises his eyebrows, and every inch of my skin threatens to set on fire.

'That *is* a very tempting offer.'

'The filing cabinet or the Christmas invitation?'

'Both . . . ' I whisper.

230

Cal's eyes glint with wicked promise. 'Great. Stay in the farmhouse on Christmas Eve night then we can have a champagne breakfast while we open our presents. Once we've managed to drag ourselves out of bed, of course.'

Presents. Damn, I've still no idea what to give him. I don't want to embarrass him or me by going over the top, not that I can afford to go over the top. But I don't want to hand over a Christmas jumper when he gives me a bracelet or necklace . . . no way, Cal would never go for that slushy stuff. He's probably thinking of a new food processor or set of saucepans. Come to think of it, we still haven't replaced the oven gloves.

'You must have something in mind for me?' I tease, hoping to get a clue about mine so I can respond in kind.

Cal's breath is warm and soft on the side of my neck. 'Of course I do.'

'Going to give me a hint?'

'It wouldn't be a surprise if I gave you too many hints, but I hope you'll like it.'

He tilts up my head and kisses my throat.

'Is it clothes?' I murmur, hardly able to breathe.

His hands settle on my waist, pulling me gently against him and leaving me in no doubt about how he feels. 'Actually, clothes were the last thing I had in mind.'

'Cal, you are imposs — ' My frankly pathetic protest is cut off by Cal's mouth. He kisses me until I feel dizzy.

'Demi!'

Robyn appears in the gap of the alley. 'Oh, sorry.'

'It's OK.'

'It's not,' Cal mutters. Glowing inside I try to wipe the smug smile off my face. I will think about moving in with him. The nights are long and cold, and I can tell by the look on his face, he wants me — and needs me.

'I'm coming!' I call to Robyn.

'Later, I hope so,' Cal says with a wicked grin.

'Shhh!' I say.

'I mean it. Several times,' he shouts.

Ignoring every impulse to jump him here in the cold alley on the cobbles, I scoot away without glancing behind.

Back at the stall, I return to my work with new enthusiasm, although it's not that easy to concentrate with Cal's words ringing in my ears and the memory of his warm mouth on mine. Making up was — and is — going to be amazing and, what's more, I can't believe how well the festival is going. So many people have asked about Kilhallon Park and even though the crowds are slightly thinner now that the younger families have gone home, the streets are still very busy with couples and young groups. Nina has taken over serving customers while I refill the mulled cider barrel and retrieve the last batch of mince pies from the crate. The pasties are long gone and soon we'll almost sell out of everything.

'There's more hot cider,' I say to Nina during a lull in the queue. 'And the pies are ready, but it's our final lot. I'll take over on the counter if you want to start clearing up a bit?'

As I turn round, Nina has just finished serving her customer and a new one stands in front of the stall. Catching sight of me, he frowns then stares at me like I'm an alien.

25

'Demi?'

I almost drop the pies onto the cobbles as the man says my name. 'It *is* you, not a double, isn't it?'

My stomach churns and I glance down at the counter. 'What can I get you, sir?'

'What do you mean, 'what can you get me, sir'?'

'I'm afraid all the pasties have sold out, but we still have cider and mince pies. You can have them with a dollop of clotted cream if you want, sir.'

'You can get me two pies and I don't want any cream, but it'd be nice if you at least acknowledged my existence.'

I want to speak to him, I want to say 'hello, how are you?' but I can't say the words. It must be the shock of seeing him here right in front of me with no warning. I can't cope unless I pretend he's just any other customer. I couldn't handle a confrontation or a big emotional scene. I just want him to leave before I totally lose it in public. Avoiding his face, I drop the pies onto a paper plate, with shaking hands.

Nina is at my arm. 'Everything OK?' she murmurs. 'I can serve this customer if you like?'

'No. I'm fine,' I murmur.

Still unable to meet my father's eyes, I shove

the plate at him. 'That'll be one pound twenty, sir.'

A woman joins Dad at the counter in front of me. She's in her early thirties, wearing a huge fake-fur coat but it can't disguise the fact that she's massively pregnant. In fact, I wouldn't be surprised if she gave birth right here and now.

'Demi? Bloody hell, it *is* her!'

'It looks like her,' Dad grunts. Coins land on the counter. 'Here's your money,' he says roughly. 'You can keep the change.'

I won't look at him; I won't. I *can't*. A hand snatches the plate and he hisses at me. 'And thanks for not acknowledging your own father. Great. Really great.'

'Wait!' I call, but it's too late. My heart sinks. I wish I'd had the courage to speak to him. I didn't want to seem callous and cold. I just didn't know how to handle seeing him like that again, out of the blue. As my dad and his girlfriend, Rachel, bustle away, I can hear them muttering and Rachel saying in a loud voice, 'What have we done to her? Why is she like this?' But their voices are soon swallowed up by all the other sounds of the choir and bands and general hubbub.

I should go after them but my legs seem frozen to the spot. I'm trembling. Seeing him again — and with Rachel — brings back memories I'd tried to bury. He must have been just as shocked as me and he did try to speak to me. But I'm not ready to talk to him yet; not here in the middle of all these crowds of strangers. Why did he have to appear now, in my new life? Why do I have to face the past when I'd buried it in a dark corner where it can't hurt me?

'Demi. Are you all right?' Nina lays her hand on my arm. Her eyes are full of concern.

'Yes. Fine. Fine . . . '

'You've gone really pale. Did that bloke and his wife give you any hassle? He acted like you knew him. Let me take over. Go and get some fresh air or sit down. Shall I call Cal?'

'No!'

'OK. OK,' she says quietly.

'Argh. Sorry, Nina. I didn't mean to be grouchy. Just a bit of a headache coming on. There are customers,' I say, seeing the older couple now at the front of the queue giving us anxious and impatient looks. 'I just need a bit of air for a moment. I'll be back . . . '

In the alley at the rear of the stall, I take a few deep breaths but the mix of fried onions from the burger bar next to ours and beer from the pub terrace makes me feel sick. Why, why, why did I react like that to seeing my dad and Rachel again? I hate to admit, but my dad looked really healthy, better than I remember him looking since Mum died, and Rachel was obviously ready to pop. Oh God, her baby will be my half-brother or sister.

Leaning against the wall, I swallow hard. That makes two siblings I'll never see if things carry on like this. My brother, Kyle, left home before me to join the army. Although we were never that close, I do wonder where he is and I've tried to find out a few times. Dad told me he was safe and back in the UK the last time I spoke to him, but I don't know which base he's stationed at. I do care about my family, even if I pretend to others and even myself that I don't. But we're still split apart, so what kind of a family does that make us? Especially this near to Christmas, when people are supposed to come together.

'Demi?'

Cal walks to me.

'What's happened? Nina said somebody's been hassling you.'

'Nothing. No.'

'Doesn't look like nothing. You're white as a sheet and your pulse is racing.'

I look down at my wrist to find Cal holding it. I snatch it away.

'Was it that bloke and his girlfriend? The pregnant one?'

'You saw them?'

'I saw them queue up, but I was busy. They were muttering when they walked off. I thought they were pissed off because you'd run out of pasties or something.' Smiling, he takes my hand again. 'You're whacked after all the preparation for this thing. Please don't feel under pressure about what I said earlier. I won't hassle you any more about moving in with me.'

'It's not that!'

My voice rings off the walls.

'Whoa.'

'Shit. I'm sorry, Cal, but that bloke and the woman — that was my dad and his girlfriend.'

There's a pause, then: 'Ah. Shit. I had no idea.'

'Neither did I. I never expected to see him

237

again. It was stupid of me. Of course, he would come to the festival, with her. Everyone for miles around is here.'

'It had to happen sometime.'

'But in public? In front of the customers and Nina? Oh, God, I went to pieces. I had no idea what to say or how to feel. I didn't even acknowledge him.'

'No wonder he was upset.'

'But he *never* seemed upset when I was at home. He never even seemed to notice me unless it was to criticise me. I may as well not have existed after Mum died. It's as if he blamed me for Mum dying, though I don't know why, and then he started drinking, he was oblivious to most things.'

'Demi. It must have been impossible for him. He wasn't a hands-on dad anyway, and your mum died and he was left with a teenage daughter who adored her. He had his own grief and he doesn't sound very good at handling emotions anyway. Your brother got the hell out of the place, didn't he?'

'Kyle wasn't much older than me. I don't blame him for joining up.'

'No, but that left you and your dad together. You were devastated and young and angry and might have blamed your father for making your mum's life unhappy. Did you?'

'I don't know. I might have. Yes, he wasn't warm and loving to her like he should have been. I hated him for that. She deserved better.'

'It sounds like a recipe for disaster. A powder keg.'

'I suppose so, but now? I still feel the same way.'

'I'm the last person to offer family counselling.' He smiles and holds me by the arms. 'But things might have changed, don't you think? Maybe now might be a good time to at least call him?'

'What will I say? I just made things much worse!'

'Tell him the truth. That you were taken by surprise and didn't know how to react. That you'd like to speak to him or, better still, meet in a neutral place.'

'I don't know if I can. I don't know if I'm brave enough to face it all.'

'Brave? You're one of the bravest people I've ever met, Demi. Do you mean that talking to him will be awkward? Uncomfortable? Sad? You told me to take a risk in taking you on. Now I'm telling you to do the same by contacting your dad.'

'You sound like Polly. She's tried to make me see him again.'

'Then for once in my life I'm happy to sound like Polly. Come here.' He hugs me, saying nothing, just holding me. My father's face comes into focus in my mind again. He looked healthy and well. He was smiling at Rachel, and I don't think I've ever seen him so at ease with himself. Not since before my mum became ill. There were good times when I was younger. Good times, calm times, and then everything started to come apart at the seams, becoming worse and worse. Cal might be right. He couldn't cope. I couldn't cope.

'You can't pretend your family doesn't exist,' he murmurs. 'Your father was obviously willing to talk to you even if he was upset that you blanked him, and who can blame him? Maybe he genuinely wanted to reach out and try to pull his family together again. It might be worth thinking about calling him again.' His voice rises in a question so I nod, even though the idea of revisiting the bad memories and conflict makes me feel physically sick.

'I'll think about it,' I say, hoping to do exactly the opposite.

26

Cal

Poor Demi. What a shock for her dad and his girlfriend to turn up like that, without any warning. Although half of West Cornwall's here tonight and we do have a prime location, so maybe it wasn't that surprising.

She's returned to the stall now, leaving me in the alley. I said I wanted to nip to one of the shops to get a scarf for Polly, but the truth is I'd seen something on a stall that would be perfect for Demi herself.

It's hard for her to have to bump into her father again and revisit bad times. Especially when she seems to be coming round to the idea of moving in with me, when I'd almost convinced her that I'm serious about us. Our conversation just now was certainly a good start and as soon as this festival's over, I'll ask her to stay the night and try and get her to open up about her dad.

For now, I need to get my purchases done as fast as possible and get back to the stall. Neither shopping nor 'selling' Kilhallon are my natural activities. I turn to walk down the alley towards the harbour when I hear a cough behind me. A man steps out from the darkness of a shop doorway and I recognise him instantly. He throws his cigarette on the ground.

'Hello, Cal. Taking a break?'

'I was about to leave, actually. I didn't know you smoked.'

'I've been trying to give up, which is the added bonus of renting a cottage in a no-smoking resort, but out here, I'm afraid I've lapsed.'

Kit smiles, which has the effect of raising my hackles instantly. It could, of course, be a complete coincidence that he's in the same alley as me. Then again, he might well have been listening to my conversation with Demi. In fact, I think that's exactly why he was hiding in the shop doorway. He only just lit that fag or I'd have smelled the smoke. It's tempting to wonder if Mawgan's lurking near too.

'I'm glad we could help.'

'You've helped me a lot already. Kilhallon has. It's going well, is it?'

'What's going well?' My reply is terse but I don't care. Kit makes my skin crawl.

He waves his hand towards the harbour. 'Tonight. The festival. It's good for business, I assume? Demi's stall has been packed all night and I see you've had a lot of interest for the resort. You must be thrilled, both of you.'

'We're pleased, yeah, but you can't afford to rest on your laurels in our trade. You have to keep up the promotion, develop the offers and find new ways of attracting customers.' I don't like his tone. In fact, I don't like him full stop.

'I suppose so.'

'In fact, I really have to get back to the stall now. I only came out for a quick chat with Demi.'

242

'Yes, so I saw.'

'And heard?'

'I couldn't help it, I'm afraid, I was standing in the doorway out of the wind, trying to decide whether to resist temptation.' He takes a drag on his cigarette and blows out the smoke.

'And decided you couldn't?'

'Life's too short not to have any vices, don't you think?' he says.

'I don't have time to think. Enjoy your lapse. I have to go.'

'Wait!' Kit's hand is on my shoulder, briefly, but long enough to make my skin prickle. This is stupid. My reaction to him is over the top. Maybe my instincts are wrong. He's just a time waster and a bore.

'I'll try not to detain you too long, but there's something I have to say. I heard you tell Demi that she shouldn't pretend her family doesn't exist.'

'What?'

'As well as overhearing you, I also saw what happened at the stall before I came up here for a smoke. That was Demi's father who turned up, I presume?'

'Yes, but I don't understand how you know that?'

'Polly also saw and heard what went on. When I mentioned that Demi and the couple seemed very upset, she told me who she thought they were. There's a family resemblance too, of course, if I needed any more confirmation.'

'I don't know. I didn't see him.' My anger spills over. If he blackens our name on every

243

holiday review site in the universe, I don't give a toss any more. 'I know you're a guest, and I'm grateful for your help on the night of the fog, but I really don't think Demi's personal life is any of your business.'

'No, you're possibly — probably — right about that.' Although Kit is agreeing with me, the smug, almost delighted expression on his face winds me up even further.

'Then I'm glad we agree on something,' I say.

'I'm sorry if you think I'm interfering, but I wonder if you'll be so quick to criticise me if we were talking about your own family. There are some people there you'd rather pretend didn't exist, aren't there?'

'My family? What do you mean?'

'I mean the Penwiths. Actually your father, specifically.'

That's it. He's pushed me too far for any attempt at politeness.

'What the hell does my dad have to do with you?'

'Well, perhaps you should ask my mother that. As you can't ask yours.'

Acid swirls in my stomach. 'What are you trying to say?'

'That your father was a lying cheating bastard who ran away from his responsibilities.' He smiles like he's offered to buy me a pint. 'If you'll forgive my bluntness, mate.'

The barb hits home and sticks deep, but I just about manage to stop myself from flattening his smug face. And anyway, why is he talking about my father? I thought it was Demi

244

he was interested in.

'I think you should stop talking right now. You're on dangerous ground, Bannen, but you're still a guest of ours so I'll refrain from smacking you in the mouth.'

'I'm only speaking the truth, but I can see that it hurts.'

'Ah. Now I see. Well, I always thought you were a bit of a tosser, to be honest, mate, but now I know exactly where this is coming from. Did Mawgan Cade tell you this? Christ, I thought you were an intelligent guy. I never thought you'd listen to her poisonous crap.'

'Hmm. Mawgan may talk a lot of crap but she's right about this.'

'Not that it's any of your sodding business, I know the gossip about my father and I know what people say. Some of it — probably a fraction — might be true. Dad was no saint, not that it's any of your business. Or Mawgan Cade's.'

'Ah. But I'm afraid it is.'

'What do you mean?'

'You really don't know, do you? It's ironic actually.'

'Ironic? Stop talking in riddles.'

'Mawgan's mother had an affair with your father.'

'What?' His words stop me in my tracks. I must have misheard them. 'What do you mean, an affair?'

'That's why the Cades' marriage split up and why Mrs Cade went off to Australia. That's why Mawgan isn't your greatest fan, I should imagine, among other things, I really don't know.'

'One, there's no proof of that, and two, what she's told you while you were shagging her can hardly be relied on. I don't think you have any idea.'

'Funnily enough, I haven't shagged Mawgan, but I do happen to believe her and if you choose to ignore her story, then you definitely can't ignore mine.'

I glance down at my wrist, though I've no idea what my watch says. 'Is this going to take long, only I'm a little bit busy for fairy tales right now. In fact there's a kids' book stall on the harbour if you want to waste their time.' I want to leave but my feet are rooted to the cobbles and Kit goes on.

'I'll start the story anyway and it's up to you whether you want to hear it.'

'Get lost, Bannen.'

I turn, forcing myself to move away from him, but his smooth voice follows me.

'Picture a young woman, only nineteen, visiting Cornwall. Picture an older man, handsome, pretty well-to-do, with land and a farmhouse and a business, albeit a crumbling one, and with a wife who was pregnant with his son.'

The words echo in the narrow alley. They clutch at my clothes and drag me back, no matter how much I want to run away.

'Picture the rich guy meeting the young woman while she's on her first holiday without her parents, and having a brief but passionate affair with her. At least it was passionate to *her*: she thought he loved her. She definitely worshipped him.'

'What are you making up now? Your new novel? I'd ditch it. Bit over the top, even for you, wouldn't you say?'

'I admit, it's not my usual style, but it's effective in this case. Shall I tell you how it ends?'

'You'd better, before I lose the will to live.'

'As I was saying . . . Of course, the older man had no intention of leaving his wife or his baby son. He never did. He was only interested in a fling with a young woman he regarded as disposable; another notch on his four poster — a conquest. The woman had been sheltered by her parents and you could say she was naïve, so when the man rejected her and told her he was married and didn't want to see her again after her stay in Cornwall, she was devastated. Are you with me, Cal?'

'Get on with it.'

'He still wasn't interested, although a little annoyed, when the young woman told him she was pregnant. Still not interested when she had the baby, another little boy, only a few months after this first son was born.'

The cobbles seem to shift beneath me. 'Tell me. Is this fairy tale the reason you came to Kilhallon in the first place?'

'One of them. Your father ruined people's lives round here. He was a lying, irresponsible coward.'

He steps closer. We're inches apart, his breath

247

is hot on my face, and not only does he smell of fags but of booze, and not of the mulled cider that Demi's been peddling from the stall. It's whisky, and beer, and a lot of it because his clothes stink. I'm not one to judge; I've been there with booze, but he's aggressive with it. Dangerous.

'So, have you worked out the ending yet?'

'It's not the subtlest of narratives, is it? There's a twist, I suppose?' I say, affecting boredom, while sick to my stomach at his story.

'Not with this tale, no.'

'How do you know you're my brother?'

'Because my mother told me,' Kit says.

'She's lying.' Even I know that's not worthy of me.

He nods sagely. 'Mawgan said you'd react like this.'

'What the hell has Mawgan got to do with any of this?'

'That doesn't matter now. My mother isn't lying and I have a DNA test to prove that your father is also mine. Even without that, your father had already accepted I was his and that's why he was paying my mother an allowance until I left university.'

I can no longer pretend I don't care about his accusations. His story has found its mark and lodged in my heart, like a barb. 'I thought you said that your mother and father lived in London. I thought . . . '

'They do. I didn't lie. You assumed. My mum married again when I started high school. I think of Roger Bannen as my dad, and have done for a very long time. He's always treated me as his own and I've never known any different. So you see, although your father rejected me and disowned me and hid my existence from everyone, I've been a lot luckier than you in one respect. My father was a decent, honest man who loved me even though I was someone else's child.'

'You've got a bloody nerve. I loved my dad. Things weren't the best between us, but I knew I was loved.'

'Maybe, but he still had all those affairs.'

Hairs prickle on the back of my neck.

'We're brothers, Cal. Though I'd rather be Mawgan's brother than yours, any day.'

'What the hell does Mawgan have to do with this?'

'From the look of horror on your face, I take it your father neglected to mention he'd fathered another child?'

'I — '

'Or *children*, of course. For all I know, I might not be the only other Penwith kid knocking around. He spread it about enough. Some of them may not even know who their dad was.'

'You bastard.'

'Call me what you want, the facts are undeniable. Even for someone who enjoys spinning yarns to those closest to him,' he adds.

I laugh at him, even though I feel sick to my stomach. What is he hinting at?

'When your father found out my mum was pregnant with me, he didn't want to see her again. He didn't want to see me after I was born,

249

even though she phoned him from the hospital. She sent him some photos and he sent them back. I've been lucky; I've had a wonderful father who brought me up as his own. Bit of a contrast with yours, don't you think?'

Only with a great effort do I restrain myself from punching his sneering face. 'Even if you what you say is true, what's brought you here now? I don't understand. If you've had such a happy childhood and you don't care about my father, why turn up here now?'

'A number of reasons. There's no special reason for this moment. I've always been fascinated by the man who rejected me and didn't want to acknowledge me as his son. I've wanted to see Kilhallon and meet you for a long time. Who wouldn't want to meet their brother, especially when he's a famous hero? I saw the magazine feature.'

'That was crap, but you know journalists. Never let the truth get in the way of a good story.'

'No. They don't.' He smiles.

'Has Mawgan Cade got something to do with you turning up now? She's been stirring up trouble, hasn't she?'

'You really don't deserve Demi, do you?' he says.

Ignoring this last piece of rubbish, I try to focus on the bile he's spewed about my family. 'You're sick. Even if your claims are true about being my father's son, what does that have to do with Demi? If you're telling the truth, I don't care who knows. My parents are dead, the news can't hurt either of them and I don't give a toss what anyone else thinks. Demi won't care. So go ahead and spread your news, if that's the kind of twisted thing that gives you satisfaction. If you'd come to me and told me this from the first day you arrived at Kilhallon, I'd have been shocked, granted, but ready to listen and talk. This . . . melodramatic way of announcing it only tells me what I've suspected all along: that you're a cunning, deceitful tosser.'

'I agree with you, she'll take the news we're half-brothers in her stride, but our being brothers isn't the only story Demi might be interested in, is it?'

My chest tightens, my throat constricts, yet somehow I manage to sneer at him. He can't know exactly what happened to me in Syria, no one can. Even if he does, it can't affect my relationship with Demi. Kit's trying to wind me up, to hurt me. Even so, I don't want Demi to hear about Soraya and Esme from a stranger who might not have the full story. I don't want to tell her what happened at all, because I can't *face* telling her. But Kit obviously has other ideas, the bastard.

'You've totally lost the plot, mate,' I say, mocking him.

My fist is tight, nails digging in my palm. His arrogant face stares back at me. The cobbles seem to shift beneath me, as if I'm losing my footing.

'I don't think so. You see, I do write thrillers and I am a freelance journalist, but not with a solar energy journal these days. For a while I've worked for a national newspaper, undercover mostly. I've been following up a story, about you as a matter of fact. You weren't just an aid worker, were you? You were captured by insurgents. But you were lucky. Someone died, didn't they, Cal? Because you got involved with things you shouldn't have. A woman you were close to, who trusted you lost her life.'

It's all I can do not to hold on to the wall to steady myself, but I have to keep it together, no matter what. 'Is this the plot of your latest novel, Bannen, because I don't know what the hell you're talking about.'

'When I found out you'd been an aid worker I decided to do a little digging about your time in the Middle East. I got in contact with a couple of war correspondents I know and one of them told me that you'd been held by insurgents.'

'How can he know that?' I snap, panicking inside.

'He has his sources. Credible sources,' Kit says. 'I met the source myself and he told me about the circumstances that led to you being captured. You may have claimed to be an aid worker, but that's only half the story, isn't it? You were a lot more than that and you ended up involving innocent civilians and getting one of them killed.'

I can't speak, my chest tightens.

Because maybe he's right.

The doubt, the fear that I was responsible, comes back to me. I definitely wasn't only an aid worker; that much is true, and one of my decisions did partly contribute to Soraya's death.

That's why his words make me feel physically sick and why I hate him for saying them.

Clinging on to control of my emotions by my fingernails, I laugh at him again. 'You're talking absolute rubbish.' Then another fear strikes me. 'What's Mawgan Cade got to do with this crap anyway? Has she been helping you make up your stories?'

'She really doesn't like you or the Penwiths, does she? She has serious issues of course — she came to my writers' talk to see me. She's no more going to write a bonkbuster than I'm going to rule over a small town and wear leopardskin, but she can look after herself. She dished a load of dirt on you and was happy to share her own story of how your father ruined her life. A regular home wrecker, wasn't he?

'You're lying about Mawgan Cade, talking crap about Syria and you're wrong about my dad and me. Liar!' I shout, losing it totally. I grab his jacket and he grunts as I force him up against the wall. I can't help myself. The rage, the desperation and fear takes over: It's been a long time since I felt this way, but at this moment I could kill Kit Bannen.

27

Demi

'Stop it! What the hell are you doing to each other?'

I fly up the alley, shouting at Kit and Cal. Cal has Kit by the collar of his coat, crushing him against the alley wall.

'For God's sake, Cal!'

Cal bunches Kit's coat in one fist. I don't think he heard me. Kit has his eyes closed like he's some kind of sacrifice. As if he's expecting Cal to hit him, as if he *wants* Cal to hit him.

I scream. I don't care if the whole town hears me. 'Cal! Don't do it!'

Cal's fist hangs in the air, inches from Kit's face. Kit's eyes are still shut. 'Go on,' Kit says. 'You know you want to. *Bro.*'

'Stop this now!'

'Keep out of this, Demi!'

'No, I won't. You total prats. I don't know what's caused this but you're like two stupid kids scrapping in the playground!'

Cal turns to look at me as if I'm a ghost. He blinks and then drops his hand. Kit opens his eyes and my stomach turns over. For God's sake, don't let him smile or laugh at Cal because that will tip him over the edge. Instead, Cal staggers backwards.

'What's going on? It's a miracle no one's

heard you or seen you.'

'You'll have to forgive Cal. He's had a bit of a shock. He's just found out he has a little brother.'

'What? Cal?'

Kit pushes himself off the wall, pulls his coat down.

'Kit claims he's my brother,' Cal says, breathing heavily.

'Half-brother, actually,' Kit corrects him, but I can hardly believe my ears. 'My name *is* Kit Bannen, but my full name is Christopher Penwith Bannen, though I rarely use the middle name. We're related, Cal and I. I'm his brother. That's my dirty little secret.'

'You're his brother? I don't understand. If that's true, why is it a dirty secret?' I say.

Cal sneers. 'Ignore him, Demi. He's just being a tosser.'

'Cal!'

'Yes, I know what you're going to say: Kit's our guest, although maybe not for much longer judging by tonight's performance.' He turns to Kit. 'You're not welcome at Kilhallon after this. I'll refund any advance rent you've paid, but you can pack your bags and get off my land tonight.'

'Cal. What's wrong? I know this must have come as a hell of a shock, but if Kit's telling the truth about being your brother, why are you reacting like this?'

'He's telling the truth about that,' Cal says quietly. 'Though I wouldn't believe a word of anything else he tells you.'

255

My confusion deepens. 'Kit? What have you done?'

'I knew you'd never tell her the truth,' Kit says to Cal, almost too quietly for me to hear.

Cal stares at him as if he'd like to blast Kit off the face of the planet. 'You wouldn't know the truth if it punched you in the face.'

I grab Cal's arm, afraid he'll push Kit up against the wall again. 'Cal, that's enough.'

Kit smiles and brushes himself down. 'Don't worry, Demi, I'll pack my bags and leave as requested. Forget the rent. I won't be asking for a refund.'

'You must have a refund. I'll arrange all that, but please, don't just go off like this. Not without telling me what's been going on. Why were you fighting?'

Kit tosses me a regretful smile, as if nothing has happened here tonight. 'I'm sorry, Demi, but I think I have to leave. I'll be gone first thing in the morning.'

He walks off down the alley.

'Wait, Kit!' I shout.

'Leave him!' Cal pulls me back and I push him away, though it's too late. Kit has already disappeared from view into the maze of streets in the fisherman's quarter. And even if I did run after him, it's obvious that Cal needs me more and has a lot of explaining to do. He lingers on the cobbles, his shoulders slumped and his face pale.

'Mind telling me what's been going on?'

Cal shrugs. 'You'd have to ask Kit.'

'I can't! He's gone because you told him to

piss off and almost throttled him, by the look of things. Whatever's gone on between you, you can't tell him to go away like that when he's shared something so incredible with you. And what does he mean, he knew you would never 'tell her the truth?' Tell who the truth? Is it something to do with your work? I know something bad happened to you out there. Is that what Kit's talking about?'

'Demi. Shut up!'

His shout bounces off the walls.

'Oh, shit, no.' Cal reaches for me but I stagger back, as if he'd slapped me. 'Kit's talking absolute crap. You must believe me. Please.' I've never heard Cal plead before and it makes me sick with worry.

'I believe anything you tell me. I trust you, Cal. Do you think Kit is making that stuff up about being your brother?'

'No. Shit. No, my dad probably spread his seed all over Cornwall. Hey, half the kids from Launceston to Land's End are probably his.'

'Cal. Please. It must have been such a shock to hear this. Maybe Kit felt rejected by your dad and can't let it go?'

'He did, but he should have got over it. He has a mother and a stepfather who love him, he has a very comfortable, cosy life.'

'Then why come down here and create trouble now?'

'Because he's an idiot. Crazy and bitter and angry about my father. Nothing else.' Cal breathes heavily. He can't seem to look me in the eye, which makes me angry.

257

'*You* don't trust *me*, do you? Or you'd tell me what else has gone on. I thought that by now, after all we've been through, you'd feel you could be honest with me,' I tell him.

His head snaps up. 'Look, I know we're close but we don't have to share everything, do we? There's absolutely nothing to tell.' His voice drips sarcasm that makes me feel mad and hurt. 'You don't tell me everything, do you, Demi?'

'I try to.'

'*Do* you?' he repeats.

'No, I suppose not.' My voice trails off, thinking of my visit to Mawgan's earlier in the year and her making me promise not to tell Cal.

'Then believe me that there's nothing more to discuss, or share, or talk about. My father got Kit's mother pregnant and then tried to forget all about it and pretend that Kit didn't exist. Perhaps, understandably, he's a little bit hurt about that. Well, boo hoo. We all have problems. He may be my brother but he's also a tosser who came back when he thought the business was doing well to piss in the pot and enjoy some kind of twisted revenge. And now he's sodding off back to London, so we can all get some peace. End of. Right?'

The last word is so loud it makes me jump.

Cal breathes hard. Then he shoves both hands through his hair and lets out a cry. 'Screw Kit Bannen. I knew he was bloody trouble from the moment I laid eyes on him!'

I'm trembling but also fired up with fury at the way Cal has spoken to me; he has shouted at me and thrown back my offers of help in my face.

'You are impossible,' I say quietly. 'Totally impossible. I'm glad I never moved in with you.'

'And I'm glad too, because I can have my own space to be as much of a bastard as I choose now without you trying to cure me of it all the time.' He shoves his hands through his hair again and groans. 'Demi! Demi. Oh shit, I'm sorry . . . I didn't mean it like that.'

'How did you mean it, then? I thought you wanted me to move into the farmhouse?'

'I do . . . but you pushed me into saying that. I was upset. Bloody Bannen! He's a fucking disaster. I do want you to move in.'

'I can't move in with you. You don't even know where you are, Cal. You're not even ready to live with yourself yet, let alone share your life with anybody else.'

28

'Hellooo, darling, how the devil are you and Mitch this morning?' Eva Spero trills down my ear first thing the morning after the festival, which I have to say, was the least festive event I've ever enjoyed in my life. Stifling a groan, I consider stabbing the off button and blaming the signal in my cottage. I'm hardly in the right frame of mind to chat about business after my sleepless night, but Eva can't be ignored.

'Fine. Good.'

'Only fine? That doesn't sound like the Demi I know. Is everything going OK with the cafe? Quiet season, I expect. Calm before the storm. Still can't tempt you to join me in Brighton?'

After last night's events with Cal, I'm dangerously close to saying yes. 'Thanks, but now I've got the place underway, I need to stick with it.'

'Well, your success is my loss, but I'm very happy to hear you're sticking with it. You need staying power in this business. Spero's would never have got off the ground if I'd thrown in the towel in the early days. Post-launch is the worst time, darling, especially as you opened at the end of the main season. Still, I trust the pre-Christmas period has kept you busy?'

'Half term was very busy, and we had a Bonfire Night supper and Christmas lunches have kept us very busy.' Slapping on a cheery voice, I snap out of my gloom and turn into the professional cafe owner again. Eva could be a big help to me, and she's already done way more for me than I could have expected.

'Great. Stick at it. Now, I have some news that should cheer you up no end. Remember we talked about doing a doggy cookbook? Well, my publisher was on the phone last night and they're very interested in the idea. In fact, they asked if you can come to a meeting in the smoke.'

'Wow. That sounds exciting.'

'It is. But the slight possible spanner in the works is that the editor wants us to go in and meet her on Monday? That's OK, isn't it?'

'Monday? We don't normally open on Monday, but we have Christmas events booked. It's a very busy time for us now December's about to start.'

'I know it's a bore, but if we don't get the ball rolling pronto, it will be too late. Publishing shuts down for aeons at Christmas. Everyone goes into hibernation until the sun appears again, darling.'

'I suppose the staff could manage without me for a day.'

'Great. Fantastic. It's at 12.30 in their central London office, which is next to Embankment tube station. I'll email all the details. I have to go. I've got a meeting with Otto and Jamie shortly and, more importantly, Betty needs her walkies on the beach. Byee . . . see you soon.'

As usual, trying to stop Eva is like trying to stop that big ball from *Indiana Jones* from squashing you. It's easier to go along with it, and this is a huge opportunity. But London? Me going to London to meet an editor of a big publishing house? That's beyond an opportunity, it's terrifying.

And that's the least of my problems.

Kit left this morning, refusing to let me refund the rest of his rent or talk about his row with Cal.

Cal's nowhere to be seen. He took the Land Rover home while Polly and I drove Jez's mate's van. Polly kept asking me if there was something the matter. She thinks it was to do with me seeing my dad again, but she gave up when I refused to speak about it, So now she's pissed off too.

Although I was shattered after the festival I didn't get much sleep last night, and I'm back in the cafe today as it's Saturday and we have some festive lunches and a mums' and toddlers' tea party this afternoon.

It's no use avoiding Cal, even if I wanted to — we have to speak sometime. During my break, I find him in the stables, rubbing down Dexter. Hanging back just outside the door, I watch him. His sleeves are rolled up and he's wearing his old riding boots. His forearms are still tanned after his summer outdoors and his muscles tense as he brushes the horse. He clicks his tongue at Dexter, whispering soothing words. The stable is warm after the chilly damp air of the farmyard and smells of leather and hay.

'Hi,' I say, stepping inside but keeping well back from the stall. I don't like horses, despite

Robyn's attempts to convert me.

'Mngggg,' Cal growls, without even stopping. Dexter pulls some hay from a basket while Cal scrapes the brush over his flanks. My upcoming trip has given me a chance to speak to him about a neutral subject and I hope we can move on.

'I just thought you ought to know that I'm going to London on Monday,' I say.

He ceases brushing and rests his hand on Dexter's neck, but doesn't turn and face me. 'Monday?'

'Yes. I know it's short notice, but Eva Spero wants me to meet an editor and it was the only time they could spare. We have a meeting about the doggy cookbook she mentioned to me at the Kilhallon launch event. There'll be money in it for us.'

Finally he pays attention to me.

'No, there'll be money for *you*, Demi. Anything you earn off this project is one hundred per cent your own. In fact, have you thought of opening your own separate business account? There could be a decent advance for this book, and there might be royalties, and spin-offs, even merchandise. You'll need a contract drawn up.'

'I know that. Eva's agent is dealing with it. But rights and merchandise? You think there will be all of that stuff? Eva did mention a line of doggy treats, but that was in the summer and I haven't had chance to think about it since then. To be honest, I thought she might have decided to forget it all.'

Especially after I decided to stay here. Just in

263

time I stop myself from saying the words.

He starts brushing Dexter again, even though the horse's flank gleams.

'So is there any chance of a lift to Penzance station first thing on Monday? I want to get the first train, but I can get a taxi or ask Polly to run me if you're busy.'

''S fine.' *Brush. Brush.* Dexter's coat will wear away in a moment.

'Cal, I hate it when we argue. Last night was very charged and we both said things we didn't mean. Kit too, I bet.'

'I meant every word I said about Bannen,' he says, sweeping his brush over Dexter's back in long, firm strokes that make me long to be stroked by his hands that way. 'But I *will* take you to the station.'

My patience snaps. 'Forget it. You don't have to.' Dropping the brush on a hay bale, he wheels round. 'I don't *have* to do anything.'

'Neither of us do. Obviously.'

We square up to each other. My skin bristles and I hate Cal in this moment. But I also love him. I love the way his dark eyes glint with fury. I love the way he smells of hard work and horse, and I love the heat radiating from his body. I love the smear of mud across his cheek that he hasn't noticed because he'd never dream of looking in a mirror for a second more than he has to. I love the fact that he hasn't shaved for two days at least. I long to feel the scrape of stubble across my cheek and his mouth on my skin. I hate him and I want him to take me right now in the stable. As long as Dexter is out of reach . . .

'Six o'clock early enough for you, or will you be having a lie-in?' he says, daring me to say it *is* too early (it definitely is), and to ask him more about his row with Kit.

'No. Though half-past five would be even better.'

'Half-five sharp it is then,' he says. 'Meet you by the Land Rover.'

'*Fine.*'

He picks up the brush again and turns his back on me. I walk out of the stable, hearing the *brush brush* in my ears, louder than ever, and Dexter snickering in pleasure. I wish I hadn't agreed to get up at five a.m., I wish Cal would open up to me, and most of all, I wish I was in Dexter's position.

29

Cal

Dexter shuffles restlessly as we walk along the cliff tops and past the engine houses. I rode him out this morning, after I'd dropped Demi at the station, hoping the fresh air would clear my mind. He seems to sense my mood and has been restive and nervy since I tacked him up. Is no one at Kilhallon my friend these days? Have I ballsed up my life — and those of so many others — so much that I deserve it? Isla, Soraya, Esme, Demi . . .

My curse echoes off the walls of the engine house and my breath mists the air like Dexter's. As I urge him to walk on, his hooves ring out on the hard earth. It's rare to have a frost at Kilhallon, but on this raw early December morning, the grass and bracken are rimmed with frost. Shrivelled leaves and ferns crunch as we walk along.

Demi and I made it all the way to the station before one of us caved in. Ten miles and neither of us spoke a single word. When we reached the car park, I bought a ticket even though I could have parked for twenty minutes free. She must have known that, but she didn't say anything. She waited in the car while I went to the machine, wanting to talk to me. She could have gone into the station, but she didn't.

So I cracked. I asked her if she was OK and she muttered, 'Yes, fine.'

Fine? That one word, 'fine', made me even more frustrated. I wanted to kiss her there and then, and a whole lot more. The thought of us making out in the back of the car has driven me wild all day. Not being able to have Demi has only made me want her even more. I can't blame her for being upset about my reaction after the festival. No matter how shocked I was by Bannen's 'revelations', I shouldn't have lost control the way I did, or taken things out on Demi.

Maybe I should have told her what happened months ago, but I can't. I don't know what her reaction will be. It's complicated, what happened, but it's also simple.

Simply put, Kit was right. I did get involved in something I shouldn't have in Syria, and indirectly Soraya — and possibly Esme — were lost. Kit Bannen may think he knows what happened out there, but he only has the story second hand. He can't know what it was like that day, or the decisions I made or how I felt. And yes, I do feel responsible for the events that unfolded. I can't help it. How do I start to explain that to Demi, who's never been further than Truro until today? How do I tell her without making excuses for myself? How can I make her understand?

What's the point in telling her when she'll probably be gone soon anyway? This trip to London is bound to remind her of the life she could have, no matter how romantic her notions

267

about running Demelza's are.

I mustn't kid myself that she's making a success of the place because I was stupid or generous enough to give her a chance. Demi Jones would have overcome any obstacle thrown in her path. I'm only a waymarker on her route to the life she deserves.

I'm holding her back by asking her to move into the farmhouse. I'm being monumentally selfish, trying to bind her to me more tightly. I won't ask her again.

30

The high roof arches over me as I step down to the platform at Paddington station. Strangely enough, the roof is as beautiful as a Kilhallon sky in its own way, but it also makes me feel very small. Everyone rushes for the ticket barriers as if they're racing in a suitcase marathon. I'm a tiny pebble stuck in the sand as the tide of people flows round me.

It's my first time in London and I hate to sound like a hick from the sticks, but it's even more of a shock to the system than I expected. My mood isn't helped by the lack of sleep I've had recently. The broken nights when I've lain awake, worrying about my dad and his girlfriend, and about Cal and Kit. I thought my life was on track, with everything going better than I could ever have hoped a year ago. Yet the things that should really matter to me, like family and relationships, are as much of a mess as ever.

For the next few hours I must try to set personal problems aside and focus on this meeting. *If* I can ever make it to the publishers' office.

Juggling a bottle of water, my bag and a laptop bag borrowed from Cal, I queue at the barrier. Am I the only person fumbling for my ticket? The only one wishing I'd worn my old trainers not the heeled suede boots I bought from the big Next at Hayle? It's hard to deal with the multiple assaults on my senses: the rumble of train engines, the announcements, guards' whistles and distant sirens. The smells: fast food, coffee and diesel. On the other side of the barrier, police cradle their guns and people hurry past, all with somewhere to go and people to see.

A young woman almost knocks my bag out of my hand and mutters something about 'looking where you're going'. Snapping out of my doziness, I try to remind myself I'm a businesswoman now, and a soon-to-be author. Like Kit — except nothing like Kit. He'd be the one telling people to look where they're going, the one with a purpose. How could I have got him so wrong?

I really thought he was OK. A bit crotchety and stressed out, but not the bitter and nasty individual he's shown himself to be. He's worse than Mawgan in one way; at least she makes it obvious she's a vicious cow, rather than hiding it under a veneer of charm.

No point dwelling on Kit now. I need to find the publishers' office.

I'd like to try the tube, but I'm so worried about getting lost and popping out on the wrong side of London that I decide to walk, with the help of an app on my phone.

Walking through the streets past the luxury shops ought to be glamorous and exciting, but you could never be alone here, never experience silence apart from the sounds of birdsong, wind and waves. London is exciting, horrifying, scary, amazing. Kilhallon is so small, so remote, a backwater. Is that right for me?

Should I be here? Or there?

It's bitterly cold out on the streets, so I tuck my scarf into my Puffa jacket, glad of the gloves I brought with me. The jacket was a present from Polly, who said it was an unwanted eBay purchase by her daughter. However, the sale ticket was still in it from the discount store in Penzance so I guess Polly must have bought it there for me. It's slightly too big but looks surprisingly stylish with the oversized soft pink scarf I treated myself to. Teamed with my smartest black skinnies and a newish plain-grey sweater, I feel quite presentable. Not that I've any idea what publishing people wear. What if they're all in power suits like Mawgan Cade? Or floating around in bohemian dresses? In the end, I decided they might look like Isla and modelled my ensemble on that, which makes me laugh at myself.

The skies over London are grey, but the sparkle around me makes up for the gloom. The windows of the shops are eye-popping with their Christmas displays. The choice on offer and the prices on display make my jaw drop. There are luxury candles in beautiful packaging, spectacular shoes that Mawgan would probably kill for, handbags that cost as much as a second-hand car and watches that would buy a house in St Trenyan. I treat myself to a pumpkin latte from a tiny cafe in a side street and thread my way through the shoppers hurrying to and fro. Some are weighed down by their bags.

A guy huddles in a filthy sleeping bag next to the tube entrance. He could be twenty or fifty,

271

he's so shrunken and grey it's hard to tell. Most people step over him, without a second glance, but his dog, a terrier, yips at me. I throw a two pound coin in his collecting bowl and long to take the dog home to Kilhallon, though I know the terrier is probably the only thing the man has in the world.

Finally, after a few wrong turns, the river looms ahead of me and I'm outside a huge glass tower that seems to pierce the sky. Security guards stand on either side of the doors and people in jackets, with huge scarves wrapped around their necks, scurry in and out.

'Demi!'

Eva waves at me and scuttles over on her scarlet heeled boots. She wears an emerald green coat and reminds me of one of Santa's elves. Oh God, I must not think that or I might burst into uncontrollable giggles. I'm already so nervous and wound up about Cal and Kit, it wouldn't take much to have me in hysterics.

What? Is that Betty in her *handbag*? It can't be . . .

Two huge black eyes peep over the top of Eva's Burberry tote. It *is* Betty! She yips at me when Eva approaches.

'Demi! You made it, you clever girl. How was your journey? Awful? You did travel first- not cattle-class, I hope?'

'Um . . .'

She grabs my arm, almost toppling over with the weight of Betty in her bag.

'You brought Betty with you,' I say, stroking the pug's ears. Betty closes her eyes in pleasure.

A little pink tongue laps my fingers, soothingly.

'Yes, of course, darling. Betty pines for me if I leave her, so I bring her with me — and the editor adores her. We'll need the dogs for the PR shots, of course. Did you not think of bringing Mitch?'

I picture Mitch racing around the editor's office, knocking over piles of books and cocking his leg up a table leg, and cringe.

'Mitch in London? You have to be kidding . . . '

'Good point. I suppose he is rather energetic.' She gazes down at Betty, perfectly at home in her Burberry cocoon. 'I must admit, Betty is such a city girl. She can't wait to hit Bond Street with me whenever she comes up. There's a darling doggy boutique in one of the arcades where the assistants worship her. We just have to go the next time we're here, but first, let's get this meeting over. Now, don't be afraid of your editor. They're all terribly glossy and bouncy, and all terribly young. Not much older than you, in fact, so just let me deal with them. You smile and nod enthusiastically to everything they say and then we'll go away and do exactly what we want anyway. Comprendo?'

'Um . . . '

How can I tell her I wasn't that afraid of my editor until she said this? The doors of the tower whoosh open. Betty yaps excitedly, but my turn churns like a washing machine.

'Smile, darling!' Eva trills as we collect our passes. 'This is publishing!'

A couple of hours later, I stagger out of the

publishers' tower, punch drunk with all the information and the surreal nature of our meeting. Eva took it all in her stride, while Betty curled up in a corner on a dog bed specially provided by our editor, who really was only a few years older than me. She also did look a little bit like Isla, or a slightly edgier version of her.

Now, we're crawling along the streets inside a black cab, with Betty sitting on my lap while Eva feeds me gossip about some of the celebrity chefs whose faces beamed at me from the covers of the books and posters in the publishers' offices.

We're going to call our book *Dog's Dinner! Healthy Treats for Canines and their Humans.* It will include some of the doggy treats I already offer at the cafe plus the summer lollies I tested for the launch. It will also include some nutritious recipes for on-the-go snacks and picnic food for dog walkers that Eva's chefs and I will develop together. The editor had already drawn up a proposed schedule and suggested I set to work as soon as possible during my 'quiet period' at Kilhallon. She may be really clever and know a lot about publishing, but she's clearly forgotten that Christmas is about to happen and that I run a seasonal business.

Eva's told me not to worry, that we have 'heaps of time' and that she and her home economics team will do a lot of the work, but I'm not so sure. In this case, I think I might have bitten off more than I can chew.

Eva takes me for lunch afterwards and starts to talk about developing a brand of healthy dog treats called Mitch & Betty's, but she says she'd need to talk to her marketing team about that and they'd have to discuss it with a manufacturer. It's all a far cry from me trailing cakes with Mitch in my cottage. In fact the world seems very big indeed. I have a sense of not being part of it, or floating above it or watching another person being me today.

'So, darling, I'd absolutely love to show you around but I have to get my train back to Brighton. I've a dinner meeting with,' she lowers her voice and whispers the name of a guy who presents a motoring show. 'A total bore of course, and a boor to boot, ha ha! But one has to suffer these people. He loves Spero's to bits so I can't afford to upset him. You don't mind me abandoning you in the big city, do you?' Eva races on like an express train, leaving me flattened on the tracks.

'No. It's fine. Really. My train leaves in a few hours and I'd enjoy a look round.'

'Oh! You've time to have lots of fun before then, I hope? You must visit that canine boutique and take something funky home for Mitch. Put it on my account, my love.'

'No, I couldn't do that.'

'You could and you will. Here's my card. Hand it over and tell them I sent you. Email me a pic of Mitch afterwards. I do think he'd look divine in one of their Pucci scarves.'

I'm sure Mitch would look divine in any scarf, but I have no intention of spending hundreds of pounds on one. So, as Eva kisses me and holds up Betty so she can be kissed too, I plan on walking around one of the parks or maybe taking

275

a bus tour or even just sitting in Covent Garden with a coffee and watching the world go by.

'Are you sure you're OK, darling? Only you seem a little absent today? Everything all right at home?'

'It's fine. We're busy with the Christmas rush and we had our Harbour Lights Festival on Friday evening, as well as Christmas trade.'

She claps her hands together in delight. 'Harbour Lights Festival? I bet it was gorgeous with all those kitsch fairy lights and rugged fisherfolk with their twinkly boats. I so wish I'd been there. It sounds utterly charming.'

'Charming?' An image fills my mind of Cal holding Kit against a wall, Kit's eyes full of hatred for Cal. 'Yes . . . it was, erm, very eventful and lively.'

Eva beams and clicks her fingers at Betty, who hops into her bag. She scoops up both in her arms. 'Well, have a safe journey back to Cornwall and we'll meet again soon. I'll be in touch. Toodle pip.'

Holding up Betty's paw in a farewell wave, Eva skips outside, or skips as much as a small woman carrying a dog in a bag can do. I think I saw the restaurant manager hailing a cab for her. After a few discreet calming breaths, I go to the loo to sort myself out. It's as I dig out my purse in the marble cloakrooms of the restaurant to check I still have my train ticket after all the surreal craziness of the past few hours that Kit's business card falls out onto the floor of the cloakroom.

Kit Bannen: Author and Freelance Journalist

He gave it to me a few weeks ago and the card is a bit frayed now and slightly soggy on one end from an encounter with Mitch's jowls, but I can still make out the mobile number.

Not that I'll be calling him.

I sit on the padded chair in front of the gilt-edged mirror in the cloakroom and stare at the card.

If I called him, he'd probably cut me off or tell me to get lost.

And Cal would hit the roof if he found out.

Not that I'm answerable to Cal.

Or afraid of Kit.

I put the card back in my bag. Kit told Isla he lived in West London, and that she and Luke must have sometimes drunk in the same pub as him without knowing it. I know where he lives: he had to give his address when he booked the cottage. I have a couple of hours to spare. I *could* call on Kit and try to reason with him. Ask him why he was so cruel to Cal . . . I faced down Mawgan Cade and nothing terrible happened so I could try talking to Kit.

No, that would be even worse than phoning him.

And Cal would go nuts if he found out.

I apply one of Tamsin's latest lip gloss samples in the mirror and touch up my face with a bit of tinted moisturiser.

Cal would never find out if I paid Kit a call, and what's the worst Kit can do to me?

Then again, Cal and Kit's relationship — or lack of it — is none of my business. And Cal would say I should put my own house in order before I interfere in his life.

Yet, I am here. So is Kit.

I pick up my bag and walk out of the restaurant. The greeter at the door offers to call me a cab, but I say no thanks.

Outside, the wind is colder and the sun is setting somewhere behind all the concrete and buildings. The shop windows glitter even more brightly and if anything there are more people crowding the pavements.

The tube station is opposite. If I set off now, how long would it take me to get to Kit's area of West London? I can use my walking app to find his house and I have his address on my Kilhallon booking app.

A text beeps: it's Cal: All OK?

I smile. He *does* care about me. Even if I won't move in with him and he's volatile and secretive and infuriating, I care about him too. I can't stand seeing him so unhappy and eaten up with hurt over Kit's behaviour.

Taking my life in my hands, I scuttle across the road between the cabs and reach the tube station. The line from here would take me straight to Hammersmith without me even changing trains. I know he lives very near a tube station because I heard him tell Polly . . .

Surely, I can't make things any worse than they are?

31

The terraced house in front of me looks a little like the one on the telly where several people were found cut up and stuffed down the drains. At least three different families must occupy this one house because there are three separate names next to the three buzzers by the glossy dark-blue entrance door with its brass fittings. I don't know why I thought that Kit might not live here. Perhaps it's because he's deceived us about so many things. However, the bottom flat has a name printed next to the buzzer. It says C. Bannen. No mystery there then.

The app made it surprisingly easy to find the building, but now I'm outside, I don't know what to do. The sensible half of me keeps shouting at me to run away and get on the tube this minute. Yet here I am, standing on the pavement, gazing up at the house. Oh my God, what if Kit's already spotted me, lurking here on the steps as if I'm checking out his flat to burgle it?

Inside my gloves, my palms are sweaty. Yuk. My heart is beating fast as I lift my finger and buzz Kit's name.

And my mind's on the frosty way Cal and I parted.

'Yeah? Who is it?'

Oh God, he sounds pissed off and he'll definitely be pissed off when he finds out it's me at the door.

'Um . . . er . . . '

'Look, mate, if you're selling something, don't bother.'

'I'm not selling anything. It's me!'

Pause. 'Who's me?'

'Demi.'

'Demi?'

'Demi Jones. From Kilhallon?'

Silence. My heart thumps. 'I was just passing, and I thought I'd pop in and see how you are . . . '

He may have sworn but the intercom crackled so I'll give him the benefit of the doubt. There's a long silence and I am itchy with tension and on the verge of running off as fast as I can.

'I suppose you'd better come up.'

Click. Burr. He's gone. Well, he was hardly hanging out the bunting, but he didn't call the police on me either. I wish I had Mitch with me, though I don't know what he could do to help.

Taking a deep breath, I push open the door and walk into the gloomy hallway.

Kit answers the door to his flat.

'If you've come to try and promote some brotherly love between us, you're wasting your time.'

'I haven't come to do that. Like I said, I was passing . . . '

'Passing? From Cornwall?'

'I came up to London to visit my publisher. I know. That sounds weird to me too. I'm writing a dog cookbook with the food guru Eva Spero and we had a meeting with our editor today in her office.'

Aware that I'm babbling, I try to stem the flow. Kit stares at me as if I'd said I'd been to the international space station. I'm not sure he can believe what I'm saying, then he grunts, very much like Cal. 'Which publisher?'

'Marchmont. Our cookbook's going to be published by their non-fiction imprint.'

He nods. 'I'm with Marchmont, but the crime imprint. My editor's office is on the top floor.'

'I had to go to the third floor. I don't know anyone else there.'

'Right.'

'Is your book finished?' I ask, worried he'll close the door.

'I'm trying to finish the first draft now. I have to send it off by close of play tomorrow, which is why I wasn't too amused to find a cold caller at my door.'

'I'm sorry to have disturbed you. Do you want me to leave?' I hold my breath.

'Not yet. Come in.' He points to a black leather sofa so I sit down. His flat is far messier than I'd expected. There are papers and books everywhere, and dirty plates and mugs litter the coffee table. In the corner of the room, a laptop sits on a small desk, the screen glowing. The high ceiling has an elaborate plaster decoration in the middle which shows me this must have been a grand house once. This situation reminds me of my visit to Mawgan Cade, except I have a horrible feeling that Kit might be an even harder nut to crack.

'You can say your piece.'

'I don't know what my piece is, except I can't

281

understand why you blame Cal so much for what his father did. Mawgan does the same, but she's got more reason. Cal rejected her, or so she thinks in her twisted mind. She *is* completely twisted, you know.'

'I'm sure she probably is but that's not my concern now, though I understand her antipathy towards Cal to a degree.' Kit's tone is as chilly as the wind swirling outside the window and I'm not sure what antipathy is but I'm pretty sure it's not friendly.

'But Cal's never done you any harm. Is it Kilhallon you want?' I ask.

He snorts. 'Kilhallon? If you think this is about money and me wanting to claim my rightful inheritance, you're wrong. I wanted some kind of acknowledgement that I existed and that I mattered and that Cal actually cared. You can tell me that I'm damaged and bitter if you like, but that's the way I feel.'

'Is it about me? Me and Cal?'

He laughs nastily. 'I don't think you understand.'

'Help me understand, then.'

'You'll have to ask Cal, not that he'll tell you,' he says sharply.

'What do you mean?'

'Nothing. If he won't share the information, I'm not surprised.'

'But you're going to share whatever it is, aren't you? Cal told me you're not just an author, and that you work for a newspaper. You're going to write something bad about Cal, aren't you? Because you don't like him and you want some kind of revenge on his dad?'

He seems surprised that I've worked this out for myself, but actually, I was guessing at best. My stomach swirls at the prospect.

'Whatever I decide won't be done out of revenge but because the truth should come out.'

'What truth? Why won't you tell me? What's he supposed to have done? And you're lying to yourself if you think hurting Cal is some kind of public service. That's a pile of crap.'

He stands up. 'You'd better leave. You're in way over your head.'

'Maybe I am, but you're as bad as Cal. Patronising me, thinking I won't or can't understand what's going on even if I don't know all the details. Cal would never do anything wicked or cruel. Not unless there was a very good reason.'

He walks to the door. 'Go back to your cafe, Demi. Make your cakes and mince pies . . . ' Then he rakes his hands through his blond mop, just like Cal does, and the likeness between them is so obvious it makes the hairs on the back of my neck tingle.

'Screw it, you didn't deserve that from me. I'm sorry for insulting your intelligence, but I mean what I say. Ask Cal what he's been involved in and don't try and stop me from doing what I think is right.'

Even though I'm trembling and Kit's clearly itching for me to leave. I stand my ground. 'What do you think is *right*? Spreading lies about Cal and ruining his life? I don't understand any of this. I will leave, but this thing you know

— would you really share this 'story' if Cal wasn't your brother?'

'I don't know. But what I really need to ask myself, is would I keep it hidden because he *is?* Go home and sort your own family life out, Demi, and don't interfere in mine. From what I heard at the festival, you have enough problems.'

'You were there?'

'I heard, though by chance. Actually, your life is none of my business. Cal's right about that. And mine is none of yours. I'm sorry if that sounds harsh. Sort your own shit out, as they say. Forgive me for not offering tea and cake.'

He opens the door and I know there's no point in staying. He really is a harder nut to crack than Mawgan, because he's clever and cool and that scares me.

'I think you're better than this,' I tell him as he shows me into the hall again.

'I doubt that very much,' he says and shuts the door behind me, quietly but firmly, leaving me in the dark.

32

Two weeks have passed since my visit to London and I could easily imagine that my trip was a dream. I haven't heard from Kit, not that I expected to after the blunt way he asked me to leave his flat.

It's past the middle of December now, with less than two weeks to go till Christmas Day itself and I've been throwing myself into the full swing of the festive run-up at Demelza's. Even though I've been up to my eyes in tinsel, turkey and mince pies since I returned from London, I've also had to plan ahead for the summer when Kilhallon will be hosting weddings. Yesterday, I booked a stall at a wedding fair in Truro in the new year to promote Kilhallon as a wedding venue and Demelza's as an outside caterer. We've also had an email from our VIP couple, 'Bonnie and Clyde' to say they're coming to visit after Christmas. That will be scary.

Our Christmas custom is boosted by a few hardy walkers and holiday makers who've come down for bargain 'turkey and tinsel' breaks in local hotels, plus the odd surfer who likes to live dangerously in the winter seas we've been enjoying. When I took Mitch for a run before work, the waves were smashing against the cliffs on the far side of the cove. I keep wondering if we're going to lose another chunk of the coast path at this rate. The surfers love the conditions though and have been in the thick of the action at local beaches.

'You're not telling me you've been out in this?' Nina asks one of them. He's part of a group of half a dozen laid-back, bronzed dudes who've been occupying the corner of the cafe and main-lining hot chocolate, pasties and slabs of Christmas cake. They'd been catching some waves just along the coast and decided to come here to 'fuel up and chill out'. I recognise a couple of the guys who used to hang out at Sheila's Beach Hut.

The guys laugh at us when we express our horror, and proudly show us terrifying footage of them riding huge waves that they've uploaded to YouTube from their GoPros. I don't mind, they can be as crazy as they want as long as they keep visiting the cafe.

We closed to the public at three and before it got dark I gave Mitch another run along the cliff tops so I could take a look at the monster surf. The waves were almost breaking over one of the old engine houses that clings to a ledge on a far headland. Though Mitch hates the lead, I've kept him on the long rein because the wind is blowing a hooley. His leg is almost back to normal now, but I still want to be super careful with him around the uneven ground until I'm confident he's fully recovered.

Seeing the huge breakers pounding Kilhallon Cove itself, I decide not to risk descending the slippery, twisty coast path. I hope the walkers I can see on the opposite side of the cove don't bother either. They could easily be washed off the bottom part of the path by a rogue wave. Two guys have already had to be rescued by the RNLI after they were swept off a rock while they were angling near Cape Cornwall.

Mitch and I stop by a stone stile and I watch the surf pounding the coastline, throwing up spray. Every now and then, fine droplets mist my face and when I stick out my tongue, I can taste salt in the air. The sea is angry, a boiling, seething grey mass battering the cliffs. We're definitely going to lose more sections of coast path one day soon. As long as the cafe is in one piece though, that's the main thing. It's stood here for over two hundred years so I think we'll be safe.

Pulling my hood over my beanie hat, I lead Mitch back towards the cafe, trying to make a mental to do list. The wind lashes my face and it's started to sleet. Icy needles sting my bare skin and I can't wait to get back inside the cafe.

With Mitch safely shut inside the farmhouse with Polly for company, I dash back to the cafe. The surfers have gone but a book club are arriving soon for a private Christmas afternoon tea. I wonder whether to ask them if they've heard of Kit, but decide against it. It's also very tempting to mention the cookbook, but Eva's agent told us not to tell anyone until we've signed the contracts and it's been announced in the book press.

When I got home from London a couple of weeks ago, Cal asked me how I got on with the publisher, naturally, but I just told him it was all fine. I think Cal was disappointed I didn't have more to say, but I had my mind on my visit to Kit. I definitely didn't mention that, of course, and now I wish I hadn't gone to see him. In hindsight, calling on him seems stupid and desperate and it definitely hasn't helped. Cal's cool and distant and I'm worried that it's not only Kit's threats that are bothering him. I know he's tired and stressed — we're both ready for a break after working flat out since autumn, and all the ups and downs.

I could be wrong, but I feel as if Cal's backed off from me since the row we had at the Harbour Lights Festival, as if he wants to cool things right down between us. We're speaking to each other again and I don't think anyone would know, from the outside, that there was anything wrong between us. Yet *I* know, and Cal is acting as if he wants to keep away from me, emotionally and physically. I told him he wasn't ready to live with himself, let alone me, but his remoteness still hurts. If we're ever going to move on, sooner or later one of us has to break the ice and I suspect it will have to be me.

33

December 22nd, morning

'*The coastal communities of West Cornwall are bracing themselves for a miserable Christmas as spring tides and high winds combine to create a storm surge that will threaten the north and west of the county. Mayor of St Trenyan, Kerren St Minver, is advising all residents and businesses within half a mile of the harbour to take action immediately as the 'hundred-year' storm is set to reach its peak in the early hours of tomorrow. Stay tuned for bulletins and information . . .*'

'I don't like the sound of that at all.' Polly turns the radio down in the kitchen of the farmhouse. 'Though it doesn't surprise me. It's been working itself up to a hell of a storm for the past few days.'

'You don't think Greg Stennack is exaggerating? You know what Radio St Trenyan's like. They love to make a mountain out of a molehill.'

'He could be, I suppose, but as I say, I've lived here a long time and I have a very bad feeling about this.'

Cal walks in from the yard, rain running off his waxed hat. 'What are they saying?' he asks, as Polly gives him a withering glare for dripping on the tiles.

'That it's going to be bad,' I say.

'I thought as much. Well, all we can do is be

289

prepared. I've serviced the generator and we've plenty of diesel for it, in case the power goes off. We should be able to power the farmhouse and guest cottages, but we'd better go round and warn everyone of what to expect.'

But what should they expect? I've seen storms and high tides before, and one of them brought a tree down on the house in the summer, but a hundred-year storm sounds very scary.

'At least we won't be flooded out up here. Apart from possible power cuts, we'll be OK with a bit of luck,' Cal says. 'It's the poor buggers down in St Trenyan I pity.'

'There was a very high tide combined with terrible gales a few years back, one February when you were away,' Polly says grimly. 'And I wouldn't want to go through that worry again.'

'I remember that, but I was working and living in Truro then, so we missed the worst of the flooding,' I say.

'That tide damaged a couple of properties round here, but we escaped a lot better than people further up the coast. There were homes destroyed and flooded out right into Devon. But I do recall a proper storm surge when I was a little girl. I couldn't have been more than four or five, but I've never forgotten it. Waves as big as houses breaking over the harbour, there were. The harbourmaster's office was wrecked and hundreds of people were out of their homes for weeks and some for months. God knows, I hope we don't have that again.'

I shudder and hope Polly's memory has exaggerated how bad the weather was in her youth. I think of Sheila and her cafe, slap bang on the beach front. Tamsin's Spa is in the back streets, a little higher up, so it should be OK. We're all in trouble if the water gets *that* high.

Cal sits down at the table. 'Let's hope so. We'll just have to wait and see,' he says firmly. 'Demi — are you opening today?'

'Yes, and tomorrow if we can, even if only for a couple of hours. There are already guests arriving for the Christmas week and they'll want a cosy place to hang out in this weather.'

'OK. You go ahead and do what you need to, but be careful on the cliff top, the wind's very strong so make your own judgement about whether it's safe to have people walking around up there so close to the edge. Shall we muck in and speak to the guests? There's no need to alarm them,' he says firmly, directing his comment at Polly, 'but forewarned is fore-armed.'

December 22nd, evening

Waves crash over the harbour wall, engulfing the spot where our stall was sited during the Harbour Lights. The lights have been switched off for safety reasons. Large trade wheelie bins are picked up and flung around like children's toys.

'Whoa! Keep back,' a policewoman warns Cal and I as we watch the water slopping over the slipway and onto the quayside. As soon as we realised that the coming storm was a significant threat, we drove down to help people prepare for the worst. We've been filling sandbags on the beach and helping people move their possessions to upper floors, but there's nothing we can do to stop the elements.

A huge wave rips one of the smaller stockings from the harbour wall and hurls it against the front of the ice-cream parlour. Luckily, the owner boarded up the windows.

Rain and salty spray batter our faces, stinging my eyes. Dirty foam tops the swollen tide and spatters the cobbles on the quay.

'What about Sheila's? Will she be OK?' Cal asks me.

'The cafe is well sandbagged, but it's not even high tide for another hour. She's elevated above the beach and we've never had a tide reach that far before, even the last two times. We'll just have to hope.'

Cal, I know now's not the time, but there's something I have to tell you. And ask you.

The words stay inside my head. I want to tell him that I saw Kit, and to ask him again about what happened to him in the Middle East. What was so awful that Kit wants to print a story about him? I believe what I told Kit: Cal would never do anything to deliberately hurt anyone.

We watch the waves, in silence, standing close together, but so far apart.

'Hey there! Could you give us a hand moving some stock upstairs?'

The man from Quayside Gallery calls to us. The water is already lapping the top of the quay, metres from his doorway.

'Coming!' I say and we run to help him. Our own problems will have to wait a while longer.

34

December 23rd, morning

'*It's the day before Christmas Eve: a day when most of us will be putting the finishing touches to the tree, defrosting the turkey and dashing out for last-minute presents. But as the sun rises over the Cornish village of St Trenyan, a less festive scene could not be imagined. In the cold light of day, the devastation wreaked by last night's unprecedented storm surge is clear to see. Scores of homes and businesses around the harbour and neighbouring streets are flooded, and debris litters the streets. Hundreds of people from St Trenyan and other coastal villages will be unable to spend Christmas in their own homes, and businesses will be closed throughout the busy Christmas tourist season. For now, the festivities are on hold and the clear-up begins.*'

A few yards away from me, the TV reporter stands next to the harbourmistress's office in his wellies and cagoule. The morning sun shines down from an almost cloudless blue sky over the harbour. Seagulls circle and perch on rooftops, screaming as they always do. But other than that, I'd hardly recognise my own town.

The waters have receded on the outgoing tide, but there's still water slopping around in hollows and crevices. The harbour and streets are littered with debris; seaweed, wheelie bins. A wrecked rowing boat lies in the circle where the Fisherman's Choir give their concerts and the twisted frame of a Christmas tree washes to and fro on the gentle swell. A group of people are dragging the shark-themed Christmas light up the jetty. Others are sweeping water from their homes and businesses and piling up waterlogged stock and furniture. Pipelines snake from fire engines into houses and shops.

It seems cruel that the sun is shining so brightly after a night that none of us will ever forget, no matter how much we want to. Cal stayed overnight in town, while I went home late to help Polly make sure our guests were safe and warm. Polly showed me how to operate the generator in case we need it over the holiday, because more high tides are predicted.

At first light, I drove down to town. From the hilltop car park, things seemed relatively normal, apart from the emergency services, electricity and water company vans. Down here at the harbour side, I can hardly believe I'm in the same town. Most of the buildings that have suffered are businesses, but a few of the cottages are holiday homes, and a handful are occupied by local families.

Stopping for a quick word of sympathy with a couple of locals, I find Tamsin in hot-pink wellies helping the owner of the pasty kitchen to clear out her shop. Her salon has escaped, though her roof has leaked in the torrential rain and damaged the ceiling in her treatment room. She's cancelled today's and tomorrow's Christmas Eve appointments to help her neighbours salvage what they can. Judging by the range of the accents I hear as people come to lend a hand lugging our ruined fixtures, lots of guests and tourists are helping too. I want to help everyone, but I know I can't so I head for the one place that may need me most.

Sheila stands outside the Beach Hut, surrounded by chairs and tables, telling her waiter, Henry, what to do with the sodden furniture. He often didn't bother to turn up when I worked for Sheila and I'm surprised but glad he's put in an appearance now. Other locals and emergency personnel buzz in and out of the building, and a hose winds its way out of the cafe, pumping water down a drain. Sheila waves when she spots me and I hurry over. Not knowing what to say, I hug her tightly. When I let her go, her eyes glisten with tears. Like many of the faces I've seen, hers is grey and drawn. I doubt if many people have had much sleep in this coastal part of Cornwall.

'Are you OK?' I ask, letting her go. She's shaking, poor thing. I want to hug her again, but don't want to make her cry.

'Yes, course I am. There are so many people much worse off than us, though I still can't quite believe it . . . ' She pauses to survey the wreckage around her. 'All these years I've lived here I never thought the sea would take the Beach Hut.'

'Me neither. I'm really, really sorry, Sheila.'

'Like I say, it could have been even more disastrous. There's been some water damage to the ground floor service area and we've lost a few chairs and tables that we couldn't rescue before the tide came up, but my flat's fine. With a lot of hard work, we'll be open again for the New Year. How are things at Kilhallon?' she asks.

'Oh, we're fine,' I say, hoping I don't sound smug. 'A few loose slates, a lot of mud and we've lost power, but Cal's rigged up the old generator so the guests are happy. Cal's helping out from the emergency centre in the community hall, but I wanted to come down here, to see how you are. What can I do to help? Shall I help you clear up?'

'Thanks, love, that means a lot to me, but my niece and the other staff are already here. Even Henry decided to forego a really gnarly day on the water, as he put it, to lend a hand. Bless him. You go and help people who need it more.'

'If you're sure. Has Mawgan been round to see the damage? This is her property, after all.'

'Mawgan? You're joking, aren't you? She's swanned off to Australia!'

'Australia? On holiday?'

'To see her mother, apparently. A spur-of-the-moment decision. The woman from The Bag Boutique heard her boasting about how dreadful it had been to try and get some business-class flights at such short notice and how much it had cost her.'

So Mawgan has gone down under with Andi and Robyn. What a turn-up — but how vile for the girls that Mawgan might be with them, even if she is at the other end of the plane. I bet I'll have loads of emails and Facebook messages about it.

'OK. Will you be all right? What about Christmas Day?' I ask Sheila.

'I was already going to my niece's. Though my own flat is dry, there's no power yet. Some people have nowhere to go. What a way to spend Christmas, eh?'

As soon as I'm certain that Sheila doesn't need my help, I leave her with a promise to return on the day after Boxing Day, and I head back to the community centre, which is acting as the hub of the rescue and salvage efforts. There are about a dozen older people, and a couple of young families, sitting on chairs or on the floor. The Rev Bev, wearing a snowman jumper, dog collar and reindeer ears, is behind the serving hatch, simultaneously trying to hand out cups of tea, soothe a distressed toddler and answer her mobile. Other people bustle in and out — the RNLI in their orange dry suits, the fire service, police, fishermen, traders, coastguard volunteers. Everyone has rallied together to help each other.

Cal walks in, his arm around the hulking inked owner of the tattoo parlour who's in bits after his place was flooded. 'Come on, mate, let's get you a cup of tea and we'll arrange a team to start clearing your shop.'

Cal mouths, 'Everything OK?' to me and I nod back, but there's no time to chat. We both have work to do.

'What can I do?' I ask Rev Bev when she disentangles herself from the toddler and the phone. She isn't wearing her make-up so I know things must have been bad.

'Anything and everything,' she says. 'We've

plenty of volunteers, but they're all out clearing up shops and businesses at the moment. Would you be an angel and take charge in here? We desperately need someone to run the kitchen and do hot food and drinks. Some of the emergency services and volunteers could really use a break and a hot drink. There's food and coffee in the kitchen that's been donated from locals, but we haven't had time to unpack or prepare it yet.'

'No problem. I can start a pop-up Demelza's if you like. I've brought some supplies of my own in the Land Rover.'

Rev Bev throws her arms around me. 'What a relief! That would be fantastic.'

Half an hour later, I'm back, lugging packets of biscuits, tea, coffee and milk and all the mince pies I could spare from the Land Rover. A couple of ladies from the St Trenyan's voluntary guild join me and immediately spring into action, along with some guests I recognise from Kilhallon. They're the family who have rented Poldark Cottage for Christmas and I'm a bit surprised to see them in here. They arrived in a brand-new Range Rover and I'd expected them to be drinking champagne in front of a log fire by now instead of hanging round the emergency centre.

'Oh, hello, Mr and Mrs Tennant. Is everything OK up at Kilhallon?'

'Oh yes, it's fine, and please call me Emma,' says the woman, an expensive-looking brunette in Cath Kidston wellies who I'd pegged as a pampered yummy mummy. 'Will's the leader of a mountain rescue team in the Lake District and

I volunteer out in the control room, so we thought we might be of some use to you. You can tell us to go away if you want.'

'How can we help?' Will Tennant asks in his rugged northern accent. He's about the same age as my dad, with thick dark hair greying at the sides, but still handsome. He looks like he has stepped out of an ad for North Face. My mum would have probably fancied him rotten. Their twin daughters stand by their mum's side. One of them seems overawed while the other can't keep her eyes off the RNLI men in their orange outfits.

'Will we need to captain the lifeboat?' the lively girl pipes up.

'Sorry, Lizzie, but not this time,' her mum replies while the quieter sister rolls her eyes.

'As if they'd let you in a lifeboat,' she says and gets a poke in the side for her sarcasm.

'Now, Nell, that's not kind and both of you can behave or you can't stay and help,' Emma says firmly and turns to me again. 'Just tell us what to do. Anything at all.'

'The reverend's coordinating everything, but we need help making some hot drinks for the lifeboat teams and rescue workers. You girls could hand out mince pies and biscuits to the RNLI, if you like, even though I can't guarantee a boat ride.'

'Cool,' says Nell.

Lizzie pushes out her lip in disappointment then nods. 'OK, as long as we can eat some too.'

'If your mum says it's all right, you can.'

Emma sighs. 'We have to leave some food for

all the people who are flooded and those who've been rescuing them.'

Nell folds her arms. 'Told you, Lizzie.'

'We can have some though,' Lizzie flashes back. 'So, nerghh.'

'That will do, girls!' Emma says and the girls subside. 'Sorry, I promise they'll behave if we keep them busy. They can be really helpful when they want to be, *can't you, girls?*' At a glare from their mum, the girls nod and start gazing around curiously at the rescuers and rescued filling the hall.

'Thanks. I'll sort some jobs for them in a minute. Reverend Beverley — she's the one in the wellies and dog collar — will take you to the rescue team coordinator.'

While Rev Bev introduces Will to the woman coordinating the incident team, Nell and Lizzie and their mum help me dish up the food donated by the townspeople and local businesses. We're all kept busy restocking the kitchen, marshalling supplies of food and taking out trays of drinks to those who can't get to the centre. There's a constant stream of people queuing for soup and hot drinks; local people forced out of their homes, the emergency services and volunteers. Not everyone is from St Trenyan, either, a few have come in from the nearby coastal hamlets and coves that have also been affected by the tidal surge.

It seems weird to be asked what to do by people of Polly's age. Some people are putting on a brave face, but a few look totally lost and on the verge of tears. I try to keep smiling, even

301

though I feel so sorry for them. The younger kids are taking it as a huge adventure, running around or building dens on the floor of the centre. Some of the older ones seem as lost as their parents, a few are whingeing and most are twitching with anxiety without their technology. Actually, the parents are twitching too and begging for chargers for their mobiles and tablets, if they managed to save them before the sea invaded.

Gradually, the room thins out as friends and relatives collect their loved ones, or people arrive to offer accommodation to help those in need find places to stay. I've not even managed to snatch a couple of words with Cal today. He's soaked with flood water and grey with exhaustion, but he also seems to be in his element, helping to organise the volunteers. I'd forgotten he used to help run the logistics for a charity. I bet he never expected to be helping out so close to home.

Mid-morning, he walks into the kitchen, followed by Will.

'Cal, you're shattered, take a proper break,' I tell him.

One of the local volunteers waves a pasty in his direction. 'Take her advice. Have a rest and get some dry clothes on. You've had no sleep and we can manage without you for a while.'

'Yeah, we don't want any extra casualties,' says Will, accepting a mince pie from his daughters with a smile.

'But I won't . . . '

'Shut up and eat your pasty,' I say, shoving a

steaming plate under his nose.

He nods and with a sigh bites into the pasty. His face relaxes and he looks relieved to be given permission to have a rest. Emma Tennant also orders me to take five so I grab the chance to have a proper chat with Cal.

We find a couple of chairs in the meeting room. 'How bad is it out there?' I say.

'Not good,' he says, brushing crumbs from his coat. 'Lots of places damaged. I doubt if some people will be back in before the end of January. Going to be a very miserable Christmas.'

'Rev Bev says she's compiling a list of people to make sure they all have somewhere to stay. Some have spent the night in the community hall and the vicarage, but most have friends and relatives they can stay with.'

'It's not the way they imagined spending Christmas.'

'No. But there could be worse.'

He looks at me intently. 'Yes, I hate to say it, but there could be even worse places. But then, you know what I mean?' There's passion in his voice, and a tinge of sadness, almost regret. He's thinking of the people he left behind in Syria, I'm sure. I wonder if he wishes he was still there with them, instead of here.

'I've had some less than festive times lately, I must admit. At least no one is hurt. Things can be replaced and we can we make sure everyone is warm and dry. That means everything, doesn't it?'

'Yes. It means everything just to be free and safe, Demi. Not that I'd say it to anyone round here who's just been flooded out of their homes, but there aren't any bombs dropping, no one trying to kill us and we'll get things back together eventually. Talking of which . . . ' With a brush of his lips over mine, he stands up. My lips zing and my stomach flips, but in a good way. This is the first time he's spoken to me with such warmth and passion since the Harbour Lights.

'I have to go,' he says and lowers his voice. 'Thanks for the pasty. I'll be dreaming of the moment I can share my bed with you again. It is Christmas Eve and you did promise to spend it with me.'

I feel almost dizzy with relief. He does still want me. We *can* patch things up. 'That was a while ago,' I murmur.

'I won't hold you to the promise if you don't want to join me, but I'd love it if you did. I think we need to try and sort things out between us.'

'Not only between us.'

He takes a breath. 'When this is over, I promise we'll talk properly.'

'Including about Kit?'

He heaves a sigh.

It's naughty of me to pin him down now, but I have to.

'OK.'

Cal finishes his pasty while more people pile into the centre. The hall is decorated with streamers and tinsel, which only makes everything seem even worse. 'Cal. We can't go off to enjoy our Christmas and leave everyone, no matter how much we'd like to.'

'You're right, but I don't know what more we

can do to help after today. All we can do is evacuate the final few homes and leave them safe until we can clear them up properly.'

'Cal?' Will shouts.

At his call, Cal stuffs the final morsel of pasty in his mouth and follows Will into the smaller meeting area off the main hall. I wonder if we will get back to Kilhallon this evening. Some of the emergency services workers won't get home, and new ones have already started to arrive for their shift. Polly and Mitch will be expecting me, and the guests might need us, but if Cal stays here, I want to too. I think about what Cal told me, about how happy he was to be free and safe and the look in his eyes when he said he still wanted to spend Christmas with me. I think he meant it. He really meant it, and not just because he wants a warm body in his bed.

Gathering up the used crockery, I'm about to head back for the kitchen when a man walks in. He hovers by the door to the main hall. His Berghaus jacket is dripping and his blond hair is damp and tousled. He hesitates, looking around him as if searching for someone, or as if he isn't sure he'll be welcome. Abandoning my crockery on a table, I meet him halfway across the room.

'Kit? What are you doing here?'

35

'I don't blame you if you throw me out but I saw the flooding on the news late last night. I couldn't sleep so I jumped in my car and drove. I've no idea how I made it. I want to help. Don't ask me why, but I want to do something, I *have* to do something,' Kit says, and licks his lips nervously. 'I realise I might not be the most welcome of volunteers, but I had to try.'

'I don't know what kind of reception you're going to get,' I warn him, which is the understatement of the year.

'It's a risk I'm prepared to take. I've things I need to do and they won't wait, no matter what the circumstances.'

'Maybe we'd better go outside and talk.'

Too late.

From the door of the office, Cal spots Kit. He frowns and with a word to Will, strides over. He's soaked and there are dark circles under his eyes. His expression is thunderous.

'Kit came to help.' It's all I can think of to say.

Cal's nostrils flare. 'We're fine, so he can turn around and go back,' he says, not bothering to lower his voice. A couple of heads turn in our direction. Any distraction must be welcome at the moment.

'Come and talk about this in the kitchen,' I say, holding Cal's arm.

Taking the hint, Will leaves us. 'I'd better get

back to the emergency committee meeting. See you later, Cal.'

Kit nods at the kitchen. 'Please hear me out. If you still don't want me around, I'll head straight back to London and I won't darken your doorstep again. All I ask is five minutes.'

Cal hesitates then grinds out a reply. 'You can have two.'

He strides off into the kitchen, leaving Kit and me in his wake.

'I hope you haven't come to make trouble,' I say to Kit as we follow. Cal is standing by the sink, his arms folded. But before Kit can reply, Cal barks, 'Right, say your piece.'

'I came back to help. Trust me on that.'

Cal laughs out loud. 'Now you have to be joking.'

I'm the referee at a boxing match. 'Should I go?' I ask, having no intention of leaving if I can help it. This kitchen has a lot of things that could be used as weapons.

'No.'

They both speak at once, Cal glares at Kit for daring to voice an opinion.

I close the door.

'Believe it or not, as soon as I heard the news, I decided to set off. I want to do something to help. St Trenyan's become my second home and I swear I'm not here to make things worse for anyone. You've got my word on that.'

Cal's intake of breath is faint and he shakes his head slightly.

'I wouldn't be here if I wanted to make trouble. I'd have already made it.' Kit glances at me. 'I've done some hard thinking and now I see things in a different way.'

Cal snorts. 'Oh, really?'

'Is it so hard to believe?'

'It is after what you said to me at the Harbour Lights.'

'I've decided against . . . ' He glances at me again. 'Doing what we discussed after all.'

Cal stares at him, but I see him swallow hard. 'What we *discussed*?' he snorts in derision. 'And am I supposed to be grateful for that?'

'No. I don't want you to be grateful to me for anything. Now's not the time, but I think we should talk, and I mean talk, not try to beat the crap out of each other. I realise that now is probably the worst time to discuss this, and I do want to talk, but I'm guessing that we have work to do first.'

'You guessed right,' Cal says sarcastically. God, I *hope* he doesn't ruin things by riling Kit now.

'Like I said, I've come to help not to make stuff worse than it is.'

Cal snorts then shakes his head. 'You can make things as bad for me as you want. I don't care, but if you hurt the people I love, I won't forget it. Understood, *bro*?'

I'm in agony and longing to know what the hell is going on between them, but realise they won't tell me. I'll just have to wait until Cal's ready.

After a few seconds, Kit nods. 'Received, loud and clear. Now, can I help?'

Cal hesitates, then a wicked smile crosses his

face. 'If you insist. We need all the help we can get and I'm sure I can find you something backbreaking, cold and wet to do.'

36

Christmas Eve, morning

It's Christmas Eve in St Trenyan. The sea laps the jetty softly, a little higher than usual, but nothing to worry anyone who's lived here as long as we have. Someone has put up a temporary tree by the harbourmistress's office and topped it with a bright yellow star. The shark-shaped light display, along with the other damaged decorations, have been carted away to a lock-up behind the community centre to be repaired ready for next year. It's going to take a lot of money to restore the lights to their former glory, but I know we can do it.

Many businesses are boarded up and hoses still pump out of flooded homes and properties. Rev Bev meets me at the community hall. There are now half a dozen sleeping bags on the floor, along with children's toys, a travel cot and dozens of bags-for-life. It's a good name for them since they really do hold people's lives: the treasured possessions and memories they managed to save before the sea invaded their homes.

Bev takes the fresh supplies from my arms and gestures me into the corner of the kitchen.

'How's it going?' I ask.

'We're coping and the last high tide was a close call, but didn't make things any worse than they are so I'm very thankful for that.' She sighs. 'It's not great. Some people will be out of their homes for weeks, and we have to get through this Christmas first. Most people have gone to relatives but there's a couple of families who don't have anyone and the hotels are almost all full. We're phoning round, trying to find places, but it's very difficult with it being Christmas Day and Boxing Day. After the holiday, most can probably make other arrangements or find somewhere temporary, but it is difficult.'

A baby cries in the corner. His mum is trying to shush him, but it's a losing battle.

'This hall is hardly the place to spend Christmas Day is it? And I can only put up one family in the vicarage with my own lot coming; we don't have big places any more. In fact, I really should be doing some stuff for work.' She smiles. 'Christmassy stuff, you know. It's a busy time of year for me. And I haven't even done my shopping or bought a turkey yet.'

I can't help laughing, even though things are so gloomy for many. 'I'll take over here. You go and do your Christmassy stuff. We've probably even got a spare turkey at Kilhallon.'

'Thanks, Demi.'

'I wish I could do more. Our cottages are full with guests and I can't put people in yurts in this weather . . .'

'It might come to that,' Bev says. 'Thanks for manning the fort. I'll be back as soon as I'm done.'

Cal walks in, almost bowed down under the weight of three large boxes. Emma takes one from him and starts to unpack it in the kitchen.

'I bet this wasn't how the Tennants expected to spend their holiday,' he says to me as we open the other boxes, which are full of cans and dried foods.

'They don't seem to mind. We'll have to give them a free short break as a thank-you.'

'Alongside her volunteering, Emma works part time for a Cumbria tourist association and knows loads of travel trade press. She's going to tell them how great Kilhallon is and put me in touch with them. I didn't ask her to do it, but isn't that great?'

Cal swings me into his arms in a rare moment when there's no one around.

'Yes. How the RNLI and mountain rescue teams manage to do their day jobs and this kind of work is incredible.'

'You've given up a lot of time to help, yourself, Cal. You look shattered and you're used to this kind of work. It's all new to Kit. How's he getting on?' Although I managed to get back to Kilhallon and snatch a few hours' sleep, Cal and Kit decided to spend last night in the community centre with some of the stranded families and volunteers.

Cal pinches his forehead and blinks. His eyes are red with fatigue. 'Knackered, wet, cold, but we haven't come to blows again yet. We're too busy.'

'But you'll talk to him?'

'Guys don't talk.'

'Cal!'

'If he wants to speak to me in a sensible way

that's not aggressive and full of crap, then yeah, I'll talk to him, but he has to get back to London tonight. He's going to stay at a motorway hotel overnight and then spend Christmas with his parents. His real parents.'

'Oh, Cal. I'm sorry about what's happened between you, and for how hurt you must have been.' I also know when to back off from hassling him about Kit. They're working together and Kit's here. That's as much as I could ever have dreamed of, and while I'm itching to know what's gone on between them, now's not the time.

'I'm too busy to think of the past. I need to think about now,' he says briskly. 'And what's going to happen later tonight and tomorrow when I have you to myself. I don't even know if you'll have the time or energy to cook Christmas lunch after I've finished with you.'

'That won't matter, because you're cooking Christmas lunch, remember?'

'Well, I think we'll just make do with beans on toast in that case. I can add a sprig of holly if I have to.'

His lips taste of salt as he kisses me, and his hair is tangled with seawater and the cold wind, but he's never been sexier to me. I hate myself for the way I'm almost trembling in his arms. It's way too late to ever back out. I love Cal, I'm in love with him. I know he wants me, needs me perhaps. I hear a cough from the door, then voices. Will Tennant and a couple of women from the RNLI walk in, smirking at catching us snogging. Cal drops his hand from my bottom

313

and we spring apart. My cheeks burn.

'How's Polly coping with the guests?' I ask Cal.

'Fine, I think. No one's checked out threatening to give us one star on TripAdvisor yet. How are the staff managing in the cafe without you?'

'Good. So well, apparently, that I wonder if they need me at all. Polly's helping out and Nina's in charge, and we close at three today anyway. I ought to go and see how they're doing, but I can't head off until Bev gets back. I hate leaving these people like this.' We take in the sleeping bags spread out in the meeting room of the centre. Most people have gone to friends and relatives by now so the remaining families have been moved into the side room for a bit of extra privacy.

'You know there are people with nowhere to go? It's Christmas Day tomorrow. Everyone's doing their best, but the storm affected people up and down the coast, not just St Trenyan, and all the hotels are full. We have to do something, Cal.'

'We can't put them all up.'

'No, but we can give it a try.'

He sighs. 'To be honest, I've been thinking the same. What about the staff cottages? Two of them aren't ready for guests but at least they're safe, warm and watertight even if the decorating is only half done. We'd need new bedding for them but with a bit of a team effort, we could put up two families for a short while.'

'Some of them could share my cottage as I'm

314

staying with you, if one of them doesn't mind sleeping on a sofa.'

'Yes . . . Demi, I know this has been a disaster for the local people, but there's one good thing come out of it.'

'You mean that we realised our row meant nothing in the grand scheme of things?' I say.

'Something like that. When all this is over, we need to have a serious talk.'

I raise my eyebrows. 'A serious talk? I thought guys didn't do serious talks?'

He gives me a peck on the cheek then whispers, 'You drive me mad, Demi Jones, in every possible way.'

'Good,' I reply, bubbling over with hope and relief, despite the circumstances. 'I'll tell Rev Bev that we can offer these people a home when she gets back and try to make some arrangements.'

37

Christmas Eve, afternoon
Cal

By two o'clock, the sun is already sinking over the horizon to the west of the harbour. The sky is that turquoise blue you get on a midwinter afternoon as the day draws in. I watch Kit help a man carry a glass and metal table out of one of the quayside cottages where we've been helping people clear out their houses with the RNLI. I found him the worst jobs I could think of, those that involved wading through freezing sewage-filled water and, far more difficult, comforting devastated people who've lost everything.

Justice? Petty? Maybe, but I don't give a toss either way.

A sodden sofa and chair lie in a skip, a rolled-up carpet hangs over the edge. The rest of the family and volunteers are still sweeping out sludge and mud from the sitting room that fronts directly onto the harbour wall. Poor beggars, they won't be back in there for a while. The middle-aged lady who owns it sweeps furiously, though I know she's been up for over twenty-four hours. It's as if she wants to sweep away the whole event, wishing it hadn't happened. The sea is unstoppable.

Kit lifts the table into a van and leaves the man loading other items while he walks over to the woman. He takes the broom from her and she bursts into tears. He puts his arm around her and her shoulders shake. He glances around at me. Does he want me to see him doing his Good Samaritan act? Are his good deeds all an act, as so much of his behaviour has been over the past couple of months? Is it a smokescreen to put me off my guard? Is it a lie? My father's whole existence was a lie . . .

The woman's husband takes her from Kit and says something. I think it's a 'thank-you'. Kit glances at me again and walks over.

He's soaking wet despite the waterproofs the RNLI found for him. His face is red with the cold and he looks exhausted.

Good.

We stand in silence for a little while, watching the husband and RNLI member persuade his wife to leave with them.

'Have they got somewhere to stay?' I ask.

'Yes. They have friends who've offered to put them up but the woman, Leanne, wouldn't leave until now. I'm relieved she's finally agreed to go. Their house is full of raw sewage. It's unbelievable. I watched the footage on the news last night but I'd no idea how bad it really was. The smell . . . It's terrible, and you can tell from people's faces that they're crushed, at Christmas too, poor bastards.'

'Yeah, the damage is what makes great pictures and footage, but nothing prepares you for the impact on people's lives. That's here long after the cameras and journos have gone.'

Kit's silent and so am I. If he's pissed off

317

about my 'journo' dig, he either isn't reacting or is too knackered to have noticed. I want to shout at him and ask him about his decision to publish his story about me, but I'm too proud. I'd rather be thrown to the wolves.

'You've seen a lot worse of course,' Kit says out of the blue.

'Have I?'

'You know you have.'

'Yes, I have. An outsider might say that the people here are lucky. No one died, though I don't know how, and we're not under fire, or being invaded, but try telling these people they're lucky when the insurance decides not to pay out or they need a mortgage on the place. We're only a little town, with little problems on a world scale, but it doesn't take much to destroy everything people have spent their lives building up.'

'You don't need to spell it out, Cal. I'm fully aware of the effect what I'd planned to do would have had on you personally.'

Planned to. I daren't hope he's really changed his mind.

'Have you told Mawgan Cade what you think happened in Syria?' I ask him.

Kit shakes his head. 'Do you think I'm completely stupid?'

'I have wondered.'

He laughs at me. 'Give me some credit. Of course I haven't. Getting involved with Mawgan was a mistake. It was cruel to her.'

I resist the urge to snort. 'She'll get over it, I'm sure she was using you more than the other way round. Mawgan had her heart replaced with granite long ago.'

'Maybe you're right. I do know when I'm being played,' he says.

'I'm sure you do.'

A trace of a smile twitches his lips but we both let it pass. One of us is going to have the last word.

'I'd love to stay on, but I have to go back to London. My parents will be expecting me.'

'Yeah, I should think they are.'

Silence again, then he turns to me. 'Cal. I've something to say to you. I don't like what your father did . . . '

Instantly my hackles rise, but I'm trying to stay calm. We both need to hear what he has to say. 'Hey, I have news for you. I'm not thrilled about it either, and I'm sorry for your mother. I'm even sorry that my father's affair with Mawgan's mother caused a rift in their family too, but I had no real idea at the time. My mum hid her own pain for a long time for my sake, of course. She must have known what my father was doing and been deeply hurt. I've often thought bottling up all that pain over the years, putting on a brave front, didn't help her illness.'

'I'm sorry for that. Genuinely,' Kit replies and I think I believe him.

'But my dad wasn't a monster,' I go on, trying to keep a lid on my emotions. Fighting won't help either of us now. 'He was a weak, flawed man and I'm not excusing what he did — but no one is perfect or innocent, as you've been at pains to point out to me. I wish I'd spoken to

319

him more, or tried to while I could — even though he'd probably have told me to shut up or laughed at me. We just didn't have that kind of relationship. But it's too late now.'

Kit listens to me carefully. I genuinely think he is prepared to hear what I have to say. A sudden noise, the grate of metal on metal, distracts us both. It's a lorry hoisting the remains of someone's belongings into a skip.

Kit grimaces. 'Look. I've come to realise that I've probably let my personal feelings get in the way of my professional life. I told myself I was pursuing you because it was an interesting story, but now I know the opposite is true. I was pursuing you because I knew that raking up that part of your life would hurt you. I was bitter, confused, envious and jealous of what you have: peace and quiet, Kilhallon, our father's love, and Demi's.'

'What?'

'You heard, you lucky bastard, and I'm not going to repeat it. I'm also not going to try to publish the story,' he says.

I snort, hardly daring to believe him or let myself realise how desperate I am for him to back down.

'Why should I believe a ruthless journalist wouldn't follow up a juicy story?'

'Because he does have some family loyalty. Because he realises that being a bastard may be part of the job, but it doesn't define him as a man. I haven't had a conversion, but Demi came to me, Cal, and spoke to me. I sent her away, I was patronising and sarcastic to her; it was too soon. She caught me just at the moment when I'd already worked out for myself what a tosser I was being, that I was probably a little in the wrong for what I'd done. So I'm sorry to her and I'll tell her that I am when I see her again. *If* I see her. But it's you she really wanted me to speak to. It was you she came to see me about.'

'Jesus, Demi spoke to you?'

'Yes. She's brave, she's interfering, she's crazy, but she quite likes you, you lucky git. I probably hate you more now than before.'

'Did you actually *hate* me when you came to Kilhallon?'

'Hate's a strong word. Not hate. Not now. Probably not ever. Shit, can we just leave this? It's excruciating enough to have to eat humble pie. Don't expect me to relish the meal. How would you feel?'

'Probably even less enthusiastic than you. Neither of us enjoys admitting we're wrong, do we? So we do have that in common. Does Demi know about your decision not to go public with the article?' I ask.

'No, and you can rest assured the story won't get out because of me. I can't promise that someone else won't find out, though, and they won't think twice about using it if they decide it would make good copy so I'd keep a low profile if I were you.'

'It's too late for that.'

He smiles wryly. 'Maybe . . . Cal, I have to set off for home. I won't be back in London until tomorrow. I owe my parents some quality time

321

and a proper explanation of why I decided to spend months down here. It *was* to finish my book — that was no lie — but as for wanting to see you and Kilhallon, I denied all of that.'

'Is your mother upset about you coming back here?'

'She's confused, I think, about her feelings for your father, but kinder on him than I am. I'm sorry, I can't handle forgiveness yet. I'm not sure I ever will . . . '

'You don't have to forgive him on my account. I don't expect or ask you to, but listen to me: he was my dad and he stuck by me and I loved him. I'm sorry he didn't behave the way he should towards you but that's how it is.' My hackles rise again, his too, I expect. I don't care. I can't lie about Dad. For all his faults, and there were many, I loved him. I won't deny that for anybody's peace of mind.

Kit stares at me. 'You're his real son. I might have half his genes, but I'm not like you.'

Demi would say he is, I think. She would say we're two peas in a pod, Kit and I.

'My mum was upset, at first, that I wanted to return here. She said I ought not to rake up the past and that my dad — my step-father — would be hurt by it, but coming to Kilhallon was something I needed to do and I'm glad I did. I am genuinely sorry about the way I handled things. Or didn't handle them. Demi was right. I was pursuing you for revenge. She said I was 'better than that'.'

'She's often right. Not always, but far too often.' My smile of pleasure that Demi braved

Kit for my sake must show on my face although I don't mean it to.

'You still haven't told her what happened out there yet, have you?'

'Not yet.'

'Jesus.' He blows out a breath. 'You really do like to live dangerously. Well, it's none of my business now, but if I were Demi and your family, I'd want to know at least part of the truth, even if it can never be the whole story.'

'No one will ever know the whole story. Not your army 'source' or anyone who wasn't there with me and Soraya that day.'

He looks at me. His lips part in surprise and confusion. 'Perhaps not, but let's leave it at that.'

I glance at the sky. It's turned gloomy now, although the emergency lighting illuminates the quayside. 'Not quite the harbour lights any of us expected,' Kit says.

'No . . . I think you'd better get on your way. There's snow forecast once you get past Bristol. I don't want you getting stuck and having to be rescued, do I?'

He smiles. 'I don't expect gratitude or brotherly love, a handshake would do.'

I take his hand and briefly, we're connected.

'Goodbye, Kit.'

'Bye, Cal. Good luck. Maybe we'll meet again in happier circumstances. I don't think either of us has finished here, do you?'

'Safe journey,' is all I can manage.

With a nod that tells me he knows I'm not ready to discuss reunions yet, he turns away and walks off.

'Thanks, Kit.'

The words escape my mouth before my brain can stop them. Kit carries on walking, but he lifts his hand, slightly and for a second. Then he's gone from sight.

My shoulders slump in relief and I have to take a moment to steady myself. Then another . . . and another. After the tension of the past few days and the discovery that I have a brother and he isn't — quite — the lying, vindictive bastard I imagined or perhaps wanted him to be, I find my hands aren't quite steady. Raking up the past in all its forms has been painful.

It will be dark in a couple of hours — especially for Kit as he heads east to London — but here at Kilhallon we get the last few rays of the sun. Sometimes in spring, the light seems to last all night. My God, how I missed these skies last Christmas; the crisp air, the gales, the tang of ozone, salt spray on my face. That's when I vowed that the moment I touched Kilhallon soil I'd tell Isla how much I felt for her. Now, here I am, knowing that I should tell someone the truth: how I feel, what happened to me. Not Isla, but Demi. But when? And how?

The wind nips my face. The temperature has plunged but we still won't have a white Christmas at Kilhallon; we never have had. I haven't seen snow settle either, not since the winter that Mum passed away. There were deep drifts that cut us off for a few days. Dad took me sledging for the first time ever. It was almost Easter. After the snow melted, she left us.

'Boys don't cry.' Dad told me that from the

moment I was out of nappies, although he didn't say it after Mum slipped away in our arms.

Grown men don't cry? They do, far more often than you'd ever believe. I've seen them. I've been one of them in my darkest moments.

That bloody wind, it cuts into me, making my eyes water. Good job it's raining again too. Hailing, in fact, from the dirtiest dark clouds you've ever seen, clumping over the ocean in the direction of Kilhallon. Great. Just what we need, a storm and leaking roofs, and I still haven't got round to painting Demi's ceiling despite promising to do it months ago.

By the time I reach the community centre again, the streets of St Trenyan are quiet and my eyes are dry. The fire service, RNLI and police are still around. Some people are still clearing up, poor sods. I don't think I can take any more weight on my shoulders today. I need Demi, because it's Christmas, almost, and I need a Christmas in my own home, with the people I love around me. It's been a long time since I had that. Perhaps a very, very long time . . .

I dig in my pocket and pull out a rain-soaked handkerchief. Oh shit, I can't go into the centre yet. I just need a few more minutes . . .

38

Demi

'Really? You'll take the two families and the two young women? I'm so relieved, I can tell you.' Rev Bev has popped back in between her Christmas Eve duties and hugs me in the kitchen of the community centre. I don't like to tell her that she has baby food on her dog collar after the children's service she's just conducted.

'Well, the old staff cottages aren't luxurious, but they're warm and watertight. They'll do for a couple of nights. I hope the families aren't going to be disappointed. It must be so horrible having to leave your own place and rely on strangers.'

'I think they're so tired and fed up of sleeping in here that any roof of their own while they try and celebrate Christmas will be a relief to them. I'll go and tell them, shall I?' Bev says. 'They're all in the meeting room.'

'Do they have transport?'

'One of their cars was flooded out and the other one's given up the ghost, but the Rotary Club can give them a lift in their minibus and they said they'd supply the bedding and some food too. They managed to salvage some of the presents for the kids and we've had donations from local businesses too. Tamsin has been fantastic, helping out and offering some spa packs for the mums.'

I smile at hearing about my friend's generosity. 'Tamsin's lovely.'

Bev mouths an apology as her mobile goes off. A minute later she speaks to me again.

'Blast. I forgot to mention the other couple who turned up while you were collecting the supplies. Apparently, they only moved into the area a few weeks ago. They'd just bought that little fisherman's cottage round the next cove and I'm afraid the tidal surge completely washed them out. Her relatives all live in Spain and there are no flights out there, even if she wasn't eight months pregnant.'

'I don't think we can take any more people unless they want to sleep in the cafe, which is possible, I suppose. We could set up beds in there.'

Bev's face falls. 'Oh dear. Someone told them that we might be able to help them find a place and they came in here this morning. I said I couldn't be sure but to come back. The man's trying to phone a hotel in Truro and the woman's popped out to the pharmacy before it shuts. Oh, there they are.'

Rachel walks in, or should I say waddles in, closely followed by my dad. Bev rushes over to greet them.

My hands shake. It can't be them. Not here. Not now.

Bev shows Rachel to a chair. Dad glances at me, obviously as gobsmacked as me that we're in the same room again.

'Hello, how are you? Any luck with finding anywhere to stay?' Bev asks them.

My dad shakes his head. 'Not yet.'

Rachel is close to tears, then spots me. I curl my hands into fists, willing my fingers to stop trembling.

'If all else fails, Demi here has offered you a roof over your head in her cafe,' Bev is telling them. The tidal surge has picked me up and dumped me in a situation I never planned or wanted and I'm floundering. I never asked for this . . .

'It's OK. We can do better than that.' Cal's hand is at my back. I didn't even notice him walk in. 'Can't we, Demi?'

'I don't want to put anybody out,' my dad grunts. 'We'll find somewhere, won't we, Rachel? We can go out of the area. There'll be a hotel or a caravan.' He takes her hand as if he's going to make her get up and leave.

'No. Wait. Dad!'

Finally I move. 'Cal's right. You can stay with us in the farmhouse. There's a spare room. Please don't go.'

'You won't want us ruining your Christmas, Demi, and I refuse to be a burden.'

'You won't be,' I say as if another girl has taken control of my thoughts.

'You won't be, Mr Jones,' Cal says firmly. He captures my hand tightly in his.

'Is it your place?' Dad asks Cal. He looks unsure and Rachel seems ready to cry. She looks so scared and tired. I feel sorry for her.

'I own it but we run it together. Don't we, Demi?' He squeezes my hand. 'There's a spare room in the main farmhouse. Nothing special but you'd be warm and comfortable,' he tells Rachel and my dad.

'Are you sure?' Dad looks directly at me. Cal squeezes my hand again, not as if he's putting pressure on me, but for support. I feel sick, confused, but I made the choice. Cal didn't make me, Bev hasn't made me.

'Yes. I'm sure.'

Bev says nothing, but looks at me hard. She seems to have worked out — in a few seconds — what's happening here.

'Shall I leave you to discuss it and work out any arrangements?' she says with a smile. 'Let me know what's decided and, Mr Jones, you and your partner are welcome at the vicarage if not. We'll manage somehow.'

'It's fine. They can stay with us,' I say.

Bev nods. 'Talk to you later. I have to go now.'

★ ★ ★

My dad takes me aside while Cal helps Rachel gather up her things. 'You don't have to do this, Demi.'

'I know I don't.'

'Don't feel obliged because of that vicar woman or your boss.'

'I don't feel obliged. I know what it's like to be stuck without somewhere to go.'

'I never turned you out,' he says quietly.

'No, but you never made me feel like you really wanted me to stay.'

'I was wrong and I've felt guilty about that ever since. I've not been the ideal dad, Demi, and after your mum passed away I was even less than ideal, but I was feeling guilty about your mum and grieving. You didn't seem to need me.'

'I did need you. I needed you more than ever.'

Two of the families gathering their stuff glance up. My face is wet with tears. This is exactly what I didn't want: a public rant.

'Let's not do this here. Or ever, if you don't want to,' he says. 'And you can still back out. No one will know that we haven't stayed.'

'*I'll* know. Cal will never agree to you leaving now.'

'It's none of his business. You don't do as he says all the time, do you?'

'Almost never!'

My dad raises his eyebrows. 'Bloody hell. I bet you're a handful to him.'

'No, I'm not! He's the handful, not me.'

Then I realise my dad has a smile on his face and I want to hit him. How dare he side with Cal? How dare he smile at me? How dare he make me feel as if I care about a single thing he thinks. How can I ever get through Christmas if he stays with us?

How can I ever get through Christmas if he doesn't?

'Demi? Are you ready to go home?'

Cal's in the doorway, weighed down with bags. Rachel stands by, watching us. She looks at me and she gives me a little sympathetic smile. I think she knows how hard this is. For me, for Dad and for her, but it's too late now. We're going to spend Christmas together and there's nothing I can do about it.

39

Christmas Eve, mid-afternoon

Cal and I carry the bags through the reception area of Kilhallon House while my dad helps Rachel out of the Land Rover. Although the chilly rain shower has passed over, it will be growing dark soon and the wind is biting so the warm air of the reception area is very welcome. Polly has placed a Christmas lantern with a festive candle in it on the desk and its golden glow and spicy smell adds to the cosy atmosphere. We push open the door to the farmhouse itself and Polly's voice drifts through from the sitting room, singing along to carols from King's on the radio. She's also lit a fire, which crackles in the hearth and lends the air a tang of woodsmoke.

I hear footsteps and voices outside, which must be my father, Rachel and the other 'evacucees'.

'I'd better go and help everyone settle in,' Cal says, leaving the bags in the sitting room. 'If you don't mind looking after your dad and Rachel?'

'OK . . . ' I say, knowing that I'm going to have to face Dad on my own some time. Funny how I find it easier to welcome strangers than my own family. My nerves make my stomach flutter, but I guess it's time to start building bridges. 'Cal, what *have* I done?'

He smiles. 'Invited half the town to spend Christmas with us.'

'I didn't notice you trying to stop me. In fact, you encouraged it so what choice did I have?' I ask.

Cal kisses me tenderly, and his fingers linger on my cheek. 'We always have a choice,' he says and then walks outside.

'Wow. This is beautiful!' says Rachel when I show her the guest room in the farmhouse.

'It's not luxury, but it's clean and comfy, I hope,' I say.

My dad and Rachel follow me inside the room. It's not been used by anyone since Cal had to temporarily move in while the main bedroom roof was repaired after a storm. Polly's aired it and put some fresh linen on the bed while we transported everyone from the village.

'It's lovely,' says Rachel. 'Older than our cottage.' Her bottom lip trembles. 'I don't know when we'll be able to get back in there. The insurance people can't even come out until the day after Boxing Day.'

'You can stay here as long as you need to,' I say, knowing instinctively that's what Cal would want, even if the situation is awkward between us.

'We'll be out of your hair soon. Rachel's cousin says we can have her holiday flat in Porthleven for a few weeks once her Christmas guests have left. It'll be all right.' Dad hugs her. She isn't as young as me, but she looks tired and thin, despite the huge bump.

'Is it a boy or a girl?' I ask.

'What?' Dad frowns.

'The baby.'

'A little girl,' he says and Rachel pats her stomach.

'She keeps kicking. She must know that something dramatic has happened.' Rachel crosses to the window and looks out over the dark moorland to the rear of the house.

'Rachel looks knackered. I hope she's not going to have the baby here,' I whisper to my dad.

He smiles. 'It's not due until the middle of January. You can stop worrying.'

'Do you want to go back downstairs and warm yourselves by the fire for a while? You can help yourself to drinks and mince pies from the kitchen. Polly's in there and I'm sure she'll take care of you both,' I say, switching briskly to professional hostess mode before I start thinking too hard about the prospect of having a little sister. 'I need to go and help Cal settle in the other families.'

Closing the door, I run downstairs, trying to put out of my mind the fact that the man I refused to even acknowledge a few weeks ago is now staying in Cal's house with me. There's too much to do to dwell on it, and even if there wasn't, I'd find some way of blocking out the momentous thought.

Polly is actually outside, waving off the Rotary Club's minibus, which dropped off our final batch of unexpected guests. They're shattered but seem grateful for a dry roof over their heads, not that they have to be. Polly has her arm around one man who's been overcome by worry and is in a right state. She offers to make him a cup of tea.

'Where's Cal? I ask her.

'Showing the kids the chickens while their parents sort themselves out.'

I jog up to the chicken house. Cal and four children, aged from about five to ten, peer through the wire fence at Polly's precious flock. The sky is darkening now and the wind is chilly, but the kids are well wrapped up and don't seem to mind. Spending Christmas at Kilhallon must seem like another adventure to them after what they've been through.

'They aren't the turkeys for our dinner, are they?' a little boy asks Cal.

'No. Turkeys are much bigger and we don't eat these chickens. We keep them to lay eggs for breakfast and cakes.'

'I can make cakes,' a little girl pipes up. 'But I don't need eggs. I only need Rice Krispies and chocolate.'

'Do you have to wring their necks?' the oldest boy demands, teasing the wire fence as if he'd like to break in. He's definitely trouble.

Cal frowns at him. 'Not if I can help it. We don't breed them so we don't have any cockerels to get rid of.'

'What's a cockellerel?' the little boy asks.

'And why do you put a ring on its neck?' adds an older girl.

'He means they strangle . . . ' Trouble begins with glee.

'I think it's cold out here and your mums and

dads will wonder where you are,' I cut in.

Cal shoots a grateful glance at me. The little boy catches my hand and gazes up at me with big blue eyes. 'What does he mean, Demi, 'wrangle the cockleshells'?'

'We don't wrangle any of the hens. They live here having a happy time making eggs for us.'

'How do the eggs get out of the hens?' he asks.

Oh shit. Cal winks at me. 'Yes, how do the eggs get out, Demi?'

The older girl pulls a face and Trouble rolls his eyes.

'Does the cockerel have a name?' the little girl asks, saving me from an awkward answer.

'Yes. Chicken McChickenface,' says Cal.

'No, it is *not*,' Trouble says with a snort.

'Wanna bet?' Cal smiles.

The boy's face crumples. He's really not sure . . .

'Let's go back to the cottages. It's getting cold.' I pull a face at Cal and take the little girl and boy by the hand while Trouble picks up a stick and swishes at the grass.

'Are we having eggs for Christmas dinner?' the little girl asks as we walk down to the cottages.

'I don't know.'

'Mum says it will have to be beans on toast,' Trouble mutters.

'That doesn't sound very festive.'

'No, but Mum says we're lucky to have a roof over our heads, even if it does smell of dog.'

I manage a smile. His family are staying in my cottage. Oh well, not everyone appreciates Mitch's hospitality.

'I like my room. You can hear the sea when Max stops moaning,' says his sister, obviously referring to Trouble.

'I don't moan!'

'Now, now,' I say, desperate to avoid breaking up any more fights. 'Let's take you home.' An idea forms in my mind. Is it a good one or the daftest I've ever had? Is it impossible? I wonder what Cal would say . . .

Max's mum answers the door of 'my' cottage. It is very strange having to knock on the door of my own place — or what *was* my own place. I'm not sure if it is my cottage now if I decide to move in with Cal.

Her face is as pale as flour. 'Thanks for taking them. We needed a break.'

'I told her about the dog smell, Mum.'

'Oh God, no. Don't be so rude, Max! Sorry, love, it's very good of you to have us.' She glares at him but Max shrugs and wanders off.

'It's fine. It's not your own house, is it? I can understand that must be horrible and I'm sorry for the doggy smell.'

'Don't be! Max can be a right little devil. I'd rather have your dog than him sometimes. Thanks for having us.'

'It's a pleasure.'

Cal and I meet at the farmhouse after he's delivered the other two little angels to their parents. Clutching hot chocolates, we both collapse around the kitchen table and don't speak for a few minutes.

'Cal?'

He glances up from his drink. 'Mmm. Do I

feel an idea about to erupt?'

'Yes, and I'm not sure whether you're going to like it or think it's possible.'

'But?'

'All the people, they're safe and dry, but it's not going to be much of a Christmas Day, eating baked beans and crisps, is it? So I wondered if we should, you know, maybe invite them to Christmas lunch with us.'

'What? Here in the farmhouse?' He sounds horrified.

'No. We could use Demelza's. I mean, I was already going to ask Dad and Rachel, so why not extend the invitation to everyone who wants to come?'

Polly bustles in. 'I hope those kids haven't terrified my chickens into stopping laying. They're very sensitive, you know, and I've already spotted one of the little horrors making gun signs at them. I'll be keeping an eye on him.'

'Shouldn't you have left for your daughter's by now? It's Christmas Eve. You'll want to spend it with your new grandson.'

'I am. My daughter and her partner and the baby are on their way to my place. I told them what had happened and they suggested it. I presume we're opening the cafe tomorrow for everyone?'

We exchange amazed glances. Cal shrugs.

'What? Have I said something amusing again?'

'No. In fact we were discussing the arrangement when you came in,' Cal says.

'Good. My Fiona's partner is a school chef, and he says he'll help us and they're bringing their food over. Now all we have to worry about is feeding the five thousand with five loaves and two fishes.'

Polly has lost me now. 'Um . . . I don't know what you mean. There's no fish in the freezer, but we've plenty of frozen loaves,' I reply, not wanting to upset her after she's given up her Christmas to cook for everyone.

Cal makes a choking sound, which is meant to be laughter. Polly shakes her head and plants her hands on her hips. 'Give me strength. Come on, you two, let's get our sleeves rolled up and get going. It's Christmas tomorrow.'

I've no idea what Polly was on about with the fish and loaves, but she's stopped mentioning them now and joined me in the cafe kitchen. It's a good job we'd already bought a turkey that was far too large for Cal and me, and that Polly and her family had done likewise. With the help of a couple of other joints from our freezers, and supplies we had left in the cafe, we should be able to eke out our stores to feed everyone.

The families have all brought what food they'd managed to salvage too. We went round the cottages before lunch, asking who wanted to join in the Christmas lunch at Demelza's and, to my surprise, everyone has said 'yes,' even the single girls, who turn out to be overseas students. I thought they'd be way too cool to join in, preferring to spend the day on their phones and tablets.

So it's all hands to the pump in the kitchens. The kids are laying the tables, while everyone else — too many, to be honest — 'helps' prepare the veg, make cranberry sauce and all the trimmings, ready for tomorrow.

In the end, with people getting under each other's feet, I decide to organise a rota so that there's at least some order. Polly's son-in-law will be here soon. Mitch has been locked in the farmhouse because he'd freak out with so much activity going on and we don't want him running off again.

Rachel looks ready to drop, but she turns out to be a dab hand at napkin folding so she's sitting at the big table showing the children how to make swans from the serviettes.

My dad walks in with Cal, carrying a crate of beer.

'I'll take that, thanks, Mr Jones,' says Cal.

'Please, call me Gary. Your cafe is really something, Demi.'

'I'm only the manager. Cal owns it.'

'Demi first had the idea for it and she designed it, project managed the build and manages the whole business,' Cal says.

My father looks around him. 'Well, you should be proud. You always did what you wanted. No stopping you when you sank your teeth into something.' I know he's thinking of my running away. 'I'm not surprised. If your mum could see it, she'd be so proud too.'

'But she can't.' I say briskly. 'Do you mind giving me a hand with peeling the veg?'

With a frown of confusion, he follows me into the kitchen.

'Sure.' He looks around him. 'Your mum

would be happy about how you turned out. I mean it.'

'Don't go there, Dad. Don't try and make it OK. Let's just leave it. It's the only way I can cope, for now.' I don't want shaky hands while I set to work on the potatoes.

'OK. If that's what you want.'

'I do.' I soften my tone and hand him a veg peeler from the rack. 'Now, could you please start peeling those spuds?'

40

Christmas Day, morning

'Happy Christmas.'

My eyes open on a man in a Santa hat and nothing else. Cal stands by the side of the bed, holding a parcel. It looks like he wrapped it in the dark while wearing mittens.

I sit bolt upright on the pillows. 'What time is it? We have to start cooking the turkeys.'

'Relax. Polly's son-in-law has already put them in the cafe and farmhouse ovens.'

I slump back on the pillows and frown. 'You haven't got any clothes on.'

'Glad you finally noticed.' He waggles the parcel and I try not to be too impressed by what waggles underneath it. 'I have Christmas dinner to cook for eighteen people.'

'Aren't you going to open it?' he says. 'If you don't like it I can take it back. It doesn't matter.'

'I do like it. I *will* like it.'

'Why the long face, then?'

I swallow hard. 'I haven't had any Christmas presents for a long time. I'm not used to having them.'

Cal flashes me a sexy smile. 'Take your time, but can you budge over so I can get into bed. I'm freezing my rocks off out here.'

And very nice rocks they are, I think as I rip off the paper like Mitch will later when he gets his new dog bed. I pull out some smooth fabric.

'It's a Christmas apron.' Laughing, I unroll it and see that it has my name embroidered across the top.

'Try it on,' he says.

Aware that I'm naked, I get out of bed into the chilly Christmas morning air and slip the apron on.

Cal sits back, his hands behind his head. 'Let's have a twirl, then.'

As I turn slowly round, knowing he can see my bare bottom, he lets out an 'ohhh' of approval. 'Another bum Christmas present, never mind,' he says, but the look in his eyes, a slow-burning intensity, tells me how he really feels. A glow has kindled under my skin and deep inside me. I'm beginning to feel that everyone can look after themselves today.

'Oh, it looks as if someone's left something in the pockets,' he says.

I dig out a small package from the apron pocket. It's a smallish oblong blue box. When I flip the lid, a beautiful bracelet nestles on a white silk interior. It's made up of tiny silver shells and starfish, interspaced with freshwater pearls that remind me of the colours of Kilhallon Cove on a still summer's day.

Before I came to Kilhallon, I'd become good at not crying when things were bad. I'd had no reason to cry when things were good, but Kilhallon has ruined me.

'You don't like it?' Cal says, probably spotting my bottom lip trembling.

'I don't like it. I *love* it. It's . . . it's dreamy. I

can't believe it's mine.'

His eyes light up with pleasure, though mine are misty. 'Good. I liked the colours. Robyn made it to my specific instructions before she left for Oz.'

A tear escapes and runs down my face.

'Bloody hell. Anyone would think I'd given you the sack!' he says, grabbing my hand and pulling me back into bed on top of him. 'You'd better take that off. We don't have to cook Christmas dinner quite yet.'

★　★　★

Against all the odds, dinner is ready. To loud 'ohs' and 'ahs' we carry the turkeys to the table. Polly and her family, and Will and Emma and their girls, follow us with the vegetables, gravy, cranberry sauce, roast potatoes — everything that a traditional meal should have and probably more. When our other 'normal' paying guests heard about the feast, they all chipped in and donated some of their wine, chocolates and other goodies.

We've had a few tears in the kitchens and there are more now as lunch is served. There are lots of brave faces while the crackers are pulled and cheesy jokes shared. Some of our guests will be out of their homes for weeks, even months, and they must be devastated, but for a few hours I hope we can give them a Christmas to enjoy and some fun times for the children.

After lunch, the little kids — and some of the big ones — point and gasp as our secret 'Santa' strides in, carrying a sack. The tiny one who asked about the cockerel has one finger stuck up his nose and the other pointing at Santa.

His dad crouches down by him and murmurs in his ear, 'Oh, look. It's one of Santa's helpers.'

'*Ho ho ho.*'

'No, it's not. It's just the man who owns the holiday park,' Max chirps up and everyone laughs.

Undeterred, 'Santa' hands out presents to the kids and even Max seems mildly impressed by his gift, a new game for his console.

'Where did these come from? They must have cost a fortune,' I whisper as Cal strips off his Santa costume in the staff cubby hole.

'Local traders donated some of the presents. Emma collected them while we were busy yesterday and she and Will also paid for some extra gifts.'

'Wow.'

'They're loaded, apparently. He owns a chain of climbing-equipment shops. They also gave me a very generous donation for the flood hardship appeal and offered all the families a break at his place in the Lake District if and when they want it.'

'I had no idea.'

'Google him,' says Cal. 'You'll see. He has an MBE for his work with the mountain rescue up there.'

We start to clear up. Some of the kids and adults play games. A couple of Twister mats have been produced, and, to my amazement, a tipsy Polly joins in.

'Come on!' I say as she falls in a heap with an 'oof.'

Slowly she sits up. 'I've gone all funny after that. I think I'd better call it a day and make myself a cup of tea.'

She wobbles towards the kitchen, making me worry about health and safety, but in few seconds, I find myself spread-eagled on the slippery Twister mat with Cal and one of the mums, shaking with laughter, far too full of turkey and Christmas pudding and in danger of collapsing at any moment.

Darkness falls outside and people begin to wander back to their own accommodation.

Max's mum, the one from my cottage, clutches the hand of her daughter who's still wearing her party hat, while the little cockerel boy dozes on his dad's shoulder.

'I didn't think, after what's happened, that we could possibly enjoy today. In fact, I think today has been one of the best Christmas Days we've ever had. Thanks, love.'

'Thank you, Demi,' says her daughter.

I crouch down and hug the little girl. 'All the best,' I say. 'Stay as long as you like.'

'My cousin's coming for us tomorrow. But I'll never forget this,' her mum says. Max is engrossed in his computer game, but does manage a mumbled 'thank you'.

'Kids, eh?' the mum says and they head to my cottage, still laughing and chattering about the party and the hens. At least they've been able to forget their troubles for a few hours. I'm happy about that.

Now it's eight o'clock and only Polly and her family, me, Cal, my dad and Rachel are left in the cafe. Even Will, Emma and the twins have gone to watch a Disney film on their TV.

Rachel rests her stockinged feet on the farmhouse settle in the cafe, rubbing her bump. Dad brings some dirty glasses into the kitchen where I'm reloading the dishwasher yet again.

'Rachel's done in so we'd better get her home, but I'll come back to help clear up.'

'Thanks but there's no need. It's almost done.'

'OK. If you're sure?'

'Yes. You can use the sitting room at the farmhouse if you like. It's not bedtime yet and the new Bond film is on soon.'

'Thanks, but Rachel's shattered and I'll probably keep her company. We've not had much sleep over the past few days.'

'When will you be back in your place, do you think?'

'I don't know. Weeks, possibly. I hope it's before the baby arrives.' He hesitates. 'I wish I'd got you a present.'

'I've managed without one for years, Dad. I can cope now. Ouch, I didn't mean it to sound like that, but I don't need gifts from you. You always made sure I was fed and had what I needed for school, even during the worst times, it just wasn't the material stuff I needed.'

'I know that.'

'Have you heard from Kyle?' I ask. 'You said he was in the army and on a tour of duty.'

'He's been at a UK base but their regiment is in Cyprus at the moment and won't be back until spring. He's been to our old house, but not to the new one — good job he can't come back for Christmas now we're flooded out. He asked me where you were in an email last week and I told him you were well and working at Kilhallon, but that we weren't speaking still.'

All I can do is nod.

'When he's back on leave, why don't you come and see him, if we're in our place by then? You can see the baby too.'

I swallow a lump in my throat. 'Yeah. I might do that. I'll definitely think about it. I'd like to see Kyle again even though we were never close. And the baby too.'

'OK.' He touches my arm. 'If you don't want to or it's too soon, that's fine. I *am* sorry. For everything. Give me another chance. Give us another chance. People can change, and it helps that I'm off the booze now.'

'I noticed you stuck to the fizzy apple juice with your lunch.'

'I thought drowning my sorrows even more than I already did would help me after your mum died. It blocked out the guilt and pain for a while and then it only made things worse. It was tough and I won't say I wouldn't love a drink right now, but I've been sober for three years. Rachel's helped me.'

'Has she?'

'Yes. It must be hard for you to see me with her. She's older than she looks, if that makes things any easier for you.'

I shrug. I still don't know how I feel about hearing any of this. Warm, fuzzy feelings are

347

going to take a while, if they ever come, but I do want to see Kyle, and the baby. Especially the baby for some reason, maybe because she represents a fresh start for all of us.

'I'd never try to replace your mother, I swear it, but I've been so lonely and lost. You left, your brother went. I'm sorry, how many times do I have to say that I've changed? People can change, Demi.'

'Yeah. I know.'

He blows out a breath of relief, but he hasn't realised that I mean *I* can change too. I can try to meet him, if not halfway then somewhere along a path that leads us much closer together.

'Demi?' he says, touching my arm briefly.

'I know you've changed. It might take me longer but Mum would want us to try so I will. Just give me time, OK?'

He nods. 'I can definitely give you that.'

Cal pokes his head around the door. 'Everything OK?'

'Fine,' we both say in unison and he smiles.

'Then let's lock up here and go back to the house.'

41

Much later, I walk into the sitting room, staring at my phone. 'Oh my God!'

'What's happened now?' Cal leans forward in on the sofa, a frown on his face.

'Nothing bad. The opposite, in fact. It's from the editor I met in London.'

'That's a relief.' Cal sinks back and picks up his whisky glass again. 'But I thought people in publishing don't work on Christmas Day.'

'Apparently they do if they really, really want you. I'm joking, this message came into my inbox a couple of days ago, I haven't had time to check it while we've been dealing with the floods. Eva texted me earlier to wish me Happy Christmas and to see how I was, but I think she was checking to see if I'd seen the note. She was worried I'd been scared off the whole idea or thought it was a crap deal. How can £20,000 be a crap deal?'

'Congratulations. You deserve it.' He pats the sofa next to him. 'Now sit down here and relax. I mixed you a whisky and a drop of water. It's the last of my dad's special malt, but I thought, if not now, then when?'

'Thanks.'

Abandoning my phone, I curl up next to him, though I can't *quite* believe what I've read. Cal slips his arm around me and I snuggle against his warm body, enjoying the texture of his sweater against my cheek and the solidity of his chest behind me. We sit in silence, sipping the whisky. I'm no big fan but must admit this glass tastes pretty good: earthy and comforting but with a fiery edge, like the man holding me. Flames dance and crackle in the hearth and the aromas of woodsmoke and whisky are mellow and soothing. We're finally alone and together, Cal and I. Life is good. Far from perfect, but if it was perfect, what point would there be in living? There are new challenges ahead for me, and for Cal, for the people we love and for Kilhallon in the New Year and the years to come. And as I imagine those years, I see myself here with him. *So* . . .

'Cal?'

'Hmm.'

'I've been thinking . . . '

'Always dangerous,' he murmurs.

I twist around and put down my glass. 'You always say that when I have an idea. Be serious for a minute.'

'OK.' He assumes a stern expression, abandons his glass and folds his arms, which only enhances his biceps and makes it even harder to concentrate. Amber flecks of firelight reflect in his dark brown eyes.

'This advance. It's not a massive amount. I mean, it *is* a massive amount of money to me, but I want to invest it in the cafe, You took a big risk in putting up the money for the building and conversion, especially when you didn't have much to spare and didn't even know we'd be able to keep Kilhallon at all. But now I'd like to have a small stake in my own business, It makes financial sense. It's an idea, isn't it?'

'An idea? You know how I love your ideas . . . ' He drops his arms, his expression genuinely serious now, which is doing seriously mushy things to my insides. 'It's your money, you can do whatever you want with it, but don't ever think you have to repay me or owe me anything. You've got where you are completely by your own efforts. I played no part in it.'

I put my arms around him, loving the feel of the rough wool of his sweater under my fingertips. 'None at all?'

'Well, maybe I provided some moral support at times.'

'Mostly immoral, actually.' Leaning forward, I kiss him and push my tongue into his mouth. As if on cue, Mitch lets out a growl, but his eyes are shut tight and he goes back to his dream, twitching as he chases imaginary rabbits.

When our kiss ends, my lips tingle from the warmth of his lips and the tang of the whisky. Cal smiles and takes my hands in his. 'It's a lot of cash. A big commitment.'

'I've already made up my mind about investing in the business so don't try to persuade me out of it.'

His eyes light up with pleasure. 'If that's your decision, I'm happy — delighted — to go along with it, but we'll have a proper contract drawn up to formalise the arrangement. You'll be a partner in the business.'

Partner? In my own business? My heart might just explode, but I try not to squeak in delight because I'm a hard-headed businesswoman now.

Cal raises his eyebrows at me. 'But remember when you're as rich as Mawgan Cade, not to screw me over and turn me off my own land.'

'I'll never turn into Mawgan Cade!' I stroke my chin Dr Evil style. 'Then again, it could be fun, having you at my mercy.'

'Fun for who?' he asks with a sexy eyebrow waggle.

'Both of us.'

Cal stands up, pulling me with him. My limbs are liquid, yet I'm trembling too. Without a word he leads me out of the sitting room, where Mitch snores softly by the armchair. The stairs creak as they always do and I follow him upstairs, my hand still in his. My breath is shorter now, desire building deep inside me at the sight of his gorgeous bum and thighs in his new Christmas jeans. In his bedroom now, he flicks the switch of the lamp and sits on the edge of the bed.

I stand between his legs and he holds me and looks up at me. 'There's no escape from the Hot Vampire this time,' he says, referring to the silly name I had for him when we first met. He bares his teeth. 'There's no tree to crash through the bedroom window and save you like last time.'

'Maybe this time I don't want to escape . . . '

He smiles. 'You don't know what I've got in store for you yet, maiden.'

'I think you know that I'm not a maiden by now . . . '

'And I'm not a vampire, but who cares. Come here!' My shriek echoes as Cal pulls me downwards and rolls me on top of him. I kiss him, actually I'm devouring him. My hands are pushing up his sweater and I'm tugging his shirt out of his jeans. There's a bit of a tangle as he pulls both off at once and soon he's naked from the waist up, his summer tan fading but his chest and abs still firm and muscled, and all mine . . .

★ ★ ★

I wake on Boxing Day morning as the first slivers of light creep into the room. Cal's eyes are shut and his lashes brush his cheek. I prop myself up on one elbow, hardly daring to breathe in case I wake him. He looks beautiful, peaceful, innocent, then I remember some of the things he did to me last night and my own cheeks glow.

'I hope you're not watching me sleep,' he mutters, opening one eye.

'How can I watch you sleep, when you're obviously awake?'

He opens the other eye and pulls me against him. Realising I'm still naked, I snuggle back down under the covers. Cal's most definitely awake from the feel of him, but he doesn't try to make love to me again. Yet. He pushes my hair out of my eyes and looks at me intently.

'Will you be staying over with me again?'

'If you want me to.'

'Just for tonight?'

'Yes, for tonight, and tomorrow if you like. And after that, let's take each night as it comes, and reassess the situation every morning.'

His smile is one of intense pleasure, almost joy. I'm worried he might hear my heart beating, then he nods, as if he's satisfied to have finally got what he wanted. We lie next to each other on the bed. Cal stares at the ceiling while I try to tame a feeling of wild happiness that is so intense and out of control, I'm worried. It's too late now to back away from Cal, from the commitment. I've flown so high, perhaps now the only way can be down, but I'm not going to crash. He won't let me.

His fingers lift my hair and tease it gently away from my eyes. 'Demi?' Cal murmurs.

'Mmm.' My voice is dreamy. I may float away at any moment and although it's probably a post-sex lull and lack of sleep, I wonder if it's possible to die of happiness.

'Did you persuade Mawgan to back off from Kilhallon?' he asks.

My body tenses. 'Me?'

He turns to face me. 'How many Demi's are there around here? Why didn't you tell me, before?'

'Because when Mawgan called me that night, she made me swear not to. She said she'd ruin us if I told anyone else and she also said some other things about your dad that weren't very nice and might have been a pile of crap. And then you assumed that Isla had made Mawgan back down and, at the time, you and Isla were close . . . I know you're still close . . . so it was easier for all of us to let you go on thinking that.'

'You should have told me.'

'No, I shouldn't. It was my decision. You know now. How did you guess it was me?'

'Isla told me it wasn't her when she came to

dinner and since then, I've been putting the pieces together and then something Kit said made me suspect it was you.'

'Please don't let on. Mawgan could still make a lot of trouble for us if she really wanted to.'

'What did she say about Dad? Was it about him having an affair with Mrs Cade?'

I nod. 'You know about that too?'

'Yes, Kit told me.' He strokes my arm. 'How did you get her to change her mind?'

'I don't honestly know. I just told Mawgan that she was hurting Andi and herself and basically she went batshit and weird and threw me out. I never expected her to drop her opposition. In fact, at any moment I expected her to fly round here on her broomstick and say I'd made things worse, so when she called to say she didn't want Kilhallon, I was even more amazed than you and Polly.'

Cal keeps looking at me. He keeps stroking my arm and my thigh. His gaze is intense and makes my skin tingle and my body fizz. My stomach is in knots, but in a good way.

'What? Why are you looking at me like that?'

He breaks into a smile. 'Because, once again, I'm gobsmacked by you. You never stop surprising me or driving me mad. Like inviting half the town for Christmas or making me desperate to share my house, with a big smelly hound in my bedroom.'

'Mitch does not smell.'

'He does after those sprout dog treats.'

'Experimental. Not everything can work.'

He laughs. 'Now you tell me you went to my

355

worst enemy, a woman devoid of a heart or a soul, and appealed to some shred of conscience that must be buried deeper than radioactive waste. And you persuaded her to stop harassing me and saved my business, home and sanity in the process.'

I shrug. 'All part of the job.'

He gathers me to him. 'No. It isn't. It's way beyond the call of duty.'

'And you won't tell anyone about my visit to Mawgan? Not Polly or Isla for God's sake. If it gets out that Mawgan has a heart after all, or at least she thought she did for a second, then she'll go ballistic and she'll come after us even harder.'

'I won't tell anyone.'

'But do you swear on your life?'

He puts on his 'serious' face. 'Demi Jones. I solemnly swear on my life and Mitch's that I will never divulge your secret as long as I live. Satisfied?'

'Hmm.'

'You don't trust me?'

'About ninety-nine per cent of the time,' I say, enjoying teasing him, but I'm also being honest. No one can ever trust anyone absolutely, not even themselves. Especially not themselves.

He whispers in my ear. 'Thanks. Whatever you did or said. Thanks.'

My throat's too clogged to reply with anything sensible so I think I say something about him owing me for a very long time. Then we hold each other, although I don't think it will be for long from what I can tell. We're still naked and there's no hiding place when you're pressed this close together under a warm duvet with a hot man you love to bits and fancy the pants off.

The inevitable happens. The wonderful, sweaty, rampant inevitable and we're lying in a tangle of duvet again, wondering whether Boxing Day is even worth getting out of bed for. I trace my initials over Cal's bare chest, although he won't know, flattening and raising the springy hair. I'm so glad he doesn't go in for waxing.

'Why are you giggling?'

'Nothing. We really ought to get up.'

He sighs. 'Do we have to?'

'Mitch will need his breakfast soon, and a run.'

'Hmm. I'll get up and feed him and take him out.'

'We can do it together now,' I say, glowing with post-sex euphoria and bursting to get up and enjoy the rest of our day together.

Cal, in contrast, frowns as if I've just suggested we should invite Mawgan Cade round for brunch followed by naked Twister. He props himself up on one elbow and takes in a breath.

'You once asked me where I was last Christmas and what Kit knew that could cause me so much pain. You haven't asked me since we had our row and I'm grateful for that. I didn't think I could ever tell you, but things are different between us now. I owe it to you — no, I *need* to tell you. I wasn't angry with Kit because he was going to tell everyone what he thinks he knows about me. I was angry because I still can't forgive myself for what happened.'

42

'There's one thing I want you to know. I wasn't a soldier or a spy, whatever Kit may have implied. We need those people and they have their own shitty nightmarish job to do, a job I couldn't do. I wasn't one. I never meant to be . . . but it *was* my fault. They'd both still be alive if it wasn't for me.'

The mention of people dying sends a shiver down my spine, but Cal needs to tell me this. I want to hear it, no matter how awful it is. 'Kit hasn't told me anything. I've no idea what happened to you, but I swore to him you'd never ever do anything wicked or cruel,' I say softly, pulling the covers back over us both.

'Not intentionally, but you have more faith in me than I do in myself.' He turns his face away from me and stares at the ceiling. My hand rests lightly on his and under my fingertips, his pulse quickens.

'There was a woman. Her name was Soraya and she had a daughter called Esme who was nine years old. She'd be ten now, of course . . . '

'When did this happen?' I ask, half afraid to break the spell, but wanting to encourage him.

'It was not long after Christmas last year, I'm not even sure of the date because each day blurred into the rest and they were all pretty awful. But I do remember that I'd just had an email — in a rare moment when I had access to a laptop and some Internet — from Robyn moaning about her dad.' He shakes his head. 'Actually, it was a relief to hear about some trivial silly problem for a change rather than dealing with life and death and horror. I meant to reply, but I never got the chance.'

His shiver is unmistakeable, but he carries on.

'I remember thinking that I'd email her back and I'd try to pick up some presents once I got to civilisation, and get a postcard for Isla.'

'Oh God, the postcards . . . ' I say with a groan, remembering the day earlier this year when I found a bundle of cards that Cal had sent to Isla while he'd been working abroad.

He smiles briefly but his expression quickly darkens. 'Yes.'

'Sorry. It was an accident that I found them in your room . . . ' My face heats up as I recall sitting on Cal's bed and reading some of his private messages to Isla. I'd only just started working for him then and I could have melted with shame at being caught by Cal.

'I *knew* you'd read them.'

'I only read a few. Once they'd fallen out of the box I couldn't help myself.'

He shakes his head. 'It doesn't matter. To be honest, I was so low at the time, I didn't really care and I also knew, even then, you'd never tell anyone else my private business.'

'I'm still sorry for prying.'

He squeezes my hand then lets it go. 'Forget it. Isla had insisted I take them all back shortly after I came home at Easter, as if to underline that it was the end of things for us. She told me it wasn't right to keep them now she was engaged to Luke. Anyway, all that's behind me, but I can't leave everything behind me so easily. I don't want to.'

'You don't have to.' I brush my lips over his, hoping the postcard reminder won't stop him from continuing with his story. 'Carry on. You can't stop now.'

'I need to go back further than Robyn's email for you to fully understand what happened. You know that I worked for a charity in Syria that provided shelter, food and medical aid.'

'I know some of it, but you've never told me the details.' Cal's mentioned his time in a desert landscape a couple of times, but never specifically. He's made it obvious he wants me — and all of his friends and family — to leave that part of his life well alone, which is why I'm so amazed to hear him talk about it now.

'We set up an aid station in a refugee camp on the Syrian border with Iraq. We were only a few kilometres from a Syrian town where local fighters were constantly battling with violent insurgents. The insurgents were drawing closer every day and shelling the town, but the locals refused to leave. Who could blame them? They were desperate not to be driven out of their homes, even though they were in great danger. Sooner or later my charity colleagues and I knew we might have to retreat even further from the town if things went badly for the locals and the town fell into the terrorists' hands. But we wanted to stay for as long as possible to help those refugees who did want to flee, and support the townspeople who insisted on staying in what was left of their homes.

'You see,' he tells me quietly. 'It's not as simple as 'them' and 'us' out there. There are so many different factions, so many people with different agendas, all prepared to kill to get their way. Insurgents, terrorists, government troops, local rebels and fighters battling their own government, UN peacekeepers — even some of 'our' own Special Forces, most of whom were there unofficially. You don't know who your enemy is half the time, let alone your friends, but Soraya *was* a true friend.'

A *true* friend. I'm not sure what Cal means by that phrase. Is he trying to tell me that there was more than friendship between him and Soraya even while he was in love with Isla? I'm still reeling from the fact that he's decided to finally open up about his experiences at all. I must tread very carefully. 'Was Soraya an aid worker too?'

'Not officially. She wasn't on the staff. She'd been a nurse before the war started but her husband, siblings and parents had all been killed and she'd had to leave her job when the hospital she worked at was bombed. She helped us by setting up a clinic in the makeshift buildings near to the hospital.'

'Oh God, how horrible for her to lose her family.'

'It's horrific, but she was one of many people to lose loved ones and she had no choice but to carry on for the sake of her daughter, Esme.'

'If Esme was nine, that's the same age as the

361

Tennants' girls . . . ' I think of the twins and myself, too, at that age. I was still secretly playing with dolls and teddies even though I made out I was way too grown-up. Then I picture Esme growing up surrounded by bombs and danger and chaos. 'Imagine being so young and afraid in such an awful situation.'

'People had to do their best and try to survive somehow,' Cal replies. 'Soraya still had some cousins and her elderly grandparents left. All of them refused to leave the town so Soraya decided to stay there with Esme for as long as she could. And one of her cousins led a group of local fighters who were trying to push back the insurgents.' He grimaces. 'I say 'insurgents' but their main aim was to reduce the place to dust or take it back to some kind of medieval hell — both, if they could.'

I shudder. 'I can't even think about something so terrifying.'

Cal kisses me briefly. 'Then don't try. Although Soraya still lived in the town, she used to help us when she could, bringing injured children to the camp, treating people and interpreting. She also acted as a bridge between us aid workers and her local fighter friends. Without her, we couldn't have treated or sheltered as many people as we did. She built up trust with the locals so that we could go into places we wouldn't otherwise have been able to. They trusted Soraya so they trusted us.'

He takes a deep breath, then carries on. 'What she didn't know was that I'd already been persuaded to help out a small UK group of soldiers. They were supposed to be there for reconnaissance and security reasons but I now realise they must have been from military intelligence or Special Forces. Looking back, I already suspected as much and chose to ignore it.

'I'd got to know their commanding officer while I'd been working. I trusted him as he'd helped us out of some very tricky situations and his guys had even saved me and my boss's life on more than one occasion when we'd run into trouble. He asked me to open up some lines of communication with the local fighters who were led by Soraya's cousin, so I agreed to persuade Soraya to broker a meeting between them.

'I knew we weren't supposed to become involved in military activity of any kind. I'm not a soldier and I was meant to be as neutral as you can be in that seething mess. But how can you be neutral when you believe that something is right and you want to protect people? The lines had become blurred — my lines, everyone's . . . you understand?' He hesitates.

'Not really, Cal, but please don't stop.'

'I was reluctant to ask Soraya to help me, but I was convinced I'd be helping the people we were caring for and she was in contact with them anyway. I'm not making excuses. I knew what I was doing and I made the call. I arranged the meeting and I started to take stuff between our military and the local fighters via Soraya on my regular runs into town with our charity truck.'

'What kind of stuff?'

'Medical supplies, mostly . . . some items of

communications equipment . . . ' His voice tails off. 'My boss must have known something was going on but she turned a blind eye, even though the supplies, antibiotics and analgesia, are like gold dust there. She probably thought they were all for civilians, but they were also used by local fighters and she had no idea about the comms and other military equipment.

'Then one day my army friend asked me to do something else on one of my runs into town.'

A door slams downstairs, startling us both. I can feel Cal's heart beating — or is it mine?

'Go on,' I say.

'My military friend asked me to take some weapons — guns, rocket-propelled grenades, an anti-tank mortar — to Soraya's cousin to use against the insurgents. This was a step too far for me — or rather, it ought to have been a step too far. I refused at first, but my military contact pleaded with me. He said that he had intelligence there would be a major assault on the town by the insurgents and that I should take the hardware as soon as possible in our truck, hidden among the medical supplies. He said that insurgent sympathisers might have already infiltrated the town and would be on the lookout for soldiers, but they wouldn't suspect me in our charity truck.'

'Oh my God. I had no idea you were so close to the fighting.'

'I told Soraya about my fears but she said that her cousin and his group needed the weapons. She said she'd take them if I didn't. She'd do anything she could to help her cousin and his group and that after she'd delivered the weapons, she'd bring Esme straight back to the camp.

'At first, I refused point blank and said it was too dangerous, but she said that the arms were vital and her group needed them. I wish I hadn't told her at all, but I trusted her judgement. In the end, I said we'd both go. But that's not how it turned out . . . '

His words tail off and he's silent. Beads of perspiration sheen his forehead. I touch his arm gently. 'What happened?'

He takes a breath. 'I started to load the guns and supplies into our truck with Soraya. There was an explosion nearby. A school on the outskirts of the camp had been shelled. I didn't know what to do. I was torn. I couldn't take the arms then. The injured school kids came first. But I also knew that the fighting was very close and that Soraya's friends would need the arms if they were to have any chance of defending themselves.'

'What a nightmare situation. What did you do in the end?'

'I told Soraya not to go without me and ran to help some of the kids. She said she'd wait for me, but I never saw her again. Not alive . . . '

'Oh, Cal.' My heart breaks for him.

He takes a deep breath and pushes on, speaking faster now. 'Even while I was helping with the school attack, word came that the insurgents had broken through the outskirts of the town faster than anyone expected and it could fall into their hands within hours. We were ordered by UN soldiers to evacuate all the civilians immediately and my boss and colleagues had no choice but to take their advice or be killed or captured. Esme was still in the town with her grandparents . . .

'I had to do *something*. The truck was nowhere to be seen and I hoped that one of my colleagues had taken it to help evacuate people. Deep down, however, I was already worried that Soraya had gone into town in it. I looked everywhere for her in the camp, but it was mayhem as everyone tried to pack up to ship out. Eventually I found a note in my quarters from her, saying she'd left shortly after I'd run to the school. I can't stop thinking that if I hadn't told her about the arms or left her on her own, she'd still be alive and Esme would be safe.'

'But you didn't encourage her. You tried to stop her. It was her decision to go alone and she must have wanted to be with her daughter too.'

'I don't know. All I know is that I should have died and not her . . . I wish I'd never become involved with the military.'

'I'm so sorry, but you can't change anything now, and beating yourself up won't help. What happened when you got to town?' I ask, though a big part of me can't bear to hear.

'I know. As soon as I realised where she'd gone, I left my colleagues to tend to the injured children and raced to the other side of town to find her and make her come back to the camp with Esme. It was like trying to fight against the rip tide. People flowed out of the town in rusty cars, on bikes and in carts — but mostly on foot with what they could carry on their backs. They were terrified. Some UN people tried to stop me and make me turn back, but I needed to find Soraya.

'I found the house where her cousin's group met. One of the fighters said Soraya hadn't been there at all so I knew that something bad had happened. I ran to her grandparents' home, hoping against hope that she'd gone there first. I ran around the corner and . . . Oh, Jesus, I saw the truck. Or what was left of it.'

'Oh God, Cal.' My hand flies to my mouth.

Cal closes his eyes. He swallows hard.

'The truck had been hit and was in pieces. I don't know if the insurgents deliberately targeted it or if it was a random hit. All I know is that I should have been driving it. It had come to rest a little way from the grandparents' house. I threw up when I saw the blackened, twisted metal, expecting Soraya to be inside.'

I feel sick myself at the image Cal has conjured in my mind.

He squeezes my hand. 'But she wasn't in the truck. At least she didn't end up like that.'

'How . . . how did it end, then?'

'I'll never know for sure but I think that she decided things had become too dangerous and made straight for her grandparents' house to find them and Esme, and drive back to the camp. In the end, I'm sure she put Esme first . . . '

Cal stops, struggling for words now. My heart breaks for him, but he takes a breath and carries on.

'I staggered forward, hoping against hope that

Soraya had survived the hit on the truck and was in the rubble around us. You could feel the ground tremble from the mortars dropping, and smell the smoke and hear the gunfire. I knew I had only minutes to try to get back to safety, if that. I was frantic. I ran into the house. I thought I was already through the door when a fresh explosion knocked me off my feet, but some of the memories have gone now . . . ' He rubs his hand over his forehead, pushing back his hair. 'I must have blacked out.'

'Oh God, Cal.'

'I was knocked off my feet and I must have been unconscious for a while. It might have only been for a few seconds or half a minute. When I came to, I saw that there had been a direct strike on the building. From who, or what, I don't know. It might have been the insurgents. It could have been our own forces, government forces. It doesn't matter now. It won't make any difference. Even if I'd been right and Soraya had been in the house trying to get Esme, it was obvious to me now that she was dead. She lay on a pile of rubble. There was hardly a mark on her body, that happens sometimes in a blast, but I knew instantly that she was gone. Her body was as limp as a rag doll.'

Tears trickle down my cheeks, but Cal's voice is now steady. 'I knew straight away, but I made sure of it before I had to leave her.'

My face is wet with tears. 'I'm so sorry for your loss, Cal. It was a terrible decision to have to make: to help her people and then to leave her. I know I wasn't there but don't think you could have made any other choice. How had Kit found out about this though? Why did he want to publish it?'

'Kit mentioned the name of a contact to me and I did recognise it. It was some guy who used to be in Special Forces. He's an ex-soldier now, apparently, and he's known for passing on information to journalists if he's paid enough money.

'While we were working together after the floods, Kit told me that he'd found out I was working in this region of Syria and that his contact had some information about me. Kit must have been delighted when he found out I'd secretly been working for the military and that I'd been involved in the death of a local woman. He thought it would make a human interest story and also make me look bad, especially as Kit admitted he also thought there might be more to my relationship with Soraya than just being colleagues.'

'He thought you and Soraya were lovers?'

'Yes, but he's wrong. Soraya and I were more than friends, but we weren't lovers. We were compatriots and I did love her, just not in the way I loved Isla — or you.'

My stomach flips. I can't believe Cal has said he loves me. I can't process the joy of hearing it in the middle of such terrible circumstances.

Cal holds me. 'I feel that it was my responsibility, my fault that Soraya drove into town and ended up in the wrong place at the wrong time.'

'But it wasn't. She didn't die in the truck

accident. It was random, in the end, and if you'd both gone, you might both have been killed. Kit can't blame you for her death, even if he wanted to expose you for working for the military.'

'That's why I was so upset with him. Not because I was worried about being in the newspapers, but I do feel responsible for putting Soraya in the wrong place at the wrong time. Kit rubbed salt in my wounds; he knew that I felt guilty and he wanted to hurt me by reopening the wound. He succeeded, until he had a change of heart.'

I groan. 'I told him he must be wrong about you when I went to London. He understands how you feel now, I think . . . What happened after you came to and discovered Soraya had gone?' I say.

'I searched for Esme, of course. I'd assumed she must still be in the wreck of the house and that was a horrific thought, but I had to make sure. There were still people running and crawling around, some horribly injured, others fleeing for their lives. The noise, the smell, the screams. I'll never forget it. But Esme wasn't there.'

'There's hope, then, that she escaped?'

He shakes his head. 'I daren't hope too much. A local fighter who I recognised arrived and tried to drag me away. He was injured himself and I think I'd dislocated my own shoulder and knee, but I carried on searching for Esme. She might have been injured or trapped in the ruins. I might have been able to help her. If the worst had happened, I reasoned, I might have found her body and at least known what happened so I could break the news to her relatives if I saw them. But she was nowhere. I carried on looking for God knows how long but the bombs were deafening by this point and the air was full of dust from the collapsed buildings.'

'You could have been killed.'

'I didn't care. I didn't think about it. I was so hell bent on finding Esme even though I knew it might be hopeless. Eventually, I heard the rumble of the terrorists' armoured vehicles and decided to get out of there, hoping to renew my search for Esme back at the refugee camp. It was barely a mile to the border where the military would be defending the camp . . . '

He pauses again. I touch his arm, but I don't think he can feel me.

'And I almost made it. I got as far as the edge of the town before I was caught by two lads — I can't call them men — in a Jeep, armed to the teeth and high on something. They overtook me and I had no choice but to stop. Later, I often wished I'd kept running and let them shoot me. In fact I expected them to shoot me on the spot. Part of me wanted them to, because I knew worse might follow if they didn't.'

'Oh my God.'

'But they didn't kill me, as you can see, and I'm here.'

'So they held you in the town?'

'To start with, in some cellar underneath a bombed-out building.'

'What happened to you?'

'Don't ask. I never thought I'd see home

again. I thought I'd end up in a YouTube video and the last thing my friends and family — Isla and Robyn — would see was me being shot or possibly even worse. But far worse than that was the guilt about Soraya and Esme. I had no idea, and I still don't, if she was still alive. She wasn't in the rubble. Someone must have taken her with them when they had to evacuate. Or perhaps the insurgents had taken her too. I'm sick at the thought of that even now.'

Can your blood run cold? It feels like it. I hug him tightly, still feeling his heart beat. His skin is cool and clammy. My mind is racing, so many thoughts, all vile and nightmarish, tumbling through it. My mind is flooded with images from the TV news, horrible things that most of us switch off to avoid. Places on the Internet we dare not go. Things so far from cosy Cornish cafes, so far from people laughing and enjoying their holidays, children playing on the sand, the oldies laughing over a cuppa and a cake in the cafe, wandering through the wildflowers, paddling in the sea . . .

'Demi? It's OK, you know. I'm here. I survived.' I lift my head. He smiles at me. 'Though I may pass out from suffocation if you don't let go of me.'

'Oh, sorry. I hadn't realised I was holding you so tight.'

I release my grip but I can't relax. 'My God, I can't even imagine what you went through. But you're here now. How did you get away?'

'The insurgents persuaded some poor local guy, who I'd actually once helped to treat, to identify me as working undercover with the western Special Forces. Which wasn't true, of course, but it wasn't *strictly* untrue because I *had* been involved with them. I don't blame the poor man: they'd probably threatened to kill his family if he didn't say it.

'Either way, I thought I was a goner. I'm amazed they didn't kill me on the spot. After a couple of days, they moved me to another house. I say house, it was just a shack that had been part of a goat farm in the desert. That was worse because of the heat.' He throws off the cover even though the bedroom's as chilly as ever. 'I could see light though the edges of the corrugated iron roof. I was there for a few weeks. I scratched each sunrise on the wall so I could keep track of the time.'

'How did you cope?'

'Part of me didn't care what happened to me, except for the pain it would cause my uncle, Robyn, Polly and Isla. I thought I should have been dead anyway. Only the thought of home and the people I loved kept me going — and even then, I felt guilty that I might live to see them while Soraya and Esme were dead.'

'No wonder you looked so thin when I saw you at the Beach Hut. I just thought you were a hipster on a faddy diet.'

He manages a smile and shakes his head. 'I wish. Put it like this, my hosts' hospitality wasn't a patch on Demelza's.' He kisses me.

'So that's why no one heard from you for a while.'

'Yes. My boss — the head of the charity

— heard from my military friend that I'd been kidnapped. She was confused and horrified.'

'How did you escape after they took you?' I ask.

'After I'd disappeared, the Special Forces guys found out what had happened. I think some of the local fighters must have seen or heard and together they formulated a plan to rescue me. They told my boss I'd been kidnapped off the street and was being held as a hostage, and they persuaded her not to tell my family I was incommunicado until they could get me out.'

He props himself up and fixes his eyes on my face. 'Demi, you must swear on my life not to talk about this to anyone. Not to Robyn or Polly even. Let's face it, most of the people here think I was exhausted and had a breakdown, and that I went AWOL. Let them think that, it's easier for everyone.'

He takes a breath, then begins again. 'I can't live my life looking over my shoulder and I don't give a toss about being abused and flamed in the papers or on social media. I just couldn't handle the guilt when Kit accused me. He was right, and that's why I was so angry.'

'I don't think Kit will publish the story now. He promised,' I say.

'You're right. I don't think he will.' He pauses.

'You know I was worried when you went back to London,' I say.

He looks puzzled. 'Why?'

'I wondered if you'd gone to see if you could get your old job back.'

'No. I can't go back unless I have a death wish

. . . and the charity doesn't want me after what happened. I'm too much trouble, but I'd like to try and find Esme, if she survived. When I went to London, I heard that the locals have re-taken the town and the camp has been rebuilt, but there was no news about Esme or the rest of her family. There are so many people displaced that it's impossible to tell . . . ' He sighs. 'I hate facing the truth but my boss is right. I'll probably never see Esme again.'

Cal is quiet for so long, staring into space, I wonder if he'll ever speak again.

'I thought when you went to London, that you might decide life wasn't exciting running a holiday resort and cafe in Cornwall when you could save the world. Sorry, that sounds stupid now. I'd no idea what really happened out there.'

'I don't think I've done much saving, though at one time, when I started out, I thought I could. I've helped a few people, and made life worse for a few others. I think it's time to concentrate on my family and friends and the people I love now.'

The people I love now.

'I spent a lot of time apart from the people I loved when they needed me as much as the people thousands of miles away did. I won't make that mistake again. Demi, you can try to get rid of me if you like, but I intend to stay put here.'

I believe him. I think I do. What if he hadn't been caught, I ask myself? If he could safely return, would he? Would Kilhallon be enough? Now I know why he threw himself into renovating it. What else was he going to do?

'If I could only find out where Esme is and if she's safe, it would put my mind at rest.'

'Is there no way?'

'I could try my military contact again, but he's told me it's virtually hopeless. My boss too. They both told me to focus my energy here, not on guilt and regrets. Slowly, over the last nine months, I've begun to come to terms with what happened. So if I've been a moody arse, I'm sorry.'

He kisses me.

'I don't blame you. I understand why now. I've always tried to understand, but knowing all of this helps,' I sigh, keeping my voice light even though I can hardly take in what Cal has shared with me. It's so big, so much bigger than our little world at Kilhallon. 'Even though you drive me mad at times, I'm glad you plan on staying here with us too.'

He smiles. 'Even if you sometimes long for me to get lost, what would Mitch do without me? Whose crotch would he sniff? Whose best jeans would he drool on? I'd definitely miss finding soggy dog chews in my wellies.'

I'm laughing now, and almost crying too, but not quite, because it's Christmas — well, actually it's Boxing Day — and I've given myself a Polly-style talking to about getting emotional, because today was meant to be the day we all chilled out and finally got to relax and enjoy our break . . . That seems hard to do after what Cal told me. Then again, what can any of us do but get on with life?

Cal holds me and we just lie together for what seems like ages. Mitch will have to wait for his run. Cal needs me for now. Eventually, he lets me go.

'Cal. I have a confession too.'

He raises his eyebrows. 'Sounds serious.'

'Not really. With all the drama over the past few weeks, I haven't got you a present. I meant to get you something but I never found anything I thought you'd love enough.'

He laughs. 'But I've got my present. You here in the farmhouse.'

'Is that enough of a present?'

'More than enough, although I hope Mitch will agree to move in too. I'd better let him out,' he says with a smile. Then he pulls on his jeans and a sweatshirt and goes downstairs to look after Mitch. I stay here a few minutes more, trying to make sense of what he's shared with me, which is momentous, moving, frightening and amazing.

The sounds from downstairs reach the bedroom — Mitch's excited yips, Cal's voice, doors opening and cupboards closing — and remind me that whatever happened in the past is over. Cal's here in the house. Safe.

He says it's the whole story about him; and there's nothing left to tell me. He says he's laid himself bare to me. So many things about Cal Penwith make more sense to me now; although some don't and maybe never will. I don't want a man I know completely; I don't want to tame him or predict him.

All I know is that what he told me was

something that he could only share with one or two people in his life: his parents, if they were still here; not Polly or Robyn or even Isla.

Just me. This is my real and most precious Christmas present. Cal's trust. Finally.

I pull on some clothes and go down to the kitchen. Cal leans against the worktop, sipping a cup of coffee. Steam curls into the air. His mug stops halfway to his mouth and he lowers it slowly to the counter. He looks at me as if I might have changed my mind about moving in, so I reach for him and pull him into a long coffee-scented kiss.

'*Nadelik Loweth*,' he whispers to me.

A cold wet nose pushes its way between us.

'Who let that dog in here?' he says.

'You, I think, and it Mitch's home now too. He's entitled to some privileges.'

There's a moment before the meaning of my comment sinks in and then I'm pulled against Cal in the biggest, tightest bear hug ever.

'*Nadelik Loweth*,' I say. 'And may it be the start of many . . . '

Cal kisses me, almost lifting me off my feet in the process, as if he never wants to let me go. After what he just told me, I know how he feels. But we have a new day here, a fresh start and a chance to try and put the past behind us, if it's possible. Cal's story has made me even more determined to try to heal the wounds in my own family, no matter how difficult.

'Have I ever told you I . . . ' Cal whispers to me, still holding me tight, but Mitch starts growling. It's his warning tone. Cal groans. 'For

God's sake, Mitch, can't I have one snog with your mistress without . . . '

Mitch leaps out of his basket. He runs towards the kitchen door and woofs.

'Mitch! Calm down!' I say, annoyed with him for making a fuss. He ought to know us by now. He nudges the kitchen door open a crack with his muzzle and we hear voices from above. Raised voices, shrieks and wails and then the sound of someone thudding down the stairs. Mitch barks loudly. I let Cal go. 'What the . . . '

The kitchen door slams back on its hinges and my dad stands in the doorway, white as a sheet.

'Quick. Will someone call an ambulance? It's Rachel. I think she's having the baby.'

Epilogue

December 27th, late morning

I have a baby sister. I'll say that again because I can't believe it myself: I have a baby sister. She weighs 5lbs 2ozs and she's called Freya Penelope, because my mum's name was Penny. She arrived in the early hours of this morning and she's a few weeks early so she and Rachel will be staying in overnight, but that's OK, apparently. They'll both be fine, so Cal has driven me home to Kilhallon Park.

A few months ago, a few weeks ago, I would have cried at the news, but not for the reason I cried when Dad came into the waiting room and told me and Cal that Rachel had had a little girl and that they were both fine and would we like to meet her. Cal shook his hand, said congratulations, and then Dad hugged me and I didn't want to vom or scream. It was OK; it felt right in that moment and I'm mindful how lucky I am to have the opportunity to start again. I'm going to make the most of it.

Freya's fingers are teeny tiny, like a doll's, and she has a little tuft of hair the same colour as mine. She's my half-sister but Dad and Rachel told me to think of her as a whole sister, a proper sister — even if she's twenty-two years younger than me.

I don't know what's going to happen in the

future. So much has already happened, and so quickly, to us all, before Dad and I have had time to talk properly and before I've had the chance to get to know him and Rachel again.

The important thing is, as Polly and my mum might say, that we've given each other a chance. We've all given each other second chances — for Dad and me, this may be a twenty-second chance — and things are different now. Not that I've changed, or he's changed, that much, not in essentials. We're made of the same stuff as we always have been, but we're both more tolerant and willing to give it a try. Lately, it feels as if everyone at Kilhallon has been through hell but come out the other side.

'We'll never ever forget Mum,' he told me again when we saw Freya.

The thing is, I thought he *had* forgotten my mum, but maybe he only wanted to forget the pain of losing her and now he's decided he's ready to remember her. He told me he regrets every day that he didn't let her know how much he loved her. I don't need to regret not saying that, so I guess I'm much luckier than him.

Christmas is never perfect. Only a fool would expect it to be. There's such a lot still to do for all of us, both at Kilhallon and St Trenyan. But Christmas at the Cornish cafe with my friends, my old family and my new — and especially with Cal — is as close to perfect as I ever dreamed.

Cal stops outside the cafe because we're supposed to be opening today, but he says, 'Demi. Come on, don't go in today. Come home to bed.'

'I can't. I have to work. If we get a move on we can open up to get the post-Christmas ramblers and people fed up of turkey. I have pasties to bake and mulled wine to serve and so many people who need a hand. There's a community to rebuild, remember?'

'I know and I'll help you in the cafe and we'll do everything we can to get St Trenyan back on its feet, but promise me too that you'll come back home to bed — with me — at some point.' His voice is almost pleading. I can't help but smile.

'OK, it's a deal, but you'll have to put on an apron again,' I say with a grin.

'You know I look so sexy. Everyone will order lots more mince pies if I'm serving.'

'Don't flatter yourself!'

He leans in closer to me, and although I know he's teasing, I could jump on him right this second in the Land Rover in broad daylight. 'You know you want me,' he says, raising one eyebrow in a cheesy, gorgeous, sexy way.

'OK, yes, I bloody want you! Now come on, put that apron on, we've got a cafe to open.'

Acknowledgements

It's been great fun to write a Christmas story while in real life blossom has been bursting out and summer has slowly arrived! Conjuring up images of frosty mornings, festive baking and fairy lights while writing this in my sunlit garden has been surreal at times. But I've had a wonderful time celebrating Christmas with Demi and Cal, and I hope you will too.

I have to thank so many people who've helped with research, support, coffee and cakes, including Nell Dixon, Liz Hanbury, Janice Hume, Sue Welfare, Marie Deakin, Hilary Ely, Ann Cooper, Kim Nash, Jules Wake, Alison Sherlock, Bella Osborne, The Budget Food Mummy and Wendy Dixon, to name a few.

Avon Maze, my publisher, has played an absolute blinder, helping to make the first Penwith novel, *Summer at the Cornish Cafe*, a summer best-seller. Huge thanks to my editors, Eloise Wood and Natasha Harding, for their hard work and sensitive editing. Thanks too go to clever copy editor Joanne Gledhill. In Harper-Collins Marketing, Helena and Louis have also been amazing, tweeting and sharing news about my book to the Twitterverse and beyond.

To all the bloggers, authors and booklovers out there, thank you for your reviews, tweets and messages. I really appreciate you reading Cal and Demi's story and telling me that you loved spending time at Kilhallon as much as I did.

And finally, to my parents and father-in-law, and my agent, Broo — and most of all, to John, Charlotte and James. Thanks for your faith in me and for sharing this fantastic journey with me.

Recipes

Mince pie cookies
Family recipe

Ingredients:
200g mincemeat (even nicer with fancy mincemeat, e.g. orange and cranberry)
100g butter
150g caster sugar
2 medium eggs
200g plain flour
½ teaspoon mixed spice
½ teaspoon bicarbonate of soda

1. Bring the butter and eggs up to room
   temperature and turn the oven to 180C. Get
   two cookie/baking trays out and line with
   grease-proof paper.
2. Cream together the butter, sugar and eggs in
   a mixing bowl.
3. Gradually stir in the flour, then the mixed
   spice and bicarbonate of soda.
4. Finally, stir the mincemeat into the cookie
   dough.
5. These cookies spread out while cooking, so
   add small teaspoons of the mixture to your baking parchment and make sure they're well spaced.
6. Check on them after 10 mins, take them out
   once they're golden on the top. Leave to cool,
   then keep in an airtight box.

Special pumpkin pie with Cornish clotted cream
From my daughter

Feeds 12–16

Ingredients
425g can of Libby's pumpkin puree
400g can of evaporated milk
170g granulated sugar
2 large eggs
1 teaspoon ground cinnamon
½ teaspoon salt
½ teaspoon mixed spice (you can substitute with chai latte powder!)
Pecan halves
Pastry (make your own or use a sheet of readymade shortcrust)

1. Pre-heat the oven to 220C. Prepare the shortcrust to fit in a 10-inch loose-base pie dish, or very deep 8- or 9-inch pie dish. Leave plenty of excess pastry round the edges as it will shrink. Blind bake it for a few minutes to stop it going soggy. When the middle starts to rise, take it out — don't let the edges brown.
2. While you do this, mix the dry ingredients and eggs in a large bowl (easy to do by hand). Stir in the pumpkin puree and then gradually stir in the evaporated milk. Pour this mixture into your pie shell.
3. Bake the pie in the oven at 220C for 15 mins. Then reduce the temperature to 180C. You can wrap foil around the top of it if the pastry

is catching. Bake for 40 mins and add pecan halves round the edge to decorate. If a knife inserted near the centre comes out clean, it's ready to serve, otherwise give it 10 more mins. Cool on wire rack for 2 hours or refrigerate (it will keep for 4 days in a plastic box in the fridge). Top with Cornish clotted cream to serve!

Simple banana bread

Recipe and introduction reproduced by kind permission of The Budget Food Mummy http://budgetfoodmummy.com/

I'm sure this is probably an obvious tip, but instead of throwing overripe bananas in the bin, make banana bread with them! It's an easy recipe to make and there is a lot of mixing to do so it's a good one to get the children to help with. It costs around £1.25 to make a loaf size.

Ingredients:
150g unsalted butter, softened (plus extra for greasing)
150g self raising flour
150g caster sugar
2 eggs, whisked
1 teaspoon baking powder
2–3 overripe bananas, mashed

1. Pre-heat oven to 180C. Grease either a cake or bread tin.
2. Cream together the butter and sugar. Stir in

the eggs and half of the flour. Stir in the rest of the flour, baking powder and banana. Put the mixture in the greased tin, smooth it out to make it even.

3. Bake in the pre-heated oven for 30 mins, or until a skewer comes out clean.

We do hope that you have enjoyed reading this large print book.

Did you know that all of our titles are available for purchase?

We publish a wide range of high quality large print books including:
Romances, Mysteries, Classics
General Fiction
Non Fiction and Westerns

Special interest titles available in large print are:
The Little Oxford Dictionary
Music Book
Song Book
Hymn Book
Service Book

Also available from us courtesy of Oxford University Press:
Young Readers' Dictionary
(large print edition)
Young Readers' Thesaurus
(large print edition)

For further information or a free brochure, please contact us at:
Ulverscroft Large Print Books Ltd.,
The Green, Bradgate Road, Anstey,
Leicester, LE7 7FU, England.
Tel: (00 44) 0116 236 4325
Fax: (00 44) 0116 234 0205

SUMMER AT THE CORNISH CAFE

Phillipa Ashley

Demi doesn't expect her summer in Cornwall to be anything out of the ordinary. As a waitress working all hours, serving ice-creams is as exciting as the holiday season is likely to get. That is, until she meets Cal Penwith. An outsider like her, Cal is persuaded to let Demi help him renovate his holiday resort, the once idyllic Kilhallon Park. Over the course of the Cornish summer, Cal and Demi grow close; and to her surprise, Demi realises she's finally found a place she can call home. But Cal has complications in his past that make Demi wonder if he could ever be interested in her. And as the summer draws to a close, she faces the hardest decision of her life . . .

WISH YOU WERE HERE

Phillipa Ashley

When Jack proposes to Beth at the end of a holiday romance, she doesn't think twice — she knows he's The One. But on their return home, Jack walks out with no explanation. Eight years on and a twist of fate finds Beth a new job — working for Jack — forced to face the man who broke her heart every day. But she really needs this job. Compelled to spend time together, the mystery of Jack's disappearance unravels. But are they both carrying too much baggage to try again — or could they finally be in the right place at the right time?

IT SHOULD HAVE BEEN ME

Phillipa Ashley

When Carrie Brownhill's fiance, solid, dependable Huw Brigstocke, suddenly calls off their wedding, she is devastated. And the final blow is struck when she finds out Huw is marrying another woman! Determined to pick herself up and get away, Carrie jumps at her friend Rowena's solution: a VW van and the road trip of a lifetime. But when Rowena has to pull out and Matt Landor, an old friend of Huw's, ends up filling the breach, she's not so sure. Will fate take the pair on an altogether different journey?